Afte... ...l was ...to say something, but he faced the man in the overalls and a large butcher's knife. The blade went through Holly's throat with an expert thrust from right to left, giving him no chance even to scream. The gunman stood well back. The knife plunged into Holly seventeen times. He counted them aloud. Holly must have been long dead by the time he stopped. The gunman consulted a sheet of paper. "Two more," he said.

The other stabbed the body twice more, then threw down the knife. The gunman crumpled up Holly's "letter" and dropped it on the ground. Rust began to understand. It was to be a homosexual murder set-up, complete with multiple cuts inflicted in a "frenzy of passion." Somebody might even be caught, sentenced, and executed for it.

IN THE COMPANY OF SPIES

STEPHEN BARLAY

FAWCETT CREST • NEW YORK

In the Company of Spies was published recently in England under the title *Cuban Confetti*.

A Fawcett Crest Book

Published by Ballantine Books

Library of Congress Catalog Card Number: 81-4674

ISBN 0-449-20378-6

This edition published by arrangement with Summit Books

Manufactured in the United States of America

First Ballantine Books Edition: December 1983

For Lucy and Albert Vajda

July
1962

"If only some seemingly insignificant and unrelated pointers had been correlated and pictured in their true context in that hot July of 1962, we would have saved face as well as lives, history might have taken a different course leaving us with one fewer war flashpoint for the 1980s."

—CIA official, London, 1980

THE TRIDENT SOARED ABOVE PARIS AND PAUL FERNAUD watched as it gored summer clouds. He hated airports and he had only come to kiss goodbye not so much his girl as his last sou earmarked for a London abortionist's pocket. A simple wedding would have cost less. But it had been her choice.

A rush of VIP photographers disturbed him. Airport regulars. They were feeding off Fidel Castro's brother Raul in transit to Moscow. Not Fernaud's kind of magazine story. More by reflex than intention he raised his camera and took a shot. And another as the man and his fiercely bearded companion ducked to fill a small and most emphatically ordinary Peugeot.

Not the car and not the faces but the beards attracted his

3

attention when he saw them again a couple of hours later. It was near his home, probably the worst house in the worst street astride the Métro to the Porte des Lilas—such an unlikely port of call of VIPs in transit. So he took a third photograph. And idled, out of sight instinctively, behind the rickety fence on the far side.

The fourth time his camera clicked was no reflex and no idle curiosity. The hurried arrival of a pair of twinned Chinamen presented him with his next meal ticket. The story was almost complete. Just one more shot. If he could catch them leaving the house together...a handshake...a furtive glance down the street....

The following morning, Paul Fernaud, age twenty-seven, single, freelance photographer, made an inch of news in just two papers. He had been fished out of the Seine. No known reasons for suicide. His pockets contained a driving license, two Métro tickets, seventy-five centimes, and a Harley Street, London, address. A long narrow mark across his throat indicated that the leather strap of his camera case might have been caught on something, perhaps strangling him. There was no film in his camera.

The crowd roared in Moscow's Lenin Stadium. Dynamo had scored yet again. They were in great form. Sandwiched between a middle-aged and an old man, the young woman in the tight-fitting flowered frock clapped enthusiastically. She loved soccer and the soccer crowd loved her. Between goals she would catch as many eyes as the center forward performing his antics of triumph on the field. But now her attention was focused on a slip of paper: "RUST, Helm, 34. The Upstairs, near Key Largo, Florida, U.S.A."

"He's still there?" she asked.

"I believe so." The old man coughed. "Am I to go ahead then?"

"We must wait. The decision is not mine."

The heavily built middle-aged man shook his head. "I'm not very happy with the choice."

"It's not our choice," she snapped. "Or it's like buying nylons at Gum. You get a choice of one."

"But will he come?"

The old man coughed again. "I believe so. It may take a month or so to organize, but he'll come."

Dynamo mounted another attack, and her eyes followed the ball. "We'd better be right. It may be our last chance."

The big man tapped with his right foot impatiently. "But even if he comes, will he do it?"

She didn't even look at him. "He won't have a choice, will he?"

Shiverishly, the old man pulled his jacket tighter on his chest. The heat of the July sun failed to keep him warm.

The phone rang and young Ercihan in the Istanbul Lloyd's agent's office answered it. He nodded, and nodded respectfully, as he listened to his master's voice. His empty gaze rested on the horizon, pinned to the twin minarets of the Selimiye Mosque. The sight of the famous flaming sunset left him cold. Something sailed into view from the left, and his eyes met it on the waters of the Bosphorus. He hung up. The freighter looked familiar even to the naked eye. He reached for his binoculars. Of course. The *Omsk*. Eleven thousand-odd tons; built and electrically welded in Osaka, Japan, only some seven months ago, in December 1961; port of registry Vladivostok; Mchy. aft, LF at btm & U dk—machinery aft, longitudinal framing at bottom and upper deck, in the language of the Lloyd's Register of Ships.

He knew the ship well because she had been a frequent passerby throughout the summer, going between Odessa and wherever. Her destination was no real concern of this office. But the sighting itself was, so he jotted down the time—one more detail for the next report to London. It never failed to warm him that he helped to provide an international intelligence service for the benefit of the insurance market as a whole and the commercial world at large. His personal notes were bound to impress Mr. Üzgünoğlu even if the ship's passage would appear in the harbor master's official movements list in any case.

The binoculars revealed bulky cargo under canvas on the deck. Yet the ship rode high in the water. The *Omsk* must be carrying something too large to be accommodated in the hold, yet valuable enough to command almost by itself the use of a fine ship. A conjecture, no doubt, but valid it must be even if

Mr. Üzgünoğlu would be quick to repeat that "we trade in facts, impartially, down the middle, no favor, no fervor." Pity. The young Turk wondered if his observation and reasoning would qualify for a Confidential Report or even a telegram in the old Pentagram code. Not because the sighting was so important but because he had never had occasion to justify any such messages, which would make them sit up in the great city of London.

The open stairs, sweeping up in a curved line from the makeshift jetty to the front door, were too grand and completely out of proportion to the building they served. They were, nevertheless, an eye-catcher and deserving of having the modest guest house named after them. "The Upstairs" was painted in black letters leaning this way and that in varying states of jolly intoxication, on all four outside walls. "So I'm not a pro," Rust would challenge any new critics of his art, and he was yet to find one to dispute it.

He worked now in the merciful shadow of the stairs. The whitewash of the house was almost completed, and it made him feel exceptionally virtuous—well, virtuous enough to deserve a small reward. He entered the kitchen and soon returned with a tumbler full of cracked ice swimming in an amber sea of rum. He urged himself to drink up fast, because even the ice would turn into instant sweat in such weather. It was too hot even for the Florida Keys. And it would be such a waste to let the ice melt in vain. So he topped up his drink, just to give the ice something to work on.

He picked up the brush. The freshness of the white dazzled him. Another couple of hours or so, and that would be the end of it. And high time, too. Friends who ventured to this lonely spot some seventy miles from Miami kept telling him he was a fool not to get a professional in for the job when he could well afford it, but he disliked strangers nosing about the house during his sometimes lengthy absences and disliked them even more for company when he was around.

Paying guests were, of course, welcome. Silent, solemn fishermen who preferred solitude to the attractions of the floating beer joints would come in a trickle until the fall and call him Mr. Rust if they had to talk. The winter crowd (maximum capacity: ten guests at a time) would address him simply as

Rust. They would be mostly women of all shapes and sizes and ages, single and married, occasionally with a male in tow, attracted to the choppy waters, the mangrove, the coral reef, the cormorants, the isolation ("you don't *have* to come by boat if you don't mind a few hours of jungle hacking"), amused by the grandeur of the stairs and the simplicity of the meals (depending on the quality of the volunteer cooks), and entertained by the bad though enthusiastic piano playing of their host, whose drinking evoked the mother instinct in all those shapes and sizes of whatever ages.

Two red dots inexplicably appeared on the white floor.

"What the hell . . ."

The sun blinded him as he looked up, then he began to see the dark skin on bare feet, knees, thighs in the floral shadow of a thin skirt, then another red dot that became a line running down a knee, and finally hands that hesitated between clutching the wounded thigh and throttling the immodesty of the skirt against his offending eyes.

"Sorry," she said.

"You okay?" He refused to withdraw his gaze from under the skirt.

"Sure I'm okay."

"Okay, then."

He dipped the brush in the bucket, whited out the red dots, found his glass, walked slowly up the stairs and led her into the house.

"Leave my thigh alone."

"Then stop bleeding on my rug."

He removed the amateurish dressing, dabbed at the seeping blood to see the torn edges of the flesh, and said without looking at her: "Might have been a machine gun."

"Just grazed."

"You ought to see a doctor."

"Why should I? I'm okay. It's my business." The singsong of her Spanish accent rose with her excitement.

"True."

He asked no questions. He could guess what had happened. Many of Julia-Rosa's family were in Castro's jails. Others, mostly the younger ones, needed her support. She whored for them religiously and made her father confessor work overtime in the church, so conveniently located behind El Paraíso, her bar base in Miami's Little Havana district, near Bay Front Park. From time to time she would disappear for a few days, even weeks. Rust knew she worked for Mongoose. She spied for them and learned to fight with arms for them. She was dedicated to the overthrow of Castro. So was Mongoose, manned by Cuban commandos, fed and trained and fanned by the CIA, and backed by Robert Kennedy, who never tired of denouncing the Bay of Pigs fiasco in public but had just endorsed the plotters' new invasion plans by his secret visit to their Miami headquarters. So Rush had heard, and he had reason to believe it. Right after the visit, two parties of raiders had gone to Cuba in those high-speed V-20's which were specially modified and armor-plated for $30,000 each. Yet neither of those two boats had returned. A party of the survivors and a few refugees had been shot up by the Cuban coast guard but made a run for it. They had been lucky. Julia-Rosa must have been among them.

Rust bandaged the wound and pulled her skirt down to cover her knees.

"Thanks."

He gave her a drink, and she noted the Cuban rum and Cuban cigars on the shelf. At last she seemed ready to tell why she had come here. She reached deep down into the cleavage of her dress and produced a sweaty sheet of paper. "Ten days ago, this was on Fidel's desk." She waited for some kind of reaction, but only the old jetty groaned as the waves hugged it.

"You know I'm not interested in politics," he said, his eyes avoiding her trophy.

"Aren't you?"

"I've burned my fingers often enough, thank you." So all right. He helped some people, mostly with advice, now and then. Politics or no politics, it would have been cruel to let simple, decent folk run into trouble blindly when he knew the possible approaches to that dangerous island so well.

She pushed the paper in front of him. Doodles of patterns and matchstick men filled the open spaces surrounding two lists of words in Cyrillic handwriting. "What is it?"

"Hard to tell."

"You can read it. You speak Russian like a native. You lived there. You told me."

"Sure. I can read the words. But it doesn't make much

sense. On the right it says 'additional advisers' in administration, land irrigation, medical training and other things."

"What other things?"

"How to establish co-ops, kindergartens, maternity homes—things like that."

"And the other list?"

Rust read it quickly and smiled. "Reads like some crazy shopping list."

"How crazy?"

"Well, it starts with wheat, oil and antiaircraft batteries."

"That's good, that's good," she enthused. "What else?"

"Shirts, boots, beef, infantry weapons, paper clips."

"Paper clips? You think it's some code?"

Rust shook his head. "Wouldn't know. Perhaps these are notes taken in the course of some long, rambling conversation."

"Anything else?"

"Sure. Beef and pork, Komar class patrol boats, er ...*porokhovyye konfety*...confetti? Some sort of powdered candy."

"You mean that sort you decorate cakes with in pretty colors?"

"I've no idea. Perhaps Castro needs them to make the new paper clips more appetizing. Anyway, it goes on to fertilizer plants, distilleries, power plants, heavy road-building machinery."

"You left out one line."

"You speak Russian?"

"No, but I saw your finger failed to stop there."

"Very observant. It was trucks and tractors, okay?"

"And you say it reads like a crazy shopping list?"

"Can't think of anything else."

Her whole face widened in a big smile. "That's just what I was told. This is Fidel's shopping list. It was written down at his desk when the Russians were there."

"They're never far away these days."

"Those were special. They talked to Fidel for two days, then the lists were typed out and the notes like this were thrown away."

"But luckily, somebody found this one?"

"That's it. It was a present for me. And now I want to sell it."

"Sell it? You, sweetheart? What about your great devotion to the cause?"

"Don't you dare." Her claws seemed to grow.

"Sorry. It's only that I'm surprised."

The claws retracted into the elegantly shaped paws. She looked away. "I'll die for the revolution if necessary. But I won't starve for it." He would have sworn there were tears in her eyes. "I gave Mongoose what they wanted. This is for my family."

"How much do you hope to get for it?"

"I don't know. A million?"

"Dollars?"

"Maybe a thousand?" she bargained hopefully. "Five hundred?"

"You can try."

"You try. I know only Mongoose, and they would want it free. You help and I pay for it. It's easier money than smuggling." She nodded toward the shelf. "Some fine *añejo* you have there. Specially imported for you along with the cigars? You're moonlighting as a smuggler, *chico*, and I know it. But I keep it to myself because you're my friend."

"Don't ever try to push me too hard, sweetheart." His voice was unnaturally soft.

"Sorry."

"I'll try to get someone interested."

She stood up and kissed his face at the top tip of the scar that ran along his chin. He smiled, and the scar disappeared in the creases of his lined face. It was not a handsome face. And when he smiled, nobody would have guessed that he had been living in it for only thirty-four years.

"You do that, *chico*, and I'll love you forever. And something else. I'll also try somebody I know. Bring your friend to El Paraíso tomorrow and I'll bring mine. And the friend who pays the most gets the shopping list."

"Okay. Keep warm."

She left through the mangrove, following the overgrown coral path. (It was not really "hours of jungle-hacking.") She must have left her car near Key Largo on U.S. Highway 1, which linked the Keys.

He was still looking for the telephone number when she

returned. "I thought I'd leave this with you. It's safer." She dropped the paper and was gone.

Rust called Jake Schramm, a quite plausible earthmoving machinery salesman of jovial disposition, and arranged to meet him at El Paraíso the following day.

"Can you give me a little hint as to what it's all about?"

Rust hesitated. Why trust the phone? "We must discuss the finest ways of consuming large quantities of golden Bacardi, what else?" He hung up, translated the notes in full, and judged them to be of no great value.

Policemen were swarming all over the bar when Rust arrived. Not a unique occasion in the streets around the mouth of the Miami River. Schramm was already on his second Bacardi. "Don't mind the cops," he assured Rust. "Some bargirl got herself battered to death."

"Julia-Rosa?"

"How did you guess?"

Rust downed his drink in one long gulp and ordered another. "She's the one who wanted to . . . show you something."

"I didn't know her."

"I wanted to introduce you. She thought what she had was too important to show anyone *she* knew."

"What was it?"

"I don't know."

"Not a clue?"

"No." That sheet of paper felt like a malignant lump pressing his chest.

"Let's go and see her."

Schramm had a quiet word with the officer in charge, and they were allowed into the little back room the bargirls used in rotation. It had four walls, a curtained window, a single bed and a washstand. El Paraíso customers were not very particular. The owner of the bar had already told the police that after hours of telephoning, Julia-Rosa had obtained his permission to use the room from closing time with an all-night john.

"She's in a bad state," said a detective, who was restating the obvious. "Must have been some goddam maniac."

Or someone going a long, long way to find out what she had for sale, thought Rust and Schramm, but neither of them said anything. Nobody knew who her client had been. Nobody knew the numbers she had called for hours. It was anybody's guess whether she had revealed the whereabouts of the "shopping list."

"Be in touch if you can suddenly remember what she tried to trade," said Schramm as they were about to part. "For if that maniac thinks that you knew something, I might have to drink alone all that firewater the Upstairs floats on." He laughed. It was a good joke. "And say no more—I'll keep warm."

Rust drove south, across the river, along S.W. 8th Street, up to the Orange Bowl and back. As far as he could tell, nobody followed him. He went into a store and looked at some electric typewriters. He tried out one, typing a few lines, then a few more, studied the result, and absentmindedly slipped the paper into his pocket. He examined the typewriter, and with exceptional clumsiness he tore the ribbon. He pulled it all out, apologized, dirtied his hands, apologized more, offered to pay for the ribbon, promised to think about his choice, and retreated in great embarrassment.

He bought some glue and two envelopes. Returning to his car, he tore the two typing tests out of the sheet. The first test said only: THIS COMES FROM FIDEL'S DESK; ABOUT TEN DAYS OLDER THAN DATE OF POSTMARK. CHECK IF DATE COINCIDES WITH VISIT OF SOME RUSSIAN TOP-LEVEL DELEGATION. He slipped it into the envelope with the "shopping list," then glued the second test—a Mr. Elliott Repson's fashionable Georgetown, Washington, address—to the outside. The second envelope he used for mailing $500 in cash to Julia-Rosa's eldest younger brother. Although he didn't even know how old the boy was, Rust hated him at that moment. Brothers. He wondered if the kid had ever blackmailed Julia-Rosa with his own helplessness and the shameless display of his dependence on her.

If only it had been made of fine brass, the curved horn could have adorned a turn-of-the-century Daimler. The shape would have been just right. But as it was a tinny contraption in the boring field gray of German World War I infantry, it was doomed to obscurity nailed to the corner of Moscow's Kalinin Prospekt and Granovsky ulitsa. Yet this afternoon, when it croaked and rattled, it might have signaled the arrival of one of those historical moments that would hardly be recognized and even less recorded at the time. To the unwieldy militiaman on point duty the wound was routine. He knew he had plenty of time: the convoy of at least four Zils, black and haughty hand-tooled limousines, would only be rolling through the Kremlin's Kutafya Gate where the KGB guard would keep his finger on the button that operated the horns and buzzers along the route.

The militiaman's tongue shifted the long, burned-out butt of his *papiros* from the corner of his mouth. He tasted the foul residue left on his lip and spat out the nicotine-gooey cardboard. A man of awakening authority, he then swaggered some seventy yards down the Granovsky to block all the one-way traffic indefinitely. Behind him, his colleague cleared the corner of pedestrians.

Both sides of the narrow street were lined bumper to bumper with black cars that ignored and obliterated the No Parking signs. Their drivers, soldiers and civilians, acknowledged the sound of the horn with almost imperceptible reflexes. Some took a respectful step or two backward. Others touched their caps, hair or ties for reassurance, as before asking a girl for the next dance on gala night at the Slavyansky Bazaar. It was not often that citizens of the capital might catch a glimpse of their leader in the flesh, and these select servants of the elite knew that Nikita Sergeyevich Khrushchev had a town home in the red-brick block of that street.

In the back seat of a parked Chaika, the penultimate status symbol rated only one rung below the Zil, a massive man with a sweaty baby face listened intently. Nature seemed to have tried to compensate him for his ugliness with a magnificently full head of wavy blond hair, but somehow it only emphasized the hog nose that filled the precious little space between his baby-blue eyes. He heard the death rattle of the horn. It slowly expired. He glanced toward the first floor of No. 2 Granovsky that bore the obscure BUREAU OF PASSES sign opposite the red-brick building, then raised some papers to his eyes only to lower and raise them once more. It was a signal that would be noted behind one of the ostensibly blind one-way windows in No. 2. If anybody guessed his reason, the death rattle would soon rise from his throat instead of the gray horn. He wondered why he had risked being there at all. Could he still back out of it?

In the wide beam of Kalinin Prospekt, police motorcycles

swept down from the Kremlin, past the Lenin Library. Intersections were blocked. Traffic in the avenue itself, never even adequate to justify the majestic expanse, would flow freely, ignoring red lights.

The convoy of Zils zoomed into view, using the narrow no-man's-land between continuous white lines in the middle which was out of bounds for ordinary citizens at all times. Such central reservations used to be the preserve of the czar's carriage. Now they were known as "Chaika lanes," where nothing and nobody must obstruct the progress of the mighty few riding in their Chaikas and Zils.

The convoy, oblivious of No Right Turn and One Way Street signs, turned into Granovsky ulitsa and soon stopped. There was a hush, commotion and slamming of car doors—and Khrushchev was already inside the red-brick.

The Zils backed out of the street, and the militiamen freed the traffic. The hognosed man spat one word toward his driver: "Wait." He then walked to the entrance of No. 2, where he flashed his pass toward the guard. It was the best of Moscow's secret stores, where access was controlled by a strict grading of the political and military hierarchy. When he had gained his first pass to this building, he knew he had arrived at the peak region and was entitled to "Kremlin rations": a wide range of ordinary but scarce and luxury goods, never seen in shops or even lower-grade secret stores, for which he would pay with vouchers that cost him a tenth or less of their market value. Above him, at the very tip of the summit, were the few who would get anything and everything offered and delivered free of charge from all corners of the globe. He glanced back toward the red-brick building. He knew that the elevator in there that carried Nikita Sergeyevich would not have stopped on the second floor, where his apartment was. It would have gone on, another two stories up, to where Frunze and other notables had once lived, a spacious apartment now occupied by bulky Ekaterina Furtseva, Minister of Culture.

The Zils, the croaky horn, the upheaval in the streets— what a lot of fuss for a bad fuck, thought hognose as he arrived at the door of the room set aside for a private "whiskey-tasting party." He entered without knocking.

There were a few armchairs and a large table packed with Scotch and bourbon, each bottle a different brand. There were a few malts, too, and crystal shot glasses, but no waiters. Three generals and a civilian greeted the new arrival with nervous nods—a cool reception by Russian standards. There was a long moment of silence. "We'd better take a drink," said the rotund marshal of the artillery, and opened a bottle. All drained their glasses in single gulps. The bottle was pushed aside, another was opened, and a second round was poured.

"Let's take it easy, shall we?" the most heavily decorated general warned them. He walked to the window and stared at the red-brick building. The thought of Nikita Sergeyevich in the arms of Catherine the Third, as Madame Furtseva was known, disgusted him. He felt nothing but contempt for the pair. Khrushchev was an upstart. All right, Stalin had been a killer and all that, but the tyrant had had stature and you knew where you stood with him. The whole country knew. Now Atyushka had gone. His people might be freed from paternal authority, but orphans they were nevertheless. His generals might have been shot or sent to the camps, but those who were permitted to serve would not have suffered the indignity of having their pay and pensions cut. And this, this Minister of Culture, relatively out of favor in the party, but worming her way back to the top, was just as despicable as her ally and lover. When she had become the first woman member of the Presidium, she used to campaign for the abolition of bonuses paid to army officers according to rank. Bitch.

The general fingered his Order of Lenin, then dusted, absentmindedly, his Stalingrad memorial medal ("Yes, call it Volgograd if you wish, but I earned it at Stalingrad!") and listened to the men clinking their glasses behind him. He turned to face them. You all despise her, he thought, but this time we ought to be grateful to her; it's because of her that he's returned to Moscow, leaving Nina Petrovna still holidaying with the rest of his family in Crimea—because of her that we know exactly where he'll spend the next couple of hours, and that we, all of us in this room, can be sure that by no freak coincidence will he summon all of us at the same time. The thought of somebody's asking questions, not to mention discovering some sort of special connection among these men, made him shiver. The stakes were high. Even if this was only their second meeting, even if nothing had ever been actually spelled out, even if each of them was present only to represent a mightier

patron who would not wish to contribute more to these pro-
ceedings than a nod of approval by proxy.

The general viewed each man in turn. One or the other
might already be reporting on them to some authority. Perhaps
he himself ought to submit a report. But even then, uncomfortable questions would be asked. Why only now? Why not
after the first meeting? Why not before the first meeting?

All of them waited for hognose to speak. He drank up. "My
friend's approved. It's up to us now to stop this harebrained
scheme of gambling. If it misfires, it could ruin our country.
And I mean ruin it completely."

Drinks were poured. The manager of the store would have
to be convinced that serious tasting had taken place.

"What if the gamble pays off?" asked the general, still
polishing his medals.

"Even worse. For then we could be stuck with the gambler
forever."

They all turned to face the window and the lovenest in the
red-brick building beyond it. Then hognose spoke about a minor
military reorganization plan and its instigator. This was the
agreed cover topic to be discussed at length as if the opening
remarks had referred to that—for the room might be bugged.
Any place might be bugged.

The general touched his combat decorations one after another. The defense of Odessa, the dash to the Vistula, Berlin.
He felt that all eyes were on him. Now it was up to him to
make the move. He had already selected a colonel for the task.
They would not want to know the name or anything else. It
was safer not to know. Damn them. And their whiskey. "I
want some Starka." He knew he could rely on the marshal of
the artillery, who always carried a leather-clad hip flask containing the best matured vodka. He was not to be disappointed.
While he drank, the others let the conversation drift toward the
safer ground of differences between Scotch and Irish.

Autumn
1962

• Thursday, August 30 •

Lord Russell's nuclear disarmament campaigners return beaten from Red Square demo. USSR denies creating "Fortress Cuba." Marilyn Monroe mourned; Lolita and Dr. No hailed. U-2s photograph SAM sites in Cuba.

R UST CUT THE ENGINE AND LET HIS BOAT, THE *HALF PINT*, drift gently to the jetty. He paused and listened to the silence of the mangroves. After a few seconds he was able to distinguish between the sounds that made up the silence. The humming of the wind. Birds tiptoeing. Leaves pushed. Something running? Mice? The discreet yattering of the water. And something else. The cluck-cluck of a tied-up boat flirting with waves. Except that there was no boat in sight. Must be hidden somewhere. He looked up. The Upstairs was in complete darkness. If he had unexpected visitors, they would leave their boat at the jetty, turn on all the lights, help themselves to cold beer and pass the time with hunting mosquitoes as big as roaches.

He walked to the bottom of the stairs, where he could not be seen from the house. After a pause, he kicked to loosen a wedge under the first stair—he really ought to fix it more permanently one of these days. The whole structure began to creak in the wind. As if someone was climbing it. He quietly ran up the concrete ramp some twenty yards farther on and, hidden by the flowers and lush leathery leaves of oleanders, reached the back of the house. As the Upstairs was built leaning onto the steep bank, it had two stories on the waterfront, and its second floor was ground level at the back. He stepped in through a window and moved noiselessly along the tiled corridor to the living-dining room. The visitor, if there was one, would be listening to the creaking stairs. Rust kicked in the door, hit the light switch and pulled back in a single move. A young man with a crewcut, gun in hand, jumped up from Rust's rocking chair. His face showed confusion: the sudden light and the sources of sounds did not tally. And Rust's voice, coming from yet another direction, mystified him even more.

"Do me a favor, Junior, put that gun away. Because I also have one."

Junior stood still. Only his eyes searched for the speaker. He noticed the serving hatch and moved slowly to pocket his gun. "Okay?"

"I'd prefer it if you threw it out of the window."

"I'm CIA. Miami station."

"Oh really?"

"No, O'Connor." He looked stunned when Rust laughed. "You want me to ident?"

"After you get rid of the artillery."

Reluctantly, O'Connor pushed the gun out of the window. Rust came in the room. He carried no gun. Only a banana. O'Connor blushed. In close-up he looked even younger. "Sorry about the surprise visit," said Junior.

"Next time maybe you'll phone first, okay? And switch on the light if you drop in and wait for me."

"It's just that I fell asleep while I was waiting."

"And got out your gun and hid your boat in your dreams? Or did you try to impress me?" And before O'Connor could think of another excuse: "Just tell me what you want."

O'Connor pulled out a notebook, cleared his throat, smacked his lips and gave the appearance of a man trying to revive the mood of a well-rehearsed act after some rude interruption by the audience. "Well, yes...er...does the name," he read, "the name...Mat-vey Sem-yonovich..." He pronounced it with difficulty, and repeated it now, remembering to watch Rust's face for signs of fright, pleasure, recognition: "Matvey Semyonovich. Does it mean anything to you?"

"No. Should it?"

"Not for me to say." He had now regained his rhythm. "It may well be a mistake."

"What?"

"The message."

"For me?"

"That's what I was told. But then, as I understand it, the man was dying and probably confused."

"And so am I. Confused, I mean."

"Sorry, sir, my fault. And probably not important at all. It's only that there was this Russki sailor who jumped ship in Havana, got himself fixed up with some refugees and tried to slip across to Key West. Their boat was picked up adrift and full of bullet holes by our Coast Guard, who towed it in to...er, us, if you know what I mean. They said the tovarish had died on the way."

"But not before he could say that he had a message for me?"

"That's right."

"And he had my address?"

"Yes." O'Connor checked his notes. "Here we are. Mr. Helmut Rust, the Upstairs, near Key Largo, Florida." Because he was reading it, he never had a chance to notice the tightening of Rust's face. "And the message ran: 'Matvey Semyonovich was very ill but he's much better now.' That's all." He looked up. "And you say it means nothing to you, sir?"

"Nothing." Rust tried to think of the quickest way to get rid of the young bungler. "Wasn't worth your trip, let alone risking your life, was it?

Schramm was raving, and Rust listened patiently. "They're crazy! We're doomed. They're fucking crazy!"

"Who's crazy?"

"Fucking crazy, my son, fucking crazy. All of them. The entire Congress of the U.S. of A. ought to have its collective head examined."

"I'm too drunk to follow you."

"Liar. I've seen you flake out but never getting drunk. Not once, not twice, so don't gimme that shit. They've just defeated JFK. Medicare for old folks? Out! School-aid program? Out! Foreign aid? Cut it! They're traitors. All of them."

"Including brother Bobby?"

"What do you mean?" Schramm's voice grew menacingly soft.

"He's been here. Looking over the Mongoose arrangements. Or so I hear."

"What else do you hear?"

"That the intelligence phase is over. Mongoose is to move into the raiding phase."

"Bullshit. You shouldn't listen to gossip."

"It bugs me."

"What?"

"The whole business. Fidel's a pain in the ass, and believe me, I have no love for him. But we can live with him. And if not, then let's just remove him like a goddam splinter, openly and without apologies. For Chrissake, why should we be ashamed of protecting our interests? Why do we need to act secretly? Ours is a great country, and let's just bang the table if we feel like it. According to our principles."

"Patriotism, Rust? Principles? You must be drunk after all."

"Maybe. But it hurts. I mean the way they're changing."

"Okay, so you dislike the Kennedys."

"You're crazy. I said nothing like that." He held out his glass: "Fill it up." They listened to the bottle giving out its soul. "Look, Jake, we worship what we were taught to worship and believe what we like to believe in. The fantastic thing about the Kennedys is that they've given us an image we could worship and *enjoy* believing in. But Mongoose doesn't fit the image. Like the Bay of Pigs didn't fit."

"That wasn't his idea."

"True."

"And he stopped it."

"No, Jake, he didn't, and you know it. He didn't prevent it. He let them go in. And then he stopped the support. He pulled the carpet and let them die or get captured for nothing. That's cheating. On us. And now again, they let the little creeps do the dirty for them. The Julia-Rosas and the rest of them."

"Still no idea what she wanted to sell me?"

"No."

"Pity. You used to be on our side."

"I'd rather sit on the fence than on fucking committees."

"But you love to come and lecture me."

"You started it. You talked about defectors and traitors."

"Okay. We'll call it quits. Now let's find another bottle."

Schramm began to rummage in cupboards full of leaflets advertising dumpers and excavators he had no intention of selling.

Rust tried to keep his voice light and casual. "By the way, defectors and all—did they ever find out the dead Russki's name?"

"What Russki?"

"The one who was picked up with drifting refugees."

"I don't know what you're talking about. Where do you hear such rubbish?"

"Let me see . . . the guy was on his third daiquiri, in the Tropicana, or maybe it was the Paraíso."

"Some Cuban, of course."

"As a matter of fact, yes."

"Come on, friend, grow up. Cubans ought to run advertising agencies, not revolutions. If any refugees are picked up around here or if any dead Russki drifts in, I'll be the first to hear about it, believe me."

"That's just what I thought." And it was a thought that worried Rust. For Junior and his tale seemed fishy. Yet the message was genuine enough to justify a little extra risk.

It took, of course, ages to get London, and then the long wait for someone to answer the phone, and then the endless questions. Who is calling, representing whom or what, what do you mean "self," sir, why the call, could anybody else help, if not why not, isn't it, after all, a matter of urgency? Rust had almost forgotten: according to Charles, the ungodly hour of 10:00 A.M. would still be reserved for utter emergencies to be handled exclusively by work freaks, masochists and certified insomniacs.

"No, sir, I'm afraid Sir Charles is not available."

"Will he be in later?"

"Couldn't say for certain, sir."

"Shall I try in the afternoon?"

"As it is long distance, you may find it a trifle extravagant, Misterrrr . . . Rust. Sir Charles has taken a few weeks' leave of absence. But if you'd care to give me the number where you could be contacted in the next couple of days . . ."

Fourteen minutes later Rust's phone rang.

"What's ailing you, dear boy?"

"Charles!"

"Full marks for an intelligent guess, full marks." The uninitiated would have found Charles's camp, nasal tone ridiculous. But then Sir Charles Stoker would hardly ever bother to admit, as he had done to Rust, that "those of us who've been blessed only with our birthwrong and marked lack of proper upbringing must cling to the authority of the caricature which people expect to be shunned by the upstart."

"Thanks for calling. It's urgent. Even if it interrupts your holiday."

"What can I say? You Yanks have no respect for people with time on their hands. We actually had to lose an empire to prove that we can also move fast."

"I must talk to you."

"You mean flesh to flesh, dear boy? What an exquisite idea!"

"Can I come and see you?"

"Eaiser done than said. Right now I'm virtually the boy next door. The venue is Mo' Bay."

Montego Bay? The heat of Jamaica? Charles would never go near it unless duty had dragged him there bound and gagged. "I thought you disliked the heat."

"It's the heart shape of the pool that tickles my fancy. That and the calypso or whatever the noise is called."

• Saturday, September 1 •

More atmospheric nuclear tests in USSR. Women's demo with empty pots and pans in Cárdenas: "We're hungry, Fidel!" Yves St. Laurent opts for the harem look with feather-trimmed hats.

IN THE MOBILE LANDSCAPE OF BIKINIS, RUST FOUND PLENTY of distraction, but even so it would have been impossible not to notice Charles, who sat at the edge of the pool, wearing impeccable shorts and shirt and Panama hat, feet dangling in the water, mind submerged in a game of Scrabble against himself.

"How goes it, Charles?" Rust stopped behind him.

"I'm getting better. When I play in French, I now beat myself almost invariably." He did not turn his head and showed no surprise. They said he had eyes in his back.

"Lucky you have the time."

"Well, you know how it is, dear boy. I'm a bit like fungi,

27

athlete's foot, let's say—cropping up everywhere but not much in demand." He then fell silent, concentrating on his circling toes in the water.

Rust sat down and took a deep breath. "The message came through."

"You mean . . . ?"

"Yeah."

"Oh." The heavy, watery eyes revealed a remarkable lack of interest, but that single syllable gave away the game. Then the voice was brought under control and the tone of concern disappeared. "And you mean to go in?"

"I promised."

"Of course."

"You think it's crazy?"

"You and you alone must be the judge of that, dear boy."

"He's my father."

"Who left you at the age of two. Or was it one?"

"It was a job that had to be done, and he volunteered."

"Ah, the allure of Eden, a do-gooder's land of promises."

"He's a broken man."

"Who now wants to get out."

"I have to do it."

"Well, dear boy, there could be difficulties. It's not cobblestones that pave the exit routes from Mother Russia."

"I'll find a way."

"Good, good, chivalry's not dead yet, only somewhat senile."

"I may need help to go in. In a hurry. There's no one else I can turn to."

"Incidentally, how's your brother? Half brother, to be precise, I know, I know. A charming man. How is he?"

"Well, I presume," said Rust.

"Presume?"

"Haven't seen him for five years. He lives somewhere in Washington, I think."

"A fine, close-knit family. Could even be English."

"If you say so."

"But he's still doing well, I hear. A high-flyer, you might say. Still able to produce magnificent pieces of intelligence just sitting in his wheelchair. A remarkable man. With a peach of a wife. What was the name? Anna?"

"Look, Charles, we've been through this before."

At length, the older man's eyes seemed to say.

It was in Moscow. Charles Stoker, not yet knighted, acted as second secretary (commerce) at the British embassy. He was known as the dithery old man who had never quite made it. Only Rust doubted that. The older man sensed his doubt and seemed to appreciate it. They became friends in a solemn, nondemonstrative fashion. Rust was working as a journalist. With a quiet CIA string attached. Charles helped and guided him. He was certain that Rust would go a long way in the Company, perhaps some *éminence grise* as a top desk man, perhaps a successful field man posing as yet another aging diplomat "who never quite made it."

Then one long night, in the telex room of the British embassy on the Maurice Thorez naberezhnaya, waiting for news about the bloodbath in Hungary, Rust told Charles about the father he never knew.

Herr Rost worked for the Red Cross in Berlin and Geneva. In an official capacity he went to Kazakhstan and disappeared after a couple of months. A year later, in 1930, his wife received news that her husband had died. After a not too respectable period of mourning, she married Hugh Repson, her American lover, and moved with her child to New York. Young Helmut became Helm. He disliked it. Then Elliott, a second son, was born. As a teenager, Helm refused to be a Repson. He translated and used his father's name.

"I'm searching for his grave," Rust told Charles during that night.

"Why?"

"I'm not sure. I just want to see it. Once. I've always had the urge. Maybe that's why I majored in Russian. Maybe because once, after the war when some German prisoners of war managed to get back home, somebody said that my father had been seen somewhere in Siberia. It was all very vague and no more than hearsay, and it was contradicted by someone else who said that my father's grave had been seen in a Siberian village. So I'm trying to find the grave, put some flowers on it and close that chapter of my life forever."

Charles was against it. It was a hopeless task. He was opposed to the whole idea, which would only call attention to Rust himself. "You don't wear fluorescent clothes in the dark, dear boy, not unless you mean to be seen." He also warned that the search might torpedo Rust's career. "Had it done just that?" was the mute question as they sat at the poolside, Charles watching Rust, Rust ogling the girls. Did Rust really quit both journalism and intelligence because he was bored with it all and wanted to enjoy life more freely? Or did the successful search have anything to do with it? For instead of a neglected grave, Rust had found an old man, broken in spirit, but alive.

"As you know," Rust said at last, "we met only a few times, always with some secrecy, usually after the early-morning service at a seventeenth-century church. The clockwork regularity of his life seemed to keep him going, but he was a wreck. Shaking nonstop. Coughing. Four years in prisons, seven years in camps. It was near Volochanka, in the Arctic, where he met a Georgian woman. They made a survival pact. And succeeded. Her husband had been killed after one of the show trials. My father adopted her family. When we met, there was no room for strangers in his life. He asked very few questions. He wasn't interested in me, my life, my mother's fate. All he kept asking about was Geneva. He longed to see it just once more. Not Berlin, not Messkirch where he was born, just Geneva. And the Jeddo, the way the natives pronounce Jet d'Eau, that spurting fountain, he never stopped marveling. 'Up, up, a hundred and thirty meters up, my son—I'll never see that again.'

"I asked if he would ever want to leave Russia. He said no, he had long forgotten how to survive anywhere else. Besides, he had a long tail. Meaning family. They'd be killed or sent to the camps; their lives and prospects would be ruined. I longed to give him something. Something special to hang his hopes on. So I asked that if his wife died and his children had grown completely independent, and if I found some way to help him, would he want to come and live with me, would he risk it? I suggested we could go to Geneva together. I told him what the town looked like these days. That excited him. He said yes, that would be wonderful.

"It was pure daydreaming, of course, because in normal circumstances, he would be both unable and unwilling to break up his life again and start all over. But, and that was a very big but, there was always the possibility of something going wrong. A mistake by him, a hostile neighbor, an informer looking for a victim and an opportunity to score, a change of policy that leads to rounding up former prisoners—any stupid change in the political climate and he could find himself on the run. So we carried on daydreaming. In fact, I had some ways at the time to help him. Why shouldn't I offer it to him? Why shouldn't he accept it? If nothing else, it gave him something to pin his hopes on. So we arranged this crazy code. A man, Vassily or whatever name, was very ill but much better now. My father would use it only as a last resort, if he was already on the run, if there was nothing else he could do."

"How would he send the message?"

"That would be up to him. Friends could help him. The authorities would never let him make a phone call to America, but he felt sure he'd find a way. And we didn't go too much into it, because we both knew it was just a dream. I'd go there, meet him probably in the church where he always worshiped, and get him out. Except that he'd never send me that message. Except that now he has. So what do I do? Ignore it? Leave him there to rot?"

Charles looked away. "You never told me how you found him."

"It was a long, long trail, hopeless inquiries, through friends' friends, and then snap. There it was."

"A miracle, dear boy, a miracle."

"That first meeting, he was shivering all the time. He could never warm up after the Arctic nights. 'Keep warm,' he said after every other sentence. 'Keep warm.'"

Rust dived into the pool and swam two lengths furiously. When he returned, Charles looked triumphant. He had just put out seven letters in *faillir*. The opposition was crumbling.

"Great," said Rust.

"I'll see you perhaps in London. I'll be back by Tuesday."

"I need a few more days. But, thanks."

"For what? I promised nothing."

• Tuesday, September 4 •

Russians send armor through Checkpoint Charlie to defy
Western powers in Berlin. Moscow embarrassed by thriving
blackmarket in cotton socks and nylon shirts. U.S. admits
accidental violation of Soviet airspace: U-2 was blown off
course.

THE WINDOWS OFFERED A MAGNIFICENT VIEW OF THE WHITE
House and its tree-lined south lawn, but the five men in
the room paid no attention to it. They belonged to the "second
layer" on the edge of the President's immediate power circuit.
The Security Committee's deliberations had just begun to seep
through to them. The presidential aide, seated behind the sump-
tuous desk, finished briefing them on the latest National Estimates by the U.S. Intelligence Board. The key issue concerned
Cuba, and, according to the final analysis, it had been found
most unlikely that the Russians would install offensive weapons, particularly long-range nuclear missiles, on the island.

That was no great surprise to these men, for they all had contributed something to the Estimates.

An Army officer brought in a file marked "eyes only." It remained unopened until he saluted and turned smartly. The door creaked as it closed after him, and everybody looked up; the sound was totally out of place.

The file contained an expert assessment by photo interpreters confirming that the SAMs sighted in Cuba "were similar to our early Nike missiles" and that their "slant range of twenty-five miles did not represent any threat to mainland USA." There were some sample photographs attached, and these were handed out. Elliott Repson, the young civilian in a wheelchair, passed them on without looking at them. He turned instead to the Air Force colonel:

"Doesn't it worry you out there, John?"

The pilot shrugged his shoulders. He commanded a small hand-picked group who flew reconnaissance missions in "utility planes," U-2s for short. Each man had been put through a process known as "sheep-digging": they resigned formally from the Air Force and went onto the CIA payroll as civilians. It was hoped it would be a face-saving formula in case they were shot down and captured. Cuban overflights had been limited to two a month until the end of August, when the program was intensified to the level of two sorties a day. The magnificent airborne cameras produced miles and miles of film in paired stereo shots in depth, and the long lenses gave such incredible details that even a face could be identified from ten miles above. The photo interpreters used an "image compensation" technique to make up for the flying speed of fifteen hundred miles an hour. Nobody in this sunny room had ever heard the name of Colonel Penkovsky, but it was no secret to them that the interpreters' work was based largely on data provided by a spy imbedded somewhere deep in the Russian defense establishment. The flights could choose any path directly over the Cuban target area until the presence of the surface-to-air missiles had been positively proved. For these SAMs were all Guidelines, the type that had brought down Gary Powers in 1960.

"Worry me? No, I can't say they do," said the pilot slowly at last. "Not too much, that is. It's more of a bother. You know we use those radar-jamming techniques, and the Russians were probably just lucky when shooting at Gary. Unless, of course, they had some secret info that would enable them to decipher our signals. Now that would change things a lot—then I'd be sitting on the gunsight of every damn SAM operator who wanted to take a potshot at me."

But did the Russians possess such information? And why were the SAMs cropping up suddenly in Cuba? They were no good in small numbers to stop a massive air raid, for instance, but they could certainly interfere with the U-2s. So was there anything the Cubans would definitely not want to be seen?

"The old man seemed worried as he left the SecCom meeting," said the presidential aide, addressing the man in the wheelchair.

"Not *too* worried, I presume."

"No." It was an obvious presumption. John McCone, director of the CIA, had expressed fears and suspicions that the SAMs would be in Cuba only to protect some new, major, most secret installations—offensive weapons, perhaps. But that was no more than reasoned speculation, not worrying enough to prevent him from leaving for his Riviera honeymoon at Cap Ferrat, but causing serious concern about another unanswered question: Did the Russians *need* offensive weapons in Cuba?

The theory of a "missile gap" in favor of Russia had given nightmares to the West ever since the early space spectaculars that had shown how far behind the United States was in that field. The military then exploited the theory in pressing for a huge research and investment program to reset the balance and tilt it in America's favor.

"Many people in the Pentagon argue that we've had missiles staring at us long enough and that it makes no difference where they're fired from," said the aide, though without much conviction. Big missiles in Cuba would reduce America's warning time to almost nothing. "And Khrushchev claimed again only two days ago that 'due to imperialist threats to Cuba' he'd send more aid and defensive weapons to Castro but he'd need no foreign bases because he could hit us anytime from his own backyard."

"Usual Soviet *vranyo*," mumbled the pilot and seemed a little surprised that he had been heard.

Three men looked baffled until Repson turned his wheelchair and explained with a smile: "A favorite Muscovite reaction to official statements, gentlemen. *Vranyo* covers a full range from inaccuracy through falsification to outright bullshitting, if you'll pardon the expression."

The lecture irritated the aide: "Of course, if the CIA gave us more precise information, we wouldn't need guesswork. For we still don't know if the Russkis are bluffing about their accurate long-range missiles."

This could not be argued. Hard intelligence sources were badly missed. Agents in Cuba had been decimated after the Bay of Pigs. The flood of reports coming mainly from exiles and refugees could contain too much hearsay. How to pick out quickly the few that would merit a mention to the President and his immediate advisers? There had been some "sightings" of *cohetes*—a Spanish word that could cover anything from firecrackers to missiles. A former Havana Hilton employee sent word about "missiles at San Cristóbal." He might have seen the SAMs. Castro's personal pilot had been overheard boasting about nuclear missiles in Fidel's pocket. Could the man be trusted? He was known as a periodically heavy drinker, and delight in exaggeration was in the national character. Senator Keating had publicly warned about the Soviet military buildup in Cuba but would only quote "private sources."

The Army officer returned with yet another dispatch. It was to make those present feel truly privileged: more than three hours before the issue of the presidential statement, they would read the full text which emphasized that there was "no evidence" of "significant offensive capability" in Cuban hands, but threatened that the "gravest issues would arise" if the situation changed.

The wheelchair moved. Repson faced the window as if he was talking only to himself. "The question is why we tolerate the presence of a threat on our doorstep. Our plans to neutralize Castro were stood down temporarily. But if, under provocation and with built-in plausible deniability, we sank the damn island or floated it away, it wouldn't matter what Moscow needed. They wouldn't have anywhere to put their 'offensive capability' within spitting distance."

The aide shook his head: "It still shouldn't concern us. The President is about to make it clear that we'll never make a compromise. We'll prevent 'by whatever necessary means' any aggressive moves and the development of a Cuban threat. And

Khrushchev knows we can lick him and the bearded fella in one go."

"Which would be a good enough reason, perhaps, to put nukes in Cuba," said the pilot. "And if we don't spot them or if we spot them only when they're operational, we'll have to start the war to end all life on earth."

The silence that followed was uncomfortable, but nobody said a word.

• Friday, September 7 •

Deadlock in nuclear test ban treaty negotiations: Soviet Union refuses to accept controls and compulsory inspection of sites of suspected illegal nuclear explosions. Kennedy requests authority to call up 150,000 army reservists "to permit prompt and effective responses . . . to challenges . . . in any part of the free world." Heart specialists call for intensified anti-butter campaign.

THE SEA WAS CALM AND TRUE AZURE AS RUST'S BOAT drew a gentle curve that hugged the shoreline of the Keys. Flying fish glittered everywhere in the sunset, and Rust approved: on his southeasterly course anybody scanning the sea from the east would have to contend with this confusing dazzle. He slowed down, slipped between yachts, jetties, wrecks and rocks near Marathon, and moored in front of a ramshackle building with a huge sign:

TAKE OUR BEER AND TAKE OUR GAS,
YOU'LL BE GLAD WHEN LEAVING US

The 225-pound owner, Hal "Jus'-juice" Sheridan ("I'll be
damned if I sell anythin' but liquid") was waiting for Rust with
several bales and crates, all packed with great expertise to be
watertight. They loaded Rust's boat, refueled it and checked
if all the auxiliary tanks were full. Until then, no words were
spoken. There was no need. Rust would take and exchange the
merchandise for goods coming out of Cuba, and the profits
would be shared. They took turns making the runs.

"I think I could use someone to watch my back this time,"
said Rust.

The big man nodded, walked up to the house almost completely overgrown by tropical shrubs, made sure that the door
was open, turned an OPEN sign to read TAKE OUR GAS AN' TAKE
OUR BEER—BUT LEAVE YOUR BUCK IF YOUR LIFE'S DEAR, and
returned to the boat without a word.

The wind picked up and the swells grew. Rust's *Half Pint*,
frequently airborne and crest-hopping, kept a steady course
across the Straits of Florida. It was one of the most deceptive
contraptions in the Caribbean. Usually underestimated because
of its meek features, it could outrun most Coast Guard vessels,
and its structure gave it an excellent chance to slip under radar
surveillance.

They were running fast toward the Double Headed Shot
Cays, flyspeck islands on the edge of the Cay Sal Bank, when
Hal said without any introduction: "I'll be leavin' the jus'-juice
business."

"Don't tell me you're going to sell solids?"

"Nope. Jus' back to work for a little while. I'm joinin' the
Green Berets."

"Never knew you had a taste for hearts-and-minds campaigns."

"It's jus' my old chief's in it. And he says we'll do coun-
terinsurgency our way."

"Introducing social reforms under pressure, you mean," said
Rust, knowing well that the irony in his voice would escape his
companion, who had won medals galore in Korea, fighting under
his "old chief," who had managed to run a kind of rat pack unit.

"Right. I mean right if you mean what my old chief means—

that if you've got 'em by the balls, their hearts and minds will follow."

He emitted a dirty laugh, and Rust joined him without much conviction. Hal was not quite the perfect companion for a stimulating conversation over a couple of drinks.

Sound and bullets could never penetrate the three-inch laminated glass, but the last of Washington's daylight entered the Oval Office with ease. The President's shadow grew longer and thinner until, like some quixotic matchstick-man, it reached across the floor toward the curved, cream sofas near the fireplace. Nobody bothered to switch on any lights yet.

"Have you seen those?" An endless shadow-finger slid across the old ship-timber of the President's desk and came to rest on a blue plastic folder.

"No." Bobby Kennedy walked to the desk and removed a series of large photographs from the folder. He flicked through them. His eyes darkened.

"We usually take it for granted that inefficiency is a typical democratic disease," said the President. "But then you look at the antics of dictatorship . . ."

"It's not the dictatorship. It's the wisdom of the military," Bobby Kennedy interrupted his brother. "Look at them." He shook his head in disbelief. The photographs were the latest batch from the CIA. The high-definition U-2 pictures of Cuban airfields showed an open display of military aircraft, wing tip to wing tip, without camouflage, without any attempt to disguise that many of them bore Soviet markings.

"It's good to know they're there for the taking. If need be, that is," said the President.

"It would have to be a pre-emptive strike. Without warning. And I doubt if you'd ever do that."

"Not unless we were pushed too far."

"I don't believe it, I can't visualize you as the Tojo of the 1960s. You'd never do a Pearl Harbor in reverse."

"I wouldn't want to." The President stood at the window, watching the distant trees as they were slowly denuded by the winds of early fall. Each dropping leaf revealed a square inch or so of the emerging jigsaw picture of the Washington Monument. "But some day, I may be forced to act."

"I can't imagine any president of this country being impeached. Not unless he's done something really criminal. Or really immoral." A mischievous smile softened the Attorney General's face. "And by immoral I mean something more serious than a bit of a tumble with a blonde, you know."

But the President refused to share the intimate joke of the innuendo. He gestured toward the photographs on the desk. "You said 'it's not the dictatorship, it's the military' or something like that, right? Well what about our own military? Would they allow a thing like that to happen at our airfields?"

"Good point. Ask them."

"I can do better." The President picked up the phone and pressed a button on his 18-line console. He did not need to identify himself. "I want General Taylor to run U-2 missions to all our military airfields without any warning. Apply the same secrecy as to Cuban operations. And I want the pictures as soon as they're in without letting anyone else see them."

Bobby Kennedy's little nod of approval paid homage to both his President and older brother. "Now why didn't anyone at CIA think about that?"

"Because most of them are very ordinary people." Which was one of the most devastating remarks about anyone in routine Kennedy parlance. "We ought to have put you in charge there. I've said it before—you're wasted at Justice."

The Caribbean became choppy, and sharks trailed the *Half Pint* as it approached Cay Sal, the largest of the barren coral dots which were hardly visible even on detailed naval charts. Rust maneuvered the boat with great caution. In the darkness it was hard to find the right island facing Cuba, just across the Nicholas Channel. Rust cut the engine, and Hal jumped out to pull the boat into some shrubs. It had been a three-hour ride without ever requiring the slightest effort from the twin Ford Mermaid engines.

Now there was nothing for them but to wait and trust Orlando, whose instinctive navigation had never failed to keep a rendezvous.

"Do you expect trouble?" asked Hal at last.

"No."

"What then?"

"I want you to go home and bring back the *Half Pint* on

Monday to pick me up. If I'm not here by Tuesday, just run and keep the boat."

"You wanna go into Cuba?" And when Rust nodded, Hal told him he was a fool.

It was an unpleasant wait. Many Cuban refugees had died there of starvation, thirst and exposure to violent storms, while waiting in vain for the occasional call by American patrols. Regular control and protection of the isolated little islands was impossible, and Cuban coast guards sometimes sent in landing parties to capture stranded fugitives.

Rust stared out across the Nicholas Channel. On the left he saw the flashing entrance beacon of La Isabela harbor. The lights on the right might have belonged to Cárdenas or Varadero. In between, searchlights kept sweeping the dark, hardly navigable mass of mangroves and coral reefs. A ship passed between him and the Cuban coast. Even with binoculars he could not identify it. But it seemed odd to see most of the hull above the water despite some bulk cargo on deck. Would the holds be almost empty? That was a pretty ridiculous idea.

They both heard a strange noise. A small boat approaching slowly, probably driven by oars. Hal moved back and disappeared among shrubs. Rust was too late to say there was no need.

"*Amigo*, you've beaten me to it." Orlando stepped ashore and warmly embraced Rust. He had two other men with him. Rust looked at them with a question in his eyes. "I'm getting too old for this game," said Orlando. As if to prove their usefulness, the two worked hard to swap their rum and cigars for Rust's wares, including radios, small electrical appliances, and clothes of great scarcity in Havana.

"One other thing," said Rust. "I'm coming with you." And when he saw surprise and reluctance on Orlando's face, he added: "I pay for the favor." He produced a large wad of dollars, which caused obvious excitement among the Cubans. The two insisted on going into a huddle with Orlando. They retreated, and there was some whispered argument in Spanish which was too fast for Rust to follow. Once Orlando shouted at them: "You're not good enough to be fed to the sharks!" Then they all approached him. The old man was white with fury: "Give them the money, you foolish dog. Haven't I always warned you never to show cash to animals?"

The two were behind him, side by side as if for mutual reassurance. Rust now saw the gun in the younger helper's hand. "Half now, half when you bring me back here," Rust said and moved slowly to his right. If they followed him, they would soon have their backs to the spot where Hal had disappeared. He only hoped that the big man had not fallen asleep. But before he could finish his move, there was a terrible crack of bones that made his stomach turn. The gun went off, the bullet whizzing toward a passing cloud. Both helpers were on the ground, blood pouring from the corresponding wounds where Hal had made their heads collide. They were yelling in pain, but only for seconds. Hal kicked one unconscious, and his hand came down on the neck of the other.

Orlando shook his head sadly. "How can we take them back? They'll report us right away."

"They'll be all right here with Hal, who'll wait for me," said Rust. "And you'll collect the second half of the money."

"How long do you want to stay?"

"Just a day. I must see Morales."

Orlando did not react to the name. He knew perfectly well that Morales ran some part of the Second National Escambray Front, an important part of the little resistance there was on the island, but it was best not to know these things. He moved toward his boat, then stopped and looked back at the still-unconscious men on the ground.

"They'll be all right," said Hal, and his voice had the sympathy and confidence an ambulance driver would try to convey to a coronary patient.

The run to the edge of the black clumps of mangroves was uneventful. Rust wondered how much the old man depended on luck and how much on bribes to the coastal patrols, but he never asked. Once they were inside the narrow channel among the coral formations, larger boats could not follow them. And Orlando seemed to know every knot and tangle in the dense vegetation, where they had to duck frequently not to be hooked and fished out by low branches.

Morales was pleased and displeased to see Rust, who woke him up just as dawn was about to break over the Caribbean. As always, there was a young, fleshy and sensual girl in attendance, and Morales shoved her out of bed to make room for the visitor to sit down. The girl stood in the corner, covering her nakedness as best she could with a small pillow until the old man lit a cigar and dismissed her with a wave of two fingers. His heavily lined, ageless peasant face revealed nothing while listening to Rust.

"I have to get someone out of Russia. It's very important to me. Can you help me?" Rust's Spanish was just about adequate, but Morales, whose English was excellent, let him struggle. It was an old game between the two. If Rust needed something, he would have to make the effort.

"I don't know, *amigo*, it's very difficult."

"If it wasn't, I wouldn't come and ask you."

That made sense. And Morales owed Rust enough favors to take the hopeless request seriously. "You haven't been here, amigo, for what, two years? Things have changed. The place is crawling with informers. Don't laugh, I know they're only inefficient Cubans, but they're Russian-trained, and they're well paid by and much afraid of the DGI."

Yes, Rust knew that. Only last March, the Russians had tried to oust Castro and annex his revolution "as though they had won it in a raffle." Those were the Líder Máximo's words when he raved and denounced the conspirators for almost four hours without stopping. Escalente, their leader, slipped out to Prague at the last minute, but other old Communists were arrested or exiled, and Kudryavtsev, the Russian ambassador, was expelled. The Soviet Union had to buy back Castro's friendship with extra weapons and goods, and had to accept the fact that Cuban intelligence, the Dirección General de Inteligencia, was a force to restrain or reckon with.

Rust had no time to argue. He had to hit Morales below the belt. "I didn't list the risks when your grandson had to get out, when you needed supplies, when..."

Morales interrupted him, raising both hands as if surrendering. He got out of bed, put on his tatty white shirt and calico pants, and pressed a raffia hat on his head. When he pulled aside the curtain that served as a door, the girl appeared, still clutching the pillow. "Get some sleep, *amigo*, I may be some time," he said to Rust, looked at the girl, looked back at the visitor, then added: "She'll give you food. Don't let your prick talk when your head knows better what not to do."

Which was not easy advice to take and remember when, after feeding him, the girl climbed into the bed next to Rust and lay there, under the one pillow, without at all pretending to sleep.

• Saturday, September 8 •

Ex-President Truman declares: Eisenhower was "the laziest President we ever had"; he blames Ike for the current Cuban situation because "he didn't have the guts to enforce the Monroe Doctrine" and "we're now paying the penalty for eight years of a do-nothing Administration." Bertrand Russell subscribes to the quaint belief that "man has a future on this planet" though it's "six to four in favor of war and the risk is growing."

THE COLORS AND GENERAL POOR QUALITY OF THE HUGE map on the wall would have been fit for a village school rather than the Kremlin's underground war room, but the details were exceptionally accurate, and that was all that mattered to young Missile General Biryuzov. His voice would have guaranteed instant sleep to confirmed insomniacs, but again, that did not matter because his audience was too anxious to hear him. He picked up a pair of wooden beam compasses and pinned one leg, with a single thrust, to San Cristóbal, west of Havana, in Cuba, and drew two circles.

"To summarize it, the first circle represents fifteen hundred kilometers, the second three thousand kilometers. Our medium and intermediate ranges. The first extends almost to Washington, beyond Ho-ooston and Mexico City; the second takes in most of Canada and almost all the 'main enemy' territory all the way to Los Angeles. Progress is satisfactory, and we hope to be fully operational by the middle of October."

A heavily decorated general fingered his magnificent row of combat medals and listened impassively. His eyes wandered toward Khrushchev and a select few of his colleagues. There was silence. Nobody reacted to the summary. Not until Khrushchev did. When his left fist hit his right palm and he snorted a single sound of laughter, everybody clapped and laughed with him. The general turned to the rotund marshal of the artillery, who looked away immediately as if they had never met. He got the same reaction from the baby-blue eyes of hognose, who sat next to Brezhnev in the third row.

Biryuzov gave a few more details. The marshal viewed him with undisguised hatred: the younger man was openly after his own job. He had buried a few such aspirants over the years, but Biryuzov was different and would have to be watched. He only half heard Khrushchev saying: "And when we're ready, the Kennedys will opt for a compromise."

"They might choose to hit us instead, hit us hard," the marshal said. He did not mean to say it. He was absentminded, off his guard for a second. Biryuzov's fault, clearly. But there was no chance to take it back.

Khrushchev's fist came down on the bench in front and sent documents flying. "I didn't invite questions and comments, did I? Did I, comrade? I made a statement. A clear statement, that they'll compromise. Why did I say that? *Why?* Because I'm a fool?" He paused, then burst into a wide smile that tried to embrace the whole room, including the marshal. "I'll tell you why. Because I know. And I have proof. That's why." He tapped his nose with his forefinger. "We know. To catch a bedbug, you must pour boiling water into his ear. But to do that, you must know where the bedbug is, and how it behaves. The best is to ask the bedbug first."

During the outburst of compulsory appreciation and merriment, the marshal excused himself. He had to go through a series of heavy, manually operated bombproof doors (Khrushchev distrusted pushbutton devices) and down a maze of vaults for selected survival. He expected to be followed, after a respectable delay, by that hognosed Brezhnev aide. It would be an innocent exchange of a few glances and even fewer words. It was a risk, but only a slight one, he hoped. After five minutes, when still nobody joined him at the urinals, he began to feel ridiculous and uneasy standing with his fly open, facing the wall. Then his nerves began to fray. He might be being watched. He might be being set up by the others. Perhaps he ought to stay away from the next meeting in Granovsky. And let the world sink into a shit pit under a mushroom cloud. He could not wait any longer and hurried back to the war room.

The meeting was just breaking up. Hognose took the marshal's arm and suggested a short walk. The marshal glanced at his watch: yes, it was past seven o'clock, there would be no more tourists or sightseers left in the Kremlin grounds, it would be pleasant and safe to talk under the glittering onion domes.

As they walked past the Czar Bell, rounding the Bell Tower of Ivan the Great, the marshal said. "So, we've failed, I suppose." He tried not to look too grave.

"In a word, yes, so far." And after a pause: "But nothing is lost. Not yet."

"What went wrong?"

"I'm not sure. But most of our communications must have been blocked somewhere down the line."

"By whom?"

"Who knows? Maybe our own men within the administration in Washington. Maybe by the American military, who could advocate armed aggression if we're seen to be arming Fidel. As you know, they're already preparing another invasion."

"What does Leonid Ilyich think of it?"

The hognose twitched and the baby-blue eyes grew several shades darker. Brezhnev was not supposed to be mentioned at all. The marshal was a fool. Perhaps it was a mistake to involve him. Too late to exclude him now. "I think . . ." He paused, only to start again. "I think that we must now explore more unorthodox channels. We're scraping the barrel in that respect, but the situation is not without hope. There're several avenues, and any of them may lead to our goal, I don't mind which, as long as it's untraceable to us. In Florida, for instance . . ."

"I don't want to know," the marshal interrupted.

"Neither do I. And I wouldn't want to tell you if I knew. I don't even know whom we've instructed to make the effort to relay the tip-off to Kennedy. But I can tell you that unorthodox channels are used even by Nikita Sergeyevich himself. In Florida we've picked up some information that he's communicated with Kennedy through a third-rate businessman."

"Why?"

"Presumably, he can't quite trust our own diplomats. Or the people who surround the President."

The marshal pulled his overcoat tighter on his chest. "I hope you know whom we can trust." The setting sun was bright and made him squint, but the breeze was chilly: it might be signaling a short autumn and a long, cold winter.

It was midafternoon and the heat was dizzying when Morales returned with a red-check sports shirt, baggy slacks and a guayabera, Castro's favorite loose-fitting jacket, for Rust. He watched his visitor and the girl, both fully dressed now, to satisfy himself that his warning had been heeded.

"Put these on," he said finally, "and leave all your own things here. Everything."

"How about shoes?"

"What shoes?" Morales laughed. "You're a drunk from the Russian camp at Sagua la Grande and lost your shoes. If we're stopped, you just keep singing and yelling at everybody in Russian."

Rust changed his clothes and noted the Russian label in the shirt. He gave Morales a look full of admiration.

The Cuban was pleased. "They all wear this," he said with pride. "Now turn around." And from behind, he poured a good half-bottle of rum on Rust. The girl giggled in the background. "Now you're genuine Russian. Russian shirts soak up Cuban rum well."

Morales drove a multicolored Dodge which was open at the back not so much by design as by bomb damage, rust and old age, and his foul-smelling passenger never thought it would make it all the way down the Zapata Peninsula.

Rust noticed a soccer field. The goal posts were freshly painted. "What's that? Soccer in Cuba?"

Morales spat out, "For our permanent visitors. They're building them all over the place." Offhand he remembered four such locations.

Rust was not interested. "Since you know so much about the Russkis here, you must have heard about the sailor who jumped ship about ten days ago."

"I haven't."

"That's odd."

"It isn't. Because there wasn't one."

"There was," Rust insisted.

"But not ten days ago. More like a month it was."

The man must have tried to get away from Cuba for weeks, until he was desperate enough to join that foolish and doomed escape attempt. Rust hoped he had died without much pain. He was grateful to the sailor for delivering his father's message, perhaps with his last breath.

Rust's olfactory nerves had been thoroughly desensitized by the rum in his clothes, but even so his nose told him that they were well into the several hundred square miles of uninhabitable marshland. Cool breezes, whiffs of citrus and pungent bell-flowers had been left behind; the stench of the swamp was inescapable. Only alligator hunters and fugitives left the road to the Bay of Pigs beyond Jaguey Grande. And, of course, the man they had set out to visit. Morales stopped the car on the shore of the Laguna del Tesoro; frightened away a pair of flamingos with his choice of a hiding place for it, and led Rust to a waiting boat.

After a few minutes out on the lake, they entered a huge lagoon, and Morales warned Rust to keep his hands away from the edge of the boat. The reason would soon be obvious: the sluggish water was alive with crocodiles. Now and again a head appeared, lethal teeth snapped at thin air, a tail gave a nudge to the boat and made Rust swear.

The man they had come to see met them at a slippery, disused pier. Half his face was in the shadow of the wide brim of a straw hat, the other half was covered by his arm. His first sentence was to ask Rust never to look at him.

"No offense, señor, but if you're caught and beaten, you'll tell them everything, and when they tear your nails out, you'll remember what you think you never knew. Why make it easy to describe me? Best if you turn your back to me."

He was some sort of manager of the crocodile farm, where baby crocs were bred in large quantities, mainly for export. He led them along shaky wooden catwalks, barely above the reach of all those mincing machines with the ancient, lifeless eyes. They stopped on a platform which seemed to have more gaps than planks, but Rust was assured that at least they would be safe there both from the sunbathing pack of reptiles and the G2 men of the *policía secreta*.

The discussion was brief and to the point. The man was indebted to Morales, who, in turn, was indebted to Rust. Help, therefore, would be forthcoming if the only possible proposition was acceptable.

Until recently, the Russians had required skins only. Now they wanted "live" consignments. The baby crocs traveled in huge, specially constructed tanks aboard cargo ships, mostly the *Omsk* and the *Poltava*, which plied regularly between Havana and Odessa. The empty tanks were always returned, and Rust's friend could make the journey hiding in one of those.

"We always have a croc farmer in charge of the babies, and he returns with the empties. Normally, he's staying at the Hotel Tsentralnaya, and your friend must contact him there. Your friend's biggest problem will be to enter the port itself and get to the ship. And that's not easy. I hear these ships bring us *cohetes* and other cargo on some secret list, and they are loaded in a restricted dock used only by the military. So how he gets there is his business. Does that help you, señor?"

"I don't know. I'll have to see. But I'll be grateful to you even for just trying to help."

The man gave Rust the name to look for in the Tsentralnaya. That was a risk he had to take. Rust shook hands with him behind his back. That gave him the added advantage of keeping his eyes on the scaly carpet of crocs. For the return journey, they took a freshly killed baby croc as an alibi for the visit if caught.

• Sunday, September 9 •

Havana's TV is filled with old Walt Disney cartoons and exhortations for greater productivity. U-2 shot down over China; pilot missing, presumed dead.

ORLANDO TOOK RUST OUT OF CUBA BEFORE DAYBREAK. He was worried about the young men they had left with Hal. "We can't just kill them. Or leave them there to die. But if I bring them back, they'll probably report me." His thumb drew a line across his throat.

Rust suggested that Orlando should go with him to Florida.

"I can't live away from home. Not that I love it, but it's home."

His problem was solved when they reached the island. Hal "Jus'-juice" Sheridan was alone. "They both ran away," he said and looked out toward the shark-infested waters.

"They couldn't swim," Orlando whispered in shock.

Hal raised his shoulders slowly, then dropped them in a

51

gesture of helplessness. Rust knew it would be pointless to question him.

At Hyannisport, everybody seemed to enjoy the peace of a balmy Sunday, everybody except the President's doctor and bodyguards. They watched the game of touch football in progress on the big lawn in the Kennedy compound. They winced every time the part-time quarterback full-time President was brought to the ground when an overexuberant player tackled him.

Few people would have been allowed to interrupt the noisy, traditional revelry of the Kennedy clan, but General Taylor was one of the few. The Kennedy sisters, acting as manic cheerleaders, tried to keep him away from the game, but he was too determined. He had a shock for the President: the U-2 pictures of the U.S. airfields. There were rows upon rows of bombers and fighters, wing to wing in the open, there to be blown up or strafed at will, with no room even to run for it, as if Pearl harbor had never taught anything to anyone. "It seems we have an awful lot of very ordinary people in charge," mumbled the Attorney General. The pictures wiped away the joy of his team being in the lead by a touchdown.

After showering in his house, the President crossed the lawn to Bobby's home where a few friends were gathered in the sunroom. He took another look at the photographs and heard his brother talking: "I don't know if we'll be successful in overthrowing Castro," said Bobby, "but we have nothing to lose in my estimate. That's why Mongoose is top priority."

General Taylor noted that the President's eyes narrowed. JFK was losing interest even in his old favorite, the development of what he called counter-insurgency units to police trouble spots in the Third World. He used to have great plans for the Green Berets who would "introduce social reforms under pressure" instead of fighting revolutions, but lately he felt that the special force was attracting the wrong men, those with a taste for action rather than hearts-and-minds campaigns.

"Then aren't we strong enough to finish off Fidel?" asked one of the Kennedy sisters. "Just wipe him out, can't we?"

"We can," said the President in a tone that made several people twitch because they all knew what was coming, "but basically, we arm to parley." Everybody in the room had heard him quote Churchill's negotiating credo several times before.

"What if Khrushchev put bombs or whatever in Cuba?"

"That would be an entirely new ballgame," conceded Kennedy. The conversation suddenly shifted back to a truly exciting and important topic—who had caught the most passes that afternoon.

· Monday, September 10 ·

The Soviet Union denounces Kennedy: the calling up of
U.S. reservists is "yet another provocation" that might
"plunge the world into thermonuclear war." Khrushchev
claims: Soviet missiles are so powerful "that there is no
need to find sites for them in Cuba or anywhere else beyond
the boundaries of the Soviet Union."

THE CUBAN KID SQUATTED UNDER A STREET LIGHT IN LIT-
tle Havana and carved his toenails with a switchblade.
He thought he might have to kill someone when Rust offered
him $10 for a few minutes' work. Rust disliked using anyone
else, but felt that the task was urgent. The kid would never be
able to describe his face hidden in the shadow of a peaked
sailor's cap.

On their way to a public phone booth, the kid understood
clearly what he had to do. Rust dialed a Washington number,
and the boy asked for Mr. Elliott Repson.

"I have a message for you, sir."

"From whom?"

"It says that *cohetes* come from Odessa to Havana." He paused to read the next line of the note held up by Rust.

"Can you hang on for a second?"

"No, I have to go. But it also says there are European soccer fields constructed near Remedios, Sagua la Grande, Guanajay and San Cristóbal."

"I didn't know that Cubans played soccer." Repson's voice revealed nothing but indifference.

"They don't, but the Russians do." Then Rust pointed at another sentence, and the kid read it. "Perhaps they mean to stay for a while."

"And how did you know my home number?" He paused, and when there was no answer, he added: "It's not listed."

The kid looked puzzled. Rust smiled at him, pressed down the cradle, disconnecting the call, and gave him a $5 bonus.

At the other end, Repson stared at the suddenly dead receiver in his hand. Then he shrugged his shoulders and pocketed the notes he had jotted down.

"Ell!"

"Yes, coming." He replaced the receiver and turned the wheelchair toward the bedroom.

"Who was that, honey?"

"Nothing very important."

The bedroom door opened, and Anna came out. "Could you zip me up, honey?" She waited for him to wheel himself to her and lowered herself quite imperceptibly to be within his reach. But Repson noticed it. He knew and appreciated the trick that was to make him feel perfectly capable and adequate even in this respect. He kissed her bare back. The zip would have to wait. He reached around her and touched her proudly prominent breasts which would catch every TV director's eyes during Bobby Kennedy's press conferences—the cameras would linger on her.

She wriggled a little with a mixture of "We're late" and "Wish we had more time for this," and he understood. They were to dine with her big white chief himself. He zipped her up, and she kissed him. "Let's move, honey, we'll be late."

"We have to stop off at the White House for a few minutes in case I'm wanted at the COMOR meeting."

"Oh no."

"It's unlikely. We'll miss our cocktails, perhaps. You just wait for me in the car."

The Committee on Overhead Reconnaissance met in McGeorge Bundy's office. Chaired by the President's security assistant, the very existence of COMOR was a most closely guarded secret, and tonight they had an exceptionally important decision to make. Only the previous day a Chinese Nationalist U-2, flying from Taiwan, had been shot down by the Communists over the mainland. The implication was clear: the Russians had done it once, the Chinese did it again, the Cubans must also be capable of doing the same. After a lengthy clash of opinions, the "restrict the flights" campaigners won. U-2 missions would be shorter and only peripheral, even though it meant that western Cuba would not be directly overflown.

Orders were issued to "those concerned." It meant that even in the White House, very few people would be made aware of the new position. The officer in chage of the U-2 missions sighed with relief. Elliott Repson was free to leave. Anna, too, would be relieved: they would not be late even for pre-dinner drinks.

Repson wheeled himself fast along the wide corridor. The presidential aide who had the room with the best view of the south lawn caught up with him.

"What do you think, Elliott?"

"I haven't been invited to think."

"You are now."

Repson shrugged his shoulders.

"Aren't you worried?"

"I would be, if it was my decision. But it wasn't."

"Come into my office for a moment, will you?" He noticed that Repson was looking at his watch. "It shouldn't take long." He held the door open for Repson and shut it firmly as soon as the wheelchair was through. "Right." He sat at his desk but jumped up impatiently two seconds later. "Okay, I'm worried."

"And I don't think that the members of COMOR have taken their decision lightly."

"No, I don't think so. But McCone is away. The pro-U-2 camp is weaker at the moment. And limiting the flights means that we're losing our last source of hard intelligence. You agree?"

"I do," said Repson with an eye on his watch.

"Our best sources seem to be drying up or offering hearsay. The CIA passes us tidbits without too much conviction. The entire intelligence spectrum is as bleak as if someone's blown all the fuses."

"I'm just as worried and annoyed as you are, believe me," said Repson. "And I agree about the quality of intelligence reaching us. Just this evening I've had an anonymous call about the Russkis constructing soccer fields in Cuba. Yes, the implication can be serious, but no, it can't be accepted as evidence of anything. And I agree, hard facts don't seem to reach us. The channels must be blocked somewhere—or else we may be worried about the nonarrival of information concerning facts that do not exist. But we've been through all this before, and right now Anna is waiting for me in the car."

"I'm sorry. I really am. I only meant to ask you if it would be a good idea to inform McCone."

"You mean a good idea for me? No, I don't think so. The Company can function perfectly well in the absence of its head. Besides, it's not for me to guess at what point the old man should be informed."

"True. But if our guesses are wrong, we may have to accept an embarrassing compromise."

"I thought the President made it clear that we'd never compromise."

"He has. But are you sure?" The aide paused to let his doubt sink in, then corrected himself, mainly for the record. "What I mean is that if Khrushchev manages to sneak nukes into Cuba and succeeds in making them fully operational before we know about it or have a chance to interfere, the threat to our cities may become so acute that we may be forced to reconsider everything."

"Better than to start World War Three, I guess."

"Maybe."

· Friday, September 14 ·

Kennedy states at news conference: currently, American military intervention in Cuba is not required or justifiable. *Pravda* appeals to people of the world to prevent U.S. aggressors from engineering war. Moscow celebrates record-breaking Vostok space flight (94 hours, 35 minutes). Kennedy backs race to the moon. Soviet grain harvest "a disaster"—Khrushchev is responsible but other heads roll.

"NO, SIR, I'M AFRAID SIR CHARLES IS NOT AVAILABLE, but at eleven A.M., he'll be at the North London Crematorium."

"Dead or alive?"

"I'm afraid he didn't specify it, Mr. Rust."

Rust attended the brief and perfunctory service only because it was raining outside. When it was over, Charles Stoker put on his gray Homburg and centered it meticulously. He apologized for dragging him all the way there.

58

"That's all right, it's fun to meet in cemeteries," Rust said, then controlled himself. "I'm sorry. Was it a friend or relative?"

"Only a colleague—not even quite that."

"And you represented the department."

"Wrong again. I came of my own accord."

"And arranged to meet me here because you thought I got my kicks out of attending strangers' funerals."

Charles smiled, and somehow it only made him look more solemn. "No, but if we stop honoring our dead, how can we ask the next generation to die for this or that cause?"

"One of your men?"

"No, no. Not really. Just a businessman. Attended some trade fair or other in Leningrad. Came back very sick. Vaguely remembered a peculiar little pinprick in the crowd milling around the Malachite Room of the Winter Palace. Or do you call it the Hermitage?"

"Was he . . . ?"

"We don't know. His illness was serious and never fully diagnosed. He suffered a great deal."

"And you are warning me?"

"But my dear boy, what on earth gave you that idea?"

"You won't help. And I'm here to understand why."

"You're here to be driven to a delightful little country pub where we have a table booked."

Charles drove a converted London cab with a door added to enclose the luggage rack, where a bucketlike contraption with adjustable straps served as a front passenger seat for a child. She must be an adult by now, thought Rust. He declined Charles's offer to sit in the back.

On their way to Hertfordshire, Charles asked about O'Connor, the agent who had brought the sailor's message to Rust. "Have you seen him again?"

"No. Schramm couldn't find him for me."

"Oh."

"Schramm says there's a tremendous turnover in junior men at Miami station. There's nothing significant about it."

"No, I didn't say there was. It's only odd."

"I didn't want him to attach too great importance to my request."

"Naturally. I only meant that Schramm is a good man, and

it's, well, a bit unexpected that he's never heard about your defector-messenger."

"Not at all. Even Schramm wouldn't know everything. Especially now that they're more than a little busy with the Cuban problem."

"Problem, dear boy? Problem? I'd call it an obsession."

"If you like."

"Don't you think that you Americans make too much fuss about it?"

"Too much or too little. I wouldn't know."

Charles dropped the subject and proved himself an attentive host throughout a very liquid lunch that ended with Irish coffee for good measure.

The rain had stopped, a pale sun came out, and Charles suggested a leisurely country walk to vent the surplus alcohol. Rust guessed that the quiet stroll would give Charles the opportunity to talk without facing him and broach a subject the older man might consider too personal and therefore embarrassing. Rust decided to make it easier for him. "So what about my trip to Russia?"

"Now that you ask, well, I have certain reservations about it, I must say."

"You think it's too dangerous."

"No. Not *too* dangerous. Not if you must go."

"You mean I don't have to."

"Nobody's going to shoot you if you stay."

"I know."

"And don't forget, whatever scheme you have in mind, you'll run into all sorts of unexpected problems over there."

"I expect so."

"In which case you may never pull it off. And with all his Russian experience, your father ought to be the first to understand."

"He probably does. But he must be desperate. And I don't think I could live with myself if I didn't even try to help."

"All I mean is that you can't assume responsibility for everything and everybody around you. Nobody can."

"No? My father used to do just that, I'm told." It was the simplicity of the countryside, the gentleness of the sun and the casualness of the breeze that urged Rust to air some thoughts that were not used to daylight. "I don't think you can understand."

"You've explained it once. I haven't forgotten."

"I haven't told you all. I couldn't. How hard it was to live with the compulsion that I must see his grave. And how much harder it was actually to talk to him when I found him."

"Yes, it must be difficult to have a relationship that ends before it has a chance to begin. But I suppose you had to try to win a father and see what made him tick."

"Him? No, it was me I was trying to understand. What I was made of. To see if I could blame that stranger for anything bad in me. To see what he might have given me apart from my German origin. After all, he was a shadow I had tried to shed all my life." The Scotch, the wine and the Irish joined forces to raise his voice, but his tone remained low, without self-pity. "It was because of him that I had no school friends and they all called me 'the Nazi.' It was no good to argue that he was known as a tough man with strong anti-Nazi views. The kids would only laugh. They kept chasing me around and shouting, 'Come on, Nazi, let's see how tough you are,' and I couldn't tell them that I wasn't tough at all, that I hated fights and hated my father. I had to fight. And to survive I had to win. Then my face was cut. It healed badly. I was marked. Just the thing to make me look sort of fierce. And if you look fierce, you're assumed to be fierce. So let's see what you're made of. It follows you everywhere, and if you try to run away, it travels ahead of you like a gunslinger's reputation. Those who don't challenge you wish they dared to."

"Like your brother?" Charles's voice was unnaturally soft, as if to give a chance not to be heard.

"Maybe. Yes, probably he, too."

It was Elliott who had insisted on that toboggan race. He had heard the name somewhere and took to calling Helm "Gatsby." He would run around the house all day shouting, "Come on, Gatsby, race me, Gatsby, race me, Gatsby, race me, race me." So he raced him. They hit a clump of snow-camouflaged trees almost simultaneously. But Elliott yelled a warning at the last second. Rust ducked and had only a finger broken. He told no one about it, and it healed leaving him with a bumpy knuckle. Elliott injured his back. Irreparably.

"So it wasn't your fault, was it?"

"Our mother didn't see it that way. I was the older one. I should have had more sense. She never forgave me."

"How old were you?"

"Just turning ten."

Charles knew that the incident must have left Rust with a self-imposed debt that would never dwindle no matter how frequently the interest was paid. You should be entitled to some remission at least for good conduct, he meant to say, but chose to chatter lightly about the conduct of the Romans whose footsteps they had been following for an hour. Rust said nothing. His silence was infectious. It was only when they had returned to London and were approaching Rust's hotel in Knightsbridge that Charles spoke again. By then his voice had been cleansed of all traces of emotions it was not trained to handle.

"I've arranged a magazine assignment for you, dear boy. It's a tremendous opportunity to travel on behalf of the Wonderful World of Transportation."

"Thanks." Deep down he had always known that Charles would help him. "It's been my lifelong desire to work for them."

"You don't seem to be impressed."

"I am. What's the gimmick?"

"They're about to open a new subway in Moscow. Khrushchev himself will cut the throat, I mean the ribbon. Sorry. *Lapsus linguae*. Showing my Freudian slip."

"Will the job speed up my visa application sufficiently?"

"That in itself won't. And, of course, I can't be seen helping you directly, but there's a chap, an osteopath."

"As long as he leaves my bones alone."

"Don't worry. Most of his manipulations are not concerned with bones at all. He has some excellent social contacts among Russki diplomats."

"Will he be doing you a favor?"

"Definitely not. It's the magazine that's going to be obliged to him."

"I understand."

"But, on the other hand . . . yes, come to think of it, you could do me a favor."

"Shoot."

"You once said your father spent a few years in the special camps near Volochanka, somewhere in the Arctic region."

"You have a terrific memory."

"Did he ever mention which particular camps?"

"Yes. VS 389/2-5 and 2-7, then BV 523/5-4 and AN 243 as well as—"

"Ah. Say no more. That's a spot of luck, luck indeed. Could you ask him to answer a couple of questions for me?"

"I could do better than that. Once we're out of Russia, I'll introduce you and you can ask him yourself."

"Lovely. That's just fine. Except . . . well, what I mean is, just to be on the safe side . . ."

"You mean if anything goes wrong and I make it but he doesn't?"

"Well, sort of. Not that I'd expect anything to go wrong, but, well, you know me, I'm selfish, I must admit."

"Okay, okay. What do I ask?"

"I'm fascinated by the security and layout of the VS 389 camps. Just roughly, how many guards are on duty at night? How deep is the outer safety perimeter in 2-5? What could be the distance between the foundry and the nearest watchtower in BV 523? And it would be particularly exciting to know if it's possible to see from the towers what's happening inside the foundry. I mean, if Papa happens to remember such useless details."

Charles made it all sound light and apologetic. Rust asked no questions. He was prepared to pretend that he had taken the request as something to satisfy an eccentric's curiosity rather than an escape planner's need of information.

· Monday, September 17 ·

Kennedy warns: Ships of NATO allies carrying Soviet cargo to Cuba could cause dangerous problems. *Pravda* warns: U.S. preparations for "armed provocation" against Cuba-bound Soviet ships could cause nuclear missile war.

MAJOR ANDREY ANISIMOVICH BOYCHENKO YAWNED AT the day's list of Moscow arrivals and fought back the urge to swear. It was a bloody insult to him and a stupid, even criminal, waste of KGB manpower to have a highly trained man like himself assigned to duties of the Second Directorate, Tourist Department. All right, all right, the job required experience and sharp eyes to spot dangerous visitors and, even more, to recognize their weaknesses. One could then select potential targets for the Anglo-American and other area departments of the First Directorate. But what on earth was there to be gained from compromising a man like Helm Rust? True, even such a trade magazine reporter could become useful one

day, but it was a long shot at best. The work would certainly
be well below Boychenko's level of skills. He was, after all,
trained for some of the most specialized tasks, including "wet
affairs," the actual physical elimination of enemies.

Still, what had to be done had to be done. Boychenko had
too many mouths to feed, too many troublesome relatives to
nurse toward more rewarding lives, too many strings to pull
to get his daughter into the Foreign Trade Ministry and more
to get young Yuri Andreyevich, that playboy soldier son of
his, off that rape charge. He could have strangled the boy with
his own hands for failing to understand that for far, far less,
without an influential father, the whole family might have been
arrested. If he must rape someone, couldn't he rape someone
other than a fairly important party *apparatchik*'s only daughter?

"Kolya!" he yelled in cold fury and noted with satisfaction
that the son of a whore orderly got the message all right, because
the door opened almost immediately. The man tried to tidy his
slovenly hair and uniform on his way in. But using both hands
for the more urgent tasks left Kolya with nothing to take the
cigarette butt out of the corner of his mouth. His eyes recognized the mistake, but he had no time to do anything about it.
Boychenko, whose small fat frame camouflaged exceptional
agility, was already on his feet and landed a blinding slap that
threatened to dislocate Kolya's jaw and make him half swallow
the cigarette at the same time. The blow had been earned, of
course, by his son and it was only the orderly's misfortune to
get it, but Kolya should have nothing to complain about: office
work was a much cushier number than "other duties" Boychenko could assign him to.

"Here." Boychenko picked up a slip of paper with Rust's
name on it and tossed it toward Kolya. "See if Records has
anything on him." It should have been done before the visa
was issued, he thought angrily, and his impatience only grew
as he watched the man leave with that irritating shuffle. Damn
him, damn the whole system, damn them all. Why, this was
1962, not the Dark Ages, and rumor had it that not only the
CIA but also the British and German secret services had their
records pushbuttonized, while he might have to wait for hours
if he was lucky, while the dust was blown away from old files.

He was lucky. Kolya returned in not quite two hours with
a slim faded-green file, marked only "secret." The folder con-

tained hardly anything. Basic personal particulars and a brief note on Rust's fourteen months as correspondent in Moscow in 1956 and 1957. Resigned to the boredom of the case, Boychenko closed the file. On the front cover, the attached "Seen/Removed/Returned" slip showed only four entries. The first three were dated 1957. The last one, August 1962. It had been seen by the "military neighbors," the GRU in KGB parlance. Only some six weeks ago. An odd coincidence.

He glanced at his watch. It was time to go to the airport to see the new arrivals. The rain was still coming down relentlessly. Boychenko picked up his short-brim fedora and dark-blue raincoat. He wished they had introduced some variations in the standard-issue plainclothes, at least for those officers who worked among foreigners. He would not object to the conspicuous plainclothes uniform for colleagues dealing with Soviet citizens, because he understood well the principle that on the home front, the obvious presence of a not too secret police acted as a deterrent to adventurous individualism.

The first breath of air, a mixture of cheap perfumes and uniquely obnoxious gasoline fumes, brought back long-forgotten memories to Rust. Sheremetyevo Airport had hardly changed since his last visit some five years ago. Aeroflot staff smiled like any other airline's personnel at the passengers descending the stairs, but armed guards made sure that nobody strayed from the group. There were three coaches waiting, but they had to be filled one by one. When one was full, the doors were locked from the outside, and passengers had to wait for everybody else from the same aircraft. The terminal building had not changed either: it still threatened to burst every time a flight came in.

Passport checkers from the KGB's Chief Border Guards Directorate sat in individual glass cages with manually operated turnstiles in front of each. The line that Rust had joined suddenly dissolved. The officer up front had left his cubicle without a word of warning or apology—his shift was over. People jostled to join other lines, which fought them off. There was no sympathy for losers. Impatient and furious glances were exchanged all around, swearing could be heard here and there, but nobody grumbled about the injustice.

Rust made good use of the extra time. He studied the faces

of men and women who were milling around beyond the customs bench, apparently with nothing better to do. Sweaty faces, wet faces; it was very hot in the overcrowded terminal, and it was raining heavily outside. He studied the eyes. Curious eyes, watchful eyes, bored eyes, suspicious eyes, eyes of authority, eyes that met his gaze, eyes that bounced away, eyes that might have been assigned to focus on a certain Helm Rust arriving from London. He had to try to spot them if eventually he might want to escape from them.

The line moved forward and shoved him in front of the smoke-filled glass cage. There was a clonk; the turnstile had locked him into position. He faced a young man whose old eyes wandered slowly from passport cover to the photograph inside, on to the photocopies of the first four passport pages that carried the visa, on to the photograph attached to the photocopies, back to the picture in the passport, down to some documents and another photograph under the desk, out of Rust's sight, only to return to Rust's face and compare it yet again with the pictures and papers.

Something must be wrong, thought Rust, but then remembered that the lengthy scrutiny was part of the technique. It would make you feel guilty. And if you felt guilty, you must be guilty, guilty of impatience if nothing else, and no one but the guilty would be impatient with the officer who was only doing his duty.

"*Roost?* Helm?"

"That's right." Rust stared at the huge No Smoking sign inside the cubicle, then watched the young officer, who squashed his cigarette this way and that way until it was extinguished irrevocably. Yes, pragmatic Russian wisdom was still much in evidence: in most public places, ashtrays were supplied together with the No Smoking signs because regulations were expected to be broken in any case.

Another clonking sound, and Rust could move on to Customs. His suitcase was opened, and he tried to look bored. He was sure he carried nothing objectionable, no presents, no printed material. Beyond glass doors he watched well-disciplined lines of people waiting patiently for transport in the driving rain. Every time a bus approached, the orderly lines broke into fierce free-for-alls.

A nod told him he was free to enter the Soviet Union. A

woman in a dark-blue raincoat eyed his shoes. Another in identical attire turned away from him. A small fat man yawned. Rust repacked his suitcase but took his raincoat out. Keep warm, he warned himself. Whenever those glass doors opened, cold and humid air rushed in, penetrating clothes and flesh alike.

On the way into town, Rust began to plan how to contact his father. The use of the telephone would be out even if the old man had managed to get one in the past few years and even if he was not yet on the run or hiding somewhere. Calling in person at his address was also out: his father would not want to let the family know about the American son, and the omnipresent *dezhurnaya*, the professional Cerberus of every building, would inevitably see, note and report the visit to the authorities. Don't rush, Rust told himself. Take your bearings. Take your time, take advantage of the ostensibly all-expenses-paid assignment, work on your fun like a tourist, enjoy yourself like a reporter. He could try to meet his father in the street. But the seventeenth-century church, the Solace of All Woeful Souls, had to be his best bet. Strange. According to his mother, his father had been an agnostic all his life. Well, at least until he had entered an atheist country. Had the old man found religious belief in the camps? Or had he started to attend the Russian Orthodox early-morning service for his wife's sake? In which case, he would not be alone there. Don't rush things. If his father had decided to ask for help and try to leave, there must be a reason. He must be in trouble. He might be watched.

Rust checked into the Ukraine, one of the four tower buildings. By Moscow standards, it would have been quite unacceptable as a railway station of Stalinist grandeur. But it seemed perfectly adequate to serve as a hotel that would ape and, perhaps, belittle what was thought to be an American skyscraper. His passport was retained (indefinitely, for registration purposes), and in return, a pass was issued to identify him and gain him permission to enter the hotel. It was to be deposited with the floor *dezhurnaya* every time he wanted the key to his room.

He telephoned the Moscow Metro Authority and arranged to visit the work in progress on the new Kaluga line, on Tuesday afternoon. He then descended to the service floor of the hotel, where only Western currency could buy unique privileges like a ticket to the Bolshoi and admission to a restaurant without having to wait on line. He also booked a sightseeing tour for Tuesday morning. It was about the last thing he intended to do but he hoped that his watcher, if there was one, would note the arrangements and relax in the full knowledge of the visitor's plans. That would give Rust the opportunity to slip away.

• Tuesday, September 18 •

CIA photo analyst studies pictures of bulk cargo carried on
deck of Cuba-bound Soviet ships, and suspects delivery of
medium-range missiles. Report is deemed "inclusive," buried in "no further action" file.

RUST ROSE EARLY, SKIPPED BREAKFAST AND, AVOIDING
the main lobby, left the hotel via the restaurant entrance
in Kutuzov Prospekt. He walked across the bridge and took a
circuitous subway and bus route to the Tretyakov Gallery. As
far as he could tell, he was not followed. He sat on a bench,
protected from the cold wind by a tobacconist kiosk, and pretending to read his *Pravda*, watched one of the smaller and
better Moscow blocks of apartment houses. If his father still
lived there and had not changed his habits since 1956, he would
soon be visible in the glass tube that was attached to the building
and housed the elevator that must have been an afterthought
by the designers. Only a few minutes later, the old man ap-

peared and began a slow descent. Rust followed him down the street and into the church. There was no tail, no company. Three old women and a crippled war veteran were begging near the entrance. Rust gave them twenty kopeks each and wondered if they were woeful souls or KGB snoops.

Inside, it was a peculiar gathering of the faithful. Most of them were older women; many of them could hardly walk, but managed to genuflect endlessly and at great speed. Younger people appeared and disappeared fast, keeping always to the shadows of columns or the thick of the crowd, mumbling a quick prayer to a favorite icon, listening to the choir, taking deep whiffs as they passed the censer-swinging acolytes, and always, always hoping against hope to remain invisible to onlookers. Rust moved up to stand behind his father. He genuflected with the rest of the people and waited for the singing to get louder. A pity he spoke only a few words of German. When he spoke Russian, people usually took his accent to be Estonian.

"Don't turn round, Vati. It's me, Helmut," he whispered. The old man went white and began to cough uncontrollably. "Don't worry, it's all right, you knew I'd come, it's all right." But it was no good. He already knew that the old man would never make it to Odessa, let alone survive the journey in that crocodile tank. "Where can we talk? Lead the way."

They stopped behind the church. Rust looked at the shivering old man and found it a painful experience. Mainly because he had nothing to say. He felt he should help. That was all. "Vati..." he began, and stopped. He was not even sure why he tried to address him in German. Perhaps that one word was the only link between them. Daddy. He searched for his own features in his father's face but found nothing. Herr Peter Rost was just an entry in his birth certificate. The man facing him was Pyotr Nikolayevich Rostonov.

The old man meekly touched his hand. "I knew you'd come, my son. It was very important. But we can't talk here. And you must meet someone else."

"Who?"

"It's very important." Pyotr Rostonov stopped shaking. He questioned Rust about his plans for the day, then decided that meeting at night would be the safest and most convenient. "Go to the Bolshoi as arranged. When you leave, try to make sure that you're not followed. But don't worry, I'll help you lose your tail. I drive a cab these days. Quite good money, you know. Just come to the street on the right of the Bolshoi, Petrovka ulitsa, will you remember? It's my name, how could you forget? I'll pick you up if it's all clear. Keep warm. It's going to be cold and rainy again."

Rust's day passed fast. He was back at the hotel in time for the sightseeing tour, and tried to look not too bored with the afternoon visit to the excavation of the new subway line. He refused to buy cheap rubles at black-market rate from the cab driver, who might easily be an agent provocateur, and discovered only too late that his lucky booking entitled him to hear *Boris Godunov*.

The same day, possibly the same hour, Oleg Penkovsky, Colonel of Glavnoye Razvedyvatelnoye Upravleniye, the intelligence directorate of the Red Army, walked out of the GRU headquarters in Arbatskaya Ploshchad. In fact, he used the heavy wood and brass gate in Frunze ulitsa where traffic was light and where he hoped to spot if he had a tail. He saw no one. Yet he felt desperate. For a few weeks now, instinct had been telling him that something was wrong. He might be suspected. Or subjected to routine investigation. He ought to lie low. Or give up the work and risk he had undertaken voluntarily.

He turned right, walking slowly, with occasional glimpses at the headquarters windows, the lower halves of which were covered by dense lace curtains. The reflection showed only an old woman behind him. He turned suddenly and walked back, past the top-heavy gate under the row of columns on the first floor, around the corner where a small old building formed part of the massive modern monster with the ominous mass of aerials and radar discs on the roof, past Gogol's statue, and sat on a bench in the green patch of Gogolevsky bul'var. The old woman had not followed him. He might be seeing ghosts. He might be just nervous and exhausted. Might be—but he knew better than that. Had he been spying for cash, he would have given up now. Had he been doing it under pressure or blackmail, he might have disappeared by now. But the film he wanted to pass on was too important. He had to deliver fresh information on the range of Soviet missiles and Khrushchev's Cuban plans.

His regular British businessman contact had been watched for some time by the *sosedi*, the "neighbors" in GRU argot meaning the secret police. A KGB official had told him that. He had even seen the watchers. He had helped his contact get out of Moscow at great risk to himself. And, instead of lying low, he had stepped up his activities in the two months since then. Now his only hope was that his fears might be groundless. If he was really suspected, they might have arrested him or transferred him to curtail his freedom and opportunities to gather information. People with less well-founded suspicions had been shot without too many questions. And he would not be played and used as a bait to catch a bigger fish: he was the big fish.

He stretched, stood up, and walked lazily in the sunshine along the old-gold walls, retracing his steps down Frunze ulitsa and rounding the block to reach the open parking lot in the square at the back.

That evening, he took the film to an American Embassy reception, but the place was crawling with KGB agents under various covers. The following day he made a desperate attempt to meet a British emergency contact, but found no safe opportunity for a hand-over.

Boris Godunov seemed more popular than Rust would have thought. At the cloakroom of the Bolshoi there was a long line, as usual. The attendant, dressed like a Victorian maid, would not be hurried. Rust could not spot his tail, but felt in his bones that there must be one. When the attendant took his raincoat, he rented a pair of binoculars. That was essential.

By the end of the performance he felt quite refreshed. Since receiving his father's message in Florida, this was the first time he had gotten some extra sleep. He was in no hurry to leave the auditorium, and so the line was very long by the time he got to the cloakroom. He waited patiently. His tail must be somewhere near, behind him. After a few minutes, anybody trying to jump the line would only call attention to himself. So he made his move. He grumbled about the slowness of the attendant. "You must be Estonian. I know the accent and your type," said the old woman next to him with mocking contempt. She kindly advised him that he could go to the head of the line right away, because those who were returning binoculars enjoyed priority. "You silly Estonians, you know nothing. It's a miracle that you find Moscow on the map." Everybody laughed, but the mood would have changed at once if anybody tried to advance with the silly Estonian. When Rust left the theater, he only watched if somebody without an overcoat followed him or if anybody was waiting to pick him up outside. If there was someone he was certainly unprepared for the miracle of Rust's finding a free cab without any delay.

"I think we're all right," said his father, who cruised around for a short while to make it doubly sure. "We'll go to a place that's safe."

Rust recognized they were in the Arbat district, where entire streets of wooden houses were being demolished to make room for modern blocks. The old man parked the car on a building site, hidden behind a crane, then led him through a maze of brick piles until they came out in another street, where a second cab was waiting. Rust caught only a glimpse of the woman who was driving, but she must have been almost as tall as Rust, and from the silhouette of a tight-skinned, finely drawn face, fiery eyes measured up the two passengers. Judging from a couple of newspaper photos and a cheap flag above the dashboard, she appeared to be a Dynamo fan. She drove off without waiting for instructions, down the poorly lit embankment, across the bridge away from the Kremlin, into even worse-lit back streets, where, Rust was sure, she doubled back several times until he had no idea where they were. That might be exactly the point of the exercise, he guessed, but said nothing.

She drove through a narrow gate with about an inch to spare on each side and stopped in a dark, fully enclosed courtyard. She then led the way up the stairs, warning Rust, "Don't touch the banister, it's unsafe," in a cold voice. As she reached the landing, she suddenly turned back to Rust and produced the slightest of smiles: "No, it's not part of the official swinging-Moscow-by-night tour." The light of the single fly-specked bulb above was enough to show Rust that she was very beautiful. No trace of high cheekbones, her blond hair a few shades too dark to match the rather Scandinavian features—perhaps a true Estonian, though Rust, except that her accent sounded Ukrainian. She was slim, yet her breasts, limbs and hips threatened to burst every seam of her dress: a careless fit or a provocative choice of a size too small—Rust tried to guess which. She wore spike-heeled shoes (an oddity for a cab driver, and

Rust had not seen her change shoes before leaving the car) and knew how to walk in them.

She went through a door without knocking, and Rust followed. The light came on, and Rust felt dwarfed by a massive bear of a man. Instinctively, he tried to step back, but his father was right behind him, closing and locking the door. She smiled again: "You have a fine son, Pyotr Nikolayevich, but you haven't even introduced us." She switched to English, spoken with a nondescript mid-Atlantic accent. "My name's Yelena Ivanovna, and you don't know how pleased I am to meet you." Then again in Russian: "And that's Florian."

"Florian Vladimirovich," mumbled the giant grudgingly from behind his fingers on his lips and bit hard on his badly gnawed nails.

"Of course, but our double names might be too much for our visitor," she said softly. It was more her voice than the explanation that seemed to pacify him. Rust noted that no surnames had been mentioned. He looked at Florian's bulging chest and concluded that the man must be armed.

"You haven't asked any questions," said his father.

"He's a wise man," she said and produced a bottle of Gorilka, some black bread, a knife and a cucumber from a box on the floor in the corner. It was unlikely that she or anybody else actually lived in the bare room, which flaunted heavy curtains on the windows as its only sign of luxury. She cut some bread, sliced the cucumber and put it all on a piece of cardboard she tore off the box.

"No glasses. I'm sorry." She smiled at Rust and gestured toward the bottle. He returned the gesture with a bit too theatrical "after you" bow. "You're very polite," she said in a solemn tone. Too solemn?

"You mean I'm suspicious?"

She laughed. The sound was free and easy. The sort that inspired trust. She picked up the bottle and drank heartily. It did not even make her face flush. Rust followed her example. He was sure the liquid would burn a hole in his throat, flow out freely and damage the floor, too. It was a Ukrainian pepper vodka.

As they were about to sit down around the well-worn table, Rust positioned himself on the big man's right: the goon was righthanded and would be at a momentary disadvantage if he tried to pull out the gun or deliver a punch. He had a feeling that Yelena was reading his thoughts. That annoyed him. "Okay, we've played the games, not let's have it," he said impatiently.

His father was about to answer, but Yelena cut in: "Can I just ask a few questions first?"

"Such as?"

"When did you get the message?"

"Let me see . . . it was the Thursday . . . er . . . yes, almost three weeks ago."

"The very end of August." Yelena calculated. "It should have been earlier."

"Why?"

She ignored the question. "What did Igor say to you?"

"Igor?"

"The sailor."

"He never got there. He's dead." There was no reaction. Just silence. So Rust told them how the message had been delivered by a young CIA agent. "It's a miracle it reached me at all."

"What exactly was the message?"

"Just what I agreed on with my father. Someone had been very ill but was better now."

"Who? What was the name?"

Rust shrugged his shoulders. "Matvey? Timofey?"

"It's important."

"Didn't seem so to me. So I forgot."

"Igor must have given your name and address to whoever he gave the message."

"That's right."

"What name did he give?"

"My name, of course."

"That's not what I meant. Did he say Helm or Helmut?"

Rust thought, then shook his head. "I'm not sure. It was so unexpected. I never really thought the message would ever come. I had a lot to think about. What I could do. How I'd go about it."

"Pity. The message might have contained a warning that he was in trouble."

"A warning to you, dear lady"—Rust's voice grew sharp— "not to me. Is that it?"

"Yes."

"You mean I was expected to come here anyway, but only you'd be warned."

"Yes." She sounded disarmingly sincere.

He turned to his father. "And you, you'd be warned, too, no matter what risk I had to take."

"I'm sorry." His father turned away and began to cough nervously.

He must be thinking about the camps. Rust felt a little ashamed. He would have liked to put his arm around the old man's shoulder. But he did not know how. He had no experience. Perhaps he could warp him in his own coat. To keep him warm. He closed his eyes and tried to think of young O'Connor sitting in his armchair in the Upstairs. He tried to recall the mood, the agent's voice. But his father's monotonous droning disturbed him.

"It's difficult to explain, my son. When you'd found me and we met in 1956, it brought back memories. It changed me back to what I must have been before I came to Russia. I suddenly realized that I was beaten. We all were beaten around here, because we did not even *think* of doing anything about our fate. I can't tell you exactly what happened next. It wouldn't be fair to the others. And it's best if you know only as much as you must. But the fact is that I became involved with a, well, a group who wanted to do something. We didn't really do much, but we began to care."

"Okay, okay, I get the message," Rust cut in impatiently. "But do I need to know all this?"

"You must," his father said.

"Why?"

"To understand why you're here."

"You mean you . . ." Rust checked himself and gestured toward the girl and the goon. "Do they know what our original arrangement was?"

"Yes."

"That you want to get out of all this?" He watched the old man's fast-shriveling face and the realization hit him that the old man's waffling had not even begun to tell the truth about the situation. "I mean, you do want to get out, don't you?"

"I can't."

"I thought it was for me to decide. Or at least to help."

"Things have changed. I'm sorry."

"Then why the hell am I here?"

"To help us."

"Us? You mean them?" He grabbed the old man's shoulders and shook him savagely. "You've cheated me. You've tricked me. You once told me how happy you were to rediscover me. Is that what your happiness was worth? Is that it? Is it?"

"I'm sorry."

Rust let him go. "And I'm sorry, too." He reached for his raincoat and glanced at Yelena. "Thanks for the drink, sweetheart. It would have been nice to meet you in some other circumstances."

"Helmut."

"Yes?"

"You . . . you can't leave us, my son."

"Can't I?" Rust kept his eyes on Florian. The big man might be armed, but the breadknife was still on the table within Rust's easy reach. "Who says I can't leave? You or them?"

"I beg of you. Just listen before you make your decision."

"I think the more I listen the less chance I'll have to make a decision and leave. And I've already heard plenty."

"Please, son. Please."

The old man was beaten. Rust could not help pitying him. It was easier now to put his arm around his shoulders. "What happened, Vati?" he whispered. "Did they beat you? Blackmail you?" When Pyotr Nikolayevich shook his head, Rust could not suppress the question that hurt most: "Don't I matter to you?"

"Of course you do. I love you. That's just what proves how important this is. Would I have risked your life otherwise?"

It was not enough to convince Rust. But he had no quick way to probe more deeply. If anybody had blackmailed the old man, it would be Yelena and the goon. Yet Rust did not feel much anger toward them. They wanted him there and they had him there. Love was not a consideration in their case. Was it in his father's case?

"We wanted to do something. We cared." The old man droned on and on as if only trying to pick up the ends of the thread where Rust's question had cut in. "Yes, we cared a lot, and there were some very influential people among us."

Rust caught his father looking at Yelena. "Like her?"

"No, no." But Yelena nodded, and the old man corrected

himself. "I mean yes. So we began to hear things we were not supposed to know about. And then something terribly important came to some people's attention. So important that even I wasn't told."

"It's best that way, Pyotr Nikolayevich. Forgive me," she said softly. "That's why, if you don't mind, I'd like to talk to Helmut alone."

Helmut. The accent of pronouncing the German name sounded familiar. O'Connor. Didn't he say it the same way?

"Say my name again."

"Helmut." Again she read the signs on his face correctly. "Was it Helmut, not Helm, in the message?"

"Probably."

"Oh." She offered Rust another gulp from the bottle; the third time around it tasted more agreeable. Perhaps it has already anesthetized my guts, he thought. While he drank, the two men stood up and moved toward the door.

"We'll be around," said Florian.

Rust grinned at him. He felt challenged and would have enjoyed making some alterations in the big man's square face.

As soon as the door had closed behind the men, she pulled her chair nearer to Rust. He liked that. Her body smelled good. The combination of her soap and skin appealed to him. The intimacy of her whisper made him think of the urgency of young love when you knew Mother might enter at any moment. But what she asked had a sobering and irritating effect on him.

"Do you care about peace?"

"Oh, for Chrissake." He switched to English in self-defense. "You play dirty, you're a cheat and perhaps a blackmailer, you trick me into risking my life, then you put on your angelic face and you have the nerve to croon about peace, goddam peace."

"I meant it. It's important for me to know how you feel about peace. Because you're here to get and take home some information that could save us all from global disaster."

"Cut out the big words, sweetheart, and let's get down to it. What's the joke?" Reacting to her sad expression, he said: "All right. I care about peace. This is my solemn and sincere testament. Satisfied?"

"Yes. So here it is in a sentence. Nikita Sergeyevich is sending missiles to Cuba."

The simplicity of it stunned him. A wild rush of memories

flooded his brain. *Cohetes.* Could be missiles as well as fire-crackers. Coming from Odessa. He needed a few moments to think. To ask the right questions. He had to gain time. "Don't be ridiculous."

"I'm very serious."

"How would you know what Khrushchev does?"

"I know."

"Okay, what sort of missiles?"

"Medium- and intermediate-range."

"What's that? I mean, what distance?"

"Up to three thousand kilometers."

Rust did not know if this was correct or not. But the manner in which she answered without the slightest hesitation was convincing. "Where will they be set up?"

"It's better for you not to know the list."

"Give me an example."

"You wouldn't know the place."

"Try me. I know a bit about Cuba." She shook her head, and Rust stood up. "If not, not. I didn't ask for it in the first place. You got me here, you wanted me to listen, you must convince me."

"Have you ever heard of San Cristóbal?"

"Maybe." Rust tried to keep his best poker face. San Cristóbal was one of the places where Russians were constructing soccer fields. "Now how about you? Who are you?"

"It doesn't matter."

"Of course it does, sweetheart. You don't think that I or anyone else will take you seriously without some evidence or an indication of source. Are you part of some resistance group?"

"Sort of."

"Big group? Small group?"

"Does it matter?"

"I want to know if you're just the messenger."

"I'm not."

"You wouldn't have firsthand information, would you?"

"Why not?"

"You're too young. And too pretty."

"What's that got to do with it?"

"The prettier the face the less ambitious they are."

"You must have met the wrong sort of women. I pity you."

She appeared sharp and unshakable. He liked that. Not only

because it made her more attractive but also because he felt he could trust her more. So he decided to probe more. "So where did you pick up all that invaluable information? I mean, in whose bed?"

Her face reddened but her voice did not change. "Do you want names, places, dates and graphs of orgasms per hour?"

"Names and positions will do. And I don't mean sex positions."

"You're a bastard."

"And I guess you knew that before you got me here. For some reason, I think, you need a bastard. An extraordinary bastard, not just a run-of-the-mill weekday bastard, someone dumb enough not to run away from risks, someone unimportant enough not to be a great loss if things go wrong, and someone vulnerable enough not to be able to say no to you, right?"

"Almost. Because if things go wrong, I may be hurt, too, and I'm very important, at least to me. Next question."

"What missiles are we talking about? Nukes?" And when she looked puzzled, he spelled it out: "Missiles with nuclear warheads?"

"Yes."

"You think Khrushchev wants to start a war?"

"I don't think so."

"What then?"

"Several things. Castro is angry because his Communist Party tried to plot against him. He's pressing for more and better arms to protect him from the probably enemy. I mean America. They say he's flirting with the Chinese to blackmail us. Khrushchev must do something positive. And missiles over there are an answer to all his problems."

"America won't tolerate it."

"No?" She smiled. "I believe that Nikita Sergeyevich has evidence that it will be tolerated. But the main thing is that he is playing strictly according to Leninist strategy. You choose maximum and minimum targets. You make maximum demands and predetermine the minimum you'll settle for. His maximum is to have missiles that can hit New York and all the other major cities. At the moment we cannot do it from here, but can do it from Cuba. The minimum is to get an American guarantee of Cuban independence. That would retain Castro's friendship, even obedience, and our foothold on America's—how do you say it?—doorstep?"

"And you don't like that."

"I don't give a shit."

That floored Rust momentarily. Both the swearword and the frankness were unexpected.

"I really don't." She smiled. "I'll be completely frank with you. What matters in the first place is that the missiles are a threat to peace, and I care about that."

"Okay, okay, cut it out. What's the second?"

"That's if he succeeds, we're going to be stuck with him forever. And he's wrong for my country. All big words but no real leadership."

"Sure, sure, you must know best."

"I didn't say that."

"No, sweetheart, you didn't. All you said is that he's so wrong you're willing to turn traitor."

"Don't use that word!"

"I can think of others."

Without any warning sign, she suddenly began to cry. Something had just snapped in her. Perhaps weeks or months of incredible strain. Perhaps years. He thought of Charles, who had once said to him that Americans had no conception of what the pressures of living under a dictatorship might be like. And that if they tried to understand those pressures in combination with that big, big Russian soul, the fear of solitude, a morbid imagination, the hate of rules and the wailing by a nation of orphans each time a loathsome ruler died, then they'd really be in limbo.

"Khrushchev killed my husband," she whispered. "Not directly. But he did. In Kiev, when . . ." Her tears were rolling down freely from widely open eyes, but there was no sobbing, no distortion of the face, no quivering of the full lips. Then the tears dried up just as suddenly as they had begun to flow.

"I'm sorry," she said in a matter-of-fact voice. "Forget what I said about my husband. It's been a long time. And I may be wrong. Sorry I mentioned it."

He touched her hair only with his fingertips to redirect an unruly wave.

"Thank you," she said in the same tone. "And now, if we're

to prevent what I'd regard as a disaster, you must get this information to your government."

"Sure." Rust began to laugh. "I'm sorry." He tried to stop laughing but could not. "I, I really am sorry. But what exactly do you have in mind? I mean, do you want me to go to Washington and telephone Kennedy, and say to him, 'Hi, Mr. President, I'm just back from Moscow and I've got news for you,' or—"

"Stop it. The missiles will be operational by about mid-October. Then it'll be too late to do anything. You must find a way."

"But why me? I'm not in government service, I'm not connected with anything or anyone who matters."

"You mean not anymore?"

For a second he wondered how much she knew about his past. "If you mean that I'm not a journalist anymore, then yes, that's what I meant."

"Good. That's why we're turning to you."

"Explain."

"Don't think we're fools. We've tried everything else we could. We've leaked information in several ways. We even supplied facts to someone who is working for the CIA, we think. But America's doing nothing. As if they knew nothing. So probably they know nothing. All the information must have been prevented from reaching the highest level. Perhaps your own hawks have stopped it. They may hope that Cuba will be attacked and wiped out if there're missiles there. Or perhaps our own spies, our KGB moles in your service, are stopping the information. Someone is. You're the last chance. You, because you're on the outside. Because you won't use the usual channels. Because we know that you'll find direct access to someone right at the top in Washington. It's a long shot. But we've no choice."

"And you're offering me some evidence."

She produced a plain sealed envelope. "Some of it is here. You must swear not to open it. You'll get the rest in America."

"I want it now. I'll talk to the embassy here tomorrow."

"No. You wouldn't ever know who you're talking to. Many people at your embassy are in the pocket of the KGB."

"Rubbish."

"I'm telling you."

He decided not to argue. The Russians' inherent sense of secrecy and inclination to see plots and plotters everywhere irritated him with their naiveté. "What if I say no to it all?"

"You won't."

"I could ruin the whole lot of you."

"Perhaps. If you had a chance."

"I could run for it."

"You won't. You're no fool."

"Would you kill me if I tried?"

"I'd hate to."

"Thanks."

"Besides, you'll help us for your father's sake. He's an old man. He trusts you. And now I trust you, too. You'll deliver the letter. Unopened."

"What about the rest of the evidence you mentioned?"

"You'll get it at the Upstairs. On the first or second of October." She stood up.

"From you?" He stood up, too. Their bodies almost touched.

"Maybe."

"If you come there, I may try to rape you."

"Promise?"

She opened the door and shouted for the two men. They came running up the stairs. Florian had a 9mm Makarov in his hand. "Don't be stupid!" Her voice sounded like a slap in the face, and the big man blushed. "Put that gun away." She turned to Rust: "How quickly can you leave Moscow without arousing suspicion?"

"I have an important interview to make the day after tomorrow. After that, I could produce some plausible excuse to leave."

"Good." She put her hand on the old man's shoulder. "You'd better say goodbye to Helmut here and now."

Rust closed his eyes. "Say my name again."

"Helmut."

"Again."

"Helmut."

"That was in the message. Not Helm. I'm almost sure." He waited. The three looked each other. "Come on. What does it mean to you?"

"There must have been some trouble. Perhaps Igor was caught and interrogated. He wouldn't be able to withhold information, but he could always make a slight alteration in the message. Like Helmut instead of Helm."

"Then why was the message delivered by the CIA? Igor wouldn't have been worried about them, would he?"

"Don't know." She sounded desperate. "That's just what I was trying to tell you. We don't know and you don't know how badly your government is infiltrated."

"Okay. You think Igor was caught, forced to confess, and the CIA was duped into delivering the message. Right? But then why hasn't my father been arrested?"

"Because Igor knew nothing about him. Or me. He was given a chance to escape with the message from somebody unknown. But something went wrong. I don't know what. But it means you must be careful even when you get home. You're probably watched." She gestured toward Florian. "Let's go. We'll wait for you two downstairs. Don't be long."

Rust sank into an uneasy silence. He had nothing to say. He had never kissed his father. It would be too formal to shake hands.

"Keep warm," said the old man idly. "I'm grateful to you. I hope you'll succeed with whatever you have to do. It's unlikely that we'll ever meet again, but I'll pray for you every day. And in return, you think of me if you ever go to Geneva. Have a look at the Red Cross building for me. And the lake. With the water jet. All that sparkling water almost halfway up the Eiffel Tower. I used to dream about it in the camps."

"Incidentally, a friend of mine is trying to sort out one or two problems about the camps. Can you remember if in camp BV 523 the guards could see from the nearest watchtower into the foundry area?"

His father hesitated. "No, I don't think so. No, definitely not. That's where we used to warm up if there was a chance."

"How far would you say the nearest perimeter watchtower was?"

"From the foundry? Oh, about a hundred meters, something like that." He became very agitated. "Can't remember. Let's not talk about it."

"How many guards are on night duty?"

"It varies. I don't know."

"One more thing. How deep is the outer safety perimeter in VS 389/2-5?"

"Twenty or thirty meters. Full of mines, of course."

In the cab, Yelena gave Rust a bottle of ordinary vodka. "Drink some. When you get back to the hotel, pretend to be drunk. No shouting, no singing, a quiet drunk. Even our police are partial and understanding toward drunks, especially quiet drunks. A man must be proud of his drunkenness and others must show due respect. Only your KGB watcher will be reprimanded for losing you for the night, but even he might be forgiven if it's found that you used your time to get drunk. It'll tell them what your weakness is."

• Wednesday, September 19 •

U.S. Congress resolution shows determination to contain
Cuban subversion "in any part of this hemisphere," prevent
the creation of Cuban military capability that could endanger
U.S. security, and work with the OAS and freedom-loving
Cubans to support Cuban aspirations for political self-de-
termination. Judy Garland is hospitalized with "an acute
kidney ailment"; drug overdose denied.

MAJOR BOYCHENKO KNEW HE HAD BEEN LUCKY. HE HAD
escaped from being held responsible. Just. He knew
that, too. And he could not have complained if they blamed
him personally. Rust was, after all, his charge, and Rust had
got away from his tail once before breakfast and once at night.
Boychenko was called by the police at dawn: a friendly detective warned him that his daughter had been seen the previous
evening in the long line at the cinema showing *Clear Sky*, that
anti-Stalinist film. Boychenko blamed the authorities for failing
to ban such rubbish, but gave a piece of his mind to that stupid

girl, too—how the hell could she expect to get into Foreign Trade with that kind of record?

That was the bad news. Other events cheered him up in the morning. He heard that the raped girl might be willing to marry his son. Her father seemed disinclined to embarrass Boychenko. Then came something positive about Rust. A telephone tap on the American embassy picked up a call from a French newspaper correspondent who, apparently, had acted on Rust's behalf, setting up a rendezvous. Because of the name reference, Rust had been traced to Boychenko, who, in turn, duly observed the lunch meeting between the American and Jim Holly, a junior on the commercial attaché's staff but suspected as a CIA operative. The two men made no effort to keep the meeting a secret—after all, visiting journalists could expect some legitimate guidance. Nevertheless, Boychenko noted in his report "the clandestine nature of making the arrangements."

In the evening, Boychenko left his number two in charge and decided to have an early night. He listened to his wife, who always knew the latest jokes. "So the *Vostok* makes another circuit around the earth, and Ivan waves with mad enthusiasm to the sky. His son says, 'Don't be stupid, they can't see you,' but Ivan tells him that he's only waving goodbye to our meat and butter for yet another year." And that was when the phone rang. For a second, Boychenko thought that the flat had been bugged. He had warned his family often enough not to spread stupid jokes about the economy. He picked up the phone, fearing the worst, but relaxed when he recognized the duty officer's voice: report at the Spetsburo. Now. Now? At once.

At nine in the evening, life was at a standstill in Dzerzhinsky Ploshchad, the square dominated by Children's World, Moscow's largest toy store, and the statue of the father of the Soviet secret police. Behind the bronze figure of that notorious Pole, a few of the tall windows were lit, breaking the ominous shadow of the two fused and remodeled buildings of the All-Russian Insurance Company, better known as the Lubyanka.

Boychenko ran along the parquet-floored dark-green corridors and wondered if he would still be around when everything was repainted light green as planned. He arrived at the Special Bureau No. 1 out of breath. If they wanted to arrest him, they would have sent for him rather than call him. And it would not be the Spetsburo. That was sabotage and assassinations.

"Wet affairs." So the news was unlikely to be as bad as all that. But you never knew.

A full colonel sat behind a desk three times the size of Boychenko's and wasted no time even to greet the wheezing major. In the glow of the white globe on the high ceiling, his face had an eerie quality as he opened a blue plastic folder.

"I see you were attached to this bureau before my time."

"Yes, from 1951 to—"

"I didn't ask, did I?"

"No, comrade."

"And you were fully trained."

Boychenko said nothing. Yes, he was fully trained for major assassination assignments, prepared and cleared for foreign missions, organization of *boyevaya gruppa*, the combat gangs that could kill or abduct targets as required, yes, he was well trained—and then wasted with what was now euphemistically described as the Reorganization, meaning de-Stalinization, damn Khrushchev.

"You're familiar with this Rust and . . . a junior embassy man, Joe Holly?"

"Jim Holly, Jim."

"Doesn't make much difference, does it?"

"No, comrade."

"Right. Well, here's your chance to get back into doing something more constructive than Tourists. We've information that the two will meet again tonight at eleven on the rampart of Lomonosov. Why the university we don't know. You'll be there only to finger them and supervise the squad from Line F, but don't interfere with their work—they have their full scenario. I think it's best if you don't show your face at all. At least at this stage. Clear?"

Rust disliked Jim Holly. He asked the wrong questions and tried to look much too important at the morning meeting. Then despite everything they had agreed on, he called again and insisted on this second rendezvous in the evening. Even his choice of place was awful: the wind threatened to blow them off the deserted hill as they walked and pretended to enjoy the sight of Moscow at their feet.

"Did you pass on my message?"

"Of course," said Holly smugly.

"To whom?"

"I thought that you'd know better than to ask. Now tell me what the joke is."

"What joke?"

"Let's not play games, Rust." He pulled Yelena's envelope out of his pocket. The seal was broken. "So what's the joke?"

"You promised not to open it." He looked inside. There were only a few empty sheets of paper. "Have you . . ."

"Yes, we've tried chemicals, the lot. So now you must tell me everything."

"You're crazy. I've told you everything."

"Sure you did, friend. You told me to use the diplomatic bag and forward an empty envelope unopened to Langley. And make a fool of the whole station over here. Come on, joker, we need to know your source, we need evidence."

Yelena was only a name with a face to Rust. He could tell nothing about her. Only his father would be evidence, but he wouldn't want to mention him. So he chose to stick to his original story. "I told you. I was stopped by a stranger in the street. He seemed to know everything about me, my work, my past. It sounded convincing that he knew something important and I must pass on his message with the evidence in the envelope. With more to come to me in Florida on the first of October. If it looks like a joke, why are you asking for a second helping?"

Holly took his arm, and his tone became very confidential. Rust could almost hear Holly's training officer instructing the recruits how to create a friendly atmosphere.

"Look, friend, you don't know how things go these days. But this bit of info you claim to have could be serious. And I mean I really mean serious. The station chief may want to see you personally. Anything about *porokhovyye konfety* in Cuba is real deadly. It can't wait till October."

Konfety. Why did it ring a bell? "*Konfety?*"

"You see, friend, you've been out of the game too long." Holly was enjoying himself shamelessly. "It's KGB slang for missiles, of course. Everybody in the business knows that, but I guess it came after your time."

Julia-Rosa's shopping list. The jotted notes and doodles must have been made by a KGB merchant. Elliott would have understood, Rust was sure.

A Skoda and a large, fully enclosed van stopped next to them. Three men in dark-blue raincoats got out of the car and approached them.

"Identity papers."

Holly produced his diplomatic passport. The spokesman of the three pocketed it. Holly protested loudly. Rust took out his hotel card. The man studied it, then pocketed that, too. "Will you come with us, please?"

They were bundled into the van unceremoniously. Holly's protests were silenced by the appearance of a 7.15 mm Tokarev, a cumbersome service revolver. The inside of the van was lit by a small bulb. It was like a cell with no windows. They drove off. After some thirty minutes, the van stopped.

The man with the gun spoke to Holly in Russian. Both captives pretended not to understand. The man kneed Holly's underbelly. The diplomat howled. The man laughed. "This place is soundproof."

"Yob tebya pereyob," said Holly, demonstrating the range of his Russian—"Fuck you to the fucking nth degree."

"That's better." The man produced a sheet of stolen letter paper with the American embassy letterhead. "I want you to write a letter, and then you can go and protest. Don't worry, you'll always be able to deny it or say that you wrote it under illegal pressure." He raised the gun and inserted it in Holly's ear. "All right?" Holly nodded. "Use your own pen." The man read some notes and began to dictate. "Dear Vassily. I won't be able to tell you this face to face and suffer the sight of pain in your lovely eyes . . . ."

"Now wait a minute."

The Russian screwed the gun farther into Holly's ear. ". . . in your lovely eyes, so this is to warn you. I'm sure you'll understand. We must break it off. Jill is suspecting us. Not only my marriage, but also my whole future is at stake. So this will be the last time. Even if it breaks my heart. Please forgive me. But don't forget. I won't. I'm sure. Your Jimmy."

Holly laughed. "And you hope to compromise me with that crap? You're crazy. What do you hope to achieve?"

"Now how could you expect me to answer that, sir?" The man tried to sound friendly and conciliatory. "I'm only doing a job. You know how it is. You write it down and I let you go. Then the big chiefs can argue."

"Don't sign it!" shouted Rust. He was pistol-whipped in the face. Why didn't they do that to Holly?

Holly watched the trickle of blood on Rust's face and signed the letter.

"Thank you," said the man and put away the letter. One of his men pulled on plastic overalls and rubber gloves. "You may go now." He got out of the van, followed by Holly and the man in the overalls. The third man drew aside his coat and took his gun out of a holster, but made no attempt to restrict Rust's view of open country and the canal bank.

After a few steps, Holly turned and was about to say something, but he faced the man in the overalls and a large butcher's knife. The blade went through his throat with an expert thrust from right to left, giving him no chance even to scream. Blood spurted everywhere. The gunman stood well back. The plastic protected the other as he went about his work efficiently, without much enthusiasm. The knife plunged into Holly seventeen times. He counted them aloud. Holly must have been long dead by the time he stopped. The gunman consulted a sheet of paper. "Two more," he said.

The other stabbed the body twice more, then threw down the knife. The gunman crumpled up Holly's "letter" and dropped it on the ground. Rust began to understand. It was to be a homosexual murder set up, complete with multiple cuts inflicted in a "frenzy of passion." Somebody might even be caught, sentenced and executed for it.

The killer pulled off the plastic overalls. He took great care not to let blood spill on his clothes underneath. Rust looked around. There was no sign of the Skoda.

"Sergeant!" The shout came from somewhere outside Rust's vision, probably from the driver's seat. The gunman walked off in that direction.

They had kicked Holly instead of hitting him with the gun. They must know that the embassy would conduct its own postmortem when the body was found. All the injuries would have to be compatible with the faked stabbing fury. Rust concluded that his own death would occur somewhere else, in different circumstances that would allow for any sort of injuries. Some accident. They might blame his drinking for it. Had he not returned to the hotel completely pickled only the night before? Or they might make him just disappear. It had happened before.

To his father, for instance. Run, run, run, instinct urged him. Wait! Schramm's teaching drifted back to him. There must be one right moment; wait for it.

The sergeant walked back into Rust's field of vision, picked up a stick, and pushed the letter under Holly's body. "Quite an original paperweight, right?"

"Too wet for documents." The killer was quick to prove his sense of humor. He stuffed the plastic outfit into a brown paper bag.

Rust kept asking himself why they had let him witness all this. They might have forgotten to shut the door. Plain carelessness. Strange. They seemed to know exactly everything else they were doing. So there must have been a reason for that, too. Of course. They had begun softening him up with the sight. Because they would want to know the source of his information. There would be interrogation. Torture. The thought suddenly made him see himself clearly, sitting there stunned and muted, almost hypnotized by the chain of events and hopeless odds. The two men started back toward the van. If he had a chance at all, he would have to take it within the next minute. His guard would not kill him. The gun was on safety. They needed him. If provoked, the man might copy his sergeant and try his hand at pistol-whipping.

"You shits, you'll pay for this," Rust hissed and kicked the man's shin.

"Fuck you!" He swung the Tokarev to deliver a wild backhand, but Rust was ready for it. He ducked and bobbed up with his outstretched hand, hitting the guard's unprotected throat. The gurgling rattle told him that he had not missed. The guard began to topple like a sack of flour in slow motion. His attacker's fist hit his temple.

Rust moved to the corner behind the door. The two men were standing a few yards away. They seemed to take forever. If they called the guard, Rust would have to shoot them and run for it.

At last he heard them coming. For maximum advantage he would have to wait until the last moment when they were about to climb into the van. Now.

The sight of the heavy gun in Rust's hand surprised them. "Silence," he whispered. He noted with a slight smile that his voice must have sounded convincing, for the sergeant dropped his gun without being told. Rust motioned them with only his head toward the inside of the van.

"Turn around." He knocked down the killer with the butt of the gun. He felt like shooting him for Holly's sake, but it wouldn't have been practical. The driver might or might not be alone, and the last thing he wanted was a gunfight.

"How do you signal them to go?" The sergeant hesitated. Rust pushed the barrel into his mouth, and the man's reaction was too slow. The crunch of broken teeth made his stomach turn. "Tell me."

The sergeant spat out some blood and pointed at a switch on the wall. The question was, would the driver know what was going on in the back? Was there a spyhole? Rust could not see any. It was no good to ask—the sergeant would probably lie. If he gave the signal to go and there was no reaction, he would know that they were ready for him outside. He could then try to trade off his hostages. He quickly went through the men's pockets. The knife man had a 6.35mm Tula-Korovin. That he took, then flicked the switch. An immediate short hoot of the horn answered it. Then nothing. What were they waiting for? Perhaps they had a warning light telling them that the door was open. There was only one way to find out.

He checked the men on the floor. All were unconscious. Two of them bleeding. He signaled once more, jumped out and rolled under the van to present a minimal target. No shots, nobody in sight. He crawled out, locked the door—and the van started. For a few seconds he would be covered, but then he would become visible in the driver's large side mirrors. He dived into the canal before he could be spotted. As the van followed the track away from the water, he caught just half a glimpse of a jovial fat face next to the driver.

He swam across the canal and ran. Well-kept paths of gravel led him to an ornamental pond. A few statues. He was shivering. There was no way to keep warm. He threw the large gun into the pond, dried the toylike Tula-Korovin—a KGB special—with some grass, then ran on. As he climbed over a high fence, he came to a bridge spanning a narrow river. The distant silhouettes of two towers to the right and one to the left with brighter lights in between suggested to him that he was on the east side of the town. The Yauza River. He crossed the bridge and ran along deserted streets.

A railway station. One of the places to be checked automatically when the alert went out for him. He recrossed the river and stopped for a breather on the embankment. The only people he saw were horizontal. Drunks.

First it was just a rumble. Then the crude firing of a heavy vehicle's engine. A water wagon came into view. The sort that sprayed and cleaned Moscow's thoroughfares every night. The sort that always seemed to have right of way, even on the wide pavements. Vehicles and pedestrians were sprayed mercilessly every time they were not quick enough to get out of the way. The drivers had their norms, and norms had to be fulfilled. There was no time to stop, slow down, show courtesy.

Rust waited until it was quite close, than ran out on the road, stumbled, and fell. He hoped the driver was good. Brakes groaned hoarsely. Rust stayed down and began to hum. When he looked up, the massive bumper was only a few inches from him.

"Fucking drunks!" The voice approached but did not sound unduly angry. "Get up, you idiot."

Rust did not move. The man bent down to lift him, and he pushed the gun into the thin, tired face.

"Don't shoot, comrade. Please. I did nothing wrong." His protests of innocence would already convict him if Rust was a policeman. "I only used the short cut because—"

"Shut up." Rust got up. "Come on. Show me how the thing works."

The driver moved without asking questions but noted Rust's wet clothes and the blood on his face, and decided that whoever the man with the gun was, police he was not. "You'd be better off if I drove," he said quietly. "Just tell me where you want to go." He was trembling as he climbed into the driving compartment.

"Don't worry," said Rust. "I don't want to hurt you."

"You must be Estonian."

Rust nodded.

"I'm from Riga," said the man and held out his hand, offering the comradeship of another suppressed minority from Latvia. "I'll help you. And no questions."

"Just show me how it works." Rust felt ashamed. The driver was most probably sincere and took a risk with his friendly attitude, but Rust could not trust him. Or anyone. He was already infected by the nationwide disease: fear and suspicion.

It was simple. A handle on the left controlled the water, on and off, and the strength of the spray, too. Rust drove and ordered the man to lie on the floor. "If we're stopped and you say a word, you're dead." Like me, he could have added, but did not. He began to think about his next move. He must try to contact his father and Yelena. It would be hard to tell her that she was right about the embassy. Perhaps she could help him to get to Odessa and into that crocodile tank. But perhaps he ought to call Washington and talk to his brother first. If he rattled off the essence of the news about the missiles, the operator might not have a chance to disconnect them in time. Elliott would be puzzled, even suspicious—after all, they had not talked to each other for just about five years—but would be bound to look into it. If then...

Two motorbikes at the side of the road. Uniformed men at the curbside. Rust stepped on the brakes.

"Roadblock?" whispered the Latvian.

"Could be."

"Don't stop. Go up on the curb and spray them if they don't jump fast enough."

The engine roared, the body heaved, the speed hardly increased, but the nozzles played their part well. The militiamen failed to jump fast enough.

"*Nedoyobysh!*" somebody yelled, calling Rust a by-product of sex, just a spoonful scraped off the sheet of his parents' bed.

"Which makes us blood brothers," the Latvian said and laughed.

Boychenko looked forward to some rest when the van left the park. It was only a fifteen-minute drive to the Lubyanka. They had just rounded Dzerzhinsky's statue, passing the heavily barred ground-floor windows on the right, when a buzzer sounded above the driver's head.

"What's that?"

"They want us to stop."

"What, here? They can't even guess where we are."

The driver shrugged his shoulders. "Do we stop or not?"

"Go on. We're there."

The scenario instructed them to bring in Rust via the club entrance. They only had to pass the main building and the huge car compound behind it. The driver flashed his lights and the first set of gates at No. 12 Dzerzhinsky ulitsa were opened for them. The KGB club and special store for secret-police personnel were housed in an eighteenth-century building which retained its pretty facade of azure with white icing.

The van rolled through a couple of internal gates and courtyards. It halted in a small enclosure surrounded by high walls. From there, the prisoner would be taken to an interrogation room in the main building via underground passages. Boychenko yawned. The job was done. It was odd why the men in the back did not climb out. The driver went to investigate, and found the door locked from the outside. When it was opened and the sergeant stumbled out crying blue murder, Boychenko knew that his son, daughter and relatives would have to wait for favors for a long, long time, and even then he could help only if his own skin was saved by some miracle. But Boychenko, despite his secret religious belief, had no faith in miracles. For no matter what the scenario said, scapegoats would be wanted and found at all levels. And who could be a more obvious scapegoat than "that incompetent man" from the Tourist Department who had lost Rust twice before? Unless, of course, that incompetent man came up trumps, recaptured the fugitive and made him talk.

• Thursday, September 20 •

Kennedy fights to restore cuts in foreign aid program. Crews of two Italian ships refuse to sail for Cuba. Pundits predict: if Nixon fails to win governorship of California, his political career will end in November. U.S. helicopters are used in Vietnam raid: "153 terrorists are killed." Soviet delegate reveals manic fear that mutual nuclear test inspections would amount to espionage.

ELLIOTT REPSON TURNED HIS CHAIR AWAY FROM HIS DESK and wheeled himself to the window. Staring at treetops and scanning the Washington horizon always helped him to concentrate. He had just finished plowing through the current Lloyd's Shipping Index Voyage Supplement. The mass of Cuba-bound traffic was ominous. The *Omsk* and *Poltava*, two of the apparent regulars, had been to Havana yet again. Lots of other sightings were reported from the port of Cienfuegos. The *Ilya Mechnikov*, *Nikolay Burdenko*, *Admiral Nachimov*, *Simferopol*, *Deputat Lutski*—all arriving from or sailing for Odessa,

Leningrad, Riga, Gdynia, Rostock. No specific report on their cargo. And these were just the Russian ships. Then there were all the charters from so-called friendly countries. Arms were carried, no doubt, but who should and who should not be alerted to bits of news about *cohetes*? Rockets? Fireworks? Missiles? What sorts? Some Congressmen were pressing for specific answers. They ought to be told to keep things in perspective and remember the vividity and power of Cuban imagination.

He pushed himself back to the telephone. The wheels of the chair squeaked. He ought to get one of the maintenance men to look at it, because oiling did not help at all. But to get anything done had become a nightmare of paperwork these days. He hated Langley, the $46 million complex the Company had moved into only a year ago. But, admittedly, some services, like communications, were much better here than in his old office of delightful obscurity behind that Navy medical outfit on 23rd NW.

Cohetes. That odd message on the phone from some Cuban kid. Almost made them late for dinner. Something about playing soccer. A few locations. The sort of message that would only confuse Washington and should never be taken seriously. He had almost completely forgotten it. Only the word *cohetes* reminded him.

Anna was already at home and answered the phone at once. "Will you be late, honey?"

"Only ten minutes and I'm off. Just a quick question, and don't say I'm out of my mind."

"You are and I love you for it. What's the question?"

"Can you remember which dinner jacket I wore at Bobby's staff dinner?"

"The new one, I'm sure. You look like a waiter in both the old ones, and—"

"And if you wanted to be seen with a third-rate waiter, you'd have married one, okay, I know. Now could you have a look to see if I left a short note in its pocket?"

A few minutes later she told him there was no note.

"Are you sure?"

"Sure I'm sure."

"Thanks."

"Don't be late."

He rang off. The note was not really important. Except that

it was another of those unsubstantiated *cohete* sightings, and he had a more than reasonable guess who the source could have been. Rust ought to be told to stop meddling in politics and concentrate on his smuggling. He had not talked to his brother for about five years, since Helm had left not only the Company but also all outward signs of normalcy. Yes, it was possible that he was still picking up bits of intelligence purely by chance. He would not want to see it wasted, so he would use his brother as a channel for it. An outlet. Elliott reassured himself that he would have certainly refused to accept any communication if it was just to help him. Yes, some of the information was useful to him, but he preferred to believe that those minute contributions to intelligence had a much more important purpose: Helm's preservation of self-respect.

On an impulse, he decided to call the Upstairs. The phone rang and rang. No answer. He could try it later again from home. No, Anna would not like that. Pity she disliked Helm so much. Though perhaps it was mutual. Perhaps it was one of the reasons why Helm had disappeared from their life. Had he once made a pass at her? She would have found it outrageous. But no, he would not have done it.

Elliott locked away his papers and started toward the door, then changed his mind and returned to the phone to try to get through just once more. This time his call was answered without delay. "No, Helm is away, this is Hal here."

Oh yes. Elliott knew who Hal "Jus'-juice" Sheridan was. Schramm, who reported to him on Helm from time to time, had mentioned Sheridan. Elliott blamed Sheridan at least partly for Helm's smuggling and irresponsible way of life.

"Who's calling?"

"Do you know where Helm is?"

"No. Who's calling?"

"When will he be back?"

"Didn't say nothin' to me. Who the hell is that?... Any messages?... Fuck yourself." Hal slammed the phone down.

Some hotel, thought Elliott. Potential guests must love it. He called Schramm, but he knew no more than Hal.

The alert had gone out, KGB investigators, special agents, the huge regular network of informers, all the police and militia were now looking for Rust. Boychenko had to sit back and wait. Being the case officer, he was in charge of the hunt—well, at least nominally. In fact, it was the formal manifestation of his past and future responsibility. There was no question of Rust's getting away. But the time element was essential. The longer he evaded the hunters the greater the chance that he could establish contact with someone from an embassy or the western press. Boychenko found it a miracle that the man had not yet been captured by dawn. A miracle? He reprimanded himself for thinking in such loose terms. There were no miracles. If Helm was not caught, he must have some refuge. Helpers. Someone to turn to. A contact provided by whoever had sent him on this mission, or some friend from the time of his press job here in 1956.

Boychenko remembered Rust's faded-green file quite clearly. It was a slim one, so slim that it must have been depleted deliberately. By whom? Why? No visitor to the Soviet Union—let alone a journalist or others arousing the slightest KGB interest—would ever be allowed to leave behind such a shallow footprint.

He sent for the file again. It had last been seen by someone from the military neighbors. The initials and a number should have identified the person. But they did not. Highly irregular. Damn them. Amateurs. He had heard on the grapevine that the powers and finances of the GRU were being slowly but radically curtailed. High time, too. It was pointless to let them have their own Residents abroad, their own agents, networks, facilities and the rest of wasteful duplication. Centralized in one hand, in the KGB's, of course, both results and security could be improved. He took the file to the colonel of the Spetsburo.

"It could be useful to know what interest the military neighbors had in Rust only a month ago," said Boychenko.

"And to discover who the actual person was," added the colonel. He filled in a Form M-17, marked urgent, requesting the answers and full details. They would do it for the Spetsburo with minimal delay. Meanwhile he instituted disciplinary procedures against the clerk in Records who had failed to ensure the appearance of proper codes and initials on the file returning from GRU HQ in August. It would be no excuse that such irregularities were the norm rather than the exception, that the Spetsburo was particularly notorious in that respect, and that the colonel himself would have heaped abuse on the busybody good-for-nothing clerk who tried to tell him what and what not to do.

Boychenko returned to his office and hoped to snatch a couple of hours' sleep at his desk, but found that he was much too worried even to close his eyes. He rechecked all factors of the general alert. Special teams at hotels used by foreigners, all western embassies and press offices, railway stations, airports, ports including those handling "Moscow from the river" tours, all roads leading out of Moscow, and main post offices from where long-distance phone calls could be made. Patrols were out in strength to scour the streets and raid restaurants. Individual officers had been assigned to watch the homes of foreign correspondents and other westerners reported at regular intervals. Telephone tapper units had received warnings and reinforcements. There was nothing else the major could do, nothing except try to guess what loophole in the unchartable bureaucratic labyrinth could be used by someone who must have help. Help. What help? That was what bugged him. That and the information withheld from him. For the colonel had still not specified why Rust was wanted so badly and why Holly had to be eliminated.

Rust stayed in the water wagon until the heavy early-morning traffic had begun to build up. The Latvian offered to drive him anywhere, but he could not risk that. Although the man promised not to report him to the authorities at all, he disbelieved him. He caught a bus, got off at the next stop, and wandered into narrow, neglected streets behind the Paveletsky railway station. He picked his way through courtyards and stopped to rummage in huge rubbish dumps in which the little that was really unwanted by the local residents had accumulated. He dug up some old and filthy rags to cover his fine tweed jacket, and buried his raincoat. Some fellow hopefully would strike gold one day. He now felt much less conspicuous to make the journey to the church. At the entrance, one of the beggars looked at him with knowing eyes, but Rust could not be sure that he had been recognized. If the beggar was not a snoop, he would be safe. But . . . there was always the but. He could be a *stukach*, one of the millions of informers, or even a *seksoty*, a collaborator in direct pay of the KGB.

Rust had decided not to follow his father from the house

this time, so now he stopped at the church door and watched the old man's descent in the glass cage. He then went inside to wait behind a pillar, burying his face in the icon that seemed to be the least venerated by the regulars. Can't you deliver miracles? he asked the Virgin.

He remained unnoticed by his father, who came in with his head down as if in shame and began to pray urgently.

"*Vati*."

The old man began to tremble uncontrollably. "I thought you'd gone."

"Couldn't. I must talk to you and Yelena. Now."

"You can't. I can't contact her. I don't know how. But maybe she'll be in touch with me later today."

"Can I wait in your home?"

"No, no. That's out of the question."

"What then?" People began to glance at them.

"Go back to your hotel. I'll be in touch."

"No good. I think they're looking for me."

"Why?" His face was withering, Rust would have sworn. A furrow a second, and the skull shrinking, too. It was pointless to tell him what had happened. The old man would only hear the wind howling through the camps.

"Don't worry." He touched the cold hand. The choir sang more loudly. Rust felt the richly robed priest's eyes on him and began to genuflect with his father. They were holding hands. For the first time, physical contact came naturally. "Don't worry. I won't tell them anything. Nothing about you. Or the others."

"You will." Down on their knees. "If they catch you, you will." Up. "You'll tell them everything." Crossing themselves. And again. "Everything you know." On their knees again. "Everything they want you to invent for them." Up again. The censer was swinging wildly. The sweet smell enveloped them. Like the sound of breaking teeth, it made Rust's stomach turn. The Virgin stared at him impassively. She was a cold lady. Or immune to suffering by now. The old man watched Rust as if seeing a ghost. Or someone just on his way to the interrogation room. "Stay here. And wait. Just wait."

Rust nodded. And genuflected. He wished he knew how to pray. And to whom.

* * *

It was noon when a first secretary of the American embassy identified Holly's body. His statement was seconded by the young widow. They were asked to read the crumpled, blood-soaked letter that had been found under the body at the scene of the crime. The police offered them sympathy. The letter had to be held as evidence. Together with the butcher's knife.

"Do you recognize the handwriting?"

"I think so," Jill said, sobbing. "But I don't under-stand . . . can't understand at all. If anything, he was always prejudiced against homosexuals. It was so stupid. He had these outbursts . . . degenerates, yes, that's what he called them."

The remark was noted with great care. "Prejudice may just be a sign, even the giveaway of latent homosexuality," the policeman tried to commiserate.

"You're crazy!" she cried and looked for support toward the diplomat, but he turned away. He was, of course, suspicious of the police, the murder, the circumstances, everything and everybody in Moscow. But, sadly, he had to suspect Holly, too. How could one tell what was in a man's heart? He, for one, had never fully believed in the clearing system, and even polygraph tests had made mistakes. Young Jim Holly. Who could have guessed?

Jill dried her eyes and asked to see the body once more. She ignored the terrible injuries and concentrated on the face. She began to look more puzzled and insulted than heartbroken. Dear Vassily. Your Jimmy. He had never let her call him Jimmy. Undignified name, he would say. Her eyes filled up with accusation.

Frequent genuflecting helped a little to keep warm, but after seven hours in the empty church, Rust knew no effective ways to keep the cold out of his bones. If the devil offered him a place in hell he would have said yes, readily. And when a beggar woman offered him a bowl of watery soup he could not say no even though he suspected it might be drugged to make his arrest easier.

In the early afternoon he tried to generate and build up some heat in a corner, but the cold of centuries was oozing from the walls. For the umpteenth time he decided to count slowly to one hundred and leave if his father or Yelena still failed to appear by then. Ninety-eight, ninety-nine, one . . . hundred. That's it. Unless he gave them another fifty. Fifty and no more.

"Come on," Yelena whispered. "You'll have to crouch on the floor of the car and keep quiet if we're stopped." Her cab was parked right at the door. A sheet of newspaper was stuck, accidentally, to the number plate. Or was it there to prevent him from seeing the number? Better that way. If they catch you, you'll tell them everything, he remembered his father's words. He got in fast, ducked, and enjoyed the warmth of the rug with which she covered him.

He watched her ankles, her heels planted firmly on the floor, her feet working the pedals. No spikes this time. Flat, drab shoes hiding the elegant arch of her feet. Sensible clothes, too, come to think of it. Nothing tight-fitting, nothing revealing. Dull, dark colors. Rough, fluffy textile. And her hair was also different, Rust remembered. Severely combed and in a knot at the back, hardly the thing to flutter freely in the wind when she would shout, "Dynamo, Dynamo!" Odd. Today there were no flags or pictures in the cab, he was sure. Why? Or why were they there the first time? Only to give him and his father something, something misleading, to remember if they were caught?

"Here we are." The car stopped. "Please keep your eyes down and let me lead you."

They were still holding hands when the door closed behind them. It was the room where they had talked before. "What went wrong?"

"I did. I passed your message and the letter to the embassy."

"You're a fool." She did not sound angry. "I told you not to."

"You couldn't expect me to act like a puppet and see snoops and conspirators everywhere."

"Why not? That's life."

"Only here." She looked hurt. As she had when he had called her a traitor. He squeezed her hand. "I'm sorry."

"Don't be." She freed her hand. "You may even be right."

He told her how he had contacted the embassy, what he had told Holly, why they had arranged a second meeting at Holly's request, and how they had been picked up at Lomonosov.

"I'm sorry," she said. "It's my fault. I had no right to use you. Or any other bystander. But I had no choice. At least I couldn't see one. We were desperate. I shouldn't have trusted you."

"You didn't. You gave me a dud."

"It was a precaution. I was planning to give you the real message after Customs clearance at the airport."

"After Customs? How?"

She shrugged her shoulders. "Somehow."

"I almost died for that little precaution. And Holly did."

"I'm sorry. But at least they still don't know whether you really had some evidence about the missiles or not." She thought for a second. "But you did tell Holly that more evidence would come to you in Florida, didn't you?"

"Yeah, and I told him the date."

"They'll try to search your place."

"Who? How?"

"They'll do it. Somehow."

"They'll find nothing."

"No. But they won't stop looking for you. And your father."

"How would they know about him?"

"It'll take time. At least a month. That gives us a chance."

"How's he?"

"Like me. Worried."

"About me? That's nice." His knees twitched under his weight. He had hardly slept since the Bolshoi.

"You'd better sit down." And when he started toward the window, she warned him not to look out. "It's safer not to know where we are."

"Sure. And . . . I'm grateful. Can I spend the night here?"

"You must. There's nowhere else to go."

"Thanks. I'll be off in the morning."

"Where to?"

"Odessa, I guess."

"You'll never make it. You'll never make it beyond the boundary of this town. You don't know what it's like out there."

"Don't I?" His dependence on her irritated him. "I got away from them, didn't I?"

"What happened?"

"Is it wise for you to know?"

"I haven't got a choice. Otherwise I can't help."

They sat down. He was shivering. She fetched the rug from the car and put it on his back. "Your clothes . . . it's all wet."

"Stop fussing. It's my angelic face that brings out the mother instinct."

She laughed: around his deep-set, tired eyes, the barbed wires of two days' stubble looked anything but angelic. He told her what had happened. She laughed again when he mentioned the water wagon and the spraying of the militia. But he felt ashamed of his subconscious adjustment to the country's climate: in his account, he made no reference to the Latvian's cooperation and sympathy. Details were not essential for her to know—but a potential risk to the man.

"You were clever. And lucky," she said.

"As well as brave, handsome and lovable."

"Yes, all that, and a fool." She looked at him straight, then turned away. "I'll have to go and get you a few things."

"Stay." He was afraid. Not so much of capture as of loneliness, waiting, uncertainty, and, above all, passivity.

"I must get you some food, a razor, a jug of water and a bucket. There's no kitchen, no toilet, no bathroom here. It's all communal, and although most of the house is empty, I don't want you to leave this room at all. Besides, I'll have to sort out what I can do for you. I'm sorry I got you into this."

"No you're not. You thought it was important. You were saving the world. With a flaming sword and Ukrainian pepper vodka."

"Don't joke about it. It's the truth."

"Can't the truth be funny?"

"No . . ." She hesitated. "Not in my country. Jokes revealing the truth can be funny. Not the truth itself. It's too often too sad."

"So? Don't you have the urge to laugh at funerals?"

"I do, but not because they're funny. It's to make the pain and tension bearable."

"And what else do you think makes me joke about your truth, your aims, your ideals and care about peace?"

She answered with a slow smile, walked over to him and kissed him with the embarrassed hurry of a young girl. "Don't go away." And she was through the door.

He heard the lock click. Twice.

Hal "Jus'-juice" Sheridan loved Rust's rocking chair. It broke the monotony of boredom, and right now he would have sworn that it was even better than television. He decided to buy one. Only it must be a little stronger. Rust's chair squeaked too much under his weight. The room swayed gently, and he felt randy. Of course. The rocking reminded him of the Japanese girl in the boat near Nagasaki. She was sweet and sad and silent, and he boasted to friends that she fucked with the abandon of an atom-bomb survivor. He knew then that he ought to stay in Japan. He did not. It was a mistake. The sky was full of stars, and the boat and the whole universe pitched and tumbled slowly. And there was none of this awful creak. He brought the chair to a sudden halt. The creaking continued. It must be the stairs. He was about to get up and investigate when the voice stopped him.

"Stay put, fatso." It was a young crewcut. In a tailored suit.

"You mean it?"

"CIA. Miami station."

"Oh yeah?" Hal heard someone moving behind him, so he did not want to be rash. Two men would not be too many to deal with if he picked the right moment. "You have means to prove it, I guess."

"That's right." The young man reached into his right inside pocket, produced a gun and fired four times.

Hal collapsed in a fast-growing pool of blood.

Within the next fifteen minutes, Hal regained consciousness occasionally. For only a few seconds each time. His vision was blurred. His ears told him that the men were ransacking the house. Looking for something. Strange. He hadn't known that Rust kept anything valuable in the house. Luckily, he passed out again when the two men returned to the room. One of them kicked his head, and his reaction was no more than what could be expected from a corpse.

Half an hour later he was found by Jake Schramm, who had come to the house after Elliott Repson's phone call to investigate whatever happened to Rust. Schramm rushed the big man to the hospital and swore heartily all the way: "Stop bleeding all over my car, you fucking fat slob."

Yelena returned with a tatty brown suitcase.

"You locked me in when you left." Rust was furious.

"I'm sorry."

"I could have broken down that door anytime."

"But the extra effort would have reminded you to think again before leaving the room."

He grabbed her by the shoulders. She winced as he shook her. "I asked for help, not protective custody."

"Fair enough."

"And no mothering."

"It's not the maternal instinct you bring out in me."

"Good." His hands went up to pull her head, crushing his lips on hers. She did not resist. Her lips were closed, but she let them part under the pressure of his tongue. No resistance and no response. She stared at him as if trying to cool him in the bright pools of her unblinking eyes.

"Better now?" she said.

"Oh sure. Thanks for the quick relief, nurse."

"It wasn't meant to be that."

"Oh no. No. Just emergency treatment. Anything to calm your patient. Thanks. I'll be glad to reciprocate any time." She tried to hold him, but he moved away. "Okay. What's the plan?"

She opened the suitcase and took out some Russian clothes. "You must change and eat, first."

"You'll have to get used to answering instead of telling me things if we want to get on while we're forced to be together."

"Okay. I'll try. Especially because we'll be here all night."

"Why?"

"Do you mind?"

"You didn't answer."

"I think I've found a way to get you out of Moscow."

"What way?"

"Is it—"

"What way?"

"An ambulance will pick you up tomorrow. It'll fly the yellow flag of contagious disease. Even if it's stopped, it's unlikely that anyone would risk taking a closer look at you."

"Clever. Why not tonight?"

"Do you mind spending the night with me?"

"Why—not—tonight?"

"Because it's safer to move in daylight. Everybody and everything look more suspicious at night."

"And where did you learn that bit of tradecraft?"

"One hears about such things."

"Can they take me to Odessa?"

She shook her head. "The journey would be too long and too dangerous. Besides, you'll leave Moscow eastward. That's the least likely route for a foreign fugitive."

She produced a chunk of cheese, greasy sausage, black bread, a bottle of fine Georgian brandy and the inevitable cucumber from the suitcase. "Help yourself."

"I presume you have some bright idea how I could leave the country." She nodded, took a big gulp of brandy, wiped the bottle on the inside of her wrist and handed it to Rust. "How?"

"Do you insist?"

He hesitated, then changed the question. "How long will it take?"

"A few days. You must be well prepared. Not only to get out of Russia, but also to get into America."

"You mean that I haven't got my passport? No trouble at all. I just—"

"Go to the embassy? I mean any embassy, when you're out of Russia?"

"Don't be stupid. Even your suspicion must have its limits somewhere," he said.

"Please yourself."

"You trust me, for instance."

"Mainly because I have no choice. And you have a long tail over here."

"You mean my father?" He drank.

"Yes."

"You wouldn't do anything to him."

"Others might. Besides, you've always been a sucker for a good cause."

"How would you know?"

"I know."

While she sliced some cucumber and offered it to him, using her palm as a tray, he tried to decide how hard to press her for answers. It was obvious that she must have some important position or well-placed, influential friends to plan his escape, arrange his exit from the country and even contemplate helping him to enter the United States. All this would increase the likely value of her information. For the first time he felt that he might really have a historical role to play. Skepticism, his old and loyal traveling companion, came to his rescue fast. Historical role? That's a good one. It amused him. That sweet kid with the brandy and cucumbers casting him in a historical role. The word "sweet" triggered off a series of association reflexes. The sweet smile of Julia-Rosa. Her list. Powdered candy. *Porokhovyye konfety*. Holly saying *porokhovyye konfety* in Cuba would be deadly.

She reached for the bottle and took another big gulp.

He smiled. "Take it easy. That brandy is sweet but strong. It may weaken you."

"How would you know? You're not drinking." She downed some more.

"One of us must stay sober. Might as well be me."

"If you say so," she whispered huskily and watched him lean toward her. Then, slowly, her eyelids grew heavy and her lips parted.

Rust's face was only a couple of inches from hers. He paused. Her warm breath touched his skin. It was a tremendous temptation to forget about risks and reality, abandon the prospect of a straight and perhaps satisfying screw for the chance of getting really involved, for the second time—and again in Russia. But it was the wrong time. And the wrong place. And she could only get hurt. And he wanted to and did believe that it was not in self-defense, too, that inch by inch he began to pull away from her.

She was still waiting. But the pause was too long. Her eyes opened and questioned him. He answered with a more puzzled than puzzling smile and picked up the bottle. He drank slowly, for pleasure, not thirst, and reduced the brandy by a good two fingers.

"Let's grow up, sweetheart." He hoped to sound convincingly callous. "To play games of falling in love is just about the last thing we want right now." He took another deep swig, then began to whistle "It's the wrong time, It's the wrong place . . ."

"Thank you, nurse," she said, struggling to regain her composure. The tune meant nothing to her.

• Friday, September 21 •

Newsweek reporters discover that an armada of sixty ships was scheduled to arrive at Cuba in September, but news conference reveals that Kennedy knows nothing about it.

THE SPETSBURO COLONEL WAS UNAVAILABLE. AND NO NEWS about Form M-17. Boychenko was growing restless. He felt cut off. He sought to see the head of his department and his request was refused. Something or someone was holding him off. It might be the system. Or a single bureaucrat. Or a saboteur. Not impossible. Now if he could discover a saboteur right inside the Center . . . He knew he might only be imagining things, but that young lieutenant in the Spetsburo colonel's anteroom had definitely been offish with him. And a colleague, too. No, nobody would know about the fiasco with Rust, not yet. But they would sense these things. And if he did nothing. . . . Anything was better than this waiting game.

Again he thought about that Rust file. It could not be so

112

thin and empty without a reason. Zemskov. Gennadi Romanovich Zemskov. The man with the legendary memory who had retired from Records only a couple of years ago. Boychenko could have kicked himself for not thinking about him sooner. And for the first time, he was pleased that Records had not yet been computerized. Tape erasure would wipe out all memories. Retirement would not. He telephoned Zemskov to announce his visit.

He walked to No. 12 Dzerzhinsky Street. At the gate he passed the deputy chief of the Special Investigation Department, and his hearty greetings were hardly acknowledged. Or was this again only his imagination? The KGB store was relatively empty. Most officers would do their shopping in the afternoon, when their wives had already told them what to bring home. Boychenko paused to think. What would please Zemskov? Things too expensive for a retired man, things reserved for the privileged on active service. Still, he would not want to spend too much out of his own pocket even if things were cheap here. He chose a bottle of Starka, a kilo of veal (and asked the man at the counter to try to put aside another kilo for him, too), and some fresh fruit.

Zemskov lived in a massive old block near the southern port on the Moskva River. Boychenko considered it a fair location for a Records clerk who had never achieved much and whose phenomenal memory had served only some slicker climbers' advancement. But the names listed on the door revealed that the apartment was shared by three families. A real surprise, but only because an ex-KGB man was involved.

"Perhaps we could go out somewhere," Zemskov suggested, but Boychenko was anxious to hide his shock.

"Why? What's wrong with this place, Gennadi Romanovich? It's a fine location with a fine view of the river, and if it's good enough for you to live here, it's good enough for me to have a drink with you."

"Oh yes, it's a fine view. Much better than what I used to have. Even if less roomy." Zemskov tried to make it sound lighthearted. "But it can't be helped. Just after I'd retired, my wife died and the building was chosen for redevelopment. So they gave me...this." His voice trailed off. He was not sure about Boychenko's reaction. "I mean, it's only fair. I'm on my own. Families with children must have priority."

"That's the spirit." His own voice made Boychenko realize that Zemskov had been half whispering most of the time. He looked around. From the edge of the window, a curtain ran across the room. He gestured toward it: "And that's your bedroom, a real bachelor's den." He chuckled.

Zemskov did not try to share his merry mood. "Er . . . well, not quite. That's where a young couple live. I mean temporarily. Until something better can be found for them."

"Oh."

Zemskov smiled to reassure the visitor. "They both work night shifts. That's why I keep my voice down a little. I mean, it's only fair. They must sleep."

"Of course. Of course."

Zemskov protested a little but was undoubtedly pleased with the presents. He wanted to open the bottle for Boychenko right away, but the major decided to go for a walk with the old man after all. Zemskov agreed. He took a key and picked up the presents. "Won't be long; just put them in my kitchen cupboard." He did not shut the door, and Boychenko heard the opening of a heavy padlock.

A woman moaned. A bed creaked. Now groaning. A suppressed cry. Boychenko stood up. Somebody must be sick behind the curtain. Some pain. Or a heart attack. He could not just stand there doing nothing for her.

Zemskov returned and picked out the sound from behind the curtain right away. He tried to smile but only managed to blush. "Well, the advantage of doing the night shift. I mean, during the day, it's only me in the apartment. I mean, they have it almost all to themselves. The family from the other room leaves early."

Boychenko had an irresistible urge to look behind the curtain, see whether she was pretty and watch her lovemaking if yes. But Zemskov was eager to usher him out.

They walked on the Damilovskaya embankment, and Boychenko decided to come to the point. "Things aren't as well organized as they used to be in your time in Records."

"Registry and Archives, you mean."

"Of course." How stupid of me, not to remember what a stickler the old man was, Boychenko thought. "Just the other day, I needed a file on a bloke called Rust, Helm Rust to be precise, and what do I find? Nothing. Somebody must have mislaid most of the contents. Come to think of it, it must have been in your time when his file was opened. In 1956, to be precise." Not very subtle, thought Boychenko, but it should make no difference to the old man. "You wouldn't remember him, I suppose. I mean, why should you?"

"An American?"

"That's right! You're really incredible!"

"A journalist."

"Go on. Let's see how good you are."

"No. Leave it alone."

"Why? It's only an exercise."

"I'm grateful to you, major. You brought me things I haven't seen for years. I don't want to be ungrateful. But there was something, er . . . something one should forget."

"Such as?"

"Something about his father. And a brother."

"The file says nothing about them."

"You see? It was all transferred to another department."

"What? From Records?"

"From Registry and Archives."

"To what department?"

"I can't remember."

"You must tell me."

"I can't remember."

"My dear Gennadi Romanovich—it's important to me."

"I can't remember."

"All right, Comrade Zemskov, if that's the way you want to play it, it's fine with me. Just fine. We'll soon sort out what you can and can't remember."

"I'm sorry. All I remember is that something important was happening and the file was kept by the First Chief Directorate."

"Which department?"

"First. I think."

"U.S. and Canada."

"But I can't be sure."

"You'd better be." Boychenko was angry. Making such a fuss about a morsel of information that might help him to save his own skin, let alone his son's! He was really tempted to take his presents back. But then he remembered the couple behind the curtain and felt sorry for the old fellow. "Well, thanks. It was a nice walk. Go easy on the Starka—you can really get sloshed if you're not used to it."

The last of Rust's American clothes were tied in a bundle. From the bottom of the suitcase, Yelena produced a white coat and some documents. "Here are your papers."

"Do I have to learn all the details?"

"Not really. Just the name, date of birth. If it comes to details, we're in trouble anyway."

She put on the white coat. Rust studied the papers. There was the dark-gray-green internal passport issued to Dmitri Gorbunov, aged thirty-five, born in Novgorod. His "social origin" was specified as working-class. The photograph showed a blank, squarish face, eyes staring straight into the camera. It would take a great deal of goodwill to mistake the man for Rust.

"I'm sorry," said Yelena, "there hasn't been time to change the picture. But I hope they won't touch your papers anyway. If they ask for them, you pull them out of your pocket and hold them out to the militia or whoever. And try to shake and look feverish."

Most of the pages of the passport were filled with stamps, proving details of his existence. The most important of these *propiski* gave him permission to go to and reside in Moscow. Another showed he was married.

"The other papers are your *spravki*," said Yelena. "Permission to be transported by special ambulance, permission to travel outside the Moscow zone, and your permission to enter the quarantine hospital in Ivanovo."

"Will I go there?"

"No."

He just glanced at her.

"I answered your question, didn't I? If you ask more I'll answer truthfully. But only if you ask me."

"Will you come with me?"

"In the ambulance? Yes." Using her crumbling lipstick, she painted "spots of fever" on his face.

It was big and ugly Florian who drove the white ambulance van with the red doors, red stripes on both sides and the back, red crosses in circles on the frosted-glass windows, flying a large yellow flag. They drove up Mir Prospekt, turning northeastward along Yaroslavskoye, and when they passed a gas station, Yelena turned to warn Rust: they would soon reach the outer ring-road intersection with the first checkpoint. Rust lay back, covered himself with a blanket and tried to shiver. He found it did not take much practicing.

Small traffic posts directed vehicles to the roadside. A wooden hut and a manually operated barrier elevated the roadblock to the status of a frontier crossing.

Yelena wound down her window and flashed a doctor's identity card toward the guards, both armed with submachine guns. "One patient, suspected of being carrier of contagious disease Category Number One," Yelena reeled off, "to be held in quarantine at Ivanovo."

The senior guard, a corporal, looked suitably impressed and kept well away from the open window. "Wait here." He walked to a boxed telephone. The other man shifted his weapon: he was now in charge.

The KGB officer supervising the roadblock sat in the warmth of his hut and listened to the whining corporal, who was obviously reluctant to come into close contact with something infectious.

"Damn it, man, when I was on point duty I had to check everything!" the officer shouted as if the telephone were merely something to hang onto. "Once I was ordered to do a body search on six lice-ridden Nazi bastards." Naturally, he had never carried out that order, but nobody would know that.

The corporal returned to the ambulance. "Open up the back door." Florian got out and walked to the rear with him. Rust grabbed the small gun under the blanket. He had seen a large motorcycle at the roadside. If it came to the worst, he could try to run for it.

"Papers."

Yelena turned back in the passenger seat and smiled at the guard: "Don't be afraid, comrade, it may not be a cholera case after all."

Rust fished the papers out of his pocket with great apparent difficulty. Unable to handle them all at the same time, he held the passport between his lips and let saliva dribble on the *spravki* as he fumbled to offer them for closer inspection.

The corporal felt sick. He glanced around furtively. Nobody could see what he was doing. Nobody except the ambulance staff and that wretched, driveling, feverish man who breathed with a rattle trying to sit up on the couch and offer his sweaty face for inspection.

"Okay. Off you go." The corporal nodded with his head toward Florian, indicating that the driver could shut the door. Why should he risk his life by touching that handle when the saliva of a Category One case might be just drying all over it?

"That was close," Rust whispered.

Yelena seemed unperturbed. "Not as close as you think. Everything in my country is an eternal combination of extreme efficiency and total negligence, individual brilliance and corporate incompetence."

Florian drove slowly through the labyrinth of traffic posts. The corporal waved toward the guard operating the barrier. The road was cleared. Still in low gear to show he was in no great hurry, Florian passed the KGB hut in the middle of the road.

"What's a Category One disease?" asked Rust.

"I don't know." Yelena chuckled. "Our people are always impressed by precise classification."

The KGB officer caught a glimpse of the woman doctor in the front passenger seat. Didn't she look familiar? Why should she? He had never known a doctor. He had never been ill or in an ambulance. He might have seen her among the gynecologists at the hospital when visiting his wife the other day. But then why should she be in the ambulance? There could be some simple explanation, of course, but if so, what was it? He picked up the phone to call the Ivanovo roadblock and alert the road patrol service.

Boychenko went straight to Registry and Archives. People of his rank and position would normally send for papers they wanted to see. His personal visit was bound to speed up procedures, particularly when the required documents were several years old and would have to be exhumed in the dusty cemetery of dead files.

He waited patiently for almost two hours in a small, damp, underground office and tried to list all the material that might contain original information and could have served as a basis for further investigation or for direct notes to be made on Rust's file in 1956. For whatever would then happen to the file itself, the original reports would probably remain untouched.

A small trolley, fully laden with yellowing documents, was wheeled in. The rising dust made Boychenko cough as he began to sort them. He selected 1/1/1/SDR-1956 to be looked at first. It represented the Summary of Daily Reports, 1956, for First Chief Directorate, First Department, from informers in the U.S. Embassy, coded No. 1. It would certainly contain a load of garbage; Russian staff to be employed by embassies for menial tasks were always selected and assigned by the KGB, but these were low-caliber agents whose brief was to report anything and everything indiscriminately and slavishly.

He scanned page after page, and by lunchtime, his diligence had won its first reward: a cleaner had overheard a remark that "some American reporter had found his father in Moscow." The reporter's name was thought to be Rost or Tost or Trust. A handwritten note indicated that the information had been referred for further investigation and cross-checking.

Boychenko was delighted. It was just the sort of detail he could get his teeth into. The Spetsburo colonel would have no difficulty tracing what happened. It might also help to explain the immense interest in Rust. He made a note and was about to close the file when a quiet, authoritative voice told him: "Hold it." Boychenko turned to face two armed civilians flanking a young plainclothes lieutenant from Special Investigations. "Your papers, major."

"They were checked at the entrance. Besides, you know me, don't you?"

"Your papers."

Boychenko handed him his KGB identity card. The lieutenant pocketed it without looking at it.

"Are you armed?"

"Of course not."

"Search him."

Boychenko's protests were ignored.

"What case were you reexamining?" The lieutenant took out a small notebook with torn edges and a German ballpoint pen.

"Rust. Helm Rust."

"Have you been authorized specifically to conduct research here?"

"I have the right."

"Have you or have you not been authorized?"

"No. I don't need to be."

"B. admits," the lieutenant said as he wrote slowly, "that he had not been authorized." He looked at the documents. "Which of those have you been through?"

Boychenko pointed at the SDR file. "Will you tell me what this is all about?"

"Let's go." The lieutenant turned to lead the group down endless underground corridors.

Boychenko recognized the place. A row of interrogation cells. Somebody must have gone crazy. Or could this be in connection with something else? His son. He might have done or said something. Or his wife. Another of her fresh crop of jokes? He had warned the silly bitch a million times. "It must be some mistake," he mumbled, already guilty, as they pushed him into a cell.

Without any warning, the lieutenant hit him in the mouth. "Shut up. Until I ask you." Boychenko spat out some blood. "Wipe it up." The young officer sat down at the desk and surveyed the major with undisguised aversion. "I don't like small, fat pigs, do you?... Do you?"

"No."

"Sir!"

"No, sir."

"So, you dislike yourself. Good. It creates some understanding between us. Right?"

"Right, sir." He had to cooperate without complaint. It was his duty. And a sign of innocence.

"Now listen. I must submit a report quickly. The less trouble you give me, the less trouble I give you. So let's have it. What's your interest in Rust?"

"I got the case and—"

"Don't give me any shit. Why did you let him go?"

"I didn't."

"Oh. You've decided to argue with me. Well, I don't want to be unreasonable. After all, the days of Beria have gone. I'll give you another chance. The men who took part in the Rust and Holly operation have already confessed that they let Rust go on your orders."

"I see." It was pointless to argue. If necessary, the men would be made to confess anything.

"So. The first question. Where's Rust now?"

"I don't know."

"You don't know." He turned to the two goons who looked on impassively. "He doesn't know."

"Shall we beg him to reconsider?" one of them asked.

"Not yet. The second question. Why did you approach and pressure Zemskov?"

Of course. It had to be Zemskov who had reported him. Boychenko was furious that deep down, he could not even blame the old man for informing on him. It was his duty. He had been approached and questioned by an officer acting without proper authorization—why else would he bring gifts to bribe him? Boychenko nodded: yes, he could see the point. "I'm sorry, sir, but it seemed a natural step in the investigation. I wanted to recapture Rust, and my reasoning was that he must have helpers if he stayed free for some thirty-six hours. His file looked unnaturally depleted, so I thought Zemskov might give me a lead as to what had happened. When he told me about the existence of a father and brother, it seemed clear that someone had removed some documents from the file. It could be a saboteur, an enemy of the state and even an opposition agent."

"A saboteur, an enemy or an agent. You mean a spy. Right?"

"Right, sir."

"A spy like you? No, don't answer. You're bound to deny everything. Let's not waste time. Just tell me why you carried on with the so-called investigation after seeing Zemskov."

Boychenko could not tell him that he had personal and family worries, that he could not afford to go on for long with an accusation of negligence hanging over his head. "I wanted to present the Spetsburo with something positive. A lead."

"And what have you come up with?"

"An indication that in 1956, Rust had found his father right here in Moscow. Now if that was the case, we'd soon find who might be helping him. All we need do is to track down the father if he's still alive, bring him in and ask him to give us a hand. He wouldn't refuse, I'm sure."

"That's enough. If you want to waste my time with such concoctions, you'll lose my sympathy. Fast." He threw his head back, and the sudden movement made his jaw jut out toward the two men. That was their cue. One of them grabbed Boychenko from behind and held him. The other used Boy-

chenko's stomach as a punching bag. The blows were coming
in fast, and Boychenko groaned. The pain had winded him so
unexpectedly that he could not find relief even in a hearty
scream. He collapsed, and the two men began to kick his
ribcage. "That's enough." The lieutenant walked out from behind the desk, unbuttoned his fly and urinated on Boychenko,
who seemed too weak even to try and move out of the way.
"Now let's start again and let's be reasonable. We can expect
a little more cooperation from a brother officer, can't we? And
let's make it quick this time, because I must write my report
before I go home. I have tickets to a wonderful poetry reading
tonight. Pushkin and Yevtushenko. What a combination! If you
make me miss that, with your delaying tactics, Comrade Boychenko, you may not find me as friendly and considerate as
I've been so far. Now back to my first question. Where's Rust
now?"

Florian drove off the main road and stopped behind thick
bushes. He handed a bottle of water to Rust. "Get out and
clean your face." Yelena had already shed her white coat and
changed into a drab quilted jacket. She put a scarf on her head
and tied it neatly under her chin. Her nails scratched the edge
of some red markings on the ambulance, and the "paint" came
off in neat strips smoothly. Florian peeled off the red crosses
and the red sheets covering the doors. With the yellow flag
removed and the number plate changed, there was an ordinary
white van with green doors proclaiming to be the property of
the Red Banner *kolkhoz* in Aleksandrov, only some six kilometers off the Ivanovo road. Rust had no time to admire their
efficiency. "Give me a hand," said Florian, picking up a hand-
ful of mud. "You do the outside." In a few minutes, the van
lost all resemblance to an ambulance.

Some approaching noise startled Rust. Without thinking, he
reached into his pocket for the TK 6.35.

Florian listened. "It must be Fyodor."

"You still have that gun?" Yelena asked Rust.

"Yes."

"I'll take it." And when Rust shook his head, she shrugged
her shoulders. "Give me your papers. And here's your new
identity." She handed him another set of documents. A horse
appeared, pulling a creaking cart. It seemed the bony animal

would never survive the last fifty yards to the bushes, but somehow it made it. Yelena waved to the old peasant, then turned back to Rust: "You'll have to change your clothes. We'll catch the Leningrad train at Kolchugino."

The changeover was swift. Rust's papers were burned. Sacks of potato and cabbages were transferred from the cart to the van. Florian walked off across the muddy fields. "We'll have to keep him in sight," said Yelena as she invited Rust to join her on the cart. Fyodor drove off toward Moscow. Anybody pursuing the fugitive would probably search for white vans leaving Moscow rather than for the muddy farm vehicle delivering *kolkhoz* produce to the capital.

The smooth professionalism of the operation aroused Rust's suspicions once again. He chose not to ask questions while the going was good, but he could not resist remarking, "If your resistance setup is as well organized as all this, your revolution can't fail."

"What revolution? I've never mentioned anything like that, have I?"

Boychenko was in bad shape. He had repeated his story and all his reasons several times, and no matter how painful the consequences of each repetition were, he stuck to his account stubbornly. For he knew the form well. The beatings and humiliation were a routine part of the investigation. They were not drawing blood or inflicting potentially permanent injuries. Not yet. And they were not really pressing him to invent a different kind of more self-incriminating confession. When that stage was reached, he would sense it right away, he hoped. Then he would have to guess the correct lines to invent. That could save him a great deal of suffering and give him more time. He hoped that time would be on his side. The lieutenant must be acting on orders following the information that had just reached them from Zemskov. Others must be making further inquiries.

The door opened, and the three men stood to attention. The Spetsburo colonel entered and took the seat behind the desk. Boychenko tried to stand, but his stomach hurt too much.

"Stand up, you bastard!" the lieutenant yelled, demonstrating his stern authority in front of the colonel.

"Let him sit down," said the colonel.

"Sit down, you bastard, sit!"

Boychenko sat in a pool of urine. He did not mind. The colonel wrinkled his nose: he did not enjoy the stench. He made Boychenko repeat his story. Yes, it did sound quite reasonable that Rust might have local help, that the slimness of the file was unnatural, that the reports from the embassy might give Boychenko a clue, and that the existence of Rust's father was such a clue. On the other hand, it was understandable that Boychenko's unauthorized inquiries had caused considerable alarm in the First Directorate, and the upheaval that followed was routine procedure due to commendable vigilance. For not even the colonel was told what the missing file contained.

"May I add something, sir?" asked Boychenko. He hoped this was the right time to stick his neck out a little—and make Zemskov sweat, too.

"What?"

"Comrade Zemskov revealed to me, without any proper authorization, of course, that Rust's file might be held by the First Chief Directorate. If that unauthorized disclosure was true, the First Directorate could have warned us in time to pay special attention to Rust on arrival." The last of his strength to sit upright had gone. He lay back on the stone floor in the lieutenant's urine.

Presumably, somebody in First had failed to scrutinize the list of daily arrivals properly, thought the colonel. And it was true, Zemskov had talked to Boychenko after corruptly accepting the presents. But the colonel was a cautious man. He could not afford a hasty reaction. Such things would have to be approved first. He stood up, stepped over Boychenko and spat his words into the lieutenant's face: "Just let him stew. No beatings or anything like that, understood? These are not the old days. Socialist legality must be observed."

The lieutenant followed him to the door and stepped on Boychenko's stomach on the way. Accidentally, of course. And Boychenko was careful not to try to cry out or even groan.

At the small station of Kolchugino, there was no crowd to provide anonymity, and Rust was conscious of the militiamen's steady gaze burning four holes in his back. There was only another twenty yards to the train. If they were stopped, they might miss the train, and the outcome of closer questioning would be anybody's guess. A guess for a pessimist, Rust had to admit. But Yelena proved herself a superb actress. Her hair flew freely in the damp wind as she hung onto Rust's arm with all the untainted devotion of the just-married, producing bubbly laughter at will, and—in her quilted jacket—treating the guards to just the picture they would know so well from every Soviet film portraying happiness. When Rust climbed the stairs of the train and looked back, he saw the guards laughing with her.

The strain, however, took its toll on the way. Yelena fell asleep on Rust's shoulder, kept shifting to find more and more comfortable positions, and curled up, finally, with her head on his lap. The similarities were inescapable, although Rust tried hard not to think of that other journey, with that other girl, some five years ago. Except then he had been returning from Leningrad to Moscow. It was the end of one of the longest weeks in Rust's life. And it had begun with the longest day of 1957.

"Penny for your thoughts."

"I thought you were asleep."

"You didn't answer," Yelena insisted.

"Didn't I?"

"That means another woman. Right?"

"Yes."

"Are you in love with her?"

"Not anymore. I think."

"Why did you think about her now?"

"Because it happened in Leningrad."

"Tell me about her."

"Are you a masochist or something?"

"No."

"Then why do you want to hear about her?"

"Because you looked sad, even hurt, when you thought about her. Did she hurt you?"

He slowly raised, then dropped his shoulders. "I don't think she meant to. And I don't think she'd have meant so much to me if the circumstances were different."

"What circumstances?"

"Hey, is this a full-scale interrogation?"

"No." She kissed him. "I mean yes." Her lips went close to his, then pulled away. "With torture, if necessary." She licked her upper lip and stretched sensuously. "What circumstances?" Rust found her naturally erotic. But a bad teaser.

He avoided looking at her. "It's just that I was probably vulnerable at the time. In a mood of exuberance. After months and months of frustrating search and inquiries, it was just before Leningrad that I had found my father. It was a shock, and we found it hard to talk. Then on that Friday morning we met at the church where he always goes. We went for a long walk, and for the first time, it was easier to talk. Oddly enough, about unimportant things. Like Geneva. The Jeddo. Then..." He stopped and stared out the window. It was pointless to tell her what happened that morning after the walk, when he visited the embassy and the CIA station chief called him into his private office.

The chief had some cheerful news for him: Elliott had been moved from the backwaters of Monitoring straight into Analysis. He would be a mere junior assistant, but it was a great opportunity. Elliott's sluggish career with the Company could really take off. Now it would be up to him. Rust was delighted. He knew how much he had contributed to that transfer. To a great extent, it had to be the result of his tenacious manipulations behind the scenes. Even their mother would have to admit that as far as possible, Helm had paid his real or imaginary debt to his brother for that crazy toboggan race and the accident.

Yelena ran out of patience waiting for the rest of the unfinished sentence. "Then?... you talked about Geneva... and then?"

"Then later I heard that quite unexpectedly, the Ministry of Culture had granted me permission to visit the bombproof cellars of the Hermitage."

"Mm, that must have pleased you."

"Immensely. I was to be the first Western journalist to see all the art treasures stored down there and never on public view. I mean, never since the Revolution. It was to be a real scoop to complete a perfect day, I thought, but I was wrong. There was more to come.

"I took the lunchtime flight to Leningrad. It was the longest day of the year, the longest of the white nights. Most of the town seemed to have abandoned all ideas about sleep, and I just loved the mood. The American cultural attaché gave a reception to end all receptions. It was at the Hotel Astoria. I arrived late, and I was bored. Everybody kept repeating the old story about the siege when the Nazis had already planned their victory ball at the Astoria and had printed those black, gold and white invitation cards which they never had a chance to use because they never occupied the city." He looked at her, and she seemed resentful. "Sorry. Did I say something wrong?"

"It's just that you don't understand. Those who have survived that siege, like my parents, cannot stop talking about those heroic days. Some mementos and anecdotes are still the most important things in their lives. Like that sign preserved on a wall in the Nevsky. It says that during the artillery barrage you must walk on the other side of the street because it's safer there. And the story of those unused invitation cards which our troops captured eventually. It's cruel not to let them repeat the story again and again. They have earned the right to relish every bit of the memory."

"I'm sorry."

"Was it at the party that you met her?"

"Yes."

"Much more beautiful than me, I suppose."

"Wrong. And you're just fishing for compliments." She was very different from Yelena. Petite and demure, constantly surrounded by a phalanx of men wherever she went. Her upper teeth protruded slightly and created a faintly visible gap between her lips. Rust found it irresistible. "But she had one thing in common with you. She had your ability to dissolve in sudden bursts of happy laughter. I remember a young reporter asking who the hell she was, and another answered, 'An apparition.' Which was right."

"Was she Russian?"

"No. I'll never forget the face of a consular second secretary's ulcerous wife who told me, 'She's on a visiting Senator's staff junket over here, and if you want to know, you're the seventeenth tonight with the same question.' And she was full of venom when she added, 'Remember, honey, I'll be holding an orgy in the ballroom just for the overflow of her court.' It was an irresistible challenge. I walked right through the group, bowed very formally and begged her for the next dance. She argued there was no music. I insisted on an answer, yes or no. She said yes. I said thanks, we must now find some music. I took her hand and she let me extract her from that tight group of men like a cork from a bottle, smoothly despite the resistance and pressure from all around.

"I led her down to the Dekabristy Square at the Neva, then down the steps right to the edge of the river, where people drank and sang and danced, and everybody tried to prove to everybody else that it was possible to read in natural light at one and two and three in the morning. It was hard to take it all in. Church spires and the gold roofs of cathedrals and the Admiralty glittered in a red sun shining from somewhere just below the horizon. The long series of low bridges were opened up and sideways to allow the larger ships to sail up the river, and people cheered and raised glasses and kissed to greet each arrival."

Rust stopped. The romantic mood of the night and the city was inescapable. Talking about it was, in a way, an admission that he was still not immune to it.

Yelena sensed the shadow of embarrassment in his voice. That involuntarily revealed slight trait of romanticism appealed to her more than he would understand. She touched his hand, then turned away. As if assuring him that there were no witnesses.

"It was impossible not to fall in love," he said in the objective tone of a standing-orders committee chairman. "And unlike most of my love life, this time it didn't all begin in bed. It was meant to end there, of course—we had both known that from that first exchange at the Astoria—but there was that added delight in the endless detours along winding canals, across humped little bridges, in and out of absurdly poetic courtyards with miniature parks and overgrown statuettes. And we drank and drank, because we talked and talked, until both our throats and the bottle ran dry.

"I think it was on the Fontanka River embankment that we were suddenly surrounded by a wild swarm of students. They were pushing an old baby carriage which was laden to the brim with magnums of Russian champagne. It was sweet and, frankly, pretty bad, but it would have been a 'base gesture of unfriendliness' not to drink with them."

"Which of course meant a few toasts, I hope," said Yelena, laughing.

"Few? We toasted America, and Russia, and Leningrad and

Petersburg in West Virginia, and Stuyvesant because he was another Peter we happened to think of, and the river, the light, the night, and all the rightful past and future occupiers of this most venerable of baby carriages we were pushing, and toasted all good men, not forgetting, not ever forgetting, all the strays, human and feline, who, by the sound of it, must have been hard at work behind every bush, determined to overpopulate Leningrad with more strays."

He fell silent again. He had never had time for other people's reminiscences, and he spared them from his own. But now the memory of those first three days was too strong.

"So what went wrong?" asked Yelena, trying to achieve what he could not in objectivity.

"She grew sad, gradually, and most of the bubbles had gone from her voice and mood by the fifth day. She had been constantly writing little 'I love you' memos. I kept finding them everywhere. Now she stopped that. She told me what a terrible pity it was and how much it hurt her that we hadn't met earlier. That week was meant to be her last fling. It was meant to be nothing but cheerful and forgettable. It shocked her that it would not be like that. I was an accident. Because her plans had been made long before that trip. On her return to America, she'd move in with her fiancé and she'd be married within a few months. No, there was no chance to change her plans. For numerous reasons. Including the fact that her fiancé was a wonderful man, she said, and that she loved us both."

On their last night in Leningrad, she got drunk. She dragged him to bed, went wild, scratched and beat his chest in a frenzy, fell asleep in his arms, and woke him up with kisses all the way down to his ankles and back. He remembered her voice and most of the words that seemed to gush from her in a gabbling whisper. "I don't know what this is," she repeated again and again. "I'm craving for your sperms. I want them inside me. Everywhere. I want to remember you by their taste."

She persuaded him to return with her to Moscow by train. And she slept on his lap most of the way.

Rust looked down. Yelena seemed to be asleep in an almost identical position. Keep warm, he thought, and covered her legs with his coat.

"Stop shifting," Yelena said.

"I thought you were asleep."

"You always think that. Especially when you don't want to say something."

"What?"

"You know what. How did it end?"

"We said goodbye in Moscow."

"And never met again?"

"Only socially."

"Did she marry him?"

"Yes."

"Do you know him?"

"Yes."

She looked away. "We never had a chance to say goodbye," she mumbled after a long pause. She was thinking of her dead husband, he guessed, but chose not to ask her.

The President seemed comfortable in shirt sleeves, but the Oval Office was definitely chilly for a man of Dean Acheson's age. Fifteen minutes earlier, Kennedy had entered through one of the huge French windows facing the lawn and the rose garden on the east side, and left the door open. He was now seated at his desk, resting one foot on the wastepaper basket, and listened to someone on the phone while jotting down a few notes. "Holly? . . . Jim Holly? . . . What was his position in the Embassy?"

Acheson was fuming. The cold breeze and the interruption failed to improve his mood. He rose from his chair, walked up and down vigorously both to warm up and imply impatience. This imperious old man, former Secretary of State, knew perfectly well that he was much respected by the President and his closest associates, that his advice was frequently sought and always valued by the Administration, and that, nevertheless, even his outspokenness must remain within limits. Yet this was not the occasion to test where those limits were. He had something to say and he was going to say it as soon as the phone call was finished. Who the hell was this Jim Holly anyway? He turned on his heels, returned to the south window, and stopped, staring at the purple-and-gold Presidential flag behind and to the right of the desk. He felt a speedy shiver race down his spine. He managed to turn just in time not to sneeze on the flag. Damned chill.

"You think there's no question of foul play or security infringement?" Kennedy asked and tapped his teeth with his forefinger a few times as he listened to the answer. "Okay, let me know. . . . And one other thing, make sure the widow's looked after, will you?"

As soon as he hung up, Acheson opened up darkly. "I hear a great many rumors about Cuban rearmament, Mister President."

"So do I, Dean. Fortunately it's not Khrushchev's policy to install offensive missiles on foreign soil."

"But if he changes his mind, will you accept it and compromise with the new situation?"

"No. No compromise. I've stated that publicly."

"Can I take it then that this is our official military policy?"

"As you well know, it's not just a matter of military policy," Kennedy said, crossing the room and then sitting on one of the sofas facing the fireplace. "I can't just disregard everything that goes beyond military realism. It's easy for the brasshats because they have a tremendous advantage: If we do what they want us to do, none of us will be here to tell them whether they were right or wrong."

That was about as much as the old man could take. He sat down on the other sofa, confronting the President. "I have a feeling, Mister President, that you're referring to some moral anguish which I detest as a moving force of politics. And I have a feeling that it is unworthy of you to be influenced unduly by, if you'll forgive me, by your brother's moral clichés about Pearl Harbor in reverse, a thoroughly false and pejorative analogy. It is a silly way to analyze a problem, and I think that the Attorney General is moved by emotional and intuitive responses more than by a trained lawyer's analysis." He stopped and took a deep breath. Now that he had said it, he was ready to hear that his advice would never again be elicited.

After a long pause, a boyish smile fleeted across Kennedy's face. "Thank you for being so frank with me, Dean. I'm lucky to have you on the team, and I'm lucky that Khrushchev is not likely to test my will and nerve ever again. And for that, I have to be grateful to you to a great extent."

He was referring to the Berlin crisis when Acheson laid

down the militant case so brilliantly—the argument to back the only possible winning stance. The acknowledgement brought tears to the old man's eyes, and he left the Oval Office hurriedly.

• Sunday, September 23 •

Che Guevara meets Khrushchev in Yalta. At the small port of Mariel, near Havana, a hurriedly built high wall hides the unloading of Russian ships. Bertrand Russell: The Russians "had it from the start. I was in Russia in 1920 and they already had this phobia. A terrible, terrible determination to keep everything secret. It's an old Eastern attitude, and it's an irrational thing. . . ."

BOYCHENKO KNEW THAT IT MIGHT TAKE WEEKS, POSSIBLY months, to breach the interdepartmental reluctance to a free exchange of information. And even if it was decided that this case merited some degree of cooperation as well as special attention, it might still take ages to agree which department of which Chief Directorate should be in charge. He resigned himself to a period of captivity and rejoiced when the entire Saturday had passed without further interrogation. On Sunday he was waked up at dawn. He was taken up to a bathroom on the ground floor. "Clean yourself up, major," said the guard, who handed him some fresh clothes. His own. From home. Things were looking up. He had just finished shaving when the lieutenant arrived and saluted him smartly.

"I'm pleased to report to you, major, that apparently some mistake has been made. I always thought, and I'm on record as saying, that you were no enemy of the people. Please go to your office now. I'm on my way to pick up a Pyotr Nikolayevich Rostonov and bring him to you for questioning."

It would have been pointless to reprimand the lieutenant or complain about his brutality. It was part of his job. If one was patient enough, one would find one's own revenge. That was Boychenko's principle. So for the time being he satisfied himself with a little gesture toward the lieutenant's neck. The young man blushed and hurriedly adjusted his loosely hanging tie. "I'm sorry, comrade."

"Rostonov?"

"The American Rust's father, I believe. At the moment you'll have to concentrate on discovering if Rust has contacted him."

"Have we got a file on him?"

"I don't know. If yes, it's held by First Directorate. And they will not release it."

"Then what are you waiting for? Bring him in, you idiot. And no slipups—I warn you."

Pyotr Nikolayevich was ready to leave for early service when the bell rang. He opened the door and went pale seeing the three plainclothesmen outside.

"Rostonov?"

He could only nod. All his blood rushed into his feet, and his drained body began shivering.

"Will you please come with us? It's a minor administrative matter."

"My kit. I mean shaving gear."

"You won't need anything. You should be back in no time."

No time. No time. His bloodstream bounced and the flood now rose toward his head. It blurred his vision, leaving him with only a slot to see through, a single beam focused on the open elevator door behind the men. He hit out with both hands and ran.

"Stoy!"

Only a few more steps. The metal door. The swish of rain-coats pulled aside.

"Stoy!"

A single leap took the old man into the glass cage. He pressed the button. The clicks of safety catches being flicked. The door began to close. The guns went off in quick succession. Some of the bullets whined ricocheting from the closing metal. Others found the narrowing gap to the cage. The old man collapsed and stared without seeing as the elevator began to descend in the glass tube attached to the wall of the house.

Some people in the street saw it coming down. A woman screamed. Two men turned and ran. They knew it was safer not to get involved even as witnesses to whatever had happened. Others just stood, paralyzed, unable to take their eyes away, as the body of the old man descended at a leisurely pace, blood spurting from several angles, obscuring the glass tube with splashes of red all the way.

The old man was definitely alive when three bluecoats ran out of the house. They dragged him inside. Two tried to stop the bleeding; the third raced to a car from which he radioed for an ambulance.

The white van arrived ten minutes later. The writing on its red stripes declared SKORAYA MEDITSINSKAYA POMOSHCH.

"Some quick medical help, pah," a plump woman mumbled. "A man can die in ten minutes." She noticed that people turned away from her. She could have kicked herself. Didn't her daughter always urge her to learn to keep her big mouth shut?

Boychenko heard about the shooting a few minutes after the ambulance had been called. He hoped the wounds were not fatal—he was itching to interrogate the man. But he was not ashamed to admit to himself how pleased he was that the lieutenant would have a great deal to explain whatever happened to Rostonov. Rostonov. The name bugged the major. It sounded so made-up. With an American son called Rust. Rustonov. Roostonov. Boychenko wished the First Directorate had given him full access to the facts on record. He felt sure he could achieve a great deal with a little help. And if there was no other way, he would get it from the old man now in intensive care at the KGB hospital.

* * *

Bossy, scheming and alluring Yelena proved to be a girlish lover. They had spent some thirty hours together—mostly in bed. She made love with total abandon, and each orgasm seemed to bring her relief, with tears and painful wailing. It was, in fact, her voice that drowned the sound of the opening front door. When at last the steps outside the bedroom could be heard, Rust reached under the pillow only to find that the small gun had gone. He stared at Yelena, who fought to control herself and whispered: "I took it. Didn't want any accidents."

A hard kick opened the bedroom door, and Rust turned to face Florian's gun. "I . . . I heard some noise." The big man looked first embarrassed, then angry.

"Wait outside," she snapped. Florian was reluctant to move. He could not take his eyes away from her. "Go." He backed out of the room but left the door slightly ajar. "Shut it!" she shouted.

Rust smiled. "You won't be popular."

"So what? This is not a popularity contest."

"Is he in love with you?"

She looked genuinely surprised. "In love? Why should he be?"

"I could think of a dozen good reasons offhand, another dozen if you gave me two minutes, and some more if you returned my gun."

"Thanks." She kissed him. "That was nice to hear."

"Except the last part of the sentence, which you chose not to hear."

"Last part?" They were getting out of bed.

"Come on, sweetheart, where is it?" He held out his hand, and when she still pretended not to understand, his hand moved jerkily. He just managed to stop himself from hitting her. "No more games. Please."

She reached behind some books on a shelf and took out the Tula-Korovin. For a second she held it, then tossed it to him. "Just no accidents, please."

"Then warn your gorilla, too, out there."

"He won't cause trouble."

"Not even after this?" He stabbed the bed with his forefinger. "No."

It was pointless to argue: probably she had not seen Florian's eyes catching the two of them in bed. Rust followed her into the marble-covered bathroom. He still could not accept her explanation that she had borrowed the apartment, about the most luxurious he had seen in Russia, from a friend who had kindly packed the pantry and the old-fashioned refrigerator with enough food for two for a week. Would be nice to forget it all and fall freely in love, he thought.

Yelena enjoyed taking long and leisurely showers with Rust, so he could not help noticing in what a great hurry she was this time. She was already dressed when he began drying himself. He reckoned she would have three or four minutes with Florian before he could join them. Dripping and wrapped in a towel, he felt like following her out, but forced himself not to. He knew that the days of waiting and more waiting had begun to fray his nerves.

Yelena entered the living room and closed the door. Florian turned away from her.

"Do you think this is wise?" He nodded toward the bedroom.

"It's none of your business." His sulking made her smile. She reached up to his head and touched his hair lightly. "Don't worry. He'll go away."

"When?"

"Soon."

"How soon?"

"It's up to us, isn't it?"

Florian looked at her. His voice was devoid of any emotion, but he leaned forward a little—a sign of close monitoring of her reactions. "He might have to be killed." He noted the flash of alarm in her eyes.

"Why? What happened?"

"They've picked up the old man."

"He can't tell them much."

"Even a little can be too much."

They both heard Rust moving in the bedroom. "Don't tell him"—she mouthed the words almost without any sound. And when the bedroom door opened: "So are we getting it or not?"

"Your cobbler's promised to do his best. I can't push him too much for obvious reasons."

"Can I talk to him?" Jake Schramm asked. He had never been squeamish about the sights and sounds of any horrid scene, but the smells of hospitals made his stomach turn.

"You can see him if you must, but it's a risk," said the surgeon, who had fished three bullets out of Hal Sheridan. "He looked a bit motheaten when you brought him in, and he must have leaked a lot of blood."

"Sure. Three slugs, three punctures."

"That's where you're wrong, man. He was even luckier than that, because he must have been horizontal by the time the fourth bullet hit him. It went in through his cheek, chipping away a bit of the bone which deflected it, and came out under his chin with just about enough force left in it to make itself comfortable in Hal's breast pocket. Which made it five punctures in all for us to plug, not to mention the stitching we had to do on his eye."

"Yuk."

Hal was in a private room, alone with a small TV set and a large CIA nurse, all arranged for him by Schramm, who asked the nurse to find a vase for the bunch of flowers he had brought.

"Here," Schramm whispered as soon as the nurse had left. He lifted the sheet and slipped a flat flask of rum underneath. He was shocked by the sight—Hal bandaged like a mummy except for one eye and the mouth—so he tried to joke. "Can you drink, or do you need a straw?"

A peculiar high-pitched laugh was the answer.

"Hope they didn't castrate you."

"Hope not." The voice remained high-pitched, and Schramm's joke was not funny at all anymore.

"Can you talk for a few minutes?"

"I'll try."

"When I brought you in, you mumbled something about the guy who shot you. Young crewcut, finely cut suit, right?"

"Blue eyes. Dark-blue."

"Anything else?"

"Yeah. Left-handed. Gun was on his right."

"Holster?"

"Didn't see. Possibly pocket. Inside pocket of jacket."

"Good man." The nurse returned with the flowers, and Schramm asked her to leave. She was not pleased.

"It's your show, mister, but you're taking a big, big responsibility," she said.

"Do me a favor, Jake," Hal squeaked, "put her in a big, big vase upside down."

Schramm waited until she left, then pulled a box of playing-card-sized photographs out of his briefcase. "You said something about Miami station."

"That's where Junior said he came from. CIA Miami station."

"Junior?"

"Yeah."

"You never mentioned his age."

"Twenty-four, twenty-five, I guess."

"Okay. Let's see if you can spot him here." They went through all the pictures, paying special attention to the younger, blue-eyed agents, but Hal could make no positive identification.

The nurse returned and, flanked by plenty of medical and administrative muscle, supervised gleefully the visitor's removal from the premises. She then proceeded to smooth Hal's sheets for the umpteenth time—and discovered the rum. "Go on, say it, I'm no lip-reader," she said to Hal. "You may have a big, big mouth, but I bet you can't tell me no new word I never heard before."

Back in his office, Schramm was in a foul mood. His desk was about to collapse under the weight of glossy literature advertising his employer's new venture, a harvester combine, and he removed it all with a swift sweep of great experience. He had long stopped using wastepaper baskets: even large cartons seemed to fill up daily with all the rubbish that was his cover.

Miami station. It would have been Miami station that, supposedly, picked up some Russki defector Rust mentioned the last time they met. Schramm had a feeling that Rust had not told him everything he knew.

Every bottle in the office was empty, and Schramm began to rummage in the cupboards, hoping to find some leftover rum somewhere. That again reminded him of Rust. Drinking Bacardi in El Paraíso where the little whore had been killed. Did she manage to sell whatever she had for sale? Or was it left with Rust? Or did her killers believe that it had been left with Rust? Was that what they were searching for when Hal was there? What could it be? And what would Rust have done with it if it was left with him? He wouldn't keep it in the house while being away for long stretches. He might . . . well, he just might send it to Washington.

Schramm dialed Elliott Repson's private number and made his report on Hal Sheridan's progress. "While we're at it, sir, there's something I'd like to ask. Just a long shot, really."

"Shoot."

"Way back in August, your . . . I mean, Helm Rust called me because a Cuban girl had something important for sale. We met in the bar where the girl worked, and found that she'd been murdered. The thing she had for sale was gone."

"Any idea what it was?"

"No, sir, but if you don't mind me saying, I had a kinda sneaky suspicion that Rust might have had it in his pocket all the time."

"You'll have to ask him."

"Sure . . . er . . . I mean, sure."

"Come on, Jake, what is it?"

"Well, to be candid about it, it was just a thought that he might have, I mean, could have sent it on to . . . er, you, sir. I mean, just as a gesture of goodwill." It was no good telling Repson that he had more than an inkling about Rust's active role in his brother's career. "I mean, if he did send it to you, it would be in good hands and all, but it could perhaps help to see what Rust might have been involved with. Sir? Are you there?"

"Yes, I'm here. Just checking. You said August?"

"Yes. I mean no, more like July. Yes, definitely."

"July then. Nope. Nothing. No communication from him, which isn't surprising, since we haven't been in touch for several years now, and there's nothing that came to me in July anonymously or under some name that could be of doubtful origin. Nothing."

Florian was late. Yelena had sent him to pick up a package from a *taynik* on Sadovoye. The conversation between the two of them had been too fast for Rust to follow in full, and she explained that *taynik* was a medieval word for some secret hole or compartment in a house or furniture to hide documents or valuables.

"Any sign of him?" Yelena asked.

"Not yet."

She seemed agitated as she walked restlessly up and down for more than an hour. Rust stood at the edge of the window, hidden by the heavy curtain, watching the wide expanse of Nevsky Prospekt. Not the shabbily dressed crowd of grays and faded blues, not the hunched shoulders and blank faces, not even the lack of glitter or illuminated shopfronts, nothing seemed to be able to eradicate the inherent elegance and grandeur of the street. Yes, No. 17, a green building with white icing, had a choice location, and Rust envied the unnamed friend who had lent this fine apartment to Yelena. He went to the kitchen to get a drink of water and admired once more the miniature park that was the courtyard. A few benches, a couple of classicist statues that had survived revolution, siege and Stalinist purification of the arts, a carved wooden gate, a small fountain, and pairs of stone lions guarding each door caught Rust's eyes. It was odd how tame these, like all Soviet lions, appeared to be. Just kittens wanting to play in the gently flowing water at the focal point of their sleepy gaze. The fountain, the jet in Lake Geneva, Vati—so Rust's associations ran. He knew he would never understand better the old man's secret, long-suppressed yearnings.

Florian arrived at last with a small, carefully wrapped packet. "It wasn't there," he complained. "I had to go all the way to the little oak to find it." Yelena sent him on another errand, and his suspicious eyes bounced like Ping-Pong balls between Rust and Yelena as if trying to figure out what the two might do when he left.

Ever since the morning scene in the bedroom, Rust had known that Florian was just waiting for the right opportunity to challenge him. He knew only too well those glances of "Let's see just how tough you really are." And Yelena seemed to know what his thoughts were.

"He doesn't count," she said when the door closed behind Florian. "He knows that you're important to me, so he'd die for you if necessary."

"I'd prefer not to test your faith in him."

She opened the package and laid out several documents on a table. She examined them carefully. "That's nice. Our cobbler's done a good job."

"Cobbler?"

"He makes the shoe in which you can walk across frontiers."
She smiled.

"You mean forger."

"It's an ugly word. This man is an artist." She handed him
a well-worn American passport, from which his own photograph stared at him. "Pleased to meet you, Mr. Foster."

"You're crazy."

"Maybe. But you'd better learn all the details by heart. If
you want to enter America alive, that is."

"Rubbish. Once I'm out of here I have no problems."

"You must still get to Washington."

"And what's the problem?"

"The neighbors have a very long arm."

"Why do you call the KGB neighbors?"

"That's what everybody calls them."

"Why are you angry?"

"Because you're wasting time with stupid questions. Study
the passport." She looked at him with growing incredulity.
"You really don't understand, or you don't care. By now
they must be ready to kill you on sight. They must have
heard about you when Igor was caught in Cuba. They had
contacts in high enough places to get a CIA agent to deliver
the message to you just to see your reaction. They must have
been watching you when you arrived. And then they had
confirmation that you were on a mission of some kind. Because foolishly you delivered our message right into their
hands when you talked to Holly, who reported it to his boss.
Do you know who that was?"

Holly mentioned the station chief. It was unimaginable that
the chief would be a Russian agent. But it was true, Holly had
been told to arrange a second meeting so that both he and Rust
could be picked up. The importance of the information was
proved quite clearly by Holly's summary execution. Presumably, Rust was spared so that he could be interrogated and
forced to reveal his source. So Yelena must be right. But he
was reluctant to give away anything about the embassy to her.
"I don't know who Holly reported to."

"And I don't believe you."

"Do you *need* to know the truth?"

"No. As long as you understand that they're looking for you
everywhere."

"Okay." He opened the passport. "Goodbye, Mr. Rust, hello Arthur Foster, much-traveled high school teacher from the Bronx. We'll have plenty of time to get acquainted." He shut the passport.

"No, you won't. I want you to learn it all now, so that you'll be ready when you need it. I'll make sure that you get it in London or somewhere else on your way to America."

"Don't I use this for leaving your beloved country?"

The irony of his voice stung her, but she resisted the temptation to hit back. "No, for that you'll need another shoe."

"Why?"

"It must be a genuine one with a genuine photo, because at the airport, the passport controller will be looking at an identical copy of the same photo. Remember? You had to hand in three pictures when you asked for a visa. The date and point of your departure are known to our authorities. The photo is already waiting for you there."

"So where will that other shoe come from?"

"Florian's working on it. Just concentrate on your passport." She sorted the documents on the table into two piles. "You won't need most of these."

"Can I see them?"

She made an attempt to stop him, but he snatched them away from her. There were "family photos" and fake mementos, employment records and medical cards, and a long detailed history of Arthur Foster, complete with photographs of places where he had spent his childhood and where he had worked. A separate list pointed out the most important details to be memorized in the pictures. These would enable him to "remember quite clearly" what color the walls and curtains were in his lodging as a student. There was enough to set up an illegal Russian with perfect cover for an indefinite stay in the United States.

"Satisfied?" She did not hide her irritation.

"Yours must be a good cobbler."

"Thank you."

"And who are you?"

She ignored the question and pushed a bunch of credit cards across the table. "Here. I'm told that in America nothing's as creditable as having credit."

"Stands to reason, doesn't it? It's like your party membership card over here." Again she looked hurt. It was pointless to keep needling her, but it helped him retain his self-respect in a situation where he had no chance to gain full control over his fate. "I'm sorry. It must be very difficult for you. You must know you'll also get your ass shot off if I'm caught."

"Martyrdom runs in the family."

"Okay. Let's see what it's like. Martyrs must take risks. We'll take a walk."

"You're crazy."

"Just a long, quiet walk along the canals, then out to the river. Leningrad is tailor-made for ruling the world and falling in love."

"Are you still in love with that girl?"

"No. Why?"

"Last night when you mentioned her it sounded as if you were. I forget her name."

"I never mentioned her name."

"Oh."

He kissed her, and for a second her lips brought back memories. The room looked different, the year was not 1962, there were no missiles on their way, and Russian soccer fields were not constructed within shooting distance of the United States.

She made a faint attempt to pull away from him. "We have work to do." Her eyes went misty. "And there's too little time left for us."

"Why don't you come with me? You could deliver your message yourself."

"If I did that, I could never return. And that or someone would probably kill me."

"Doesn't martyrdom run in the family?"

"It does. But we like to survive so that we can savor every minute of it."

Che Guevara was entertained in a grand style throughout his visit, Khrushchev had made sure of that. On this last evening, they dined together aboard the Soviet leader's yacht, repainted and renamed the *Havana* to commemorate the occasion. In less than twenty-four hours, the boat might again be repainted and renamed the *Aswan* to honor Nasser, but Che was not to know that as they sailed slowly along the Soviet Riviera.

The Cuban, not a renowned connoisseur of food or occasion,

was itching to get down to politics, but Khrushchev played him with patience, plied him with vodka, and induced him to toast Cuban-Soviet friendship again and again. It was in the middle of these repeated exhortations of eternal and unbreakable camaraderie that he produced a small folder with a theatrical gesture: "And this is to prove that our faith and trust in Fidel is unshakable, despite gossip, despite appearances, despite photography." Che opened the folder, and his face tightened with embarrassment. There were pictures, arranged in sequence. Raul Castro at an airport. Raul in Paris. Raul with some Chinese. Some Chinese Che knew, too. Raul shaking hands. "Please don't bother to examine them too much, they're not worth the time. Just give them to Comrade Castro with my compliments and tell him to forget about it. When it comes to true friends, we Russians believe what they tell us, not what we see. Besides, Raul may be so young that his mother's milk has hardly dried on his lips, but my dear and beloved Fidel is an old owl who knows that it's unwise to make friends with the poor and the amateur when the hand of the rich and the professional is offered in all sincerity." Che tried to give back the pictures, but Khrushchev insisted: "Please, please keep them. Make it a memento. One of the three I wanted to give you."

"What are the others?"

"One is the news that the first warheads will be on their way within a couple of days."

"They were supposed to arrive by now."

"I know, I know, but there were delays, not only on our side, I understand, but on yours, too."

"The construction of the port is progressing well."

"But are the launch sites also progressing satisfactorily? Or could it be that there are saboteurs among the workforce assigned to this important task?"

"That's impossible."

"I hope so, I do. But of course we'd feel happier if our experienced men could be given a greater opportunity to participate in the selection, vetting and security arrangements."

That was just the opportunity the Cuban was waiting for. "Perhaps you don't trust us sufficiently, Nikita Sergeyevich. Is that why you don't want us to have the missiles under our direct control?"

"Not at all! How could you say that? It makes no difference who's controlling what, not among friends."

"Fidel would be happier if we had direct control over at least some missiles. After all, the American Mongoose plan is going ahead fast. They might invade us again, and they'd hit us hard if they knew about the missiles."

"No, they would not. They wouldn't dare."

"Are you saying then that the Soviet Union is strong enough right now to fight an all-out missile war?"

"It depends whose opinion you accept on this matter. When a forest is cut down, chips will fly, but there's no need to take a defeatist view. Not unless you talk to defeatists. So who have you talked to? Perhaps scheming old Mikhail Andreyevich or young and restless Leonid Ilyich?" Khrushchev laughed heartily to emphasize what a good joke the random reference to these names was, but the meaning was not lost on his guest. For Guevara had talked to both of these and others. He did meet Brezhnev the young and restless, and he did visit Suslov, the old and scheming, in his town home above Madame Furtseva's in Granovsky ulitsa. Khrushchev rested his puffy fingers on Guevara's shoulder. "What I mean is, there is nothing to worry about. You and Fidel listen to me and you'll have me as a friend for life. So just to reassure you, take this little note as my third memento."

It was the translation and photocopy of some parts of a memorandum in English, dated April 19, 1961, the third day of the ill-fated Bay of Pigs venture. "If we don't want Russia to set up missile bases in Cuba," it began, addressing President Kennedy, "we had better decide now what we are willing to do to stop it."

"Why are sections missing?" asked Guevara.

Khruschev turned his palms to the sky in a gesture of helplessness: "That's how we received it." There was no need to feed Castro with all the details. "But it should answer all Fidel's doubts and problems."

The memo recommended calling on the Organization of American States to prohibit the shipment of arms to Cuba from any source. "At the same time they would guarantee the territorial integrity of Cuba so that the Cuban government could not say they would be at the mercy of the United States."

"Note the signature," Khruschev urged his guest.

"Is the memo genuine?"

Khrushchev made no attempt at concealing his anger. "Of course it's genuine! The original is in the White House, the first copy is in my desk in Moscow, and the second copy is now yours. What the fuck do you expect me to present you with? All the Kennedys on a plate, with bullets between the eyes, and their heads stuffed ready for a butcher's window display?"

The visa trace had taken four days, and the delay as well as the outcome infuriated Major Boychenko. It was obvious that there had been some irregularity. Rust's visa was granted by an accelerated process at the request of a lieutenant commander, a high-ranking GRU agent on the naval attaché's staff at the London embassy of the USSR. The London KGB Resident was clearly trying to minimize the importance of the incident. Boychenko threatened to create a real stink about it, but received a stiff warning that the officer involved was the son-in-law of the chairman of the Supreme Court, a crony of Khrushchev himself. Although Boychenko understood and played well the advantages of mutual backscratching and nepotism, and although the new legality had probably saved him from a great deal of unnecessary punishment during his arrest, he now resented the protection extended to the lieutenant commander and blamed Khrushchev for it. During the Stalin era it would have been easier to break the man's career as well as neck. Now he was told to let the matter rest, and he knew it was sound advice. But it did not help him. Not when he was summoned to the First Chief Directorate to receive his orders: Rust must be found and neutralized.

They refused to give him any further information about Rust or his background or his father. That implied to him that he must be working somewhere on the periphery of an intelligence operation at the very highest level, an operation that was regarded as even more important than the message in Rust's possession. If he uncovered too much it would be more dangerous than uncovering too little.

"I request permission to interrogate Pyotr Nikolayevich Rostonov at the earliest opportunity."

"Why would you need permission for that? It's your right

to interrogate him. As long as you observe the rules of socialist legality, of course."

"The doctors tell me that his injuries are very serious and he's under heavy sedation. If the degree of sedation is reduced, death due to shock may occur within minutes."

"It's a risk you'll have to assess, of course. Nobody here has seen the doctors or the patient. You're the one who's most familiar with the problem—you must make the decision. And we have complete faith in you, of course."

Of course, of course, of course—damn you. Boychenko tried to make sure that his face would not reveal his reaction to everybody's usual tactics of dodging responsibility. But this total lack of help and guidance did help and guide him. It indicated that he, in turn, must avoid the crushing weight of making irrevocable decisions. If he insisted on getting the opportunity to conduct an interrogation and then the old man died, it would be his responsibility irrespective of the direct cause of death. If the old man died, the trigger-happy lieutenant would be held responsible in any case. But if the old man died before Boychenko had a chance to interrogate him, some of the blame could be laid on the doctors whose overanxious care of the patient had prevented the authorities from gaining invaluable information through asking some harmless questions. To vindicate his own position in this way, Boychenko would have to be at the man's bedside, applying hard, though not too hard, pressure for permission to ask those questions. The degree of pressure to go on record could be adjusted later on, in retrospect.

• Monday, September 24 •

Castro announces on TV that Soviet Union plans to build
new port in Havana Bay purely as a base for its "Atlantic
fishing fleet." Teddy Kennedy wins Democratic nomination
for JFK's vacant Senate seat; opponent claims: "If your
name was Ed Moore, your candidacy would be a joke."
Muscovite is sentenced to three years' hard labor for remark
about space flight: "A bathroom would be worth fifteen
orbits to me."

"**W**ON'T WORK," REPORTED FLORIAN, WHO WAS LATE,
yet again, from his errand. "You'll have to think of
some other way to get him out or get rid of him." He nodded
toward Rust.

"Damn you!" For the first time, Yelena appeared to be on
the brink of losing her self-control.

"It's not my fault," Florian protested like a child. His eyes
avoided Yelena's. He thrust four fingertips in his mouth and

chewed the well-worn stumps vigorously until they began to bleed. "It's not my fault."

"What's wrong?" asked Rust.

"Oh, it's just that we seem to be having a bit of a problem."

"Listen, sweetheart . . ."

"Why do you call me sweetheart every time you're angry with me?"

"I might call you many other things, too, if you try to treat me like that gorilla." He was itching to hit the man to vent some of his frustration. He was not to be disappointed. Florian threw himself at him blindly. Rust had an easy chance to slip out of his way at the last second and kick his shin in the same move. Florian crashed against the wall howling. But he managed to whip out his gun before Rust could reach him.

"Stop it." Her voice was almost inaudible. "At once. And put that gun away." She turned to Rust: "And you're a fool."

"Then you've made a bad choice, sweetheart. So will you tell me what the problem is?"

"Okay, I'll be completely frank with you."

"Anything but that, please. Every time you offer to be completely frank with me, you give me another pack of lies."

"All right. We're having problems with your exit passport. I thought we had it all worked out."

"Had what worked out?"

"There was an American tourist here. He was taken to hospital with, er, some sudden illness."

"Food poisoning," Florian volunteered. And he was much too keen to explain it. "Can happen to anyone anywhere. I had nothing to do with it. Honestly. It's just that it would have been so convenient—"

"That's enough," she interrupted him and turned to Rust: "We were hoping to use his passport for you. There was a quite passable likeness between the two of you. We'd have tinted your hair and supplied you with a neat mustache."

"You're crazy!" Rust grabbed her shoulders and squeezed her furiously. "You want to gamble everything, including my fucking life, on the strength of a fucking false mustache?!"

"You don't understand. You're against it only because disguises may sometimes look ridiculous. But it would work in this case. You're not to go unrecognized by some friend of yours. It would only be scrutinized by a border guard for a few seconds. His main job is to compare your picture in front of him with the picture in your passport. He's trained to make the identification by looking for similarities, not the possible differences. He's conditioned to see what he's supposed to see. Believe me. I've—I mean, I know how they're trained."

"Ridiculous," said Rust, twiddling his nonexistent mustache, but he did not sound fully convinced by his own doubts anymore. "What happened to the man with the food poisoning?"

"Intourist flew him to a Moscow sanatorium. We'll have to find another one. That's all, but time is, well, not running out, but pressing. You understand?"

"I do. You should have taken me to Odessa right away, just as I suggested."

"It wouldn't have worked. Going by boat the delay would have been too great. There could be war by the time you arrived."

Rust turned away and walked to the window. He pressed his forehead against the cold glass and stared out on the Nevsky. Florian began to say something, but the American's back twitched impatiently and silenced him.

"We'll sort out something. Don't worry," she said.

"I have a feeling that right now you're more worried than I am, and that's quite something, I tell you. No, don't interrupt. I'm impressed by all that you've done, and I've been good, I haven't asked many questions. I don't know what your game is, and I don't know if this is simply a government-backed charade to pull off some monumental bluff and plant some disinformation on us. Are you working for *dezinformatziya*?"

"Now you're being silly."

"That's right. Maybe it's silly not to press you more for the source of your missile information, for an explanation of how you could help Igor or whatever the name of that sailor was, how you obtain marvelous facilities like an empty room in overcrowded Moscow, various false papers and an ambulance, and why you talk about America as the 'probable enemy'— remember?"

"You play guessing games."

"That's right. There's nothing else I can do. Only to use the little I know, remind myself that in KGB parlance America is always the 'main enemy' while the 'probable enemy' is the GRU's phrase for it. Shall I go on?"

"Only if you're trying to avoid doing what I've asked you to do."

"Now who's silly? You know only too well that you've got me by the balls in more ways than one, even if I overlook the literal interpretation." Florian moved, and Rust pointed a finger without looking at him. "And you stay out of this."

"It must be your decision," said Yelena.

"Sure, sweetheart. Like it was my decision to come here in the first place and now to risk my father's life or not. Apart from that, I must admit, you put forward a pretty convincing argument when we first met. So it seems I'll have to go through with it. I'll need my own clothes."

"Florian can get them."

"Then tell him to get on with it. And get my money. Anybody's money, as long as it's American. Then we'll go for a walk."

"You can't."

"Can't I?"

"The risk is too great."

"It's even greater to stay here. We must get a passport, and as you said, it must be the real thing."

"They must be looking for you everywhere."

"All right, we'll reduce the risk. You'll watch my back, and if it looks as if I'm running into some sort of trouble or getting myself arrested, you tell your ape to shoot me." He walked across the room and touched Florian's nose with his fingertip. "You'll have only one chance, but I'm sure you won't miss, will you, darling?"

Florian grabbed Rust's wrist, squeezed, digging his thumb into the artery, and let go of it—all in two seconds. "I'm looking forward to saving you from interrogation and prison, Mr. *Roost*."

All traffic at and around Kharkov's grand railway station was at a standstill. Even express trains were halted and shunted onto sidings. Armed guards lined the platforms. People in the know stared down the tracks southward. They had almost an hour to wait for the special from Yalta for which the route had been cleared. When it arrived, it swept through the station without slowing down. Those who were quick enough would be able to tell their children and grandchildren how they caught a glimpse of a cheerful Comrade Nikita Sergeyevich. They might even add, "He was not more than a good arm's length away, fresh from Crimean sunshine and smiling at all of us with loving warmth in his eyes." They would never know that the loving smile was permanent on the wax face of a dummy and the warmth shone unerringly from the glass beads embedded in unblinking eyes. The effigy traveled first-class. It was positioned strategically at the rear window to beam at all good citizens, all the way to Moscow.

Khrushchev was, indeed, on that train, only a few yards away from his benevolent alter ego. Raving about fascist bastards, he promised to crush the Turkish government, which had decided, according to confidential advance information, to request Turkish shipowners to stop carrying Soviet cargo to Cuba.

"I'll show them, I'll show the bastards. Is that what they call democracy? Is that the freedom of the sea? They must be acting under American pressure. But we'll soon see who can apply the greater pressure. I want an immediate report on our options to counter this . . . this insult." He suddenly stopped and threw himself back in the red velvet armchair. "You . . . you don't think that the Americans are pressing them because they know?"

Everybody in the study compartment of the train tried to look somewhere else, as if the question could not possibly be addressed to him, but there was not enough room to exclude the leader from anybody's field of vision. Khrushchev swung around to face Semichastny, a tall figure on the verge of flabbiness but not yet overweight.

"Do you think the Americans know?"

"According to our information—"

"Never mind your information. I asked what you think."

Semichastny had been head of the KGB for only ten months. He was still riding, as in every previous job, on Shelepin's coattails, still trying to feel his way, still dreading moments like this, still unprotected from this fat peasant and his harebrained schemes. "I do not think they know about our Cuban *konfety*, if this is what you're asking, Nikita Sergeyevich."

"Why not? Are they stupid?"

"I wouldn't think so."

"Then what?"

"First they're experiencing a scarcity of reliable information. We have friends who can cut out a lot in time, as you know. Then there's the question of wishing to know—I mean, really wanting to know the truth. Many of the American hawks would, in fact, welcome missiles on Cuban soil. They think it would give them a chance to invade, this time in force. But of course we must remain vigilant." This was an excellent opportunity to snipe at the GRU and make another step toward restricting intelligence operations by the military and expropriating all their resources. "This is why I believe that the entire security arrangement should go through my own Residents in every country involved rather than through the less reliable representatives of our military neighbors. One of them, for instance, has just helped to accelerate a visa request for a foreigner's visit to Moscow." Khrushchev was waiting, but Semichastny paused for effect, combing his sandy hair with outstretched fingers. "That foreigner obtained some information in Moscow about our shipments to Cuba and tried to pass it on to the American embassy."

It was as if even the train had gone silent.

"Tried?"

"Yes, tried. We were, luckily, in a position to intercept."

"Why wasn't I told?" Khrushchev whispered.

"It didn't seem important enough."

"Not important enough? Not important enough?! Are you out of your mind? Everything about Cuba is of extreme importance. Our preparations are delayed. We may not be ready until late October. If we're caught out before we're operational we could be humiliated by Kennedy. We'd get no guarantees, nothing, just a good spanking. And I won't be spanked, you understand? I won't be spanked publicly, not without some good reason." He laughed heartily. "Not without something that would show both Fidel and his beloved Chinks who's boss and who can deliver. Who was that foreigner?"

"Some American journalist."

"Has he confessed his sources?"

"He, er, he hasn't been caught yet, but his arrest is imminent, I'm told." That, of course, could later be denied and somebody could be punished for misleading information.

"Good." Khrushchev turned to his side. "Gromyko is lunching with Dean Rusk next week. If Cuba is mentioned, he must deny most vigorously any shipment of missiles. Later he could claim that I never tell him anything."

Everybody laughed, and Semichastny wondered if there could be a grain of truth in the joke. Was Gromyko on his way out? He decided this was another good moment to score and demonstrate his efficiency. "The question of arming Cuba with modern weapons has just been discussed by Kennedy's inner security council. Through our 'contact' we managed to introduce the argument that it's not Soviet policy to station missiles on foreign soil, because if it was, we could have installed them easily in East Europe."

"You managed to introduce this point in their discussions?"

"Yes, we did."

"You're a fool. They'd argue that it would be too dangerous for us to have *konfety* even at Soviet bases in Poland, for instance. If we'd had them in Hungary in '56, they might have fallen into enemy hands and they could have turned them around to threaten Moscow. But it can't happen in Cuba—it's too far from us and too near the Americans. That was very stupid. It may give them ideas about our plans. Make sure that Gromyko denies everything, and that nothing happens in respect to the Cuban operation without my personal approval." Khrushchev got up and walked to the tinted glass, behind which the University Hill and the outskirts of Kharkov were receding fast. Some people waved toward the train and Khrushchev almost waved back, forgetting that he would not be seen anyway. He thought of his tireless effigy in the last window of the carriage, and that reminded him of Potemkin, the prince, who had erected fake village fronts along the road where Catherine the Great used to travel. His aim was to conceal the squalor of the real villages behind the hoardings and to please her majesty. We create figures to wave to and sights to please our people— that's Communism for you, thought Khrushchev, and it amused him. He was still smiling when he turned back to the Chairman of the KGB: "Let me know when that journalist has confessed. The source of his information interests me."

Rust could not stay any longer in the marble-paneled, marble-pillared, marble-floored hall of Aeroflot. Not if he did not want to attract undue attention. He had already managed to chat with half a dozen British and American tourists and businessmen. Only one of them was of similar build to his own (a pair of heavy black-rimmed glasses would have probably created a sufficient semblance to the man's passport photo), but then it turned out that he was traveling with a group, which ruled out the possibility of stealing his identity.

Rust was walking toward a Beryozka store when he spotted a likely solution. The man was about his own height, five foot ten, with a massive, bushy beard, wearing an unmistakably Western anorak. He went into the store, where it would have been easy to talk to him, but as the shop sold select goods only to Westerners for hard currency, identification had to be shown at the door. Rust walked on, stopping to tie his shoelaces, looking at some buildings, and finding it difficult to hang about unobtrusively because there were hardly any shop windows, the easy excuse, in the Soviet Union. He observed that Yelena and Florian had the same problem watching him.

At long last the man came out and walked down toward St. Isaac's Cathedral. In the square he looked at his watch, turned again and went into the Hotel Astoria. Cocktail time. An excellent opportunity. Rust glanced at Yelena and started toward the hotel. She seemed alarmed. Rust would be stopped and questioned at the door. Rust smiled as he came face to face with the elderly doorman.

"And how are you today?" he asked in his imitation of broken Russian.

The doorman nodded, obviously confused by the clash between a stranger's face and the key word, "today," which had implied that they knew each other, that the same question had been asked by the same foreigner on perhaps several previous occasions. He would still have to ask for the man's pass to authorize entry to the hotel. Embarrassing. Fortunately, the familiar stranger knew the rules and reached into his pocket for the hotel *spravka*.

But Rust's hand stopped halfway. He asked the doorman about those Victory Ball invitation cards. "I've just heard about them," he said. "Could you tell me what happened? I mean, is the story true?"

It was a perfect choice. A true citizen of Leningrad, he could not miss the chance to regurgitate that glorious nonevent.

The doorman talked for a good five minutes—and by then, even the two plainclothesmen watching the doorman had lost interest in the foreigner coming through the door.

Rust ordered some tea in the somewhat faded grandeur of the corner lobby. From the comfort and privacy of his highback armchair he could watch the entrance, the reception desk and the door to the garish, fully modernized—that is, plastic-coated—bar where an illuminated glass panel listed the only bona fide currencies—anything but those circulated by Russia and fellow Communist countries.

There was no sign of the bearded man. Rust talked to several other tourists. He knew he had to be patient in his search because his basic requirements were exact: he needed to find a man of similar build and not too different face structure, someone traveling on his own and planning to leave the country soon. The timing was essential: date and time of departure would already be known to the border guards and airport authorities.

Boychenko had several men checking airport, port and railway-station logs. Noted departures, irregularities, anything vaguely unusual or suspicious was to be reported to him right away. A squad of six men concentrated on the records kept by all controllers of Moscow exit roads. By the afternoon a short list of events deserving special attention had been drawn up for him. Among these was a mention of an ambulance with a suspected disease carrier destined for the isolation unit at Ivanovo. There was some reference to a Category One disease.

"What's that?" Boychenko asked, but nobody had the answer. He marked that and another dozen entries in the log for further investigation. He then changed into uniform and ordered a staff car to take him to the KGB hospital.

"The old man is in bad shape," said the colonel in charge of the ward.

"That's not the question, comrade."

"I know. I'm just telling you."

"Will he survive a brief interrogation?"

The colonel shrugged his shoulders. "It's a risk to question him at this stage." He stopped and thought about the risk he himself was taking by expressing a view that could be used against him later on. "I mean, a lot would depend on the interrogator."

"So you're against interrogation," Boychenko said, trying to pin him down.

"Not at all, major, not at all. All I'm saying is that I don't know how urgent an interrogation is. I know nothing about his case. And we can't judge how much he'd be able to withstand. Come and see him for yourself. If I reduce the sedation, he may lapse into a coma or just die."

The old man was in a windowless cubicle, watched at all times by a nurse and a guard. He was mumbling in his sleep. "It's so cold, so cold."

"Can't you give him an extra blanket or something?" asked Boychenko.

"It's no good. The cold is inside him."

A nurse came in. "Comrade Boychenko is wanted on the telephone."

The call was from the First Chief Directorate. It urged Boychenko to carry out an interrogation at the earliest possible opportunity—yet not to forget how essential the suspect's survival remained. He tried to disguise his fury as he passed on the order and, preferably, the responsibility to the colonel: "Considering the relatively low level of risk you've outlined to me, I must ask you now to prepare the patient for a brief interrogation. How long will it take?"

"A few hours."

"I'll wait here."

The smell of cheap plastic permeated the air in the bar. The ill-conceived lighting effects created gloom rather than ambience. A scratched record of the Don Cossacks blared desperately from a large speaker to complete what was meant to be nightclub decadence inducing foreigners to feel at home and part with their money merrily.

"We must be a wee bit crazy to pay one pound sterling for that," grumbled Andrew call-me-Mac McGregor and held his shot glass to the light. "Look at it, just look." He rolled the drops of liquid around. "Not enough to wet the glass."

Rust could not have agreed more with him, and he helped the bearded man to cope with the mathematical puzzle: if a whiskey and a gin and tonic cost two pounds five shillings and sixpence, how much should Mac get back from a five-pound note in Greek drachmas and Bolivian pesos, the only small change the barman claimed to have?

"Stop blathering, me lad, just keep the money and give us another whiskey, a gin and a wee tonic," said McGregor and turned to give Rust some useful advice for life: "Never cut that Gordian knot, me friend, if you can liquidize and drink it."

Rust felt sorry for him. It was too easy. McGregor was naive and hungry for companionship after three weeks in Russia, spent mostly in mud-bound *kolkhozi* where whiskey was consumed only by fat capitalists in the occasional visiting film shows, and where his interpretor truly believed that Bonnie Prince Charlie was "some Englishman."

Back at the apartment on the Nevsky, Rust told Yelena that he would dine with the Scotsman that evening. "Can you get me a beard like his?"

"Yes, but that won't be enough. Your hair will have to be tinted gray, and Florian will give you an injection in your gum to make your face swell. When is your Scotsman planning to leave?"

"Tomorrow evening. It's the six-forty P.M. BOAC flight to London via Helsinki and Copenhagen."

"Could you get him here tomorrow morning?"

"Yes. On one condition. You must guarantee his safety."

"That's all right. There's no reason to believe that he'll be more than inconvenienced."

"Not good enough. I want your word on it."

"Okay. You have it. I never thought you'd be so deeply concerned about the safety of complete strangers." She smiled.

"And I never thought you'd be so callous concerning the lives of innocent bystanders." Rust's voice was even sharper than his words, but she did not seem hurt. If anything, she looked surprised. The way Charles might be surprised in a situation like this. Or Schramm. Way back in the days of training him, Schramm used to hint that hurting the innocent was sometimes inevitable. "You've got to learn to sin without guilt." Rust wondered if he could ever come to terms with a principle like that. "You must be pragmatic about such things," Schramm said. "That's what makes generals and other executives. And good agents destined for glory." Rust hoped he could still say wholeheartedly what he had answered to Schramm. "I doubt if the glory can ever match the guilt."

"How will you get him here?" Yelena asked.

"Easily. He's keen to come."

"Why?"

"I've promised him an introduction to a very beautiful Russian girl. I didn't tell him how callous she might be. But I said he might be able to date her when he comes back to sell more of his milking machines over here."

At midnight, the colonel promised Boychenko that it would not be long now. "Your man is delirious, with a very high temperature, but he should be able to answer a few gently put questions."

While waiting, Boychenko phoned his wife. There was no news about the raped girl, which was good news, and there was positively good news about his daughter's job prospect at the Foreign Trade Ministry: Boychenko had signed a rather complimentary political character reference for a surgeon who wanted to apply for permission to seek a job in the capital; the surgeon's son, in turn, had arranged a little advantage for a friend's aunt on the waiting list for a new set of bath faucets, and she had then had a word with her next-door neighbor, the widow of a general, who owed her a favor and could obtain from the privileged department of Voyentorg, the army store, a couple of long zip fasteners and a pair of Czech spike-heel shoes for the parents of a Foreign Trade Ministry clerical supervisor.

"Do you want me to be present during the interview?" asked the colonel.

Boychenko thought for a second and decided against it. "No, just stand by with a full emergency unit. You must not allow him to die."

The old man was shaking all the time. The sight of Boychenko's uniform forced him to try to sit up. He made a superhuman effort. "Ask me, major, ask me anything. We're on the same side."

"Naturally."

"And keep warm."

"That's right. We must keep warm. And keep away from all the cold places. You know what I mean?"

"I do. Just ask me. What do you want to know?"

Boychenko stepped to the bed and leaned forward until their faces almost touched. "I have only one question. Where's your son?"

The old man opened his mouth, but could not speak because his jaw was twitching so badly.

"You don't want to answer me? Fair enough, I understand." He tore the blanket off the bed and threw it on the floor. "Fair enough. If that's what you want." He opened the window, and icy rain sprayed him, which made him furious. The old man's twitching must be pure hysteria and an excuse not to answer the question. A hearty slap in the face was, in his experience, an effective remedy for both.

"Where's your son?"

The shaking stopped. The old man's eyes popped wide open in a fixed gaze at the window. Not even the rain made him blink. "He's not my son," he whispered.

"Liar!" Boychenko's fist went hard into his kidney.

Pyotr Nikolayevich curled up in slow motion. In the cold wind his parchment skin began to turn blue.

"Don't you dare die on me!" He beat the emergency call button frantically.

While the doctors worked on the patient, the colonel asked Boychenko what had happened.

"Nothing. You said he was delirious. Well, he was not. I asked a simple question. He kicked off the blanket and lied to me like any normal healthy person." Wouldn't I lie to get that damn kid off that rape charge? But he quickly qualified his remark just to be on the safe side when the colonel would make his report. "I mean, he tried to lie to me, like any enemy of the people would."

The old man was given some oxygen and an injection. Waiting for the effect of the sedatives, Boychenko telephoned his office to make arrangements for charging the young lieutenant with negligence in carrying out the arrest or, alternatively, with the unnecessary killing of an important witness. He had just put the phone down when he heard the old man mumble again.

"It's not my fault . . . I don't know where he is. . . . Florian gave the orders. . . . Please, Yelena Ivanovna . . . please don't make me do it. . . . No, I won't argue, you're right. . . . They're the greatest . . . Dy-na-mo! Dy-na-mo! . . . I must keep warm . . . . Please, please . . . Florian, please . . . you're so big and strong, so big . . . please help. . . ." He was staring at the wall, but Boychenko guessed he was seeing ghosts.

The major pushed a doctor out of the way and leaned over the bed. "It's all right," he whispered soothingly. "It's all right now. I'm Florian. I'm here to help you."

"Help me."

"Here." He pulled the blanket tight around the curling body. "Keep warm. I'll help you. But I must know where your son is."

"I don't know."

"And where's Yelena?"

"In her cab. The cab . . . she'll run me down if I don't support Dynamo. She will."

A doctor, his hand on the patient's pulse, tried to say something, but Boychenko made him shut up with a wide wave of his hand. "I'll help you. I promise. But I must know where your son is."

"The cab . . ." Pyotr Nikolayevich tried to sit up to escape the cab running fast toward him, then fell back, still staring in horror, and not seeing even ghosts anymore.

The charge would have to be unnecessary killing of an important witness, Boychenko concluded. That and perhaps negligence and breaking certain aspects of socialist legality. What particular aspects was something to be decided later on. Florian and Yelena. They must be found somewhere. There could not be all that many women cabbies who were ferocious Dynamo supporters, Boychenko encouraged himself. He wanted to get on with the search fast, but first he ought to have a word with the colonel in charge of the ward. Perhaps their accounts of the events leading to the death could be coordinated. He asked several people, but nobody seemed to know where the colonel was. Boychenko guessed he must already be working on his report of the unfortunate circumstances. Which left Boychenko no time to spare before delivering his own version.

• Tuesday, September 25 •

U.S. State Department reserves 28th-floor suite in Waldorf for Dean Rusk-Gromyko lunch. NATO exercise in Greece for half a million men. Kennedy writes to Nasser and confirms his conviction that "it's possible to find an honorable and humanitarian solution to Arab-Israel dispute." Wall Street prices fall. Sterling sinks to $2.80. Dollar sinks to DM4.

COLONEL OLEG PENKOVSKY DECIDED TO WALK TO HIS office partly because it was an exceptionally bright, sunny morning and partly because he wanted to see if he was followed. He said a few cheerful words to the *dezhurnaya* (knowing full well that even his mood might be reported and subjected to scrutiny). He left his home, No. 36 Maxim Gorky naberezhnaya, and stopped to send a few ostensibly joyous glances up and down the glittering Moskva River. This gave him a chance to take in the sight of the few cars parked along the embankment. Yes, the one he thought might be there was still there. It was an ordinary black-on-yellow number plate, MC35-45, a Moscow registration. Although the car seemed to be empty, he was sure that somebody was watching him from inside it. It was no good to pretend that this was just the routine periodic check on him. It had been going on too regularly for too long in the past few weeks. But then why did they not pull him in for questioning? Did they suspect that he had accomplices? Were they GRU security or KGB? Must be KGB. He wished he could do something against them. He hated the neighbors. They had begun to dismantle the GRU, Penkovsky's own people, quite ruthlessly. Several important GRU agents in the West had been eliminated by brother officers. The KGB wanted it all to itself. Penkovsky wished he could repay them in kind and expose some of their own agents. Or at least make sure that his last dispatch about the Cuban buildup and the very limited capability of the Russians' home-based rockets would reach the right people. But he had no way of knowing that.

He turned left and walked at a leisurely pace along the awakening embankment.

Leningrad, too, had a sunny morning. Rust was leaning on his elbow, watching Yelena's peaceful sleep. Throughout the long night, she had said goodbye to him with every inch of her body. He wondered what lovemaking with her without lurking threats and pressures might be like. Would she be equally attractive and her sex equally exciting if his life did not depend on her? She stirred and, as always, was awake from one second to the next. She had the ability to cross the boundary into and out of sleep without any gradual process. It was a soldier's art to fall asleep and wake up just like that. "Hello, soldier," he said. "Welcome to this world."

"What time do you have to pick up McGregor?" she said, sitting up and looking at her watch.

"Plenty of time."

"There's never enough time. Especially not this time." She moved, then smiled, noticing his eager eyes. "Would you mind turning away while I get up and find at least a shirt to put on?"

Her shyness amused him, but it was pointless to tease her with it yet again.

"You didn't say what time you had to pick him up."

"Ten-thirty. He'll have packed and checked out by then. The plan is that I bring him here. He thinks we'll spend a long, boozy day with that beautiful girl—you'll do, I guess—then we'll take the London flight together."

"Good. Florian will be ready."

"How do you plan to keep Mac here until the flight leaves?"

"We'll pump him full of fast-acting sedatives. That should knock him out for twenty-four hours at least. He'll then be found, probably in a daze, with your papers in his pocket. It may take him a day or so to prove that he's not you, but then they'll let him go."

"Sounds easy."

"It better be."

She returned to the bed, wearing only his shirt. He greeted the sight with a wolf whistle. She seemed not to understand.

"Looks sexy on you."

"Does it?" It was a straight question. The art of light flirtation was not in her armory. She walked to the cupboard and studied herself in the long mirror on the inside of the door. "Is that what you find sexy?"

"Mm."

"Has she ever worn your shirt?"

"Who?"

"The girl you were in love with in Leningrad."

"Can't remember."

"Liar."

"Honestly."

"Then you're not in love with her anymore."

"No, probably not."

"Why?"

"It's gone."

"How long does it take you to fall out of love?"

"I don't know. There're no rules." The question and the mood of the moment pleased him, he admitted to himself. And he knew that both of them were acting out of character. There were no ties, no conventions, nobody else to consider, not past commitments, no future. Falling in love on the moon could be like that, in a state of weightlessness. She took another hard, searching look at herself in the long mirror as if trying to memorize the picture, then shut the door and sat on the bed.

"Did she leave you?" Her voice was clinical but not cold.

"No." He had not told Yelena any details about the breakup, and he did not want to lie to her now. "It, just . . . you know."

"Do you wish she was here now?"

"What a silly question."

"Is it?"

"You're not jealous, are you?" he asked lightly.

"I don't know." The matter-of-fact answer bore the hallmark of sincerity. "I don't know what jealousy feels like. Do you?"

She was drifting toward a deeper, more emotional conversation, and he knew he had to steer her clear of it. "No, I specialize in vacation affairs with women who visit the Upstairs. It's their vacation and my affair. I can spot them as they come through the door. Jealousy is no part of the deal, so nobody gets hurt, sweetheart."

"Are you angry with me?"

"No. Why?"

"You called me sweetheart again."

"Did I?" If anything, he was angry with himself. Let yourself go, he urged himself. Enjoy it to the full while it lasts. He kissed her.

She kissed him back, but remained distant and thoughtful. "If this is jealousy, I don't want to know any more about it."

"It's a deal." He tried to pull her back into bed.

"You know something? Nobody had seen me cry since Kiev, not until you saw me in Moscow."

"Am I supposed to be proud of that?"

"I don't know."

The chances are that it just doesn't matter what state I do and do not see you in, thought Rust. Once we get off the moon . . . "What happened in Kiev?" He knew it had something to do with her dead husband. But she said nothing. When he tried to kiss her again, she wriggled free and retreated to a safer distance.

"Time isn't on our side." Her objective tone could have sliced ice cubes when she added: "Pity." She stood up and ran her hands down the shirt as it followed the curves of her body, from her breasts to halfway down her thighs. "It would be nice to keep it. I'd never wash it. Perhaps it would always smell of you."

"Keep it."

"Not worth the risk." She took it off and dropped it on the bed. He followed her to the bathroom, but she asked him not to touch her. "We must run through the plan once more before Florian gets here."

He watched her showering, and rattled off the simple sequence. "Finally, at five to six, I enter the airport shop. I select some souvenirs, but not chocolates or dictionaries. I pay and do not open the sealed bag the girl at the counter hands over. Where will you and Florian be?"

"It's not important."

"How much does he know about the plan?"

"Enough." She did not ask him to turn away but kept covering herself as much as she could. Rust had a feeling she had begun to enjoy being watched.

"Don't you trust Florian?" he asked.

"I do."

"Would he confess everything if he was caught?"

"Of course. Like anybody else."

"Would I tell about you?"

"Yes. You'd have no choice. But luckily, you know nothing about me. Except my face."

"And your body. I won't forget that."

She faced him, let the soap slip away, and dropped her hands. "That's nice. I'll remember that." Again that sincere voice, no trace of flirtation. "Just don't describe me to anyone."

"If I was caught and forced to tell as much as I knew, what chances would you have?"

"Not much."

"Could you get away? I mean, out of the country?"

"Perhaps. But unlikely."

"You could try Odessa. With my father. All you'd have to do—"

"Don't tell me." She turned off the tap and let him wrap her in one of the thin, well-worn towels. For a second, he could visualize her rolled into one of his soft, luxurious bath towels at the Upstairs. He wondered how she would fit in there. How long she would last with no danger, no dependence, no surplus adrenalin flow except that induced by the occasional trip to Cuba and the frequent arrival of vacationers.

Despite her protests, he told her about the Odessa arrangements. It made him feel better. And less dependent on her. He tried to convince himself that she had to know the escape route for the sake of his father and not because he felt desperate to do something for her. "Hotel Tsentralnaya. Don't forget. The man in charge of the crocodile tank will arrange everything. And once you're in Cuba, you'll be looked after." Morales would help her, he felt sure.

"How would I get out of Cuba?"

"They'll let me know you're on your way. Then I'll meet you there and get you out."

"And take me to the Upstairs?"

"If that's what you want."

"Nice dream. I'll remember it."

The door opened and Bobby Kennedy swung around in his red leather chair. "Come in, Anna, come on in."

Anna Repson walked up to his desk and deposited a thick buff file. "It's the stuff you wanted on the Mob." She opened the file and pointed at some markings at the top. "It's all under separate headings for their deals with the CIA, Castro and Hoffa. The last section lists their own operations in Cuba."

"Good. That was quick. Thank you."

"You said you wanted it urgently."

"That's why I asked you and nobody else to chase it. How's Ell?"

"Fine, thanks. Always busy. Too busy."

"I understand and I don't envy you. It can't be easy to live with him." He noticed her eyebrows rising resentfully. With embarrassment, he hurriedly clarified himself: no, he was not referring to Repson's wheelchair and disability. "I mean some of these guys in intelligence seem to be married to their work, and it's not easy on outsiders like wives and families."

His eyes were riveted to her alluring gait until the door closed behind her—the Attorney General was not alone in Justice to envy the luck of Elliott Repson. He then turned to the file and examined a few pages—slapdash CIA schemes in Ike's last Presidential year to kill Castro or at least make his charismatic beard fall out; Castro's attitude to Cuban trade in narcotics, the arrest of Trafficante, a Mafia smuggler in Havana. They let him live in a luxurious jail, Kennedy thought, obviously because they have plans for using him. But who the hell is this Jack Ruby who visited him? Is he Castro's contact to the Mob? Is he preparing the reopening of the drug-routes to the United States?

No matter how tempting and juicy the file promised to be, it had to wait. But the Attorney General looked forward to yet another long night's reading that should provide further inducement and motivation for Mongoose.

The squad working on the Moscow exit logs delivered the details of a "departure of yellow-flag case." Boychenko was convinced that Rust, accompanied by "a woman doctor" and the driver (described as "big, ugly and muscular") must have made his getaway in that ambulance. The KGB officer in charge of that roadblock was summoned to his office for questioning. When he implied the possible negligence of one of his men, the corporal, too, was brought in for "intensive interrogation." Fifty minutes later, it appeared certain that the man was not an accomplice and he was transferred to the prison hospital.

The officer remembered that the "doctor" had seemed vaguely familiar to him. The log proved that he had alerted the road patrol service as well as the Ivanovo roadblock for a second check. What puzzled Boychenko was that the ambulance had simply disappeared: nobody had seen it on the road or at the Ivanovo checkpoint, and it had never arrived at the isolation unit.

He made his report to the Spetsburo as well as the First Chief Directorate, and it was decided that the *kolkhozi*—several of which were known to be harboring passively hostile elements—would have to be searched. Everybody would be required to account for his movements from September 20 onward, and everybody whose alibi appeared suspect would be brought in for further questioning. Boychenko expected at least forty or fifty suspects. He knew that the large number might be a disadvantage, but there was no other way—that was how the system worked.

There was no joy in the report about the women cabbies. There were only a few known to be interested in football at all. Irrespective of what team they supported, all were to be brought in for preliminary interviews. Boychenko assigned the KGB officer of the roadblock to this task. He hoped that the man might identify one of the cabbies as the "woman doctor" in the ambulance.

* * *

"A wee bit early to start on vodka," McGregor protested, but he found it difficult to say no to Yelena. She was hiding behind dark glasses, complaining about conjunctivitis and claiming that light would make her condition much worse. She wore a totally nondescript gray skirt and white blouse, and beyond giving the overall impression of being a pretty woman, she provided Mac with nothing he could eventually recall and usefully confess about her.

Florian kept out of sight. Rust went to talk to him in the kitchen. He wanted reassurance that Mac would not be hurt. "He's a powerfully built man," Rust said. "How do you propose to hold him down while you give him the injection?"

"We don't hold him down. It's just a pinprick, then four seconds to wait," Florian said with a proud smile and produced a slim metal tube, not larger than half a pencil. "It fires a tiny pellet which might carry poison—or fast-acting sedative. Would you like to bet which it will be?"

"You'd better make sure that it's a sedative."

"And if not? What do you intend to do about it?"

"I'll kill you."

"You won't be here—with any luck. Or will you come back to us?"

Rust pushed him out of the way and slammed the door as he returned to the room. Yelena looked up, but Mac was too busy watching her. Another drink, then one more. It seemed to have no effect on Yelena, but Mac's eyes were glittering dangerously.

Florian entered almost noiselessly. The pinprick on Mac's neck lasted only a fraction of a second. Florian pulled back at once and turned away so that he would not be recognized later on.

"What was that?" Mac was on his feet.

Two . . . three . . . Rust counted silently.

"What the hell's going on?"

Four . . . five . . . Mac did not seem to react to the drug at all. Six . . . seven . . .

In fear and fury Mac moved toward Florian but collapsed in midstep as if all his muscles had snapped simultaneously.

They carried Mac to the bedroom and laid him on the bed. "He should be out cold for at least twenty-four hours," said Florian. "But there was a moment when I thought he'd never drop."

Rust took Mac's clothes and began to study his passport. He would have a few hours to memorize all the particulars. He went through the Scotsman's luggage to weed out anything that might delay him at customs. There were a couple of novels by Graham Greene, and Yelena advised him to take them out, mainly because one was *Our Man in Havana*. Mac's Bible also had to be left behind.

"This place; he may remember this place," said Rust. "Why didn't I think about this before?"

"Don't worry," said Yelena. "You brought him here by cab—it's unlikely that he'd remember the number of the house."

"You told me to get out of the cab a couple of streets farther down so that the driver would not see us at this place. We got out somewhere off Sadovoye and walked."

"That's all right then."

"But if he's interrogated, he might remember the building. The lovely colors, the courtyard, this room."

"It doesn't matter. By then this room will look entirely different, I promise you. Nobody will believe him."

Rust did not want to press it any further. But it remained a frightening thought: Mac might give away Yelena—or sign his own death sentence by trying too hard to prove that he remembered the place correctly. Rust forced himself to stop thinking about the vicious circle in which the life of the innocent had to be risked to protect the guilty only because Schramm's rules of pragmatism were inescapable. He began to feel a peculiar hatred against the Scotsman. We love those we've helped, not those who've helped us, and hate the ones against whom we've sinned, he thought. But he felt no guilt. Just shame. For there was nothing he could do for Mac except pray—and pray he could not.

Florian brought in a plastic carrier bag containing some jars, a few bottles and a full beard. Yelena started mixing colors to match Rust's hair to the grayness of the beard.

Major General Yemelin stared at the mountain of papers his orderly had brought in to him. He was disgusted. Ever since he had taken over the First Chief Directorate he had tried and tried to cut down the paperwork, but there was no way to succeed. He could not even introduce a system to mark the documents demanding his most urgent attention. Classification was no guide, because everything had to be either secret or top secret, and the latter alone demanded a man and a half if he did nothing but read all day. He spotted a red-and-green folder and pulled it out of the middle. He had to break the red seal on it and would have to reseal it after reading and signing it. Within the First Directorate he was the only one entitled to open that folder: it contained tidbits from GRU personnel who were also KGB informers.

He looked at the first slip of paper, and he would not have been surprised if he had suffered a stroke there and then. Signed by the code number of the informer, the note merely told him that a GRU forger had supplied a complete "shoe" (Arthur Foster, American citizen) to an unnamed GRU superior. Yemelin picked up his phone marked No. 1, which was a direct line to the head of the KGB, but the call was answered by Semichastny's duty officer.

"Where's the chief?"

"On his way back from Yalta."

"Do we have any further details on the report about that American shoe the military neighbors had ordered?"

The officer checked and came back with a no.

"Has Comrade Semichastny seen it yet?"

"No, it only came in last night."

"Take a note, will you? His attention should be directed to this report on his return immediately."

There was nothing else he could do. The existence of informers could not be revealed or acknowledged under any circumstances. If further information was required, only the head of KGB could obtain it, and only through the head of GRU. Yemelin was furious, but there was nothing to do for the time being apart from swearing at his GRU colleagues, who, apparently, were about to break the recent ruling that they would not place any of their own illegals into the United States, where only the First Directorate was to operate. He could have requested immediate radio contact with Semichastny, but it seemed pointless: if the shoe had been supplied only within the last couple of days, the GRU would still be busy training that "Arthur Foster," whose full preparation might take several months.

Yemelin hung up and read the rest of the brief reports in the folder. That was when he almost suffered his second stroke.

There was a follow-up from the same code-numbered informer saying that the shoe had been delivered via a *taynik* in Leningrad. Even when Semichastny was back in Moscow, it would take at least a couple of days to discover the full details, who was running that GRU operation, who had ordered and received the shoe. "Come!" he shouted when he heard knocking at the door. He closed the folder and nodded to a Spetsburo colonel who entered with Major Boychenko in tow.

Yemelin listened to Boychenko's report and hoped that the major would slip up in some way. He loathed the small, fat loudmouth, who was skillfully extricating himself from all possible responsibility for his suspect's death.

Mac's clothes turned out to be a little too roomy for Rust, but otherwise he felt he had a fighting chance to get through passport control without trouble. What infuriated him was that he could not find an opportunity to say goodbye to Yelena in private, because Florian would be away for only a few seconds at a time to check Mac's condition. The beard had worried him at first—he had kept catching it in everything—but by the time he had learned his new identity, he began to grow fonder of his hairy face. Sadly, he handed the Tula-Korovin to Florian. Carrying a gun would be an unacceptable risk.

Yelena looked at her watch. It was 3:30 in the afternoon. "Get the syringe," she said to Florian. As soon as the door closed behind him, she kissed Rust in a hurry. "You'll look devastating with real white hair," she whispered. Rust tried to hold her, but she slipped away. "Mind your beard," she said. "Our spacecraft are fantastic, but we're yet to produce a decent glue."

Alarmed, Rust touched the beard, but it felt reasonably secure.

Florian returned and prepared the syringe gleefully. "Open your mouth."

Rust tried to look indifferent. Florian stabbed his gum hard. The throbbing began at once and got worse and worse. Rust hoped that the pain did not show.

"Looks good," she said and touched his face as the flesh began to swell.

A few minutes later, Rust could hardly see out of his left

eye. He took a look at himself in a mirror and compared his face with the passport photo. "It'll do," he said. "I hope."

Yelena touched his face once more. She was about to say something, but her voice faltered. She cleared her throat and tried to sound very objective. "Yes, I'm sure it'll do. Don't worry. And take care. And don't buy chocolates or dictionaries."

Florian watched them. Rust started toward the door. "Thanks for everything. See you later," he said finally and walked out. He was to take the subway to the Finland railway station. Florian would deliver his suitcase there by car.

At four o'clock, Rust stood in the crowd milling around a huge glass cage. It contained the engine that had brought Lenin back from exile. He felt a light touch on his back. It was Florian, who put down the suitcase next to him, then disappeared. Rust stayed on for a couple of minutes, picked up the case and walked out to look for a cab.

Yelena checked Mac's sleep and Rust's clothes once more. She put his papers and some money in the pockets. When Florian returned, she left in a hurry.

Florian poured himself a drink. He did not like the arrangements. What if Mac remembered him or Yelena or the apartment or all three after all? It would be much better not to take chances with him. But if Yelena thought it would be all right, well...He shrugged his shoulders. He downed his drink and began to dress Mac. It was not easy. Rust's clothes would not quite fit. Dammit. The unconscious man felt heavy, as if resisting everything that was done to him. Florian swore and knelt on Mac to hold him steady while pulling the shirt on. He had never thought the worst parts would be the buttons and the tie. He walked to the mirror, took off his tie, experimented with the knot on himself, then returned to Mac and tried it again, leaning closer and closer.

It might have been the pressure on the throat or a jerky pull on the reluctant body—Florian never knew what made the Scotsman come to. It was just that suddenly the eyes were open and the body moved. All Florian could do quickly was to kneel on Mac and head-butt him. Fear, despair and recognition mingled in the eyes still glazed by the drug. The mouth opened and bared a fine set of strong teeth.

The head butt must have dazed Florian as much as the

Scotsman. That was why he broke his own well-tried rule to hit hard, draw back fast, and hit again. The hesitation cost him dearly. The Scotsman was gasping for air. His jaw convulsed with a powerful, jerky reflex that threatened to crack his own teeth. But his teeth caught flesh. Florian screamed. The pain was excruciating. Blood spurted and sprayed them both. Still screaming, he battered Mac's face. He never knew which blow had killed the Scotsman. He staggered back and ran to the bathroom. Blood was gushing from his nose so fast that he could not see the damage in the mirror. But his frantically searching fingers felt out the picture. Mac had bitten off the tip of his nose.

Florian used up two towels, then folded a small towel for a makeshift bandage, but blood was still seeping through. He felt panicky and tried to remember Yelena's precise instructions. A glance at his watch told him that he had wasted half an hour. He would never be able to follow the plan to the letter now.

He brought in a heavy tarpaulin sack from the kitchen and struggled to stuff the dead man, the tweed jacket and the rest of the leftover clothes inside it. He then tried to shift the bag, but it was too heavy. He felt weak. It might have been due to the shock or the loss of blood. He knew he would not be able to lift the sack. So he dragged it along, through the door, bumping it down stair by stair. He opened the door of the car, which he had parked, luckily, right at the foot of the stairs in the courtyard.

In the twilight, an old woman was approaching. She noticed Florian's blood-soaked bandage. The horror in her eyes reminded him of the Scotsman, and he was on the verge of pulling his gun and shooting her. But instinct compelled her to look elsewhere fast. She scurried away, pretending not to have seen anything. Florian continued his battle with the heavy sack. He pulled and kicked and shoved it into the car at last. His feet were trembling from the effort. Heavy drops of blood were thudding on the door handle, the ground, the steering wheel as he made his way to the driver's seat.

It was 4:50. The tumor of panic grew and grew in his throat. Rust must be at the airport, about to join the line confronting the passport checkers. By now, Florian was supposed to have finished dumping his unconscious victim. Unconscious, not dead. And according to the timetable, he should have been well on his way back to the apartment, where things would have to be rearranged. Only rearranged, as planned, not cleaned of monstrous bloodstains. But time was running out. Florian knew he would have to improvise, and that had never been his strong point. It worried him.

He drove along the canal, away from the Nevsky, and stopped at a park, adjoining a steeply humped bridge. A couple of schoolgirls were crossing the canal. They stopped to giggle. Their full thighs sticking out of the short skirts of their uniform caught Florian's eyes. It's the wrong time, he reprimanded himself, but the flesh held his attention. Another two minutes had been wasted. At last they moved on. He dragged the sack out of the car and pushed it off the embankment. It fell onto the narrow ledge of concrete at water level. He jumped after it and pulled it under the foot of the bridge. Again he had to wait for people to pass. Blood was oozing from the sack and also through the bandage on his nose. He heard the engine of a small boat. The sound was approaching. Could be police. He did not feel like giving them long explanations. He crawled under the bridge and lay down on the sack. He would have sworn that the Scotsman was still squirming under his weight. The boat stopped, with its engine idling, somewhere beyond the bend of the canal.

The line in the airport was snaking slowly toward the passport controller's cubicle. Rust tried to look bored. He had Mac's passport in his hand and felt compelled to open and study it just once more. He resisted the urge despite his overbearing conviction that he would not remember even the name correctly if asked.

The guard took his passport without looking at him. The noise of papers shifted and flicked. Rust could not see what the guard was doing. What if the photograph and copy of Mac's visa were not there? Excuse me, sir, will you step aside for a moment, please? No, he would not say *sir*. He might not say *please* either. Facing downward, the guard looked left, right, left again. He was comparing things. A glance up at Rust. Just as Yelena had predicted. He was looking for features of similarity. The passport appeared in the narrow gap under the window. A half-grunt—and Rust was to move on. Easy.

He had thirty-four long minutes to kill before he would have to enter the duty-free Beryozka shop and buy a random selection of souvenirs. Pity I can't call my father and say at least good-bye, he thought as he passed a bank of public telephones. Out of order—out of order—out of order. Probably they had never even been connected. They were there only to look good. Because airports were supposed to have public telephones. Potemkin's not dead yet, he concluded and walked over to the bar.

"A brandy, please."

"No brandy." The barman gave him an elaborate, leather-bound menu card.

Rust scanned the long list. "It says brandy—here."

"No brandy." The barman shrugged his shoulders. "No brandy, no whiskey, no wine. Nothing. Only beer today. Export beer."

"I'll have a beer then."

The barman poured it from a bottle which had already been opened. The liquid failed to fill the glass. The man opened another bottle and topped it up. "Here you are, sir. Anything else?"

Rust forked out $3 and waited for his fifty cents change.

"Sorry. No American money." The barman offered him a choice of Russian, East German, Danish and various African currencies. Rust did not want to argue. He noticed a man in a blue raincoat watching the scene at the bar. Rust pretended to pay no attention to him as he pocketed a few strange coins and walked away. The man was still keeping his eyes on the barman, his thumb and forefinger smoothing away his thick short mustache incessantly.

The dead Scotsman seemed to refuse to get out of the tarpaulin sack. Florian had to fight him every inch of the way. The effort made his nose bleed faster again. He tore a strip off Rust's shirt for a second bandage, but it kept slipping off until he tied it at the back of his head, covering the entire lower half of his face bandit-style. He remembered the list of his duties and checked Rust's papers in Mac's pockets. Yes, everything was there. With a bit of luck, the body under the bridge would not be found for at least a couple of hours. That would give Rust plenty of time to get away.

Florian stood up, and his nose started throbbing. In blind fury, he kicked the corpse and it slipped into the water. Fuming and swearing, Floriau grabbed it by the ankle to pull it back, but the idling engine began to purr harder somewhere out of sight. The boat might appear in the bend within seconds. He had to let the damned Scotsman float away. The boat was approaching now. Inevitably, it would pass the corpse. Florian climbed up the embankment, ran to the car and tried to force a racing start out of the old workhorse.

At 5:27, the small motorboat hit something in the water. The two workmen on board peered in horror at the corpse. Using a hook, they pulled it to the concrete ledge and satisfied themselves that yes, it was a corpse. For five minutes they argued what they should do. If they reported their find to the militia, it would be known that they had left their job, repairing the landing stage farther up the canal, too early. They might also be accused of having something to do with the death of the man. No, it was much safer to wash the blood off their hands and return to their worksite as fast as possible. If they met someone on their way, they would report the body; if not, they would just forget about it.

At 5:45, Florian drove into the courtyard. The place was deserted, but instinct warned him that somehow it was too quiet. I'm too jittery, that's all, he reassured himself. He parked the car again at the foot of the stairs. He turned off the engine, but silence did not follow. A car was coming through the arch of the gate. It stopped. Something moved at the far end of the yard, behind the fountain. He recognized the old woman who had seen him on his way out with the blood-soaked bandage. He should have shot her, he knew. Now it was too late. She stood there, trembling, and nodding toward his car. Two militiamen appeared behind her. Florian started the engine and threw the lever into reverse, but remembered that the gate was blocked by that other car, from which now the two plainclothesmen emerged.

Florian stuffed four fingers in his mouth and began to chew eagerly. He had never been blessed by vivid imagination. But he had the talent for recalling details. Right now, his instructions from Yelena flashed through his mind. And the sight of that corpse in the canal. And the state of the apartment above. And all the information he would give away if he was questioned. Too bad. He could do nothing about that. Even Yelena would understand. She would forgive him. But then he remembered all the interrogations he had conducted or witnessed. The smells and the sounds and the eyes. And the toenails. And the teeth. He pulled out his gun. The militiamen saw it and dived for cover. Florian screwed the barrel into the soft underside of his jaw and pulled the trigger. The explosion spattered the inside of the car with blood, brain and fragments of skull.

The militiamen were glad that their plainclothes colleagues were at the scene. They could leave it to them to handle the body, search in vain for any documents in the pockets and examine the weapon. And it was the gun that startled them most. A 7.15 Tokarev. The heavy service revolver. Its registration number could be traced, no doubt, but it might raise rather than answer questions. Except that the gun introduced a cheerful prospect, too. For now the case would have to be reported to the KGB right away, and the police could take the more comfortable back seat.

At 5:55 precisely, forty-five minutes before takeoff, Rust walked into the airport Beryozka shop. He picked up some lacquered cups, pretended to ponder over the price, then replaced them on the shelf. The cashier's desk at the exit came into his view. Three uniformed girls were on duty there. One checked the passenger's purchase, another took the money, and the third put the items in a plastic bag which she sealed with metal stitches. The third girl looked up. It was Yelena. For a second, her eyes held his, then she turned to her next customer.

Rust took an amber necklace, an art book about the Hermitage, two bottles of pepper vodka, some souvenir matches and a box of the best cigars, which he recognized as third-rate Cubans. He then joined the waiting line at the exit. The girl checking his selection dictated the prices to the cashier, then handed each item to Yelena, who slipped them into a plastic bag. He paid, and while he waited for his change, he tried to catch Yelena's eyes, but she was too busy sealing the bag. Again he noticed the man who kept fingering his thick mustache, standing now just outside the glass panel behind the cashier. Yelena held out the bag, Rust reached for it, and their hands touched.

"It's the thirteenth dot on page thirty-one," she whispered

and smiled as if wishing him a safe journey while the cash register opened with a clank.

Rust walked out of the shop and, feeling the man's eyes on his back, sat down on a bench, hoping that he appeared sufficiently bored. Although Mac's briefcase was only half full, he decided not to squeeze the plastic bag into it. Better to carry it in full sight of everybody. Yelena had warned. He put the bag next to him on the bench and felt its contents while doing so. Yes, there was a box in it, containing chocolates, presumably, and another small package he had not selected. Must be a pocket dictionary. After a couple of minutes, he looked around, checked his watch as if contemplating how much time he had, then strolled lazily across the room toward the bathrooms. He saw that the man in the raincoat was following him.

The canal police found the documents in the dead man's pocket. Helm Rust. From Florida. It rang alarm bells. An American corpse was not just any ordinary corpse. There was a whole set of precisely laid-down procedures to follow, and the officer knew there must be no mistakes. So he made some notes before calling the station. The body had been seen floating in the canal at approximately 17:35 P.M. by two printers on their way to work; police had reached the scene at 17:47; the body had been pulled out of the water at 17:51; the identity of the victim had been ascertained at 17:53—details were now ready for reporting to the station. The officer in charge walked back to his boat to radio headquarters. He told the desk sergeant to call the KGB Tourist Department right away. It would show that he was fully familiar with the procedures. He was told to stand by and wait for instructions.

The two printers were anxious to move on, because if they were late for their night shift they would be penalized heavily. But the officer was in no hurry. Although he had taken their names and addresses, and had checked and double-checked their identities, it was safer to have witnesses on hand. For who knows? These two might have tried to rob the American and called the police when something went wrong, causing them to panic.

At 17:56, the boat radio came to life. It was a call from the Leningrad KGB directly. The orders were simple: hold witnesses, hold everything, keep passersby away, don't touch the body—wait for a KGB unit already on its way.

"Excuse me, please." The man in the raincoat struggled with the English word. "You . . . English?"

Rust almost protested that he was American, but checked his instinct and nodded. "Yeah. Sort of. Scottish, in fact." He hoped that this would explain his accent, too.

The man produced an identity card. "Captain Barch, Economic Crimes Department." He bowed stiffly. "Can I see your papers, please?"

"Of course." Rust gave him the passport. "Do you mind if I . . ." He gestured toward the urinals.

"Please, please." He stood close to Rust, studied the passport, page by page, then returned to the photograph. "Tooth pain, Mr. McGregor?"

"Mm." Rust covered his swollen face, then turned to wash his hands.

"You tourist in USSR?"

"No, I was working here, me lad." He was glad that only this captain was there to hear his poor imitation of an accent. "Working here, understand? I've brought you a few good milking machines."

"Oh. Thank you. Thank you very much, Mr. McGregor. Now will you help me, please?"

"Of course. What can I do?"

Above their heads, a speaker began to emit some noise. It was the distorted voice of a woman. Although most of the words came through garbled, the message was clear: Rust's flight was being called. But it was in Russian. And he had to be careful not to react: Barch might know that McGregor did not speak the language.

"Are you on the London flight, please?"

"Yes, why?"

The noise now began to resemble English, calling the flight to London via Helsinki and Copenhagen.

"I may have to ask you to . . . to, how shall I say? Not to fly away? We have the best doctors for tooth pain."

"What the hell do you mean?"

"I . . . we . . . we investigate economic theft, yes? And I think people at the bar and in the shop theft things from the nation."

"And how can I help you with that?"

"Can I please look at your bag? The things you've bought in the shop?"

"Why not? But be quick, because I don't want to miss the flight." He handed over the plastic bag. Yelena would not be foolish enough to put Arthur Foster's American passport or other naked documents in the bag, and the microdot would be invisible.

While the captain began to open the stitches, Rust stepped back a little. In the limited space to maneuver, he would have to hit the man hard the first moment of apparent trouble. His back touched the door.

The captain emptied the bag, placing all its contents on the floor. Two bottles of pepper vodka, an amber necklace, a box of cigars, a book on the Hermitage, a box of chocolates, a slim set of souvenir matches, and a multilingual restaurant dictionary. He wagged his finger triumphantly. "You see? They thief! I told you."

"But it's mine. I didn't steal anything."

"No? Here's the list from the machine. Look—you paid for five things and you have here seven things. Why?"

"I don't know. Perhaps they added them up. I mean, the two bottles as one item and the two boxes as just one other item."

"Item? Maybe, maybe. But perhaps they just took it and gave it to you. As a present? Or you pay them under counter for it? Ugh? Maybe?"

"Look, I don't know what you're talking about. I picked these things, they put them in the bag, and I paid what the bill showed. If they made a wee mistake, it's your problem. If they're thieves, it's still your problem. But I must go now. Your government would not be pleased to hear that you held me up with groundless accusations. I'm a distinguished visitor. They asked me to come back and bring more milking machines."

The captain began to sweat. He obviously knew the risk. But he also knew that after weeks and weeks of patient watching, he had at last cracked the system, and that he was now holding both the evidence and a key witness if not a culprit. He replaced the bottles and souvenirs in the plastic bag. "How much did you pay for all this, Mr. McGregor?"

"Have a look. It's on the bill."

"How much?"

"I can't remember."

"You can't remember?" Captain Barch felt like jumping with joy. The suspect had said he could not remember the price! Who on earth had ever heard of anyone who forgot how much he had paid for such gifts and souvenirs of considerable scarcity value? "You must wait in here, Mr. McGregor."

"Why?"

"I must call a colleague. We must take a—what do you call it?"

"Statement?"

"Yes, statement. Thank you. Please, stand over there."

Rust did not move from the door. "But I'll miss my flight."

"We hope that will not be necessary. Because we have the proof!" He raised the plastic bag. "It's here!"

By now Rust knew that it was only a matter of time, that he would have to run or fight for it. But he couldn't run with the captain holding the bag and chasing him. "I shall report your behavior to your government." Rust chose to look worried and defenseless. "I shall have to tell them that you've made some impertinent and groundless accusations." It worked. He could tell. It was the captain's turn to look more and more worried.

"Look, Mr. McGregor, I am not against you. We could be friends."

"Good. Let's be friends. How?" He noticed that the captain slowly transferred the plastic bag from the right to the left hand. If and when he tried to draw his gun, both his hands would be occupied momentarily. Rust had to wait for the moment.

"You make a statement and we let you go."

It gave Rust a flash of hope that something could be worked out. But he was wrong. The captain did not bother to draw his gun. He knew he could deal with the man in his way. He would not even need to hit him and risk eventual complaints of unnecessary brutality. He just grabbed the beard and pulled hard. Reluctantly, the head would follow. For half a second he was amazed how little resistance he had met. For that half a second the two men faced each other, both silenced and immobilized by that shared surprise. Rust's face felt cold in its sudden nakedness. The captain stared at the bunch of hair in his hand; his lungs were already filling up, ready to yell for assistance.

Rust had no choice. He went for the throat with both hands. His thumbs pressed hard. No sound could escape. But that left his body undefended against the captain's knee. The kick exploded in his loins and made him feel faint. The natural reaction was to protect himself, but he fought it off. A groan spurted from his chest, bringing up bilious vomit into his mouth. And the knee was driven into him once more. The third time it was less like an explosion but hard enough to drain away his strength. His arms felt heavy, and his fingers loosened their grip. The captain staggered backward, into an open cubicle. A painful rattle was the only sound that could pass through his damaged throat. He grabbed at thin air in search of support. His calves were stopped in their movement abruptly by the toilet bowl, and he found himself seated. The beard and the bag fell out of his hands as he groped desperately for his gun. Rust knew he had to do something fast. But his arms would not be raised, and he could hardly stand up straight. All he could do was to push the captain off the seat and kick his temple when he was down.

There was some noise behind him. The door. They had been in there for about five minutes by now. It was a miracle that nobody had come in before. Rust stepped inside the cubicle and pulled the door shut.

The captain lay there stunned. He would have to die. Silently. But pain had made Rust too weak to kill. From behind the door he heard the gurgle of the urinal. Somebody was whistling. The tap at the washbasin was turned on. Rust looked down at Barch. His eyes caught the toilet: it was full of water almost to the brim. The man outside was whistling more and more enthusiastically. Rust stared at the toilet. He knew there was no other way. He grabbed the captain by the hair and hauled him up, only to force him face down into the water. The speaker above began to crackle. It was the second call for the BOAC flight to London. He leaned on the captain's twitching body with all his weight. But he tried not to think about it. Yes, he had killed before. In fights. Not like this. Not in cold blood. Captain Barch tried to raise his face out of the water. Rust held him. "Sin without guilt!" Schramm bellowed at him from somewhere in his past. "Go on! You see? It's easy." Barch stopped wriggling. Rust felt no guilt. Or shame.

The speaker in the ceiling crackled again. The second call for the flight was not repeated in English. Rust remembered Yelena's warning that the calls were expected to be answered without any delay. He was not to attract attention to himself by being late.

The pathologist hated the bearded man on the marble slab. His assistant waited patiently for the chief's standard joke to come. Inevitably, he had not long to wait.

"Damned corpses. They just know how to turn up at the wrong time. After six P.M., this place ought to be quiet as a morgue."

The KGB officers who had brought it in eagerly watched every move he made. The pathologist could read their faces: they were inexperienced juniors who would expect instant pronouncements about the cause and time of death, and all sorts of other details providing clues to the identity of the killer. But he was not to be rushed.

"You say he's an American. Mm, must be a poor one."

"What makes you say that?"

"Don't you see? Ill-fitting clothes. Might have been bought secondhand. You know, in . . ." He was about to say something about New York and his visit over there, but changed his mind. None of these young thugs' business where he had studied in his youth. The phone on the wall rang. He answered it, listened without saying a word, hung up—and began to swear heartily. "Another one's coming in! What's going on?"

One of the KGB men was standing right behind him, breathing down his neck. The other took over the office, laid out all the papers found in the dead man's pockets, and put through several "trace and ident" calls to find out more about Helm Rust, U.S. citizen. To cover himself against any possible accusations of delay that might arise, he carefully jotted down the time, 18:13.

He called the department and talked to the duty officer. "Anything about those witnesses?"

"They're processed."

"What do they say?"

"Nothing. As yet. We've checked some of their statements,

and those are correct. It's true that they're printers and that they were on their way to work. And they say they had nothing to do with the American or his death. Which may be true."

"Maybe. We'll find out." He hung up. His guess was that the printers were innocent, but thorough interrogation could do no harm. It might even uncover something else the two men might be guilty of.

Dead, Captain Barch would not sit straight on the toilet. So Rust tore off the long chain and tied him to the pipes on the wall. If somebody peeped into the cubicle through the gap under the door, he would see a pair of feet in a position only to be expected. Rust felt shaky. It was no good to keep telling himself that he had had to do it. It was murder nevertheless. And the pain persisted. He could not stand up straight.

Outside, the tap was turned off. Then the door was opened and shut. Rust picked up the beard and pressed it back into position on his face. He hoped the glue would last through the next thirty minutes. With his penknife he forced and twisted the lock. It would be jammed when he slammed the door shut from the outside. That might give him an extra few minutes.

While he washed his hands, a man came in heading straight for the locked cubicle. Rust was ready to jump on him from behind. But the jammed lock held. The man mumbled something and went into the next cubicle. Rust picked up the plastic bag and took it with him, but he left his briefcase behind. It was his excuse for returning.

In the main lobby nothing had changed. The barman was busy; people wanting a drink read the long list on the menu only to be told about the export beer, their only option today. Rust passed the telephone booths, stopped as if looking for something in the bag, and slipped an Out of Order sign off a door handle. He then returned to the bathroom. The speakers above sprang to life once more: it was the third and final call. He hung the sign on the locked door. The man in the adjoining cubicle pulled the chain and swore heartily. The rush and over-flow of water must have splashed him. A routine problem. Except that the washroom might be flooded, and if the cleaners were called . . . Rust chose not to think about it. There was nothing he could do. He left in a hurry and almost bumped into Yelena. She wore an ordinary overcoat and looked very pale. She might have guessed that there was trouble, but she was unable to help. Rust nodded, reassuringly and imperceptibly, he hoped. She answered with an emphatic look at her watch. Yes, Rust knew, he was late. But the pain slowed him down. Two plainclothesmen and a Russian stewardess were checking lists at the single gate. Rust was ushered to a near-empty bus and the doors clanked shut behind him.

It was a short ride to the aircraft, where another two buses, one crammed, the other half full, waited with their doors locked. The three vehicles were watched by armed guards. Officials aboard each bus began a head count. The time 6:24 P.M. Rust doubted that they could take off at 6:40. The numbers did not tally. Officials from each bus conferred, then a recount was carried out. At 6:27, the doors were still locked. Some passengers exchanged glances, but nobody complained.

Telephone bells shattered the solemnity of the morgue. The pathologist looked up. One of the KGB men was already running toward the office. It was a call from Moscow. "Yes, we've found Roost, Helm Roost, American, on the lists."

"Which lists?"

"Both the visitors' and wanted lists."

"Wanted for what?"

"Perhaps you could tell me, comrade, why you've put through the trace in the first place."

The Leningrad man thought for a second. If Rust was on the wanted list, this was an important case. Being in charge and being successful could bring him accelerated promotion. If he answered this duty officer, the case would be taken out of his hands before he had a chance to talk to and make a good impression on the man who mattered. "Who's the case officer?"

"Major Boychenko."

"I'll talk to him."

"He's not in the building. We've already checked."

"Then find him. And get on with it! What the hell are you waiting for? You're wasting my time." He slammed the phone down. As he looked up, a rolling table with a body came into view. A big man with a gaping wound. As if half the skull had been blown away. The officer fought to avoid throwing up.

* * *

The doors of the buses were opened at 6:28. Boarding between armed guards began immediately to allow passengers the minimum opportunity to view and memorize the layout of the airport.

Aboard the aircraft there was a final head count. Russian personnel left, and the doors were shut. Welcome aboard. Rust resisted the temptation to talk to the captain and ask him for help. The man could do nothing if the airport authorities ordered the evacuation of the aircraft for some "technical reason." The big machine began to roll smoothly. 6:39. Unless there was some unexpected delay, takeoff might commence at 6:40 after all.

Boychenko's call went straight through to the morgue. The pathologist answered it, using the set on the wall.

"You have Helm Rust in there?"

"Yes."

"Dead?"

"Yes."

"Are you sure it's him?"

"That's what his papers say. But that's not my department. Do you wish to talk to the officers who brought him in?"

"Are you sure he's dead?"

"Yes. He was fished out of the canal."

"So it's drowning."

"Probably. But first he must have taken quite a battering. There're several vicious lacerations. Even under his beard."

"What beard? Rust has no beard."

"He has."

"It must be false. Take it off."

"Look, major, I don't try to tell you how to do your work, you let me do mine. I can surely tell if a beard is false or not. I'm holding it right now."

"Pull it."

"That's ridiculous."

"Give me one of the officers."

The pathologist handed the phone to the KGB man, who listened intently, then grabbed and tried to pluck the dead man's beard. "It doesn't give. . . . Yeah, it seems real. . . . Yeah. . . . Yeah. Gray tweed jacket, that's right. . . . No, it's a very full beard, it wouldn't grow in six days." The officer shrugged his shoulders and tugged at the beard ferociously. A few hairs and a strip of skin peeled off. The pathologist turned away in disgust.

Boychenko's investigation was now concentrated on Leningrad. That was how he heard the news right away when Captain Barch's body was found in the lavatory at 7:20. Rust. It had to be his doing. But it meant that Rust had definitely slipped through customs and passport control. Which turnstile had he passed through, and how? The stack of "departures" documents revealed the answers by yielding the visa photograph of a bearded man. Andrew McGregor. Staff of the Astoria were to be summoned to identify the corpse. The border guard responsible for clearing the man was arrested and charged with negligence. Boychenko ordered his intensive interrogation leading to a confession of complicity. Boychenko could have requested fighters to be sent after the plane, except that the flight had long been out of Soviet airspace. But Rust was certainly not going to be out of his reach.

At 8:10, a hurriedly convened meeting began at the First Chief Directorate. Boychenko proposed to ask for Finnish police cooperation to apprehend the murder suspect. The meeting decided against it, for the request would involve Foreign Ministry bureaucracy, and by the time the police could be contacted, the flight would probably have left Helsinki. It could be much more profitable to contact British authorities.

The Spetsburo colonel raised objections to that course of action, too: "Once we're seen to be interested in the man, any more definitive action on our part would be prejudiced."

The last thing Boychenko wanted to do was to argue with him. But he had no choice. It was not enough to track down and kill Rust in a day or two. By then he might have passed on his message. "If we alert the British police, we'll know, at least, where he is."

Major General Yemelin arrived. Boychenko was asked to give him a summary of the discussion. In his final sentence he repeated his proposal, and the Spetsburo colonel tried to torpedo it right away: "The British might refuse to arrest him. A mere questioning would only warn Rust."

That gave Boychenko the chance to score: "They'll have to arrest him. He must be traveling with a stolen passport. His own is still in our possession. He's probably killed McGregor, and we can claim that he murdered Captain Barch, too."

"Are you sure he's left the country with that McGregor's passport?" the general asked.

"Yes, sir. I mean, it appears—"

"Not an American passport in the name of Arthur Foster."

"We'll check it at once."

"Do we know where he'll be taken if he's arrested?" the colonel asked to regain the limelight. An urgent call was put through to the London specialist of the Directorate. He thought the prisoner would probably be held and questioned at Staines or Hounslow, particularly if all charges were restricted to criminal ones. As a result it was decided that a large, as yet unspecified, amount of missing money must also be mentioned to both the Foreign Ministry and the British authorities. Meanwhile, the Spetsburo would instruct the Helsinki KGB Resident to check if McGregor was on the flight from Finland to London. The Resident at the London embassy would also be alerted. A coded telex message would give him a top-priority order: a "wet squad" must eliminate Rust alias McGregor alias Foster at the earliest opportunity.

"Ideally, it should appear to be an accident while the suspect is in British police custody at Staines or . . . whatever the other place is," said the colonel. He would have liked to elaborate on it a little more, but the telephone interrupted him. It was a call for Boychenko from the Leningrad morgue. The KGB officer there was anxious to inform him that an "unindentified Russian corpse" had also been brought in.

"So what?"

"I've just been told that he was to be arrested following a tip-off at No. 17 on the Nevsky, when he committed suicide."

"And? Come on?"

"Nothing else, really, but he killed himself with a Tokarev 7.15."

"Oh. And you say he hasn't been identified?"

"Not yet."

"Are you sure he's Russian?"

"Yes. His clothes, general features, dental fillings . . . excuse me, the pathologist is saying something . . . yes, the man's front teeth have silver cappings and the doctor says it's not done these days in other countries."

* * *

Rust struggled with an overwhelming temptation to leave the flight and try to disappear in Helsinki. He could feign some illness, perhaps appendicitis, anything to get him to a hospital, from where he could escape. He had just decided to make his move when it occurred to him that Finland might be a greater risk than Britain. If he was caught, Finnish authorities might yield more readily to their powerful neighbor's pressure and the KGB might kill or abduct him more easily.

When the aircraft took off again, Rust relaxed but kept asking for cups of coffee to make sure that he would not fall asleep. A young English social worker, who had joined the flight in Helsinki, tried to enthuse about the Finns, the Russians, the Swedes, the Poles and anyone except her countrymen, but Rust was not in a talkative mood and rudely checked her outbursts.

Some twenty minutes from Heathrow, the head steward emerged from the flight deck and stood surveying the passengers. Rust felt sure that his beard was the object of the search. The steward returned to the flight deck and closed the door. Then the copilot came out. He walked halfway down the aisle, past Rust, then back.

Captain Barch must have been found, the Russians must have informed the British, the pilot must have received instructions to land normally but not to allow disembarkation without policemen at the door. Rust prepared to run for it if necessary. Maybe he could use Arthur Foster's passport and credit cards. The package must be in the box of chocolates, he guessed.

After landing, there were only the usual announcements. Please remain seated. Thank you. Hope you enjoyed the flight and next time...

The aircraft stopped. The doors were opened almost immediately. Disembarkation was quick. Everybody seemed to overtake everybody else as if they could save time that way and be first to pick up luggage. Rust followed them slowly. He felt he deserved a breather.

As he approached the long line at passport control, he spotted two plainclothesmen peering at passports over the immigration officer's shoulder. Then farther up, another two. They might have been waiting for somebody else, but Rust did not want to risk it. He tapped his pockets as if looking for something. "Must have left it on the aircraft," he mumbled and turned to retrace his steps along the corridor, searching left and right for something he had never lost. The corridor turned and twisted. Then it forked out. "Transit Passengers" was the sign he wanted.

He found only four pound notes and some loose change in McGregor's pocket. He ought to have borrowed the Scotsman's traveler's checks, too. He called Charles at his home. He was lucky. "Rust here. You must come and get me out of here right away. I'm . . . well, just come."

"Do I need warm clothes and magazines for the journey?"

"What?"

"I mean where are you? Odessa?"

"Transit lounge. Heathrow. Bring a bottle of Glenfiddich and we'll celebrate with triples."

By the time Charles arrived, Rust had taken the beard off and washed his face. "Are you just visiting, or have you lost your passport, dear boy?"

"Both." He noticed that Charles kept scanning the crowd around them. "Are you looking for someone?"

"Yes. Your father."

"He isn't here."

"What went wrong?"

"There's no time to tell you now. I'm carrying a message, and I must get it to Washington no matter what."

"That important?"

"Not really. Only a matter of war and peace."

"And what's keeping you?"

Rust pulled out McGregor's passport. "That's what. It's, er, borrowed, and I have a feeling that they're waiting for me. We haven't parted on friendly terms. I mean, the KGB and I. So how do we get out of here?"

Charles hesitated.

"I mean, I assume you want to help."

"Yes, you may assume that. Which doesn't mean that I can help. Wait here." He gave Rust his leather-covered hip flask. "Busy yourself."

"Thanks."

Charles was away for fifteen minutes. "Spot of trouble, dear boy. I can help only if I level with the police."

"Why?"

"They want you badly."

"What for?"

"Murder. Two murders, to be precise. And a large sum of cash."

"Okay. One murder. No cash."

"McGregor? Why?"

"No, he's only drugged. Twenty-four hours and he'll be good as new. I've made sure of that. Can't say the same about Captain Barch, unfortunately. But I can explain."

"I'm sure you can. But it must have been a rather odd chemical if it allowed a drugged Scotsman to beat himself up, inflict some terrible wounds on himself, fall into a canal and drown."

"That's a lie."

"Maybe. But you're wearing his clothes, and that's what the Russkis say."

"You can't believe that."

"I'm willing to listen. But I can't get you out of here without police cooperation. Besides, you may be safer in their custody. I mean . . ."

"I know what you mean. How long will it take to clear me?"

"Depends, doesn't it?"

"There's no time."

"You want a lawyer?"

"Do I need one?"

"I don't know. Depends what you tell me in the morning."

"Make it dawn."

They walked down the corridor. Rust stumbled and dropped McGregor's beard and passport in a trash can. He was sure nobody had noticed it. They reached the hall with passport control at the far end. "Go ahead," said Charles. "I'll see you in the morning."

Rust stopped in front of the immigration officer. "Good evening. My name is Rust. Helm Rust. American. It seems I've lost my passport."

The two plainclothesmen closed in. "Excuse me, sir, did you say the name was Rust?"

"Yes."

"Also known as Mr. McGregor?"

"No."

"Which flight were you on?"

"Moscow, Helsinki."

"Under your own name? I mean, Mr. Rust?"

"Excuse me, gentlemen." Charles joined the group and turned to Rust: "I think you've lost something on the way." He handed him the passport and the beard. Rust was suddenly forced to sense that this was not the time to celebrate his escape with triples because his ordeal might have just begun. From now on, if he failed with his mission and war broke out, he would have only himself to blame for mistakes—such as contacting Charles instead of buying his own whiskey.

• Wednesday, September 26 •

Aviation Week and Space Technology magazine reports: Some "Pentagon strategists consider the present arms buildup in Cuba the first step toward eventual construction of intermediate-range ballistic missile emplacements. They point out that the defensive nature of armaments arriving from Soviet Russia is aimed at preventing aerial photographic reconnaissance, not at preparations to fend off invasion." Pentagon refutes validity of such speculations.

"YOU FUCKING CREEP."

"No need to become agitated, dear boy." Charles searched for a dustfree spot for his gray Homburg. "Had to deal with some urgent mail first and didn't realize it was already half past ten. Sorry."

"And why did you need to find and hand over the beard and the passport to immigration?"

"I thought it would be best and safest to have everything under one roof."

"And I thought I could trust you." Rust felt like killing him.

"You were right. I'm your only hope to get away with, er, let's say a bit of this and that. For the Russkis are screaming blue murder, which, in fact, may just be the operative word." Charles knocked on the door and asked the policeman outside the cell to take him and Rust to a detention room that would be more comfortable. "And can we have some coffee, please?" He turned to Rust: "You've had some breakfast, I presume."

"Your hospitality is touching."

The detention room was a small, bare office, with a desk and two chairs. Rust glanced around. The window to the courtyard was barred. There was a perforated brick in the wall. "I don't want to be overheard."

"You won't be. You must trust me."

No doubt, thought Rust, but the question is, to what extent can Charles or anybody else be trusted?

"Incidentally, you've decided against asking for a lawyer at this stage, right?"

"Right."

"How about the embassy?"

Rust remembered Holly. "Not at the moment."

Charles was a good listener. He would not need notes to remember details, and he had the self-control to refrain from asking questions until Rust finished telling him everything—everything except the information he had to convey to Washington.

"So they tricked you into going to Moscow and risking your life."

"Yes and no. They didn't think that the risk was that great. It was my fault that I approached Holly despite their warnings. Besides, they took an even bigger risk."

"Have you had a chance to talk to your father alone?"

"Yes, briefly."

"What was your impression?"

"He's a worried, broken man."

"Yet brave enough to participate in some resistance operation."

Rust slowly raised and dropped his shoulders.

"Or do you think that he might have been blackmailed into it?"

"I thought about it."

"And?"

"Discounted it."

"Why?"

"Because if he was cornered, he could have made some mistake in his original message to me to alert me."

"Yes, I think I agree. For even if he hardly knew you, he wouldn't expose you to a suicide mission in vain—no honest father would, right?"

"Right."

"Which means that he must have cooperated in the scheme willingly. The question is, did he know that his associates were GRU?"

"Are you sure they were? Why not KGB? Why not cops or disgruntled dental technicians?"

"Come off it, Helm, you must have guessed it yourself. You mentioned several obvious clues to me. There must have been dozens more. They spoke about America as the 'probable enemy.' The KGB refers to the 'main enemy.' They spoke about using a *taynik*. It's their word for a mail drop. By the way, did they show you that American passport?"

"Yes."

"What was the name?"

"Arthur Foster. Why?"

"I'll try to check if it's a stolen one. Have you got it here?"

"N-no." Rust hoped that Charles had missed the hesitation in his voice. He cleared his throat to explain his faltering and added: "They've promised to get it to me in London. Together with some proof."

"Mm. They must have been a pretty high-powered bunch."

"Probably."

"How else could she . . . what's her name?"

"Yelena."

"Her full name."

"She didn't say."

"No. Anyway, how would she be able to help that sailor's defection if she wasn't GRU or KGB? And how come she knew somebody who might be a CIA agent over there? She said they had tried but failed to get their message to Washington through that channel, didn't she? Incidentally, you haven't mentioned what the message was, have you?"

Rust smiled. "That was beneath you, Charles. You know perfectly well what I have or have not mentioned."

"Sorry, dear boy. I must be getting a little feebleminded in my old age."

"I wouldn't bet on it."

"That's kind of you. I appreciate it."

Charles was play-acting, and Rust did not like it. A little earlier he had been almost ready to tell him everything.

A policeman brought them some food. Charles apologized profusely for the quality.

"It doesn't matter," answered Rust, "as long as it's the only lunch I eat here."

Charles began to ask more detailed questions. Rust was more and more disinclined to answer. He first blamed his Russian experiences for that. Their paranoia must be infectious, he thought. Or was it that once the seed of suspicion had been planted it spread like weed? That must be it. For there was no reason. On the other hand, there was Holly's death. Somebody high up must have betrayed him. On the other hand, Charles was no Holly. On the other hand, Charles himself might be a traitor. On the other hand, that was lunacy. On the other hand, it was now Charles who was preventing him from carrying out his mission. On the other hand, Charles was only doing his job. It was part of that job to suspect Rust. On the other hand, he could still be more helpful if he wanted to. On the other hand—how many hands were there?

"You seem a little absentminded."

"I'm tired, that's all."

"I'll have to go soon. At least it'll give you a chance to sleep a little."

"I thought the police might also want to question me."

"I . . . I've asked them for some cooperation. To leave you in peace for the time being." Charles said it lightly, but for the first time, there was some menace in his voice.

"Wasn't I supposed to be seen by some judge to make my detention official?"

"A magistrate, you mean."

"Whatever you call him."

"Yes, you'd come up for a minute or two in court if your detention was made official. But then my chances to help you unofficially would be more limited."

Charles asked several questions about Yelena. What was she like? Were there any clues to her position? Rust's answers were vague. She was a Dynamo supporter. She knew what she was talking about. She was very feminine.

"How did she behave toward your father? Was there any sign of tension between them?"

"No. He seemed to respect her, that's all."

"Incidentally, have you had a chance to ask him about the camps?"

"Yes."

"Good. What did he say?"

"It's important to you, isn't it?"

"You know it is."

"Can you tell me why?"

"I thought you could guess."

"I did."

"And?"

"I have his answers." Rust stared out of the window.

"I see."

"What?"

"That you're trying to sell them to me."

"Whatever gave you that idea?"

"Look, dear boy, it's no secret that I want them badly. We're trying to spring one or two people from those camps. But if the price is unconditional help, I'm not in a buying mood."

"Now you're talking. So tell me what you mean by 'unconditional.' Or rather what your conditions are."

"It's simple. I want to know what your game is. What your role is. What's so important that made you kill at least one man? Who am I helping if I help you? Are you being used? For what? By whom? Have they duped you? Have they sold you a pup? Are you trying to sell me one? Have you sold out? Please don't protest, it wouldn't be enough to convince me. Do you see my problem?"

"I do. And I'll be frank with you. I can't help you. Not unconditionally. For I can't be sure what your game is. What your role is. What is so important that made you kill at least one friendship at the airport? No, please don't protest, it wouldn't be enough to convince me. But I appreciate that you've made at least a limited attempt to be honest with me. And no, I'm not trying to haggle with you over the fate of some wretched people in those camps. So here's what my father told me. And it's free of charge."

Rust told him that in camp BV 523, the guards in the tower could not see what was going on in the foundry, that the nearest tower was about a hundred yards away, and what the depth of the mined outer perimeter was in VS 389/2-5.

"Thanks. That's most helpful."

"I hope you won't misuse it."

"Anything I can do for you?"

"Yes. For one thing, you could arrange the return of my belt, shoelaces and handluggage. I promise I won't hang myself or cut my wrists with my own toothbrush. And if they return my duty-free shopping with the briefcase, I could smoke my Cuban cigars and give you some pepper vodka which I brought for you. You're of course welcome to check it all first."

"I'll see what I can do. Anything else?"

"Yes. Send a warning to Jus'-juice Sheridan. He's staying at the Upstairs, and I don't want to expose him to some surprise visit."

"What visit?"

"Ah! I caught you at last. You've missed a detail."

"What?"

"Holly knew that some evidence might be delivered to me at the Upstairs. If they want to check out the place, Hal might be in trouble. I want him to stay away from there."

"Okay. I'll see to it."

Rust waited. But Charles was already preparing to leave. Why didn't he suggest trapping those visitors? Was he afraid to mention the idea? Or was he just protecting those bastards?

As they left the office, Charles turned right and Rust was led to his cell on the left. He looked back. Through the gap in the slow self-closing door he could see the reception room and the courtyard. Charles's specially adapted cab was parked right at the door, facing a narrow passage to the street.

Keep warm, Rust was about to say, but the door closed. The camps, the shiverish old man, Moscow, Geneva, the dreams of sparkling water shooting up, up, 130 meters, the camps, the old man—Rust's associations ran in circles. Something he could not define bugged him. If there was any reason to mistrust him and the purpose of his Moscow trip, an old hand like Charles would not risk revealing to him that something dramatic was about to happen at certain Siberian camps. And if he was suspect, the same would apply to any information he had brought out. So Charles must be up to something. Could he be working for Them? If yes, why didn't he stop me while I was there? Rust kept asking himself. What if he did? What if Yelena and my father are already being interrogated? Or dead.

A policeman brought in his briefcase and the plastic bag with his duty-free goodies. Rust took out a cigar. That gave him a chance to glance through the contents casually. Everything was there. It had been checked thoroughly, no doubt, but Rust could only hope that nothing had been found. It would have taken ages to examine every item for possible microdots. He was itching to take a closer look at the dictionary and chocolates, but if he was now watched by some hidden device, it would only call attention to Yelena's presents. Damn you all, Rust swore silently. He hated the lot of them. Them and their trade. And his own involvement, too. So it was painful to admit that he loved every minute of it. Risk and double cross and murder notwithstanding. It was like coming back to life after a long period spent in a coma.

Boychenko reread the brief message that had just been decoded for him. "Target at Staines police station. Waiting for suitable opportunity. Target has been visited by driver of specially adapted taxicab." It had come from the "wet affairs" team assigned by the London Resident. Boychenko wished he were there himself to complete the job. But he had enough to do in Moscow.

The specialist from the First Directorate U.K. desk called him on the phone: "We've identified the owner of that cab. It's a Sir Charles Stoker, who used to be in Moscow at the time Rust was here. We've alerted everyone who might be able to block Stoker's channels of communications if Rust passed the message to him."

"You think they can do it?"

"It's hard to tell."

"Thanks." Boychenko hung up and buzzed for his orderly.

Kolya took the cigarette out of his mouth and smartened himself up a little before answering the call. His boss had been in a rather bad mood lately.

The GRU "cobbler" was shown in to Boychenko, who wanted to know everything about the American passport for Rust. He was furious that it had cost him a full day to get permission to question the cobbler. He took an instant dislike to the fat and jolly little man, who revealed an artist's self-indulgence in explaining the work.

"No, comrade major, it wasn't a stolen passport. It was a good fake. I used the best materials. The U.S. State Department has just recently introduced them to prevent forgeries." He chuckled. "The cover is original Lexide, a simulated plastic produced by Payne-Jones and Co. in Lowville, New York. It's made by a secret process and at the moment we cannot duplicate it satisfactorily. The pages with the antiforgery sunburst pattern are supposed to come from the American Writing Paper Corporation, somewhere in Massachusetts. I've brought you some samples, comrade major." He held up a sheet to the light. "Here—that's the otherwise invisible Great Seal watermark which appears on every page. You'd never tell the difference between this—which is the original—and this, which was made in Poland, would you? Our comrades in Lodz do a truly outstanding job. But for some reason, they're still having problems with the first four and rather crucial pages where the American eagle is superimposed. Here, that's the one."

"You mean immigration officials could spot it if your passport is used for entry?"

"Never. For I've used originals. And I took great care with the prefix to the numbers which are perforated into each passport. I didn't want to give him an X series, for that's diplomatic, or a Z, which is only issued abroad and could be suspect, and I took care not to make it too old, because of the recent changes in coding which show the year of issue. So I chose to make it a B, which dates it 1961."

"Yes, thanks, that'll do." The cobbler seemed disappointed, but Boychenko had run out of patience. "What was the name?"

"Arthur Foster."

"Who'd be using it?"

"I never know."

"Did you fix the photograph yourself?"

"Yes, of course, because the stamp—"

"Have you got a copy?"

"I'm not allowed to keep one."

Boychenko nodded. He took half a dozen photographs from a folder and dropped them on the desk. "Recognize any of these?"

"Yes, comrade major." The cobbler picked out Rust's picture without any hesitation. "That's the man whose picture was in the Foster papers."

"Papers? You mean there was a full set?"

"Of course. Credit cards, driving license, the lot. I work strictly according to specifications."

"Whose specifications?"

"Whoever issues the orders."

"So who was that in this case?"

"I wouldn't know. I only received the usual requisition chit."

"I see." Boychenko made a note to try to follow up the origin of that chit. It would require General Yemelin's permission. That pleased him. Any contact with the general would probably strengthen his position. "Then what? I mean, what happens when you've completed a job?"

"Normally, it's picked up by a security messenger, but in this case, I had to take it myself to Leningrad."

"To whom?" Boychenko pounced.

"Just to drop it in a *taynik*. But there was a mix-up and so I met the comrade who came to collect it, and he was very satisfied."

"Was he really?"

"Oh yes. And quite obviously he knew what to look for when he examined the passport."

"And what's your fucking excuse for not mentioning this before?"

"Nobody's asked me before."

"Don't give me *vranyo*!"

"Honestly—it, it just never came up."

"All right. It'll be in my report. You said"—he was writing it slowly—"that I was the first to ask that question. Correct?"

"Yes, comrade major."

"Good. Very good. Now tell me the man's name."

"I don't know."

"You don't know or you don't remember?"

"I don't know."

"Describe him."

"Very tall, about that much taller than me. Age about thirty-five, forty. Dark hair, heavy build, with big hands."

"What eyes?"

"Dark, I think."

"Good." The description matched the details Boychenko already knew about the second corpse in the Leningrad morgue. "Was he alone?"

"Yes."

"Did he mention a woman?"

"What do you mean?"

"Something like 'She'll be pleased,' anything like that?"

"No."

"Did you see him leave?"

"Yes."

"On foot? By car?"

"Yes, now that you mention it, I think a cab was waiting for him."

"Driven by a woman?"

"I don't remember."

"Are you sure?"

"It didn't seem important."

"You wouldn't have seen the interior of the cab, would you?"

"What do you mean?"

"You know, the usual things. Perhaps a few pictures from the papers. Some footballers. Moscow Dynamo colors."

"What? In a cab driven by a woman? No."

"Pity. But you'd recognize the man if you saw him again, right?"

"I think so."

Boychenko called the Leningrad morgue. The KGB officer in charge had good news for him. The bearded man had been positively identified as Andrew McGregor. The other corpse with its extensive head injuries caused many problems, but the serial number on the Tokarev, with which the man had killed himself, helped to solve them. As it was a standard-issue 7.15mm service revolver, it was on record showing its current user, a Captain Viktor Antonovich Khomenko of GRU security.

It took Boychenko another hour to obtain a photograph of Khomenko. The cobbler identified him as the recipient of the forged Foster passport. Boychenko requested an immediate and full investigation of Khomenko's background and life-style, female companions, friends, known associates both at work and in private. One fact was already known: Khomenko had been on official leave for ten days. That was no help to the investigation. But it made it imperative to identify Khomenko's potential group of traitors and catch the ringleader. General Yemelin agreed to see Boychenko right away, and authorized the major to proceed.

Accordingly, further orders were telexed in code to the London Resident. If the assassination squad could capture and interrogate Rust without undue risk of escape (the word "undue" was Boychenko's insurance policy), every effort must be made to extract a confession concerning the identity of a woman who might have been or posed as a doctor or someone connected with the ambulance service or a cab driver and Dynamo supporter. As it was a "wet affairs" assignment leading to the target's elimination anyway, no limitation was to be imposed on the interrogation technique.

The KGB Resident in New York, a member of the Soviet UN delegation, was also altered. He must arrange surveillance at Idlewild airport in readiness of an Arthur Foster's possible arrival from London. Moscow would dispatch a two-man "wet affairs" squad to New York to stand by in case the London squad had failed in some way or needed backup.

Then Boychenko had an idea. Rust might try to contact his brother in Washington. Would it not be possible to watch Elliott Repson? It was not an unreasonable chance to catch Rust that way. But the general vetoed it without any explanation.

• Friday, September 28 •

Mississippi State University continues to disallow Negro student J. Meredith's enrollment; Bobby Kennedy threatens to enforce government order. London *Economist* scorns U.S. obsession with Castro and Cuba; the fuss over some twenty missiles with a thirty-five-mile range is deemed to be semi-hysterical.

THE MOMENT CHARLES ENTERED THE CELL HE KNEW THAT Rust's patience had been stretched to the limit or beyond. "I'm sorry I couldn't come earlier."

"That's all right. I spent a quiet Wednesday evening, relaxed all day Thursday, and had a nice stroll from wall to wall this morning. What else could I ask for?"

"I'm sorry. But we'll have an excellent lunch sent in." Charles threw his trench coat and gray Homburg on the bed. "I'm trying to help, believe me. If only you'd let me, I could provide security and help you contact whomever you want to."

"I'm sure you could." Rust pulled a bottle of pepper vodka

206

out of the plastic bag. "We'll drink to that." He poured a large shot into his tooth glass, which he handed to Charles. He raised the bottle to his lips. "To friendship." Charles tasted the liquid, and it made him cough. Rust drank and clumsily hit the edge of the stone washbasin. The vodka bottle shattered. He was left holding the neck of it like a dagger. Charles looked up startled and was about to step back, but Rust gave him no time. He rushed at the older man, spun him around, grabbed his hair from behind with his left hand and held the jagged glass to his throat.

"Now you're unreasonable, even stupid, dear boy."

"I know, sweetheart, but you gave me no choice."

"You can't get away. A guard is right outside the door."

"I know. I want you to call him in."

"I won't. Not unless I shout for help. So put that stupid thing down, and we'll forget about it, right?"

"You're underestimating my problems, Charles. I'll never forgive myself for it, but I'll cut your throat if I have to." Just as he pressed the sharp edge closer, Charles tried to turn and face him. The result was no more than a scratch. But it drew blood. "I've warned you. Now call the guard." He dragged Charles to the corner, where they would be unseen when the door was opened. "No cries for help, just a call—you only want him to take us to the little office."

Charles reached out to knock on the door. "Sergeant!"

An unarmed policeman ambled in. Rust had never had a very high opinion of British security. Now he saw no reason to change his view. The sergeant turned and was about to say something. "Shut up. You tell him, Charles."

"Keep quiet—please."

"Tell him to shut the door, then face the wall and put his hands up."

Charles tried to nod, but that brought him into contact with the crude weapon. "Please," he whispered.

The policeman hesitated, then turned and raised his hands. That was the crucial moment. Rust knew he had to move fast. He let go of Charles, picked up a chair with his left hand and hit the sergeant on the head. The man went down without a sound. Charles was too slow to take advantage of his few seconds of freedom. By the time he could have reacted, Rust was holding him once again. "Car keys." Charles fished them out of his pocket and dropped them on the floor. Rust stepped back and hit him hard on the chin. The older man collapsed. "I'm sorry," Rust whispered involuntarily. He bent down to check his condition. Charles seemed unconscious. Rust hoped he would not be too bad off. He picked up the keys, his briefcase and the plastic bag, put on Charles's trench coat and Homburg, and hurried out. The key was in the lock on the outside. Rust turned it, then slipped it behind a radiator. He restrained himself from running down the corridor and through the deserted reception room.

The modified cab was parked right outside the self-closing door. He drove through the narrow passage to the street without anybody trying to stop him. Somewhere in the back of his mind he noted that it had been easy. Surprisingly easy. But he had no time to reflect on it.

On the third floor of the CIA headquarters at Langley, a photo analyst waited impatiently. For more than two weeks since the suspension of U-2 flights over Cuba, he had been studying earlier photographs of the missile sites, and the results began to worry him. The positioning of the surface-to-air missiles near San Cristóbal appeared to show a geometric pattern. A trapezoid. He checked the photographs taken near other Cuban towns for comparison. He connected the dots representing the SAMs and found more trapezoids. The worst of it all was that he knew that pattern only too well. Gary Powers and other U-2 pilots had photographed it over and over again around ballistic-missile silos in Soviet territory. To him the implication was that the SAMs in Cuba might be ready to defend eventually some intermediate or long-range nukes.

His chief agreed with his reasoning and saw a good case for the urgent resumption of reconnaissance flights. The meeting that was to consider the proposal had now been in session for almost three hours. The analyst was waiting to be called in. He would explain his theory and illustrate his argument. At last the door opened. It was his chief.

"Negative."

"What happened?"

"They've blocked it. The suspension of flights was the decision of COMOR itself. It's for them or USIB to reconsider your interesting though somewhat farfetched hypothesis."

* * *

The police sergeant was taken to the hospital for a checkup. Charles Stoker stood among broken glass and washed his face.

"You okay?"

"Quite. It's just that I haven't caught one on the chin since my schooldays." He picked up a towel and turned to Jake Schramm. Every time he met the sandy-haired, avuncular man with the big white hands, he admired whoever might have made the inspired choice of earth-moving-machinery salesman to be Schramm's cover.

"He's a hard hitter, my boy Rust. I trained him myself in the old days."

"He's still a credit to you," said Charles and massaged his chin. "How did it go?"

"No hitch at all. He drove toward the airport and kept checking if he was followed, but of course we watched him from the traffic police chopper. He dumped your cab at Heathrow and took the bus to town. Now it's your Special Branch squad on his tail with cars, motorbikes, station wagons, what-have-you. But I still think you're gambling."

"I had no choice."

"And I'd suggest that—"

"I know, Jake, I appreciate your help and concern. But it's my show, and you know it."

"Sure, sure, no argument at all, except that because it's your show, if anything goes wrong, it's you who may have to shoot the boy, and shoot him dead before you can be sure of his guilt."

"Lucky you. It's me who'll have to live with that decision ever after." He looked for his hat and coat.

"Oh yes," said Schramm, leering at him, "he took the Homburg."

"I'll kill him twice if he loses it. Let's go."

In the unmarked police car, Schramm sat back and tried to think of a gentle way to declare that sooner rather than later he would have to report the situation to Langley. At the moment, Schramm was on official leave, visiting Europe as a tourist, but that couldn't be kept up for long. Only three days ago, he came over, paying his own fare, worrying about Rust, hoping that Charles might know something about why the Upstairs had been raided by two men posing as CIA and why

Jus'-juice had been shot. Now he knew only a little more and had every reason to be worried much more about his friend.

Charles sensed his mood. He put his hand on Schramm's arm. "Let's hope he'll turn out to be clean."

"Hope. That's not good enough. He's my friend. And I'm inclined to trust friends."

"And I've always treated him as a son. But I'd shoot my own son without any compunction if he did what Helm might have done."

"Okay, okay, I know."

"But you still refuse to go over the facts logically. Remember 1956? I knew that something was very fishy when quite out of the blue, his old man was found alive and well and living in sunny Moscow. I told you then, right?"

"Right."

"Then what happens next? Rust resigns. With a father in Russia, he'd have been hounded out of the agency anyway, he claims. I argue that his is a special case. He's not interested. Had enough, he says. Enough of what? He was just about starting two careers with every promise of turning out to be brilliant both as a journalist and as an agent. But no, he'd had enough. He wanted the simple life. But we both know that he's led anything but a simple life. The Upstairs and the smuggling might have been lucrative fun. But he kept turning up information, channeling it through you and me and who knows who else. Why? You tell me, Jake."

"I don't know. Perhaps just couldn't keep his hands out of the till. It's habit-forming."

"Agreed. It's hard to give it up. Once a spy always a spy and all that. Granted. But whose spy?" Schramm moved, and Charles squeezed his arm. "Sorry. But that's exactly what I meant. Questions must be asked, and if possible, answers must be found. So okay, he was helping us with tidbits. But then one day, a mysterious message via a defector and an alleged CIA agent, neither of whom we can trace. And then this little escapade to Moscow. What could I do? Out came my old list of questions. Did he really find his father? How? With whose help? What happened between the two when they met? Was his father the victim, the poor ex-prisoner, he claimed to be? Or was he KGB? Did he squeeze Rust? How? With what? Was it a forced resignation? If yes, why? If not, did he tell us the real reason?"

"We've been through that before."

"Right. But what do I do? I help our friend with the visa and ask him to supply a few answers about camps if he can. He couldn't be more obliging. He doesn't forget. He returns with all the answers. Except that it's all false. In BV 523 there's never been a foundry. VS 389 has never had a mined outer perimeter, and its satellite camp 2-5 had been closed down before the years of the old man's alleged imprisonment. So now I have proof. Someone's trying to fool me. Helm? Daddy? Who? Why? Which leaves me with my original suspicion that Rusty boy's involved in a major operation. He may be guilty or not guilty. He may have to die for nothing. That's the gamble. But if we let him run and we see where he runs, he may, just may, take us to the hidden goodies on Treasure Island. Now you tell me where I've gone wrong and I call off the whole operation."

"Well, I can't really fault your logic."

"But?"

"I didn't say 'but.'"

"You didn't need to."

"All right. I think you haven't explored all your options before letting him run."

"What options? Beating the fillings out of his teeth, or what?"

"Me, for instance. Couldn't I be an option?"

"You mean he might have given you the message. And eventually the proof, too."

"Possibly. I'm sorry, I didn't mean that he'd regard me as a better friend or that he'd trust me more, but, well, I'm American. And I'm Company."

"Yes, I've thought about that. But I couldn't accept it. And there's no need to apologize. My personal feelings have nothing to do with it. It's a matter of logic. Look, he claims that he's carrying a vitally important message and that some proof to support it will be delivered to him. How? When? He doesn't know. Or he doesn't want to tell me. Okay. But even if we accept that all this is true, we know, at least we have his word for it, that he badly burned his finger when he contacted Holly against the girl's alleged warning. One thing is certain. Holly is dead. If Rust is telling the truth, that experience must have convinced him to go directly to the top. He'll trust no one. Not me, not you. After all, he claims to have been betrayed by the Moscow station chief himself."

"Incidentally, don't you think we ought to try to check out that story with Holly's widow?"

"It won't run away, Jake. But if we move now, we'll have to explain to everybody how we know about Holly's death and the rest. Besides, if Rust is a plant, he may be part of a smear campaign against the station chief."

A radio call came through. The surveillance team reported that "suspect has just stolen two apples from a street stall." The officer asked if Sir Charles wanted to have Rust apprehended.

"No, just add the theft to his charge sheet. There'll be plenty more on it. Continue the watch, but do not interfere with anything he does. We'll soon be there."

"What the hell does he want with those apples?" Schramm turned to Charles: "You think there's something hidden inside?"

"You mean the proof?" Charles shrugged his shoulders. "The proof is in the eating."

"Very funny."

"He's started eating one of the apples, sir."

"Let me know if he doesn't eat them both. And if he passes the remaining apple on to someone else, hold them both."

The officer went off the air. "He hasn't eaten anything today," said Charles, "and he can't have more than a couple of pounds left."

The car was speeding down Cromwell Road when the surveillance team reported that "suspect is sitting on a bench munching chocolates in Kensington Gardens."

The chocolates were gray and dry and had the texture of fine sand. But Rust was hungry, and eating gave him a chance to examine the contents of the box without calling attention to himself. He knew he could not be watched, but he tried to take precautions as if he might be. Under the second layer of chocolates, through the base plate of the box, he could feel the outline of the passport. He tore up the paper and there it was. Tom Craig, Jr. She'd cheated him. She'd made him learn all about Arthur Foster only to swap the "shoe" afterward. He could have killed her. But it might have been a mistake. Rust closed his eyes. He could visualize Yelena clearly. He could hear her self-assured voice. You need help, Helmut. You must trust me. I must take precautions. Was Tom Craig, Jr., another of her precautions? Rust relaxed. It might have been a safeguard even against Florian. If you're caught, they make you tell them everything. And her "cheating" had already begun to work in Rust's favor: Charles would now be busy alerting all British exit controls to the possibility of an Arthur Foster, American citizen, trying to leave the country. Rust's mood swung to euphoria. He could have kissed her now.

Evening mist descended on the park. McGregor's ill-fitting clothes failed to keep out the damp air. Rust ate his second apple. Keep warm. He closed his briefcase and broke into a brisk walk. Keep warm. In a public bathroom he pocketed the passport and flushed down the remains of the chocolate box. He examined the multilingual dictionary. There was nothing to reveal its importance. The thirteenth dot on page thirty-one was a perfectly natural camouflage for the microdot that might be a guide to several more hidden on other pages.

He walked, made sudden stops and turns, checked the street behind him in shop windows, doubled back on his track several times, and used all the tricks he had once learned from Jake Schramm to be reasonably certain that he could not be followed except by a truly professional and sufficiently large squad. On his way, he finalized his plans. First he must obtain money or a ticket to fly to America. He would then choose a safe place for depositing Yelena's dictionary. Finally he would try to arrange a meeting with someone as close to the President as possible, probably a member of the Security Committee or the U.S. Intelligence Board. He decided not to trust a diplomat or anyone who was just a high-ranking member of the Company. After all, that was why Yelena had chosen him for the mission. Only when such a high-level meeting was arranged would he recover the microdots.

The strict criteria he had set for his choice of eventual trustee to receive and handle the message and the proof imposed a severe limitation on the contacts and channels he could use. For apart from his brother and Jake Schramm, everybody would be likely to ask too many questions first and offer help only if satisfied.

From a public phone booth he called Schramm's office in Miami. The call was answered by a machine. Rust had no money and so he couldn't leave a message. It was 10:30. In Washington it would be 4:30 in the afternoon. His brother might already be at home. He gave Elliott's number to the operator. "Could you please make it collect?"

"You mean transfer charge, sir."

"Right."

There was no answer. Rust walked around for another twenty minutes and tried again. He asked for the Washington number. "Could you transfer the charge, please?"

"Sure, sir, we'll make it collect, right?"

Anna answered the call. She hesitated, then accepted the charge. Rust recognized her voice immediately, though it was a bad connection. His mouth ran dry. His tongue stuck to his palate. She helloed impatiently. The operator urged him to speak. "It's your number in Washington, go ahead, caller."

"Oh . . . hi . . . Helm here."

"Hi, where are you?"

"In London. Is Ell there?"

"Sure. Hang on." He heard her shout, "Ell!" Then distant sounds. She returned: "He'll take it in the den."

Elliott's voice was strange. "What are you doing in London, Helm? And what great event can I thank for the pleasure of hearing from you?"

"I need some cash."

"Don't we all?"

"Very funny."

"Well, at least it's nice to know that your brother comes to mind when you're broke."

"It's no joke, Ell, and it's urgent. I need a ticket in the name of Tom Craig for the first flight to New York. And I mean the first flight, even if it's got to be first-class."

"How about a private charter, Mr. Craig? Are you a member of the Playboy Club?"

"I'll call you again in half an hour. Let me know then which flight I'm on. Then meet me at Idlewild. And I'll need protection."

"Go to the embassy. I'll give them a call."

"No good. And I'm serious."

"What's it all about?"

"I'd rather not discuss it on the phone."

"Give me a clue."

Cuban confetti, Rust wanted to say, but controlled himself. "Think of the odd expression in the shopping list I sent you."

There was a moment's silence. "What list?"

"The one in July."

"You sent it to me?" There was another pause. "Can't remember."

It could not be just the bad line. The voice was strange. "Ell?"

"Yes."

"You sound peculiar. As if you were somebody else."

"Anybody I know?"

"What was Mother's favorite color?"

"Don't be a fool."

"Tell me."

"Mauve, of course."

"Sorry. I must be seeing ghosts everywhere. And your voice was odd."

"I've got a cold."

Half an hour later Rust called again. Elliott gave him the number of the first New York plane in the morning and asked him to take a connecting flight to Washington.

"No good. I must meet you in New York." He did not want to spell out his suspicion that Elliott's home might be watched. It was unlikely, but it was just possible that Moscow, having discovered his real identity, would try to track him down through his brother. To tap Elliott's line at short notice could be ruled out even if they had access to some specialist's services in Washington. So the phone was reasonably safe. "Ell? Are you there?"

"Sure. It's only that I've been trying to figure out something. But it's no go."

"Must be."

"I'll be on special twenty-four-hour duty, and there's no way to get out of it. You'd have to wait all day for me."

"It's really urgent. And don't suggest the embassy."

"Mm. What if I sent a couple of guys to meet you? I mean guys whom I trust as much as myself. They'll be briefed. And they'll know Mother's favorite color. How's that? You just tell them whatever you want."

"No. But I'll tell them what I want from you."

"Okay. They'll be authorized to do anything I could do."

"Thanks. I'll meet them at the Hertz desk. Got the name?"

"Tom Craig, Jr. Beats your own hands down. The ticket will be telexed to the TWA desk, Heathrow. Take care."

"Keep warm."

Rust walked around shivering through the night and swore at himself for having dumped Charles's coat in the cab. Steaming cups of coffee at a night stall tempted him, but he wanted to save his money for the bus fare to the airport. He knew he could drink the coffee and then run away without paying, but that seemed too great a risk to be worth it. So he walked faster.

• Saturday, September 29 •

Republicans demand Naval blockade of Cuba to stop further arms deliveries. Vice-President Johnson warns: "Stopping a Russian ship is an act of war." Upheaval in Belgium: drivers will need a license! Foreign journalists will need special permission to venture outside Havana. On Moscow's Gorky Street (the *Brodvey* in local "jet-set" parlance), new *kokteil* (wine with milk) is the craze. U.S. decides to send missiles to Israel to counter-balance Nasser's new Soviet bombers.

THE TICKET WAS WAITING FOR RUST AT HEATHROW. HE had no difficulty going through passport control. Charles, you're slipping—in the old days you'd have been here, trapping me personally, he thought and decided to warn him at the first opportunity. At the same time, he was grateful to Yelena once again. He wondered what her real name could be, and what she would be like if she ever turned up in Florida. It was reassuring to know that he had helped her with the details of

217

the Odessa run and the Cuban contact, but he could not decide whether or not he hoped that she would ever need or want to make use of them.

With the last of McGregor's money he bought a half-bottle of Scotch in the duty-free shop. It was yet another long wait for the flight to be called, but this time, he was the first to answer it. He ate the largest breakfast the stewardess had ever been asked to serve on first class, then slept for three hours. The aircraft was not even half full, and apart from him, there were only two other passengers up front. Both were midmanagement executive types who spent most of the flight, probably their first in first class, guzzling free champagne.

Near New York, Rust asked for a postcard. He scribbled a few lines to "Dear Hal," signed it "Tom," but did not address it. He slipped the card, a bar of soap, an unused notepad, a pen, a pair of sunglasses, the matches and the multilingual dictionary into the plastic bag from the duty-free shop. Then, sadly, he added his razor to the contents. There had to be something of some value in the bag. During disembarkation he appeared to be sleepy. He was the last off the plane. In the corridor he stopped a ground hostess and handed her the plastic bag, saying that he had just found it. Together they glanced through its contents. The postcard to Hal with no address was insufficient to help trace the sender who had lost the bag, but good enough for identification if the owner ever claimed it. The hostess promised to take it to Lost Property, and Rust watched her all the way. The bag would be safe in there for the time being.

As he had no luggage to wait for, he would have been the first at immigration control, but he waited for a small crowd to gather before joining the line. He didn't quite trust Yelena's cobbler. But his doubt was unjustified. He was passed through without any hitch.

Somebody touched his back lightly. "Hi."

He spun around. "Anna."

"Long time no see." She smiled. And when he said nothing, she stepped closer and whispered, "Ell thought you sounded worried about the arrangement. So he sent me to pick you up and reassure you. And yes, I do know that the color is mauve."

"Are you alone?"

"Is this a decent question?"

"I mean . . ."

"I know what you mean, you fool." She turned and nodded toward a tall, pancake-faced man with cauliflower ears. The man nodded back. "That's Lieutenant Lanigan. He's to observe that we behave ourselves. And to make sure that nobody is trying to follow us. It's all very hush-hush."

"Is Ell coming over?"

"As soon as he can. But he'll call us in . . . what's it called? A safehouse?"

On their way to her car they tried a couple of conversations, but it was no good. Both of them knew it would be hard to talk. So she drove in silence. Rust kept looking back. Lanigan with the mashed ears was right behind them, driving a heavy old pickup. They turned west along the Long Island Expressway but kept the speed down. She pulled up at the Queens Midtown Tunnel and paid the toll. "Keep your head down," she whispered in a mischievous tone. "Ell said this would be where we've got to lose them."

"Who?"

"Whoever's following us." She accelerated. "Isn't it exciting?"

Behind them, the pickup had pulled up awkwardly. It was blocking the entire lane. The other lanes were also blocked by some stupid drivers. Anna was well into the tunnel by now. Rust heard the ever-increasing volume of hooting behind them, but they were moving away from it fast.

"Did we have a second backup?" he asked.

"I don't know. Ell didn't say." They emerged from the tunnel. Still no cars behind them. She turned right, and right again and stopped. "We have to change cars."

He followed her without any questions. Elliott had made the arrangements; it was okay with him. In Manhattan they had a chance to disappear in any direction. She drove up on Second Avenue, then turned onto the Queensboro Bridge to double back toward Long Island, along Queens Boulevard and Northern Boulevard all the way to the Glen Cove intersection. Eventually she left the main road, and Rust lost track as she negotiated narrow lanes with hardly any hesitation.

"You know the area pretty well."

"Ell told me to drive around here while waiting for your flight."

The house was completely cut off from any other habitation in the mature forest. She had the keys and led the way in. The place was damp, and obviously nobody had lived there for quite some time. "Could you bring that in?" She pointed at a large open cardboard box full of food and bottles. It reminded him of Yelena's emergency supplies.

"How long are we planning to stay here?"

"I don't know, but I'd love a drink even if it's only five minutes. You might find some glasses in there."

He moved to the far end of a large living room. The phone rang in the adjoining room. Through the open door, Rust heard Anna talking. "Hi, honey. Yes, everything's okay. Yes, fine."

Rust raised his hand to signal to her that he also wanted to talk to Elliott. She didn't notice it. He crossed the room and called, "Hold it," but she had hung up by the time he got there.

"Sorry, he was in a hurry." She turned to apologize and bumped into him. For three long seconds they said nothing. She then stepped back. "He . . . he said his man would soon be here, and if necessary he'd come over himself."

Charles was swearing. He and Schramm flew into Idlewild only five minutes after Rust's plane had landed. Rust's collect calls had been traced, and so they knew he had been in touch with his brother. It was considered best not to sit on Rust's tail but arrange a "reception committee" at the airport.

"Idiots. How the hell did you lose him?" Schramm raved and ranted. "I gave you his name, flight and picture."

The men had no excuse. They saw Rust coming through immigration, saw him being met and driven away by a woman whom they described as "a real knockout." They admitted losing her and Rust in the jam at the tunnel tollgate. "He had no luggage, just a briefcase, and he was one of the first out," one of the men said, only to infuriate Schramm even more.

"A briefcase and a plastic bag from the duty-free shop, you mean."

"No, just a briefcase."

"You didn't look."

"There was nothing else. Maybe he put the bag in the case during the flight."

Schramm turned to Charles. "Could he?"

"Not unless he threw away a few things. That case was absolutely full. But is it all that important?"

"Isn't it?"

"Look, even if he has some proof, it may be meaningless without him and the message itself."

Schramm was losing his patience with Charles. "That's why I thought it was wrong to let him escape in the first place. Because if he's joined the opposition for blackmail or whatever reason, he's now free to carry out his mission and cause all the damage he might be assigned to cause long before you can trace him and gun him down."

"It wasn't I who lost sight of him, was it? And it isn't for me to find him. We're in your territory."

Schramm did not need to be reminded of that. He had already decided to alert a few people, just quietly for the time being, to search for Rust. But he would soon have to make it all official and accept responsibility for the delay.

This time it was a Cognac and Armagnac tasting party in No. 2 Granovsky ulitsa. The heavily decorated general raised his glass. "Comrades, I have reason to believe that the matter we've approached with considerable concern is being concluded—just about now." The other two generals and the two civilians present avoided the eyes of each other. They stared at walls or the floor gravely, not giving away the slightest sign of elation. If the general was right, the harebrained scheme of gambler Khrushchev would soon be in ruins. The missiles in Cuba were not yet ready to threaten America. If Kennedy acted firmly within a week, Khrushchev's power would evaporate by mid-October. Yes, Cuba might be lost, but the generals and all those in favor of a strong traditional army would gain an unassailable influence. Their power position, pay and pensions would be restored; creeps like Furtseva would be no menace to any of them anymore.

Glasses were clinked and brandy snifters were drained unceremoniously.

As was his habit, the general fingered his Order of Lenin, then dusted his Stalingrad medal with a quick succession of flicks. The hognosed man with the sweaty baby face watched him surreptitiously. Yes, it seemed that the general, or rather his men, had done a good job. No doubt Kennedy could be expected to intervene without delay. Get out, you spongy Ukrainian peasant, or we'll rap your stubby fingers. That's what the President would say if it was up to me, he thought. And then, under new management, the age of sanity will dawn. Sanity will mean quiet and systematic but total re-equipment with *porokhovyye konfety* and other modern weapons until nobody, but nobody, can argue with us. Yes, the general's done a good job. But what he did could be regarded as treason. And if he's done it against Khrushchev, he might do it again, against others. He must not be trusted. He and the others in the room.

The others refilled their glasses and waited for hognose to speak. If Brezhnev succeeded Khrushchev, this man would wield vast influence. But if the bid for power failed, if Suslov, Mikoyan and the rest of the kingmakers withdrew their backing, the mere fact that these men in the room were known as booze brothers at the Bureau of Passes could ruin them all. Hognose raised his glass: "To Mother Russia, may she keep us in Napoleon V.S.O.P. forevermore."

As they knocked back the fine brandy in single gulps, the rattle-and-croak of the brass horn outside seeped through the windows. Nikita Sergeyevich must be on his way from the Kremlin. The men in the room turned to watch the street and reassure themselves that he was coming to Granovsky only to visit the red-brick building opposite.

"Mr. Rust?"

Rust nodded.

"Lieutenant Lanigan at your service, sir. Colonel Mann's been delayed but will be here soon. If you need anything, I'll be outside, patrolling the grounds." He nodded stiffly toward Anna. "Ma'am."

"It's cold in here," she said when the door closed behind him. She looked at the yawning fireplace and the wood piled high next to it. "You think we could build a fire?"

"Why not?" Rust was determined to sound casual. "We've nothing better to do."

Kneeling side by side, they began to work together. Inevitably, their hands touched. Both withdrew hastily. "It's strange," she said.

"What?"

"To be with you in daytime. I remember you only in moonlight."

"Don't."

"Sorry."

"Go and sit over there." He blew furiously at the faint glow at the end of some twigs.

"I only wanted to help."

"Well, don't." Rust's eyes nursed the infantile flames. "Sorry. I didn't mean to be rude."

"I know." She moved to stand up. "Oh, my knees."

"What's wrong?" He reached out to help her up.

"Only old age."

"What old age?" He feasted on the sight, still holding her arm, as they stood in front of the reluctant fire.

"D-day, or rather the longest day plus six years, give or take a few months. And don't say that it doesn't show."

"It does. To your advantage."

She stood still, looking up at him. "Thank you." Then, after a pause, she took his hand to remove it from her arm. "As I once said, we should have met earlier and in different circumstances." She held his hand until he snatched it away.

"But we didn't. And we'd better not forget it." She walked away and lit a cigarette. He watched her neck—was her hair shorter now than it used to be?—and cursed himself for remembering every curve, every bulge, the color and the fragrance of her skin. "In the six years, nothing has changed, Anna. Nothing. So let's not play games." He turned back toward the fire.

He heard some noises. The clasp of her handbag. The rustling of paper. Then soft steps. A slip of paper slithered under his arm. Then the steps moved away. He looked at the paper. And it made him smile. "Sorry, sorry, sorry, doyling." Upcurving lines—fat, cursive letters. "I never meant no haym, I pyomise. Let's make up and be friends again. Pleese, pleese, pleese!" The note and her peculiar, individual handwriting brought back memories. In Leningrad she used to put such notes next to his bed to greet him in the morning, should he wake up before her. He found "I love you" memos in his shoes, and "Still love you, doyling" stuck to the soap. She used to spell out sounds, but that was because her spelling was atrocious, and she knew it: the "jokes" were a cover-up. When he laughed now, she laughed with him.

He dropped the note into the fire and watched it burn. "That's the last one ever, okay?" She did not answer. He walked over to her. "Can I have a cigarette, please?"

"You don't smoke."

"I do now."

She offered him her own cigarette. "Have a puff. See if you like it."

He only touched it to his lips. "I do."

"So do I."

"Ell shouldn't have sent you here."

"I know. I didn't want to come. But he insisted. He said he was worried about you and this was a favor to him. I told him it would be a very special favor because, as I'd told him again and again over the years, I'd always disliked you. He kept asking why. I said there was no reason. I said I couldn't understand it myself. But somehow, for some reason, we . . . we just never hit it off. There was this . . . this odd animosity that I felt toward you from the moment we'd met." Once more, she offered Rust her cigarette. He held it between his lips for a couple of seconds, then gave it back to her. She pressed the stub to the corner of her mouth, without smoking it, until it began to burn her fingers. "I thought I'd faint when he introduced us in the restaurant."

"I noticed."

"You were a real bastard. You shouldn't have allowed it to happen. Not ever."

"Couldn't help it. Believe me."

He returned to the fire and shoved more twigs in with furious energy.

She lit another cigarette. "You never told me what happened at that lunch."

"I never had a chance to tell you. I hoped I never would."

She turned to face him. "Tell me now."

"There's no time. Lanigan will be back soon. What was the name of that colonel?"

"Tell me."

"Mann? Is he Ell's friend? Mann. Colonel Mann."

"Fuck Mann. Tell me."

"Better not. Ell is my brother."

"And don't I know it? Didn't I keep away from you just as much as you kept away from me? But your brother's making it more and more difficult. He's . . . he's as if he was schizophrenic or something. It's getting real hard to live with him. I even heard that he's doing some odd things at work. People talk. I always try to silence them, but in my job I keep hearing things."

"What things?"

"Better if you don't know. He's your brother, remember?"

"What things?"

"No dice. Not unless you tell first."

"What?"

"About that lunch."

He shrugged his shoulders, then kept his hands busy with the fire. "It was a couple of months after Leningrad. I had to visit Washington, and he took me to lunch. He was a changed man. Lighthearted, bubbly and optimistic, everything that used to be alien to him. I attributed it to his new job. He was going up in the world. I was delighted. But he told me that it had nothing to do with his job. There was something else. Or rather, somebody else, to be precise.

"He ordered champagne. 'Here's to me,' he said. 'I'm getting married.' He drank, and I kept my eyes away from the wheelchair. I didn't want to pry, but it was a question mark. I mean, he might have visited call girls sometimes, but he never mentioned it. And I never knew if his injuries had made him impotent or not. So I drank to his engagement heartily, but he read my thoughts. 'And if you're worried about me or if you think that my disablement may prevent us from having children, don't. I can reassure you that it's been checked out in more ways than one.' He said it with a childish, mischievous smile. Every time I think of him, I see him with that smile. And I remember the words. They keep coming back."

He was squatting, staring at the fire, and Anna sat down next to him. She offered him her cigarette. He hesitated, then gently pushed her hand away.

"Did he tell you right away who he was about to marry?"

"No. That was the worst of it."

"He mentioned Bobby Kennedy or that I was on a Senator's campaign staff or that I had just been to Leningrad, and you guessed."

"Worse. He kept saying what a wonderful girl *She* was. Never mentioning the name, always referring to *Her* and *She* with a capital H and S. *She*'s fantastic. Everybody looks up when *She* comes in. Everybody listens when *She* talks. And *She* doesn't mind the wheelchair. *She* says it's a good thing because it'll slow him down chasing other girls. And he spoke about his great love. 'Imagine, Helm, *She*'s jealous of me. As if I wanted anyone else. As if *She* left me anything to spare for even a one-night stand with any other girl. *She* wants it all to herself.' Ell's words, not mine." Rust paused, and the creases on his face grew deeper. The old scar attained a red glow. "In a way, I enjoyed listening to his panegyrics about *Her*, because it was marvelous to see how happy he was. And then he leaned across the table and lowered his voice to make a confession. 'Look, Helm, I know we never talk about such, such personal things, but I must talk now, I must share the joy, and there's nobody else to whom I could say this without being suspected of boasting. I mean *She*, *She*'s just crazy about me. I never thought it could happen. Can you imagine, in bed, *She*, *She* gets into a sort of frenzy. *She* scratches and beats my chest, kisses me all over, and tells me again and again that *She*'s never felt such a thing before, that *She* has some sort of ir- resistible'—"

"Stop it," she interrupted Rust.

"I haven't finished."

"I've heard enough."

"No, no. You wanted to know what happened at that lunch. Now you've got to hear what Ell said to me. He said that his fiancée had some sort of irresistible craving for his sperms. That she wanted them inside her, everywhere. And that if he died, she'd always want to remember him by the taste of his sperms. That's exactly what he said. So there was no need for me to guess, right? I had heard those sentences before and remembered them clearly."

"I'm sorry."

"I don't believe it."

"And I can't blame you."

"That's kind of you."

"And I don't think you'd ever believe me if I explained what happened."

"No, I don't think I would." He left her at the fire and

poured himself two fingers of bourbon. "You haven't touched your drink yet."

"It's too early for me."

"You asked for it."

"I was at a loss. I didn't know what to say." She took the glass and drank up. "But about that . . . craving—I really meant it at the time."

"Every time?"

"Bastard."

"Sorry. I was only trying to clarify it."

"I said what I felt."

"At the time."

"Yes."

"Pity you had to add that you had never felt like that before. Because at least in my case it wasn't true."

"It was more true then than ever before or after."

Rust watched her lighting her umpteenth cigarette. "It really hit me at the time," he said. "I mean, hearing your words from Ell. It was stupid, because there had been no reason to believe you in the first place. But it hurt. Even though I knew why. Because of plain and simple male vanity. And I knew how gullible we tend to be when it comes to seemingly genuine praises of our sexual prowess. And it still hurt, even though I knew perfectly well that professional whores had always exploited that imbecile gullibility."

"Thank you."

"I hated myself."

"Yourself?"

"Yes, because I still found it difficult not to love you. At the time."

"I'll have another drink now."

"I thought it was too early for you."

"Not today. It doesn't seem too early for anything."

Rust poured. "It was thoughtful of Ell to make the bourbon Kentucky for me."

"It was my choice."

"How did you guess that I liked it?"

"I don't know. Perhaps you mentioned it in Leningrad. No, I think you drank Kentucky at the end of that lunch. I joined you for coffee, remember?"

"Yes. You appeared just on cue."

"And when I came in, looking for Ell, and saw you with him, I almost died. Too bad I didn't."

"Why? You had nothing to fear. I think I even managed to say how delighted I was to meet you at last."

"You said more than that. Ell guided my hand into your palm and said, 'Anna, meet my big bad brother in the flesh.' Then he told you that I was the dream girl. And you were so sweet it almost made me puke. 'Pleased to meet you, Anna, I've heard such a lot about you that I feel I've known you well for quite a long time. Congratulations to you both. An excellent choice, Ell, she'll be a dream of a sister-in-law to me.' That's what you said. Correct?"

"Probably."

"And we just smiled as he explained why he hadn't mentioned to me before my trip that you were in Russia. Simply because he wanted to be there when we met. And because he was afraid that we might meet accidentally at the Moscow embassy, he never mentioned that his brother's name was Rust, not Repson."

"He wasn't the only one to blame, Anna. You never mentioned his name either in Leningrad."

"Why should I? You were meant to be only a—yes, don't smirk—a fast fling. Too bad that it turned out to be more. But I couldn't have broken it up with Ell. And you wouldn't have wanted me to."

"No."

"Because he was more vulnerable than you."

"I guess so."

"You were a fool. You should have pushed him off a cliff or something. Anything to get rid of him and let us be happy. But no. You were the considerate brother. You chose to disappear. And you resigned right away. From everything. Even from life."

"I survived."

"Why did you opt out altogether?"

"It seemed the best choice. If I worked with him, if we had mutual friends in the same town or even if I had to just visit Washington from time to time, we'd have met now and then. And I didn't want that."

"Everybody says you threw away a great career."

"That's kind of them."

"Even the little occasional help you still gave Ell helped him to make a career he didn't deserve."

"I didn't help much. It's you he ought to be grateful to. You made him a different man. You brought out the best of his talents in every direction."

She ignored the undertone. "Yes, he's done very well for himself, at least until recently."

"What's wrong now?"

"I'm not sure. It's hard to put my finger on it."

"Try."

"It's unfair."

"To him?"

"To both of you."

"You promised. It was a deal."

She drank and held out her glass for more. "I don't know what's happening. He may be under a lot of pressure, but he's changed. He's acting strangely. He's become big-headed. He always knows best. Everything. I heard somebody saying that he wants to judge and decide everything by himself. You know what I mean. He gets some orders—he may or may not carry them out. He hears something, gets some information—he may or may not pass it on. He loses things. He forgets things."

Rust was staring at her hard. She did not seem to notice. The words "loses things, forgets things" kept echoing in his brain.

"Don't misunderstand me." She stepped closer to him. "He's a wonderful man and I wouldn't ever want to hurt him. Or leave him."

"I hope you never will."

"But what if he left me?"

"He won't."

"You don't know. You haven't seen him for a long time. And I know it may happen. And if it does, could we . . . could we meet again?"

"Don't be silly. It was wonderful at the time, and it hurt when it ended, and again for a while after that lunch, but it's over."

"You never think about me?"

"Not really."

"Not even in Russia?"

"What do you mean?"

"Ell said you'd just returned from there."

"That's odd."

"Why?"

"He didn't know I was there."

"Well, he must have known."

"But why did he mention it?"

"Ask him."

"I will."

"Did you go to Leningrad?"

"Yes."

"There you must have thought about me."

"I didn't think about you. I remembered you. That's all."

"Because you thought about somebody else?"

"Others, to be precise. I hope it won't shock you, but my life in Florida is not exactly given to celibacy. The Upstairs isn't popular because of its firm stand against promiscuity."

"Anyone who matters?"

"Yes, now and then. In Russia, for instance..."

"You're a poor liar."

"Am I?"

"You were still angry with me when we talked about that lunch."

"Yes, I suppose I was. It's not a particularly pleasant memory, you know."

"You wouldn't have been angry if I didn't matter to you anymore."

"Please yourself."

"Don't worry, I don't want to start again with you. Not any more than you do. And not unless it's all aboveboard."

"Why did you say it's becoming hard to live with him?"

"All sorts of reasons. His behavior, his complaints about not having any children."

"Why haven't you had any?"

"We couldn't."

"I'm sorry."

"Are you, Helm? Are you really?"

"Yes, of course. Why couldn't you have children?" She turned away, then spun around to face him with defiance. Rust thought he understood. "Was it because of Ell?"

"No, because of you, you fool."

"How do I come into this?"

She crushed her cigarette and lit another one. "I suppose you might as well know."

"What?"

"I was pregnant after Leningrad. And I was tempted to keep the baby. But the strain would have been too much for me. To live with that kind of reminder forever. So I went to Switzerland. I have friends there. They arranged an abortion for me. And the guy made a mess of it. And a mess of me. That's all."

Rust took and squeezed her hand, then let go of it. "I'm sorry."

"It's all right. Didn't mean to make you feel guilty. It's been a long time. It was tough when it happened, but friends helped me to get over it. It was good to see them all again, and that made it easier."

"How come you have so many friends there?"

"I lived there for quite a while."

"Where?"

"Are you trying to shift the conversation to neutral ground?"

"No. It was a genuine question."

"Oh yes, indeed. I didn't recognize it; we've never had time to indulge in small talk. But it's never too late, I suppose. So, hello, Mr. Rust, how nice to meet you, do you come here often? And where do you take your vacations? As for me, I usually go to Switzerland, I just love those mountains, you know, but that wasn't what you were asking, was it? Oh yes, you wanted to know where I lived over there. Well, mostly in Zurich, but also in Geneva which I loved so much. Do you know Geneva, Mr. Rust?" His hard gaze stopped her. "Did I say something wrong, Mr. Rust?"

"My father loved Geneva."

"Oh."

"When I met him in Moscow a few years ago, he kept remembering the town, the Red Cross building, the lake with the Jeddo. He had a tough time . . . I mean since then. And he's forgotten most things, but that building and that hundred and thirty meters of jetting water still represent his past, a different life."

"Hundred and thirty meters?"

"Yes, well over four hundred feet."

"When was he there?"

"Oh, about 1930, I guess."

"There was no water jet there at that time."

"There was."

"It was constructed after the war."

"No. He's been in Russia since about '31 or '32, but he remembers the jet, so it must have been there much earlier than you think."

"I don't know. You may be right." She stopped to listen to some noise outside. It was the front door. "It must be Lanigan."

"And the colonel, I hope."

"I don't. It's been nice to be with you. Even when you were rude. and cruel to me. But as you said, it can't be helped. Nothing's changed. So it's goodbye time again, I suppose."

He looked her up and down with a mixture of undisguised warmth and lust. The noises of movement grew louder outside. A door was banged shut. He slowly adjusted his face. His mouth stretched into a smile. "How about . . . I mean, let's try to be friends."

"Let's. It seems we have a lot in common."

The door opened. Two men came in. The first, a small, dapper character in a conservative gray suit with a bottle-green suede vest, faced Rust. "Mr. Rust? Alias Craig?"

"That's right."

"I'm Mann." He didn't bother to introduce his tall companion, an ascetic figure with deep-set eyes and endless limbs. "And you must be Mrs. Repson. Please to meet you, ma'am."

"Colonel."

"I thought you two knew each other," said Rust.

"No, I haven't had the pleasure. Right. Can I have your passport, sir?"

"What for?"

"Identification."

"I thought Mrs. Repson's presence would be good enough."

"Are you trying to make things difficult for me, Mr. Rust?"

Rust took out his passport but did not hand it over. "No. How about yourself? I haven't seen your card yet."

Mann nodded. "True." He took out his CIA card but did not show it to Rust.

Anna laughed. "How stupid men can get."

"That's right, Mrs. Repson," said Mann. "And we might

prefer to conduct our stupid business in private, if you don't mind."

"I don't."

"Stay," said Rust. "The colonel and I won't discuss any secrets."

Mann continued to address Anna: "It's on your husband's orders, ma'am, nothing personal, and no insult intended, you understand."

She started toward the door. With no more than a twitch of his head he motioned the tall man to go with her. "See to it that Mrs. Repson has everything she needs." He held out his CIA card to Rust when the door closed.

"Okay, colonel, let's not waste time, I believe you. Now could you please arrange a meeting for me?"

"With whom?"

"The President."

"Very funny."

"It wasn't meant to be."

"No? Oh, I'm sorry. Maybe I should have asked which President you had in mind? Lincoln? Roosevelt? Take your pick, sir."

"My brother said you'd do anything he could do for me."

"That's right."

"Well, I'll settle for someone very close to the President."

"I'll see what I can do. But Ell, I mean your brother, said that first you'd tell me what it's all about."

"It's information of utmost importance."

"Concerning what?"

"That I can't tell you."

"Then how can you expect me to help you?"

"My brother promised. He knows me well enough not to imagine that I'd try to waste anybody's time if I didn't think it was something important."

"But I'm not your brother. So with due respect, sir, you ought to try to convince me."

"Okay, let's get him on the phone."

"He can't be reached just now." The tall man returned, and Mann questioned him with an almost imperceptible raise of his eyebrows. The man nodded and positioned himself in front of the door.

"Anna, I mean Mrs. Repson, will know how to contact him."

"What's your opinion, George?" Mann asked. "Would she know?"

"Not just now." The drawn, tight-skinned face produced a grimace that might have been mistaken for a smile.

"I'll ask her."

"Don't," said Mann. "Come on, let's sit down over there. George will give us a drink. George, have a look at what's in the box."

"I'll have the Kentucky," said Rust as he walked toward George. "Pour me a large one while I talk to Mrs. Repson."

George did not move from the door. Rust faced him. Would he need to fight his way out? They stood almost nose to nose.

"Mr. Rust. I said, come over here."

Rust ignored Mann and concentrated on the tall man at the door. "Go on, pour, George, there's a good lad." He stepped back a little to give him the distance he needed for hitting the man hard if there was no other way. There was a soft click and almost immediately a tremendous explosion next to his right ear. Rust froze. He saw a huge hole torn in the wall. Powdered plaster made the air foggy. He spent a split second waiting for the pain. It didn't come. He was not hurt. He turned slowly toward Mann, who was retreating, holding a .357 Magnum. "What's..." Rust began but stopped. The explosion had temporarily deafened him. His own voice was strange. He was not sure if any sound had come out of his throat. He tried again. "What's the joke?"

"Joke? It was no joke. I could have blown your head off."

Rust could not be sure whether he was hearing or lip-reading the words. "With artillery like that? Sure you could. Why didn't you?"

"It was just a warning. I had a feeling you might want to hit George. Now let's sit down and be friends again. You were going to have a drink and tell me about that message."

"I didn't mention any message. I only said information. It must have been Ell who said message, right?"

"Message, information, whatever it is." Mann motioned him with the Colt toward an armchair.

"You're bluffing, sweetheart. You didn't shoot me because

you're not authorized to shoot me. Because Ell wants you to ask questions and deliver answers, not a corpse."

"Don't bank on it."

"Shouldn't I?" Rust started slowly toward him. "Let's see your hand. I don't think you hold that royal flush. No. I'll credit you with a pair of aces, if that." Rust was shuffling inch by inch toward him. Mann raised the gun. Could that be on Ell's orders? Rust stopped. Although the pressure and the ringing in his right ear blurred his hearing, he picked out the creaking of floorboards behind him. He knew that George could not be more than a couple of feet away. If they were not supposed to shoot him, he might have a chance to knock down George and escape. "Didn't you hear me? I'm calling your bluff."

From somewhere upstairs, probably through several closed doors, came a piercing scream followed by Anna's cry: "Helm!" With a reflex reaction everybody looked up. Rust made a millisecond faster recovery than the others. He whirled around, swinging the back of his right fist blindly in the direction where George ought to be, hoping to follow up with his left. He calculated the height and distance well. His knuckles caught the taller man on the side of the mouth. He knew the damage he must have inflicted from the pain shooting up his own arm.

"Helm! Lanigan! Help!" She was hammering on a door. "Help!"

Rust was halfway to the door when a crippling kick landed on his kidney. He collapsed and rolled to the left to face Mann, who was about to kick him for the second time. Rust caught his foot and twisted it hard. Mann did not resist the force and went flying down. He knows what he's doing, thought Rust, and for a flash, reminded by Anna's yelling, he wondered what on earth had happened to Lanigan. Then something dark rose above him, dark as George's heavy shoes, and everything went black.

The door opened. The orderly stared at it, then jumped to his feet. Led by a general of the GRU, several men stormed in. A full colonel and a small fat major of the KGB, two civilians, border guards.

"Is Colonel Muratova in her office?"

The orderly, winded by the unexpected visit, managed to nod before he could conjure up a *da*.

"You wait in the corridor in case we need you." The general pushed the door in and led the men into the office.

Yelena looked up in anger, then quickly stood to attention. "Comrade general." She was wearing her GRU uniform. The general silenced her with an irritated snap of his fingers, then rounded the desk and sat in her chair. The KGB colonel took the other chair, and the other men formed a half circle. A lieutenant and a corporal of the KGB border guards scrutinized her openly.

"Major Boychenko of the KGB has a few questions for you, Nina Ivanovna. Answer them with precision. It's very important."

Boychenko would have preferred to question her in some other place and in more formal circumstances where he would sit and her greater height would not belittle him, but the choice was not his, and he had to make a good impression on the general and the Spetsburo colonel. "Colonel Muratova," he began in what he hoped would be the voice of authority, "where have you spent the last ten days?"

She looked at the general.

"You may answer," he said.

"I was investigating Colonel Penkovsky's background."

Boychenko was about to say something, but the Spetsburo colonel cut in first: "I thought that case was in the hands of KGB security."

"It was and it is," said the general, "but as he's on the staff of GRU HQ, we've found it prudent to carry out a general background check and establish how or where the traitor might have compromised our operations. After all, he might have had associates."

"That would all be covered by security. KGB security."

Answering Boychenko's questions, Yelena accounted for her movements in the past nine days. She said she had worked mostly on her own but had been in contact with various officers who could verify her statements. She struggled to disguise her initial shock: how had they got to her so soon?

"Where did you go when you left Moscow?"

"Are you suggesting that I did leave Moscow?"

"Didn't you?"

"No."

"Where did you spend the last six days?"

"On observation duty. Using a plain pool car, registration number MC 35-45."

"Can we verify that?"

"Of course. I was seen by others. And I was in regular contact with Arbatskaya Ploshchad on the phone and by radio."

"You called?"

"Sometimes. But sometimes HQ called me." She smiled with great confidence. The woman who had acted as her double throughout the past nine days could never be found. "Is there any question about my activities? Am I under some sort of investigation?"

"No, no, not at all, Comrade Muratova, just routine." Boychenko smiled. "It's a standard set of questions I'm obliged to ask." He looked at the lieutenant and the corporal of the border guards. Both of them shook their heads slightly. "No?"

"Don't think so, comrade major," the lieutenant said. "But I can't be positive, of course. It was just a glimpse."

Boychenko asked a few personal questions about her background, then a few more casual ones about her favorite pastime. "Do you play any sports?"

"No, not regularly."

"Do you follow any? Gymnastics? Soccer?"

"Soccer? Yes, that's something I'm very interested in." She could sense the suddenly rising tension in the men's faces. "Whenever I hear that there's a match somewhere, I run as far as I can from it."

They all laughed. Boychenko was still laughing when he asked: "What do you know about Roost? I beg your pardon— Rust, that's how they pronounce it, don't they?"

"Roost? Rust? Oh yes. I remember now. It must have been five or six years ago."

"We all know what her role was in setting up the operation in 1956, don't we?" asked the general.

"Yes, of course, general, but I thought she might . . ."

"Remember?" she asked. "Yes, I do. It was quite an interesting idea. Unfortunately, an abortive one. At least as far as I know, we've never followed it up—or did we?"

"You met him at the time?"

"No. Never."

"But you'd recognize him."

"Yes, I suppose if I saw a picture, I might."

"This one?"

She looked at a photograph. "No."

"This?"

"No." She kept shaking her head as he produced more and more photographs. None was Rust's. Then she saw a face she knew. Florian. "This is Captain Khomenko. He works in this building."

"Really?"

"You must have checked it, surely."

"Do you know him well?"

"He used to work for me."

"Where's he now?"

"He's been transferred to facilities, field operations, that is."

"But where is he right now? I mean, physically."

"I saw him a few weeks ago when he mentioned that he was to be awarded for good work with a fortnight's holiday in Sochi or Yalta or somewhere around there. I can't remember exactly, but we could check this easily. Do you want me to?"

"Not just now."

"What's he up to? I mean, is he involved with something?" She felt she had to show some interest, or at least natural curiosity. She knew that there was something wrong with Florian, because he had not been in contact as arranged. But the question was, what was wrong? Was he suspected or under routine investigation? Couldn't be routine, not in connection with questions about Rust. So was he free or under arrest? If captured, was he alive? If yes, that would explain how Boychenko and his pack had got to her so fast. But no, Florian would not be taken alive. He would not want to be subjected to interrogation. "I don't want to be nosy, of course, but I found Khomenko a good and conscientious officer, not particularly bright, but extremely reliable." Well done, she patted herself on the shoulder: a favorable statement about a man under investigation could come only from someone who was completely in the clear.

"Any idea why he would have gone to Leningrad?"

"Leningrad? No. Well, I mean no reason I can think of." Now she knew that Florian was in serious trouble. Her next question was, had they already connected him with her or were they just checking out possible female associates who might have had a chance to be with him in Leningrad?

"In your opinion, Comrade Muratova, why would the captain need an American 'shoe'?"

"I had no idea." So that was it. Either the cobbler had reported the request to the KGB or they had searched Khomenko's home in Moscow—or both. For Yelena had taken the precaution of hiding the Arthur Foster passport in Khomenko's Moscow home. If he was captured and interrogated, he would be forced to confess that he had passed the papers on to Yelena—a confession that would not be borne out by the fact that the passport was found in his home. It would prove Khomenko a liar and reduce Yelena to a figment of his imagination.

"Do you think he might have wanted to use the passport himself?"

"What for?"

"Perhaps he was planning to escape."

"I wouldn't know."

"Wouldn't he tell you?"

"Why should he?"

"Because he was in love with you, wasn't he?"

She knew that she was watched closely by all the men in the room. Boychenko must have picked up some old gossip, and, she had to admit, he had introduced it quite cleverly, quickly and without warning. So she parried it with a carefully controlled slow smile. "Oh, that. Yes, that used to be a standard joke in the section. I mean, when he worked for me. People kept teasing him about it."

"Why?"

"Why not?"

"Why him? Why not somebody else?"

"I don't know. Perhaps once he said something nice about me. Certainly not to me. And I have a feeling that they never tired of teasing him only because he reacted so angrily."

Boychenko did not believe her. There was something here. There had to be. And he could get it out of her in no time. But they would not let him. This was just a routine questioning. One of many to discover if any woman officer had had an opportunity to be Khomenko's associate and play, for instance, the doctor in the ambulance. This Colonel Muratova seemed

to have had at least half an opportunity, even if it was covered
by a reasonable alibi. It was killing him that he had to apologize
for asking her to notify him if she had to leave the capital for
any reason in the next few days. He felt it in his bones, and
all his experience was telling him, that her connection with
Khomenko could not be just one of those things; her involvement with "setting up the original operation with Rust in '56"—
whatever that secret operation might have been—would be just
too much of a coincidence.

Yelena accepted his apologies with comradely sympathy.
No, it was no trouble at all, she would be glad to help in any
way if that was required. Of course she would contact Major
Boychenko if she planned to leave Moscow for any reason, but
at the moment, she had no such plans. Which was not quite
true. In the last few minutes, she had begun to think about
Odessa. Hotel Tsentralnaya. It would have been very difficult
to make the journey with Rust, but she, on her own, could get
there and enter even the restricted port area without too much
trouble. It was reassuring to know that should she need it, there
was at least somewhere to run to.

Rust tried to swim, but his hands and feet disobeyed him.
No, they did not disobey him. It was he himself who could
not move them. Though he knew he must be drowning. There
was water in his nose and ears, but not in his mouth. He could
not open his mouth. Only his eyes would open. More water
rushed at him, and he had to shut his eyes quickly.

"Come on, come on, you've rested long enough, come on!"

The voice reached Rust as he moved and water ran out of
his ear. He began to feel pain in his head where he had been
kicked, and regained consciousness. He was lying in a pool of
water. His mouth would still not open. It was taped firmly.
His hands and feet were wired together so tightly that the raw
metal had drawn blood at several places around his wrists.
Mann, with his back to the window, loomed above him, swinging an empty bucket lazily. Rust had some difficulty breathing.
One of his nostrils was blocked. Might be catching a cold—
it was just a subconscious reflex thought, and the absurdity of
worrying about such a minor ailment in the circumstances almost made him chuckle. It could only be his eyes that gave
him away.

"What's so funny?"

Rust could not answer. Mann did not pursue it, because the door opened and George returned. The thin face was completely distorted by the still-swelling lump and the cut at the corner of his mouth where Rust's backhand had caught him.

"What happened?"

"It's all right." George spoke with obvious difficulty. It gave Rust the hope that the man had at least a few broken teeth.

"I said, what happened?"

"She must have scraped her face against the floorboards until the tape came off. Her face is full of scratches."

"Okay now?"

"Yeah. I fixed her."

"You mean . . . ?"

"No, no. Just ran the tape around her head. And restricted her movement a little." George began to laugh, but stopped right away because of the pain it caused.

"Good. We may need her later."

"How about this one?" George kicked Rust in the ribs.

"I think he'll be more sensible now."

"Shall we start?"

"No, not yet. He might want to volunteer some answers. Let's not make it hard on him. Just remove the tape, George."

The tall man pulled off the tape slowly.

"Where's Lanigan?" Rust asked.

"Ugh." Mann frowned with disgust. "He's an awful mess. Don't even mention him." He turned to his partner. "It's not nice, George. What's got to be done has got to be done; there's no need to overdo it." He pulled a chair up to Rust and sat down. "Now, Mr. Rust, let's have your story."

"What story?"

"Don't make it hard on yourself, please don't. Ell won't be pleased when I tell him about the delays you've caused."

"I don't believe that you're reporting to Ell. And I think you're making a bad mistake, whoever you are."

"You hear that, George? He doesn't believe us. He thinks we're making a mistake. You know something, Mr. Rust? I know some brutes who wouldn't allow you to doubt their word. They'd kick your balls until you had three Adam's apples. You're lucky that I'm not one of those. So why not tell me what the message is? All right, all right, you want to call it information, although I'm sure that Ell said 'message' to me."

"Did Ell also mention that you must hurt his wife?"

"Well, not in so many words."

"He loves her."

"He used to love her. True. But it's not a very good marriage these days, as eventually he'll tell you himself, I'm sure."

"Bullshit."

George stepped nearer.

"Not yet, George, not yet. I'm a firm believer in the power of reasoning, and I think Mr. Rust is a reasonable man. So let me just put all my cards on the table, Mr. Rust. After all, you were calling my bluff, weren't you? Okay, I'll be absolutely frank with you."

Rust was stung by the promise. That was how Yelena would introduce all her fibs, half-truths and absolute *vranyo*.

"Yes, I think you've guessed it. We're not what you'd call regular CIA. But you and we are on the same side."

"It doesn't seem to be much fun to be your ally, Mann."

"I won't accept that. Don't forget, you started the rough stuff. Look at poor George. It's not nice what you've done to him, is it? So be reasonable. We can't allow you a repeat performance, can we?"

"Cut out the bullshit, will you?"

"Right. I like you, Rust. You're a man of action. Like me. So here you are. We know that you're bringing a message from Moscow about *porokhovyye konfety*." He allowed himself the pleasure of taking gleeful notice of the blood running out of Rust's face. "Cuban confetti, to be precise. Which, we both know, means 'missiles' in that most obnoxious KGB parlance. You once forwarded a stolen document about this, and when a stupid little Cuban whore died for it, you should have been warned not to dabble in other people's games. But you failed to read the writing on the wall. Pity. Now you're trying it again, against all odds. After all, as you see, we already know what's going on, and we know the message."

"Amazing." Rust expected the pressure to increase. Sooner or later he would have to admit a few things. The question was what to say. And that depended on what they already knew. It was essential to find out more about Mann's hand. "Okay, tell me what you want to know."

"Why did you go to the Soviet Union?"

"I had an assignment for a magazine."

"Just...out of the blue."

"That's right."

"And when you got there somebody approached you and asked you to deliver the message."

"Sort of."

"What sort of?"

"He said—"

"He?"

"Yes."

"One man?"

"Yes."

"Your father?"

"No."

"No. Just a man. A stranger?"

"Yes. But he seemed to know a lot about me. That's why he approached me, he said."

"What did he know about you?"

"That my brother was working for the government."

"He knew that?"

"Yes. He wanted me to deliver the message to my brother."

"So what was the message?"

"Just what you said. That nukes are going into Cuba."

"And you took his word for it?"

"Not quite, but it sounded interesting."

"You didn't ask for proof."

"I did, but he said no proof was necessary. Only a warning to the American government. They'd know what to do."

"And who was the man?"

"I don't know. He said he was a friend of America, and he wanted to help."

"That won't do, Rust, and you know it."

"That's all there is. I can't remember any more."

"Well, you'll have to try harder. George..."

The tall man brought in a shabby suitcase and unpacked a large tape recorder, an amplifier, an assortment of wires and adjustable earphones. He half-lifted out a Plexiglass container, about the size of a shoebox, and stared into it. "Poor, poor Fidel, you're getting very bored in there, my pet, but don't worry, you'll soon be out of that box."

Rust could not see what Fidel was.

"Leave it alone and get me the beaker," rasped Mann.

The two of them worked with fuss-free, well-rehearsed efficiency. George got out a beaker, Mann filled it with water. Mann dissolved several tablets in the water, George affixed a large bulldog clip to Rust's nose. His nostrils blocked, Rust had to breathe through his mouth. "That's how bad little boys are made to drink their medicine, Rust. So be a good boy." George held Rust's head firmly, and Mann forced the liquid into his mouth. "Don't worry, it's only a laxative. It'll give you the biggest bowel wash you can dream of. You'll see how nice it is."

Softening up. It must be part of a planned process of softening up. Rust tried to pay no attention to the preparations and forced himself to concentrate. The problem was when to begin to talk and how much to say. People who did not want to give away any secrets and held out under torture would break at some point and confess everything—or die first. Rust did not want to die. He knew that Yelena had taken precautions. "If you're caught, you tell them everything." So eventually, he could tell them her lies, everything she had obviously made clear and memorable for him. That she was a cabby. A Dynamo supporter. But not the occasional slips of GRU language. The ambulance? Yes. And the Foster passport. Things these two might already know. But if Yelena had an alibi for these potential confessions by Rust, he must convince them that he had reached the breaking point and was telling the truth at last. Which called for a double bluff. He must feed them with his own lies first, and tell Yelena's lies as the final version. But how could he gauge the amount of pain he would have to withstand to make it all believable?

Muffled, distant screams pierced the ceiling. They came probably through several doors. "That's how you fixed her?" Mann was fuming. Rust thought he would hit George, who now stood up, determined to fix her more effectively. "I'll do it," said Mann. "You get on with this."

Anna's screams could still be heard when George removed the nose clip and put the large earphones on Rust. He adjusted the metal strap until the pads became airtight, pressed to Rust's face and skull. He returned to the tape recorder, threaded a tape through, started the machine, fiddled with various knobs on the amplifier, then flicked a switch. Tons of thunder fell freely on Rust's eardrums and made him cry out with pain. George nodded. "Just testing," he mumbled, and switched off the machine. Relieved from the pressure, Rust's eardrums felt as if they were trying to bulge outward.

George connected several gauges to the amplifier. He looked up and listened. His hands paused in midair. Then a satisfied nod, and he carried on with his job. Presumably, the screams had stopped upstairs. His pouting indicated to Rust that he was whistling, like so many other good craftsmen, totally absorbed in his work.

Rust began to shiver intensely. His body had given him no advance warning. As if his guts knew ahead of his brain what was to come. His lungs tried to release an immense bubble of air. His throat wanted to cry. *No! Please don't!* He closed his eyes and tried desperately not to think. But his brain cells obeyed his subconscious. "Keep warm. Don't let yourself be tortured. Beg them to listen. Tell them everything. Admit to yourself what you've known since Anna's first scream, that these men cannot be CIA. They must be Russians. Or working for them. For the people who've killed Holly. But Moscow wouldn't know how or where to find you. Not unless they've got it out of Florian or Yelena. Not Florian. Only Yelena. Florian knows nothing about the Craig passport. In which case it's no good to suffer trying to protect her. But Ell knew the name. And your time of arrival. And Charles might know it. Charles might have tracked you all the way, after all. As Mann tracked you, despite Lanigan's tactics, from the airport."

Rust's shivering became uncontrollable. Like his father's in the church. It was not the cold. It was fear. It would be no good to keep warm. He wished they had taped his mouth. It would prevent his cries giving them satisfaction.

Mann returned. He checked what George was doing, then took a roll of wide adhesive tape and closed Rust's eyes with it. He stuck on layer upon layer until all the light was excluded. Total darkness and total silence. Disorientation began right away. Then a spasm of colic. The pain was accompanied by nausea. He broke out in cold sweat. What if the drug made him vomit? What if they taped his mouth and it could not come out? He would drown. Without a chance to cry for help, beg for mercy, confess anything and more. Stop it, Rust, stop it at once, he scolded himself. Your own imagination is their strongest weapon. Stop it. Suddenly he was not quite sure if he had talked to himself aloud. So it was dangerous even to think.

The thunder hit him from both sides once again. The pressure was unbearable, yet increasing. It had a mind-numbing, paralyzing effect. The shivering stopped. His neck muscles tightened dangerously, as if trying to snap in defiance of the blaring onslaught. *Cry out! Cry out! Tell them they've won!* His throat and mouth were too numb to obey. Because for the first time, he was hit by the certainty that once he broke down and told them what they accepted as truth, they could not allow him to live. And what about Lanigan? And Anna? Did Ell want them all dead?

"Nothing, nothing, fucking nothing." Schramm brought down his fist hard, intent on hammering the small bar table into the floor, but forcing only the glasses to hop. The few late-night drinkers made a point of paying no attention to him: this was not the place for table-banging or foul language. A worn man, obviously disinclined to leave and face home, did not even look up. The middle-aged couple in the corner, with illicit love written all over them, had eyes only for each other. The butch executive, queening over a bunch of office juniors, ordered another round and spared only a glance for the entrance: was it the wind that had banged the door?

"Fucking nothing," repeated Schramm, because he hated to be ignored. He had just returned from the telephone, and "nothing" was the summary of information he could offer to Charles. "My guess is that he's still here. It's reasonably certain that he hasn't taken a flight, train or Greyhound to get out of New York. But he might have driven a car. Or walked."

"Or taken an ambulance," said Charles.

"Right."

Schramm waved toward the barman. They had been drinking in there long enough for the man to know their orders. "I'll have to phone Repson."

"Do you think that's a good idea?"

"You mean you don't?"

"Yes, you could put it that way."

"Then why the fuck don't you say so in the first place, Sir Charles, dear boy?"

"Because after a full day's frustration cum drinking, I think we're getting on each other's nerves even without sharp pronouncements on right and wrong."

"Thank you, Sir Charles. So I take it that you're diametrically opposed to calling Repson and asking if he knows where Rust is."

"Correct."

"So what the hell do you suggest we do?"

"Call Repson, of course. But only because I have nothing better to suggest."

"Great."

"Just don't tell him, at least not at this stage, what we know."

"Agreed."

Repson answered the phone so promptly that it suggested to Schramm he must have been sitting right next to the instrument. "Where are you, Jake?"

"In New York."

"Still on vacation?"

"How did you know I was?"

"I called your office a few days ago and they told me."

"Anything specific you wanted, sir?"

"No. I mean yes. I wanted to ask you about Helm. I mean, if you knew where he was."

"I don't. And that's exactly why I'm calling. I've just come back from London, where somebody mentioned that Rust might have been there."

"He was. And for all I know, he might still be there."

"What do you mean?"

"He called me. He said he must see me urgently in New York. I couldn't go, but promised to send a couple of guys to meet him at Idlewild."

"Guys? A couple of guys?"

"That's what I said."

"And?"

"We arranged he'd meet them at the Hertz desk. He never turned up. That's all."

"But your two guys were there."

"Do I have to repeat everything? Is this a bad line or something?"

"No. Sorry."

"Who told you about Helm in London?"

"Er, I think..."

"Don't bullshit me, Jake, of course you remember."

"Yeah. Sir Charles, I think."

"Okay, I'll put through a call to him. Call me back later if you like."

Schramm hung up and told Charles what Repson had said. "Will London tell him where you are?"

"No, they'll take a message so that I could ring him back. Which is good. Keeps us in touch with him. Rust may contact him again."

"He may. Or he may already be with his brother in Washington."

"You think Repson lied to you?"

"I don't know. He sounded odd. Tense. But it could be anything. Maybe it's only that I called at the wrong moment. Perhaps he was just screwing the delectable Anna."

• Sunday, September 30 •

Brezhnev's visit to Tito leads to frequent embraces and spate of speculation: Can Khrushchev contain internal opposition and rivals' aspirations? McNamara announces: U.S. and Allied aircraft armed with nuclear weapons are on stand-by near East German frontier to guarantee Berlin access. Mississippi University riots: 400 U.S. Marshals and 3,000 Federal troops enforce registration of first Negro student; two men killed, 70 injured, 150 arrested. Two Soviet diplomats are made *personae non grata*: they were caught buying U.S. Naval documents from American sailor in roadside restaurant in Larchmont, N.Y.

THE PITCH AND VOLUME OF THE AUDIO BATTERING KEPT changing. It never gave Rust's ears a chance to adjust and seek refuge in numbness. The first time the colic threatened to burst his guts, he fought it off. Then the spasmodic griping pain grew in intensity and frequency. Let me go to the john, he thought he said, but could not be sure. Then his mind escaped

249

from the pain in a pipedream about glorious bursts of diarrhea. He was not even sure when the floodgates had broken down for the first time. His clothes absorbed some of the foul liquid, but he knew he lay in a growing pool. He sat up and shook his head violently, but the earphone strap held. He knew he shouldn't have done that. He knew from experience that his punishment would be prompt and cruelly measured to cause maximum pain without permanent damage. And there it was: the volume increased and made him cry out like a baby. Baby! Baby! Toddlers taunting. Was it just hallucination? His urine flowed freely. The pool grew yet again. And then he threw up. The nausea was only the cause. The stench and helpless humiliation were the trigger. He was wailing, at least he thought he was. Vomit erupted again and again. The high pitch once more. That was the worst. "The art is to know when to admit defeat." What was that? Who said that? It came from a distant and improbable past when somebody's remark would have seemed like crazy speculation. In total exhaustion, he threw himself back, knocking his head hard against the floor. Sinking, sinking, fainting or falling asleep—it made no difference at last. His mouth popped open. "Schramm, Schramm said it. Cutting your losses could be your first step toward recovery. Good old Schramm . . . ramm . . . am . . . ammeter . . . Monsieur Ampère . . . Rust, you're not paying attention. What have you done, Helm? You know you mustn't do things like that—you must tell Mummy when you want to go out. And when the plops, and when the plops, and when the plops go marching out . . ."

Something burned his tongue. No, no. It's ice. Melting. Flooding his throat. He had to fight off drowning. And that woke him up, returning him to a world of pain.

He was convinced this had been going on for weeks. And then it would be too late to admit defeat. But he might be mistaken. The whole thing might have lasted no more than minutes. When it would be too soon to cut his losses. They would not believe him.

Mann returned to the room to take over from George. He was tired and hated the sewer air of the room. "Shall we give it a try?"

George shrugged his shoulders. Thirty hours of the "treatment" was not bad for starters, but it was no more than that. Except that time was pressing them.

"Okay. Cut it off."

The sudden silence brought a new type of pain, but that was gone soon. Rust fell asleep. For a few seconds only. The fear of a restart woke him up. But sleep overcame fear and imagination. For a few seconds.

"Okay, let's start again."

"You're the most rotten interrogator I've ever had," Schramm grumbled but did not object. For the past twenty-four hours, he and Charles had taken it in turns to question the other on his knowledge of Rust. By now they had established a likely behavior profile—what Rust would or would not do in various situations, due to background, character and experience.

"Never mind, dear boy, let's just start again. You were largely responsible for his original training."

"It was too short. He'd have long forgotten most of it."

"Not the original instructions. That's when you're the keenest. So you remember all the futile and the trivial, everything you'd call, no doubt, bullshitting."

"Bullshit."

"Fifteen love, Jake."

"What?"

"I mean I'm winning. You said what I guessed you would. And I still remember my first instructor, a right old Colonel Blimp, saying, 'When you think you're followed, you must start whistling, because men whistling in the street are not only ill-mannered louts but eminently carefree, too.' Not the sort of stuff you'd expect me to memorize, right?"

"I wouldn't know."

"Thank you. But never mind. Let's see what the great stuff you taught Rust was."

"I can't remember."

"Try, Jake, try. You wouldn't change your ways of thinking. The basic attitudes. Now suppose I'm a new recruit. And you want me to hide something. What would you suggest?"

"I don't know. Depends what you want to hide."

"A plastic bag, for instance."

"Give it to somebody you trust. Failing that, find an outsider. Somebody with no ax to grind."

"An air hostess?"

"Perhaps."

"She might think you're smuggling."

"Then a passenger. Find an accessible hiding place. Make use of obvious facilities."

"What facilities?" Charles pounced.

"Anything natural in the circumstances."

Forty minutes later they stood at the airport Lost Property office, another forty minutes later they managed to convince the stickler in charge that Schramm must inspect the plastic bag "lost" on Rust's flight. The unaddressed postcard to Hal made Schramm laugh. "Yeah, yeah, it's the trick I taught him, all right."

One bar of soap, one blank notepad, one pair of sunglasses, souvenir matches, half a bottle of scotch, one multilingual dictionary, one razor, one pen. It had to be the razor, the pen, the matches or the dictionary.

"If it's the pen or the razor, we'll know in five minutes. If it's the matches, it won't take long to find a microdot or two. But if it's the dictionary, you can start swearing now," concluded Charles. "Next summer we may still be at it."

They took the pen and the razor apart. Neither yielded any clues. Schramm slipped a miniature bleeper into the razor. Anybody carrying it could be followed with a receiver from even a few blocks away. Two men were stationed to watch the office and a third was inside, helping at the counter. The expert Schramm called in could not hold out high hopes for quick results. Charles was right: the search might take ages. Their best hope was to wait and watch for Rust. He would have to come and claim his bag.

It hurt when George removed the tape, and Rust's eyes took ages to adjust to the light even though the room was in semi-darkness. He moved his head. It caused thunder in his ears. He knew that the earphones were off, yet he kept feeling the pressure of the metal strap. He saw that Mann was saying something but he couldn't figure out what. Painful whining and thudding floated around inside his skull, bouncing back and forth, hammering and grinding the bones. "Water," he whispered. He would have never believed that he was shouting.

George's face came into focus. "Say please." The mouth conveyed the words through exaggerated articulation.

"Please!" He still thought he was whispering.

George brought in some water and held it a couple of feet above Rust, who tried to sit up. It was an enormous effort. His entire body felt like jelly. The almost continuous diarrhea had drained away all his strength. He tried to push himself up by the back of his head. It was no good. It only made painful echoes worse. George reached down, grabbed his collar and pulled him up. He gaped like a fish, and George laughed as he poured the water too fast for him to swallow. Half the water just flowed down his face. The other half began to run through him by the time George let go of his collar, allowing him to fall back with a thump. The exercise made him dizzy. If only he could sleep a little. He closed his eyes. The whole world was in a mad swirl.

The next time he saw George's face he knew he had slept a little. Something like five minutes or two days. "Sit up," a mouth seemed to say. Rust tried to obey. His hands felt free. He heaved, and almost fell off the bed to where, apparently, he had been moved. Together with his sense of time, his balance must have gone. He grew conscious of the stench. It was sickening. George propped him up with a couple of cushions but had to push him, eventually, into the corner, for Rust was unable to maintain a vertical position without help.

Mann began to ask questions. Rust had to rely mostly on lip-reading. From time to time, the questions had to be written down for him. When he answered, he was incapable of regulating his voice.

"You're lying, of course," said Mann. He did not seem angry. He had expected nothing else at this stage.

Rust protested meekly. No, it was true, they had given him no proof, but it would come to him in Florida. And it was true that he had gone to Russia because of the magazine assignment. And . . . He stopped. If Ell was behind Mann, and if Ell was a traitor, he would probably contact Schramm and enlist his help. Because Schramm knew Rust well, because Schramm might guess how his former pupil's mind worked, because Schramm might be able to figure out how and where some evidence could be hidden. In which case it would be a waste to suffer anymore trying to protect that damned plastic bag. Which would leave

Rust with only two aims in his remaining brief life expectancy: to minimize Anna's suffering and protect Yelena.

Mann was looking at the Tom Craig passport. "Where did you get this?"

"In London."

"Liar."

"All right, in Moscow."

"That's better. What happened to the other one?"

"Will you make a deal?" Rust asked.

"What deal?"

"I'll tell you the answer and you let Mrs. Repson go. She knows nothing about all this."

"I'll think about it."

"You let her go first."

"Are you trying to dictate to me, Mr. Rust? Are you really?"

"No."

"Then tell me. What happened to the Foster passport?"

Mann knew the name. He might know a lot more. Was Yelena in trouble? "You see, I told you the truth the first time. I got the Craig passport in London. I swapped it for the Foster papers."

"Then why did you kill McGregor?"

"I didn't."

"Somebody did."

"I don't know."

"The question is why. You needed his passport to go to London?"

"Yes, but I didn't kill him."

"Tell me about that cabby."

"What cabby?"

"The woman, of course."

"I never mentioned a woman."

"I know. I'm only trying to make it easier for you. There was that woman cabby, don't you remember?"

"Oh yes, you're right. Some soccer fanatic."

"Which team?"

"Locomotiv? Dynamo? I don't know."

"Was she driving when you left Moscow?"

"No."

"Who was?"

"The man."

"What was his name?"

"Florian."

"But she was there, too."

"No. I mean yes. I'm not sure."

"You think some music through earphones could refresh your memory?"

"No. I remember now. She was there. Yes, she sat with me in the back."

"The back of what?"

"The cab, of course. With all the football pictures."

"The cab with the pictures. Aha. And who gave the orders?"

"He did."

"And she obeyed without questions?"

"That's right."

"Then why would he kill her?"

"Kill her?"

"That's what I asked."

"I don't know."

"It was quite a vicious murder."

"Can't be."

"Why not? Was he in love with her?"

"No."

"Perhaps he was her husband."

"Her husband was dead."

"Rust, you're still lying to me."

George grinned and walked over to the suitcase. He slowly lifted out the lid of the Plexiglass box and stirred the contents with a stick. "Come on, Fidel, you may go for walkies. Or play with the gentleman, eh? Would you like that?"

"No, George, Mr. Rust doesn't want to play just now. Probably he's hungry. And thirsty. Look after him, George, he's our guest. And then perhaps a little music, Mr. Rust?"

Even the sight of food was enough to make Rust's stomach turn. But he decided he must eat. Force it down if necessary. And drink, drink, even if they put more of that dreadful laxative in it. While Mann helped him to drink, George reset the tape, then returned with the earphones.

• Monday, October 1 •

The Russian ambassador reassures Kennedy that no offensive weapons have been sent to Cuba. "Berlin wall is sign of weakness," says Chancellor Adenauer. Dean Rusk entertains Foreign Minister Gromyko on 28th floor of Waldorf; chicken Marie Antoinette serves friendship and détente; Laos is discussed, Cuba is not.

THE KREMLIN'S UNDERGROUND WAR ROOM SEEMED EERIE and deserted. Six generals, clustered around the large map of Cuba, tried to look not too hot or embarrassed under the strong spotlight as they answered the endless questions put to them by the single silhouette occupying one plush seat among rows and rows of empty armchairs.

"No, Comrade Nikita Sergeyevich, nobody's trying to sabotage the preparations." "Yes, Comrade Nikita Sergeyevich, the guilty ones will be found and made to account for the dreadful delay." "Yes, Comrade Nikita Sergeyevich, everything's being done to restore momentum and salvage as much as possible of the original schedule." "No, Comrade Nikita Sergeyevich, there's no doubt anymore that by the middle of the month, we'll have our Cuban-based nuclear-strike capability. The only question is whether Kennedy will be willing to use force or accept some sort of compromise."

Khrushchev smiled but did not bother to answer. He knew what the Kennedy attitude would be. He knew for sure.

The way Rust's hands and feet were tied allowed him to throw himself around when the noise or the colic hurt too much. In the evening he fell off the bed, which infuriated George, who had to move a filthy sheet of plastic and kick and push him onto it once again.

Mann slept through the early part of the night. George amused himself poking with a stick at Fidel in the box. By midnight he began to feel the effect of his long stretch on duty. His eyelids grew heavy. Rust had been twitching and twisting quite a bit, but by now, he was almost worn out to the point where no painful noise or diarrhea could keep him awake all the time.

"Are you resting, George? Are you feeling charitable toward him?" Mann had returned very quietly, and his sharp voice startled George.

"I'm sorry."

"He seems to be sleeping."

George reached for the volume knob. "That'll wake him." Rust reacted violently.

"Turn it off," said Mann. "Remove the earphones, peel the tape off his eyes, untie his feet and get him back on the bed."

"It'll make me puke." George tore off the tape. This time it took Rust even longer to adjust to light and silence. Exhaustion and fear fought to control his body. Exhaustion kept winning. He fell asleep again and again.

"Go on, George, puke," said Mann. "It'll keep you awake."

George's angry prodding and rough handling woke up Rust for seconds. Mann placed the Plexiglas box on a low coffee table. Rust could see nothing inside it but bark and withered leaves. Mann put on the thick gardening gloves and reached into the box. He shouted, "George!" The tall man turned. "Catch!" George went white and ducked. Mann laughed heartily. It was a good joke. He had nothing in his gloved hands.

Rust's mouth was so parched that he had to struggle to open

it and ask for water. George gave him some bourbon. Rust drank, coughed, felt renewed pain gripping his bowels, thought, What a waste of good bourbon, and fell asleep. When he woke up again, he was seated on the bed. He was naked from the waist down, his head was surrounded by cushions, his hands and feet were spread-eagled and tied with rope and wire to the bed. Castration! The fright forced his tormented eyes to scan the room in search of sharp instruments. He saw none. Mann came into his field of vision. "Can you hear me?" Mann asked. There was no reaction. He stepped closer and faced Rust. He articulated slowly and clearly. "Can you understand me?"

Rust nodded.

"Good. You'll now have to try to be more positively helpful to us. Otherwise we'll introduce you to Fidel. He's a *Scolopendra gigantea*, a most distinguished member of the arthropod class Chilopoda. He's a uniquely large and magnificent specimen from the East Indies, and he has these venomous little fangs." Mann removed the gloves. "Now, when I say 'venomous,' I don't mean fatal, because his bite hardly ever kills directly, but, and it's a big but, it can cause probably the worst pain anybody's ever had. Some people who were bitten found suicide preferable to suffering. Others smashed up their skulls in a mad effort to relieve the pain at least temporarily. But we wouldn't want you to do any such stupid things. That's why you're surrounded by those lovely cushions, right, George?"

"Yeah, yeah, now let's get on with it and get out of here."

"A fine intention, George, but you forget that these things can't be rushed. Mr. Rust must understand what's going to happen. And he wants to understand—don't you, Mr. Rust? Or may I call you Helm? Perhaps Helmut?"

Helmut. The word and its pronunciation conjured up memories of his father and Yelena. That first meeting in Moscow. Do you care about peace? Cut out the big words, sweetheart. If they get you, you'll tell them everything. Sorry, Yelena, the time's come.

Hardly any of Mann's voice penetrated Rust's ears. When he did not watch the mouth, he heard nothing. Only Yelena's voice. Asking about the girl in Leningrad. What happened to her? Do you still love her?

"Anna," Rust shouted, firmly convinced that he was whis-

pering. "She knows nothing. You promised to let her go. We
made a deal, Mann."

"A deal? What deal? Do you know about any deals, George?"

"Yeah. He wants to tell you everything."

"Okay, let's try."

The temptation was tremendous. Rust longed to pour out
everything he could think of. But would they now believe the
truth? Or would they accept lies that there was no conspiracy,
the information came from an individual, and his father was
not involved, that he could not describe the cabby, and that
they gave him no proof?

Mann repeated his earlier questions, then introduced some
new ones. These revealed that he had detailed information that
must have come from Moscow.

"You didn't leave Moscow by taxi, did you?"

"We did."

"You left by ambulance."

"If you say so."

"Where did you abandon the ambulance?"

"Will you let Mrs. Repson go?"

"Okay, Helm, you're a good in-law. Now, where did you
abandon the ambulance?"

"At the railway station."

"Where?"

"Kolchugino."

"Impossible. The ambulance would have been seen at the
Kolchugino checkpoint when coming off the Ivanovo road. But
it wasn't."

"It's amazing what you CIA boys know."

"And you're impertinent, Helmut." Mann stepped closer to
the bed.

George leaned over Rust to speak right into his face: "We'll
send Fidel on a walkie-talkie. He walkie, you talkie!" He found
the joke side-splittingly funny. "And perhaps we'll send Fidel
for another walkie-talkie on Mrs. Repson's cunt!" He guf-
fawed and picked up the gardening gloves.

"No," Rust protested. "Why don't you ask more questions?"

"Because you're wasting our time with lies," said Mann.
"But I'll give you a fair chance. We'll give you a jab which
is just a diluted version of Fidel's original." He picked a shiny
metal box out of the suitcase and filled a syringe with some

dark liquid. "I guess you'll have a minute to talk to us before you go mad. If in that minute you give some satisfactory answers, I'll give you a second jab to knock you out for a few hours until the worst pain's gone. When you wake up, we'll ask you for some more details. And you'll answer. Or else it won't be a little jab but a real walkie-talkie, right, George?"

"Right."

Mann turned his back on him. Rust tried to lean forward, but his head was taped firmly to the cushions and the bed. He felt no more than a pinprick in his groin. Then nothing. Just the colic. It squeezed a few more drops of liquid out of him. Then an urge to howl. But he could not. A gripping, nerve-writhing torment spread fast with the rushing blood through every vein from his groin. His teeth crunched and cracked. His arms and feet strained against the ropes and wires holding him until his skin split open and blood spurted in a mad effort of multiple self-amputation. And the pain was still increasing.

Mann was already firing questions. He knew he had to be quick. Rust made a superhuman effort to separate his teeth and squeeze words out with the gale of agony that rose from his lungs. He did not know what exactly he was saying. There was no control. Words ran out freely. The cart came from the Red Banner *kilkhoz* in Aleksandrov. So did Fyodor, the old man who drove the van to Moscow. Florian was in love with Yelena. The Foster passport came from her. But she must have swapped it for the Craig passport in the last second to cover her tracks. She gave him the evidence to go with the message.

"Where?"

"At the airport."

"When?"

"Just before the captain died."

"Where's the evidence now?"

"At Idlewild!" Rust screamed. "In a plastic bag."

"Where?"

"In Lost Property."

"How can you reclaim it?"

Rust tried to answer. There was nothing in this world he wanted more than to answer fast and truthfully. But the urge to wail was stronger. And it left no room for any other sound in his throat. He was squirming nonstop as if driven to dance by machine-gun bullets, and he would have smashed his head into anything only too gladly to stop the pain at any cost.

"Give him the jab," Mann urged George.

"Didn't you want to ask anything else?" George broke off the tip of an ampule and filled a second syringe. "He didn't tell you how to reclaim the bag."

"Later. He can't take any more now."

George sought out a vein and injected the antidote with expert firmness. The effect was almost instantaneous.

"I thought the dilution was weaker," Mann mumbled. He looked at his watch. "We had only fifty-seven seconds. I'll complain about this."

Rust sank into comatose sleep, free of pain, questions, decisions and self-accusation.

"He'll be out for several hours, but you keep an eye on him, George," said Mann. "I'll make the call to the office."

• Tuesday, October 2 •

Kennedy and OAS foreign ministers issue communique: Cuban people must be helped to regain their freedom; "Sino-Soviet intervention in Cuba" and expansion of Communism from Cuba remain most urgent problems of hemisphere. Commander Schirra, fifth American in space, completes six-orbit mission. General Taylor is sworn in as Chairman of U.S Joint Chiefs of Staff.

ONLY TWO HOURS AFTER RUST'S ORDEAL IN NEW YORK, the morning rush hour traffic was at its height on the Moscow-Ivanovo road. The Moscow-registered black car was delayed, but Major Boychenko was determined not to be unduly angry. After all, at long last, things were moving again. It was 9:30 when his car rolled through the gates of the Red Banner *kilkhoz* in Aleksandrov.

A few minutes later, old Fyodor Galakhov was summoned to talk to a small, fat and friendly civilian in the back seat of the black car. On demand, Fyodor produced his internal passport. He knew he was not supposed ever to be without it, and he had always complied with the rule. Recently, however, he had not done it only because he was a good citizen, but also because of the new, special value of the document: it had now a truly cherished and enviable "permission to move to Moscow" stamped on one of the blank pages reserved for internal visas and other *spravki*. It was that kindly big bear of a man from the GRU who had arranged it for him. In return, Fyodor only had to take part in that little charade of swapping his cart for a van and driving the van to Moscow. He would have done it for nothing. Anybody would have done it if asked by an officer of the GRU. Fyodor had nothing to fear. Not until this fat civilian asked the ominous question: "Do you want to live in Moscow, then?"

That could spell disaster. For it was known to all that only a fool would not want to live in Moscow, where life was better and easier, and where all the unavailable might sometimes be obtainable, but the invitation to declare his intention brought the Russian Catch-22 into play. For if he said he did want to live in Moscow, it might indicate that he was trying to run away from the small community where he and perhaps his crimes/sins/hostile views/mere laziness were too noticeable. But to claim that he did not want to live in Moscow would reveal that he was trying to hide from the capital's more alert authorities and that he was banking on the inefficiency of the local party and militia that might fail to discover that he was an enemy of the people.

Fyodor had no choice this time. The *spravka* in his passport revealed his intention. And the next trap, he knew, lay only one question away. "Yes, it's an honor to have the permission."

"Indeed. I'm glad you see it that way. And may I ask where you intend to live in Moscow?"

So there it was. Catch-23. "I shall apply to the Moscow Soviet to grant me a room or the share of a room, as they see fit."

"Naturally. Because you've already got a job in Moscow, I presume."

Fyodor did not answer.

"Haven't you got a job? Oh."

"I, I was told that I can get a job there if I'm already a Moscow resident."

"But you can become a resident only if you have a job there. You must know that. Yes, I'm sure you do. So the question is, how do you hope to get that first job or room? Do you have friends in high places? Are you supplying them with a little fruit and meat and vegetables? Perhaps some illegally brewed vodka?"

Fyodor began to protest his innocence, but Major Boychenko—who never bothered to tell him his name or rank— cut him short. "I know, your friend must be the one who arranged this *spravka* for you. Correct? What else did he promise, and for what favors?"

Fyodor knew no more than that the man, who called himself Florian, carried a card with the letters GRU printed on it. It would have certainly been an unimaginable impertinence for him to ask for a closer examination of the card or demand Comrade Florian's full name.

"You're not very cooperative, Fyodor Galakhov." Boychenko grinned. "It might be best if you came to Moscow with me. We'll see what accommodation we can find for you."

George viewed Mann gravely and planned his revenge. He could not yet think of any definite form, but he knew that one day, somehow, Mann would have to pay for all this. For Mann had slept through the early part of the night, then again through dawn and early morning, and now ordered him to make some breakfast. So George rummaged in the cardboard box, found some food and took it to the kitchen. He was inclined to burn Mann's toast, but abandoned the idea because he would only be told to make some more.

To wake up Rust turned out to be a major effort. The persistent din in his ears helped to protect him from the outside world. His entire system was determined not to let him leave the refuge he had found in sleep. Eventually, George had to give him a caffeine injection, and even then they had to walk him up and down to keep him awake while some more questions could be asked. Rust answered them slowly and with great effort. He knew he had no choice left anymore. But his greatest struggle was to think, think clearly and fast if at all possible. He told Mann about the plastic bag. About its contents. About the way of producing identification: the half-finished letter to Hal.

* * *

"It would be easier if you took me with you to Idlewild," Rust mumbled.

"Why?"

"It would be easier to get the bag."

"If you told me the truth about it, I would have no problems. And I do hope, in your interest in the first place, that you did tell me the truth."

Although Rust would not offer a good reason, he tried to persuade Mann again and again, until inevitably, suspicions were aroused.

"You don't think that in your state you could get away from me on the way, do you?"

"No."

"Then why are you so keen to go?"

"It would be better."

"Why?"

"It would be better."

"Don't be stupid," George said with a yawn that threatened to burst his lungs. The air in the room made his face distort: Rust stank as badly as the hole in the frozen ground he had once helped to fill with bodies. "Even if you could get away somehow from Idlewild, I'd still be here, holding Mrs. Repson! You remember that, don't you?"

"Oh yes. I do." Rust almost added, "Thank you." For that was all he wanted to know. That Anna was still held somewhere in the house. Left alone with George, he might have a chance. Half a chance. If, somehow, he could stay awake.

Mann prepared to leave.

"Do we let him sleep?" asked George.

Mann hesitated. "Yes. Why not? From now on he'll talk to us anytime, won't you, Helmut?"

Rust did not answer. His body went limp, his eyes closed, and his urine flowed freely down his legs. George was disgusted. He let Rust collapse on the floor. Although before leaving for the airport Mann had told him to clean up Rust a little, he decided not to touch him. Why should he? Why should a man soon to die need to be clean? Death in the warmth of his own shit might even be comforting to him. George thought he was nodding only because he was in full agreement with himself. He was, in fact, falling asleep.

Rust forced himself to open his eyes. He knew that Mann had left the house, and now he saw George's gaping mouth, drooling in an exhausted stupor. This was his chance. Better than the half-chance he had hoped for. He raised himself on one elbow. His entire body responded to the effort with shiverish trembling. Keep warm. And sleep. Just for a few minutes. He noticed George's watch. 11:35. If only he could sleep for five minutes. No. Don't sleep. Don't sleep. Don't.

It was the cold that woke him up. George was snoring, and Rust was pleased that he could hear it. George's hand was in the same position as before, hanging over the side of the armchair. Rust looked at the watch. 12:45. Alarmed, he moved. He could not remember how long it had taken Anna to drive here from the airport. Mann might be back soon. Rust knew he could deal easily with George, find Anna and get away in time—if only he had the strength to get up and move. He grabbed the edge of the bed and tried to pull himself up. It seemed an impossible task. His arm itself felt too heavy for him to support. Dryness burned his lips and glued his tongue to his palate. He closed his eyes. Pull. Pull. His grip slipped and he was back on the floor with a thump. George turned his head but did not wake up. Rust rested a couple of minutes, fighting all the way not to fall asleep again. The constant trembling of his hands made him realize that he might not be able to deal with George even if he managed to get up and over to the armchair. If he punched George, it might not be more than a tickle on the thin, pointed chin. And he could not hope to be able to lift a chair to hit him on the head.

He noticed the Plexiglas box on the coffee table. Whatever it contained, it might be his only ally. The lid was on, the stick lay across it. And that table was low enough to be reached from the floor. So all Rust needed was to be able to crawl to it. George moved. But he was only shifting his uncomfortable posture. Rust decided it would be a waste of effort to watch George: if he woke up too soon, he would have all the advantages.

Inch by inch he approached the table. He looked up—the sight made him recoil in disgust. Inside the lid, curved like a new moon, a huge centipede hung motionless, upside down. It bore no resemblance to the rubberized ones used by children for pranks. It was thicker than two fingers and as long as Rust's forearm. Its antennae quivered, then the whole segmented body moved sinuously. To stand up, pick up the ghastly creature and drop it in George's shirt at the neck would have been easy—except that Rust could not trust his own balance. If he fell, he might wake up George or drop the centipede on himself. He would have to use the stick. With that he might reach the largest and easiest target: the bare expanse of face with the gaping mouth.

When Rust lifted the lid, the centipede moved again. A pair of fangs appeared, poised to attack. Rust was desperate to allow himself a breather, but he had no idea how fast the centipede might be able to move. He lowered the lid to the floor, forced the stick under the slowly stretching body and began to raise it. It was a maddening balancing act. Raising himself on one elbow, Rust was sweating profusely. The last inches up were agony. At the end, Rust could not see whether the head or the tail hovered above George's mouth. He shook the stick a little—and felt it go lighter as the extra weight dropped. He fell back and his eyes closed. There was nothing he could do.

The silence must have lasted a second or two. Then a horrific cry of anguish broke through the din in his ears loud and clear. George was on his feet, tearing the centipede away, dancing in a craze as if hoping to shake out the spreading pain. He yelled at Rust inarticulately as he noticed his prisoner on the floor. With one hand he was lacerating his own flesh at his mouth, with the other he was reaching for his pocket. Violent convulsions ruined his coordination. At last he managed to pull out a snubnosed gun, but he could not hold it straight. He began shooting wildly, aimlessly, collapsed, then banged his head several times against the wall. Rust crawled toward the door. There was yet another explosion. He turned. George was lying in a pool of blood. Rust had no way to tell whether he had blown his brains out accidentally or deliberately. Sweating and shivering, Rust made his way slowly across the room. He picked up the gun, but it kept slipping out of his hand. He looked around. The centipede was nowhere in sight. He only hoped he would not meet it on his long and arduous way to the door.

"This is bureaucracy at its worst," Mann was fuming. "My friend lost the bag, he had to go on to Detroit and asked me to pick it up for him if it was at Lost Property. You asked me about the contents, and I told you. Even about the half-finished postcard. So what else do you want to know?"

The man at the counter was polite and apologetic. He explained that the regulations required answers to all questions on Lost and Found Form C37. "You see, sir, some forms need only ticks, but this is a real dog. Now I could tell you stories..."

Mann agreed to identify himself rather than argue any more. Luckily, he was carrying a spare set of driving license and credit cards. There was nothing for him to worry about except the waste of time. Because he had hoped to be back at the house by now.

Rust knew he had lost too much time. He shouted and shouted, hoping to get some answer from Anna, but nothing could be heard from upstairs. He tried to climb the stairs, but it exhausted him to the point where he feared he might pass out or fall asleep only to be found in a heap when Mann returned.

"Anna!"

A vague premonition grew into firm conviction: Anna did not answer because she was not alive. They had no use for her. She could tell them nothing. But she could identify them if they let her go. So she had to die, probably with Lanigan. Rust had to know the truth. He wiped the blood off the gun: it had three bullets left. As long as he was awake he was not defenseless. The urge was tremendous to leave the house and try to escape. But Mann might arrive at any moment, and outside, Rust's chances against him would be even worse.

Rust grabbed the upright of the banister and began to crawl up the stairs. Every one of them demanded the determination of a solo venture up the Himalayas. He reached the first landing. Fourteen stairs. It seemed hopeless ever to get farther up. He heard something. Could be the gravel crunching under the tires of a car. Or perhaps, induced by the effort, it might be the din restarting in his skull. He turned to face the front door below. He tried to take aim. But all his limbs were shaking. He lay on his stomach. If he held his feet dangling in reverse behind him in the air, he had enough room to rest both outstretched arms in front of him, holding the gun with both hands.

The door opened and Mann appeared. He had the plastic bag. Blinded by the incoming light, Rust shouted, "Don't move!" At least he hoped he was shouting.

"What the hell." Mann stopped. Then a slow smile spread over his face. "Don't be stupid. Your hands are shaking." Mann began to advance slowly. "You couldn't hit an elephant. Not even a dead elephant."

"Don't move."

Mann jumped to the right, and Rust fired. The bang and its echoes in the confined space reverberated, renewing the painful pressures on his eardrums. Instead of dying out, the noise grew and grew until it sounded like an approaching helicopter, rotor blades roaring, then groaning, then whining and chirping. If it wasn't all in my mind, it could even be a real chopper, thought Rust. His vision began to blur. He could just make out Mann's silhouette against the wall. And the shadowy figure was watching the door. Did he also hear that helicopter-like noise? Then silence. Mann flung himself on the stairs, presenting a minimal target, climbing fast on all fours. Rust had to turn quickly. He knew he was about to pass out. He heard the click of the safety catch. Or he thought he had heard it. He fired. And fired again.

The combined session of CIA and Pentagon experts reached a deadlock. They were to advise COMOR, the President's Committee on Overhead Reconnaissance, but the gulf between clashing views was too wide. The photo analysts' latest report was deemed to be "speculative." Some hawks campaigned for the immediate resumption of unlimited U-2 flights all over Cuba, but the majority were opposed to it. The risk was considered to be too great. A provocation. Just what some of the generals wanted. Provoke some extreme reaction, such as missiles fired against American aircraft, and the President would be forced to sanction retaliation. The Cubans, trained secretly in Florida for an invasion, were said to be ready to go in— except this time, unlike during the Bay of Pigs, the President would have no chance to deny them full air cover and pull the carpet from under them. But the hawks were the minority. "There's plenty of time" was the prevailing view.

Repson agreed with the majority. He emphasized that McCone, director of the Company, was due back from his honeymoon in a couple of days. "Let's wait for him and let him decide."

"If he wants to resume the flights, he'll need backing and evidence to convince the President," argued the Air Force colonel.

"And how exactly do you propose to provide that evidence?" Repson sneered. He was bored with pilots who could not see much beyond the limits of their gunsights. "Come on, how do you propose to get the evidence?"

"Certainly not by waiting for nukes to become regular parts of the Havana skyline."

Some people laughed. The majority agreed that Khrushchev could not afford to take serious risks, such as placing long-range missiles with nuclear or conventional warheads in Cuba. Certainly not after the President's categorical statement that the appearance of aggressive weapons in Cuba would not be tolerated by the United States. No bargaining, no compromise. Not even if it meant war.

The meeting ended inconclusively—or rather with the conclusion that nothing should be done. The decision, taken by COMOR on September 10, after the loss of a U-2 over China, was to remain in force. No flights to be routed over western Cuba.

The telephone rang. "It's for you, Elliott."

Must be London or Miami, thought Repson. He had waited in vain all day for Sir Charles to return his call. But it was a CIA agent from Miami station.

"What's the problem?" Repson asked.

"No problem, sir. We're still at the Upstairs, but we've done it."

"That was pretty quick—it's quite a house to search."

"We were lucky, I guess."

"You mean you've found something?"

"Just the thing you've anticipated, sir. It was hidden in a box of contraband Cuban cigars. What do we do with it? . . . Sir? Are you there, sir?"

"Yes. Er . . . catch the first flight and bring it to Washington. Let me see, you should be here by about, say, ten P.M. I'll be at home. Have you got my address in Georgetown?"

The tinkle of metal on glass, the soft hiss of rubber wheels turning on linoleum, muted voices over a distant hum, the glitter of chrome or stardust blotted out now and then by the whiteness of angels' wings or nurses' coats—Rust knew he had to be in heaven or in a hospital. Schramm's face was the first he recognized, and that eliminated the former. From then on, he was recovering fast. A few hours' sedation had restored much of his strength and hearing. And he felt hungry. A good sign. He tried to sit up.

"Take it easy," said Schramm.

Rust looked around. Charles, grave and concerned, stood in the background. Rust smiled at him and turned back to Schramm. "Where did you find me?"

"In that weird house in Long Island."

"Where's Anna? I mean, Mrs. Repson."

"I don't know."

"Didn't you find her? She must be there."

"Only you were there and the two bodies. Did you shoot them, Helm?"

"Males?"

"Yes. Two."

"Anybody upstairs?"

"No. Correct?" Schramm asked Charles.

"Nobody upstairs, dear boy," Charles confirmed.

"Then they killed her. Together with Lanigan. Have you searched the grounds? Any sign of fresh digging?"

"We've got the FBI out there."

"They might have been dumped in the sea."

"Who? Mrs. Repson? And Lanigan? Who's Lanigan?"

"Ell's man from the Company." Schramm looked bewildered, but Rust ignored him and addressed Charles: "Why the fuck didn't you trust me?"

"Why didn't *you* trust *me*?"

"Does Ell know what happened? I mean, to me and Anna?"

"Not from us he doesn't," said Schramm. "You want to call him?"

"I want to see him. Now." A nurse tried to fuss over him. He brushed her hand aside and sat up. "I have no time for that, honey." He felt dizzy and had to hold the edge of the bed. His grip felt firm. Another good sign. "Get rid of everybody apart from Charles and yourself, Jake." Two nurses and a doctor left on Schramm's nod. "Just get me some food, please."

"Okay," said Schramm. "Tell us."

"You first."

"There isn't much, really." Charles stepped closer. "We tailed you and some idiots lost you at a tollgate when you were driven in by an attractive young lady from Idlewild."

"That's when you called in Jake."

"No, dear boy, he was with me all the time. When we lost you, he remembered an old trick he had taught you."

"I thought he might if he was called in. Have you got the bag?"

"Yes."

"Have you examined it?"

"Just the dictionary."

"What have you found?"

"Only a microdot on page four. It's . . . well, it seems to be a memo by Khrushchev, authorizing the installation of some SAMs in Cuba. It doesn't seem genuine, I must say."

"It probably is. Anything else?"

"Not yet. But a friend in a Company lab is working on it," Schramm said.

"It's on . . ." Rust stopped. "So what happened?"

"We ran a big search for you, and kept an eye on that Lost Property office. We knew that you'd have to return sooner or later. When someone else turned up, our guys delayed him long enough for us to get there. We tailed him by chopper to that house. Except when we landed on the front lawn, we heard several shots from inside. We found the guy dead in the hallway. And another body in the living room. Incidentally, what was that dreadful creature by the fire?"

"A centipede."

"Well, I didn't count how many legs it had, but it sure had a lot of lives. It took endless kickings to die."

"I hope it felt the pain."

"Why?"

"Never mind."

A nurse brought in food, and Rust needed all his self-control not to gobble up everything in sight. Some intestinal spasms returned, but it was not too bad and he could keep the food and water in. He asked the nurse to leave.

"You eat like someone who's starved for a week," said Charles.

"They've purged my bowels clean as new, I guess." Grabbed by sudden panic, he stopped. "What day is it?"

"Tuesday." Schramm looked at his watch. "Not that much is left of it."

Charles sat down on the edge of the bed. "I think it's your turn to tell, Helm."

"In a sec. Jake said it was a friend in a Company lab working on the dictionary."

"Correct."

"Does that mean that it's unofficial?"

"Well, yes, in a way."

"In what way?"

"Charles and I thought that first we had to figure out what you were up to. I mean, we had no way of telling who to trust and what your game was."

"Particularly not when you told me what information your father gave you about those camps," added Charles.

"What about it?"

"It's all wrong. He either didn't know the answers himself, or, well, you know . . ."

"What?"

"He might have lied to you. Quite deliberately. I have no idea why he would do that. Perhaps it's just that his memory was failing. Camps can do a lot of queer things to people. What was your impression? Was he, er, okay up there?"

The food froze in Rust's mouth. What Charles had said brought back the memory of the brief conversation with Anna about Geneva. She was probably wrong. She had to be. He forced himself to swallow. "Does either of you know when the big water jet in Geneva was built?"

Schramm shrugged his shoulders.

"Late last century, I believe," said Charles. Rust sighed with relief, but the older man continued, "But it wasn't much more than a good spurt, I think, at the time. They kept improving it, but the really big jet was not installed until, oh, well after the war. I remember I was there in 1950 or '51; they made quite a song and dance about the height. No, it might have been '52. Anyway, what's the relevance?"

Why? Why would the old man lie about the water jet? The Jeddo, he called it. And he mentioned even the height. Why? A hundred and thirty meters. How did he know? He wouldn't.

Not unless he had only heard or read about it and confused the information with his own memories. Or else he might have revisited Geneva after the war. But why would they let him? And if they did, why would he lie about it? To convince his son that he had ever been in Geneva at all?

Charles watched Rust's shocked expression. "I take it you didn't know that the information he gave you was false."

"No, I didn't."

"I'm sorry."

"Not your fault. It's . . . it's just that I wanted to know what I was made of. What I've inherited from him. To see if I could blame that stranger for anything or everything bad in me. So now I know." He stared at the ceiling. "And that's not the worst." He paused. It was hard to say it. "Ell." The friendly familiarity of the name was wrong to use this time. "My brother is a traitor. He's probably ordered his wife's death. And authorized my torture and death."

"Repson?"

"He fingered me at Idlewild to those thugs. He sent along Anna to allay any suspicions I might have, and probably to get rid of her, too, in one go."

Charles and Jake avoided his eyes. They knew how much those few sentences must have hurt Rust.

"Okay, what do we do? Do we pick him up? What?" Jake was itching to go into action.

"First you've got to get that dictionary. Lucky it's not in Company hands—I mean, officially." Rust stopped again. A memory flash brought back a fragment of the telephone conversation with Ell from London. *Porokhovyye konfety.* Castro's shopping list. Ell denied that he had ever received it. Rust now knew why. "Anyway, here's briefly what happened." In a matter-of-fact voice he summarized the last three weeks' events. He cut out most of the traumatic experiences, though obviously, both his listeners sensed the gaps. He was ready to tell them the little he knew about the missiles when a thought ran through him like a shudder. What if these two were on Mann's side? What if they had returned with Mann only to finish off the job? When Mann and George were found dead, these two could have tried to continue in a different style. Except that by then, they had nothing more to gain from keeping him alive. He could not dismiss the thought completely, but decided that if these two were also working for the opposition, he would not have much left worth fighting for.

"You were saying." Jake broke the long silence. "About that dictionary."

"You've got to retrieve it. And the microdot that's already been blown up. It'll have to go right to the top. I mean McCone."

"He's away."

"Okay, his deputy then. The thirteenth dot on page thirty-one is a microdot. I guess it could be a chart to help you locate some other microdots on different pages." He paused, then mumbled mostly to himself: "What a joke: I planned to deliver it to the President through Ell."

"Yeah. We'll have to pick him up and bring him in. Shall I arrange it?"

Rust shook his head.

"I mean, I could do it sort of unofficially if that's what you preferred."

"Before you move, I've got to go and see him. I think I've earned the right to judge him first—at least to my satisfaction!"

"Don't. The risk is too great," protested Charles.

Jake agreed: "It's crazy."

"It's my skin. And as of now, I'm dispensable. So give me an hour with him. Can you be ready by then?"

• Wednesday, October 3 •

Revealed in Miami: Pentagon asked Jose Miró Córdoba's
Cuban Revolutionary Council for 150 escapee officers to
receive advanced training at U.S. military schools; twelve
men already selected. Increasingly heavy traffic (mostly
Russian ships) at Havana and Cienfuegos; reports of unloading at night in screened-off "security" areas.

I N MOSCOW IT WAS 3:00 IN THE AFTERNOON, AND MAJOR
Boychenko had a feeling that the day would never end.
There was nothing he could do about his headache—he should
not have experimented with all those western *kokteil* concoctions everybody seemed to drink at the party. And there was
nothing he could do about the sudden silence from New York.
Yet less than twenty-four hours ago, there was sunshine for
him whichever way he turned.

By Tuesday lunchtime, old Fyodor Galakhov of the Red
Banner *kolkhoz* had told him everything. Boychenko exercised
his power of persuasion and never needed even to approach

the limits of socialist legality. He reported directly to the Spetsburo, and the colonel praised him for his clear and concise summary of the situation. Only half an hour later, he was formally relieved of all his Tourist duties and transferred temporarily to the Spetsburo. He was not particularly keen to join an assassination squad, even if it would give him a chance to travel abroad, but the assignment was recognition for his hard work and dedication. And there was more to come. As if the news of his success had already been spreading along the grapevine of Moscow's potentates there was a sudden slurry of telephone calls: the bath faucets and the scarcity goods from the Voyentorg had been delivered, his reference for the surgeon had been useful and the Foreign Trade Ministry official, whose favors Boychenko had been seeking, suddenly found an "unexpected opening" for Boychenko's daughter.

Then came more news from New York. Boychenko did not know much about the details of the setup, but even he was impressed by what the KGB Resident could conjure up over there. He did not fail to be most complimentary about all this when he and the colonel were summoned to make their progress report to Major General Yemelin, head of the First Chief Directorate. The general was beginning to like him. That became obvious when at the end of the day, the general said to him: "Come and have a drink with us, Andrey Anisimovich." The party was held at the general's huge apartment on Kadasevskaya embankment, overlooking the river and the wall of the Kremlin beyond, and judging from the quality of the drinks and the quantity of the caviar, Boychenko knew he was "in," at last. The *kokteil* business was unfortunate—on vodka, he would have stayed the full course in any company—but he did not disgrace himself unduly, and there was still no cloud on his horizon at dawn.

He reached his office at 7:30 in the morning, telephoned his wife not to worry about his all-night absence, and asked the radio room for the latest news from New York. It was then that somebody, somewhere, must have switched off his personal sun. The prospect grew bleaker and bleaker every hour. No news from New York. There must be. Sorry, nothing. Then call the embassy Resident. Suddenly, the Resident was not available. Try the KGB Resident at the UN mission. Sorry, impossible, not his operation.

General Yemelin had encouraged him to report directly if he had any problems. He tried. Sorry, the general was not in and it was not known when he would be. The adjutant and Boychenko exchanged knowing glances, but that did not help anyone.

Boychenko then gave hell to the duty officer of the radio room, and that was reported back to his superiors. "Careful, major, don't upset too many people—not yet," said the Spetsburo colonel. "I can't tell you all the details, but obviously, you must have guessed that your case has a bearing on the continued security of 'Sapphire,' possibly our highest-ranking agent in America. It's an entirely independent network that services Sapphire's needs and activities, and every move affecting security must be their responsibility, and theirs alone. It's that important. So tread carefully."

Which again was no solace to Boychenko. For the New York squad, his sole source of leads, remained silent as if the two men had never existed or were dead.

The day's first New York–Washington shuttle banked to starboard to make its final approach and land. Rust woke up and squinted as the pale sun that lit up the Potomac below glittered on the window. "I'm hungry," he mumbled.

"Not again!" Charles exclaimed with mocking consternation. He opened his briefcase and produced yet another of the sandwiches the hospital had packed for Rust. "Judging from your ceaseless breakfasting since midnight, you must be on the mend."

Rust began to munch away and glanced around surreptitiously. There were at least half a dozen semi-familiar faces. He had been promised an hour alone with Ell, but it appeared that Schramm was not prepared to take chances. Whatever was to happen between the brothers, these men would be on hand to prevent Ell from getting away.

"What have you done about the Upstairs?"

"The Upstairs?"

"Yes, Charles, the Upstairs. I asked you in London to arrange something and have it watched."

"Oh yes, that's done. You said you expected it might be raided."

"That's right. From Holly's boss, or whoever their man in

the Moscow embassy might be, they would know that I expected some proof to be delivered to me at home. If they turn up, I don't want Hal to be unprepared and alone."

Charles looked distinctly embarrassed. He cleared his throat and looked away. "Well, I haven't had a chance to mention it before. There was, in fact, some sort of raid."

"What about Hal?"

"He's in hospital."

"What happened?"

"They pumped some bullets into him. Luckily, he's a strong boy."

"Do you know if anything was found?"

"Don't know."

"Who were they?"

"Claimed to be CIA, at least until they started shooting."

"When was that?"

"Oh, let me see. It was definitely a Thursday." Charles took out a diary. "That's right, the twentieth."

"Can't be. I expected the evidence to be delivered on the first of October. That's what I was told. That's what I told Holly. So that's what he must have passed on to whoever it was. It would have been pointless for them to raid the Upstairs earlier. They wouldn't take an unnecessary risk like that."

Charles shrugged his shoulders. "The raid was on the twentieth."

"It doesn't make sense. How's Hal?"

"He'll live. Wish I could be so sure about your prospects."

"Don't worry."

"I'd prefer to go with you. I mean, you could talk to Ell on your own, but he'd know that I was there."

"We've been through that before. Let's stick to our agreement."

They took a cab from the airport. Rust noticed that the men scattered around them aboard the aircraft now followed them in two chauffeur-driven cars.

Charles dropped him off on the corner of Ell's street in Georgetown. "Take care. And don't take chances."

"Keep warm." Rust nodded to him as if they were in full agreement. In fact, perhaps they were. Ell might not be completely unprepared for his visit. It would be crazy to give him any more advantage by taking chances. "Just get straight on with it," Charles had warned, "and gauge his reactions. If he tries to shoot himself, let him. Otherwise he might change his mind and shoot you first."

The street was deserted. This part of Washington was the precinct of late-nighters rather than early-risers. The cars parked opposite the house and farther down the street seemed empty. But there was no way to tell. Rust pressed the button of the intercom. It was only a few seconds later that a buzzer sounded and Ell's voice rattled through the metal grille of the speaker. "Just push the door and come right up, Helm."

Rust looked up and faced a small, closed-circuit security camera. From the speed of Ell's answer it was obvious that the visit had been expected. Rust walked through the door. He was surprised to see a neatly dressed crewcut just inside.

"Right through and up the stairs, sir."

It was a spacious, elegantly furnished yet homey living room with two tall French windows beyond which some fine wrought iron closed in the nonexistent balconies. Rust's eyes had to search for Ell, adjusting slowly to the semidarkness of the room, and discovering that the hominess was probably due to all the mucky leftovers of a long night's vigil. Half-empty coffee cups and glasses, half-full ashtrays, the sour-stale air of smoke, sweat and dust. Ell's wheelchair squeaked as he rolled out of the darker end of the room.

"Where have you been?"

"Good question, Ell. Anything else you want to know?"

"Yes. Why didn't you turn up at Idlewild?"

"I was there. You know that."

"At the Hertz desk?"

"No, not there."

"That's what my men told me."

"Really?"

"At least you could have called me."

"Let's not play games, Ell. There's no time for that." Rust was irritated by his brother's feeble effort to defend himself by going on the attack. He found it a pitiful performance.

"I'm in no mood for games, I can assure you."

"I'm not surprised. Even if you don't know all the facts, you must suspect, even expect, the worst. And I'm not in the mood to give it to you gently."

"There's no need either. I know everything." Repson looked

at his watch. "And the final bit of proof should be here any moment now."

"You mean the bodies?"

"Whose bodies? What are you talking about?"

"Your men."

"What men?"

"Mann and George. At least that's what they called themselves."

"Who are they?"

"Suit yourself. I'm not your prosecutor, Ell. I only wanted to see a traitor in the flesh. To hear your excuses. To try to understand you. So that one day I'd remember you with some sympathy. I wanted to see you blush. But I was wrong. You must have forgotten how to blush a long time ago. Or feel embarrassed. That's why I'm sorry to say I have at least some news that may please you: you've probably managed to get rid of Anna if not me."

"What the hell are you talking about?"

"It was clever of you to send her to Idlewild."

"I didn't."

"You mean she just decided to come and meet me there? And she proved herself a mind-reader to discover that I'd be there at all. Not to mention the code. Had she just guessed it? Mother's favorite color—that's right, Mrs. Repson, you win the jackpot. Or have I suffered too much to remember clearly? Perhaps 'mauve' was not the code."

"It was. And that's what I gave the men who were waiting for you at the Hertz desk."

"Why did you send Anna?"

"You're crazy."

"You could have killed her yourself. Or they could have done it here. Or was it more convenient that I should be implicated in some way?"

"You need a doctor, Helm. A psychiatrist, to be precise. And I pity you. Even though I shouldn't. You've thrown away your right to my sympathy. I know you wanted Anna to meet you at Idlewild. I know how you tried to force her."

"That's a good line—I mean, knowing that she won't be able to contradict you because she's dead."

"You poor, poor man. Anna! Anna!"

The door opened, and Anna came in. She was wearing a

long silk dressing gown and at first did not seem to notice Rust. She looked tired. He started toward her.

"Don't!" Repson barked and waved at Rust with a gun. "Just stay where you are."

Anna shook her head in disbelief. "No, no."

"I'm sorry, honey," said Repson. "You were right. He did have the nerve to come here after all."

Rust was in a state of shock. Were these two in collusion? And if yes, why did they try to keep up some pretense? He turned to Anna: "How did you get away?"

"From where?"

"Long Island."

"I haven't been to New York for at least a couple of months. Come to think of it, I haven't been away from Washington since May."

"Then where were you on Saturday?"

"Saturday? Hm . . . Saturday . . ."

"It's all right, honey, you don't have to answer him," said Repson without taking his eyes away from Rust.

She stepped behind her husband and put her hand on his shoulder as if seeking refuge. "There's no reason not to answer. I was in the office. There was some urgent extra work to be done for Bobby. I was there most of the day and met you for dinner."

"That shouldn't be difficult to check," said Rust, thinking hard in case he had made a mistake about the day. Was it Saturday? The days in the house on Long Island had fused into an endless one in his memory.

"There's no need to check. We spoke on the phone at lunch-time. We dined together in the Army and Navy Club. We met in the Farragut lobby. And we came home early because of you, Helm. At that time I was still worried about you."

"But you were on duty all day," Rust pounced as he spotted the gap in the story.

"That's right."

"So you had no way of telling what time she left the house in the morning."

"N-no."

"Except that somebody in the office will be able to confirm what time I got in on Saturday," she said.

"I hope you'll have a watertight alibi, sweetheart. It will

try to prove, no doubt, that you've never had a chance to fly to New York and spend some of the morning with me. And if it does prove that, we'll know at least one of your accomplices."

Repson raised his shoulder so that her hand, resting on it, touched his face. "You don't have to stay here and listen to all this, honey, when he's obviously bluffing."

"I'll stay. I don't need to be afraid of him anymore."

"Anymore?" asked Rust. "What's that supposed to mean?"

"Cut it out, Helm, she's told me everything."

"Really?"

"I always knew that you could be pretty ruthless, but I never thought that you'd stoop that low."

"How low?"

"Are you trying to deny that you had an affair with her in Leningrad?"

Rust hesitated. She looked right through him. He shrugged his shoulders. "No. When did she tell you?"

"On Sunday."

"Why only now?"

"I didn't want to hurt Ell," she said.

"But now you've changed your mind, right?"

"You forced me to."

"Did I?"

"Yes, with that call on Sunday. When you told me that if I didn't pay, you'd come here and tell him yourself. It left me no choice. I haven't got that sort of money."

"Fascinating."

"Stop it, Helm!" Repson raised the gun. "And don't forget, nobody could blame me if I shot you now."

"But you won't. Because you're no fool. Because you know that I wouldn't have come here without some insurance."

"You mean the negatives?"

"What negatives?"

"We've already found them. So it's no good to deny things anymore. And the guy who let you in is a fed. Other agents are next door. They have all the evidence they need. They're waiting for me to finish with you." He paused, then added very quietly: "I only hoped you'd have the decency to apologize to me."

"I didn't know that she was your fiancée at the time."

"I know that."

"Then what do you want me to apologize for?"

"The blackmail. The extortion of money. The anguish you caused her. The final threat on Sunday."

"I didn't call her on Sunday, or ever since Leningrad. And she knows that. Because she knows where I was on Sunday." Rust was beginning to understand. She had returned from Long Island as soon as Mann and George had taken over. So she had to be working with those two. Which made her a Soviet agent. In which case their meeting and affair in Leningrad were no coincidence. Perhaps that's why he had received that unexpected permission to do the Hermitage story. It took him to Leningrad. It was a setup. And he fell into it because it was plausible and, above all, flattering. It helped to ensure that if he ever grew suspicious of his sister-in-law, his word would carry no weight because he could be proved to be a jealous, jilted lover. Even his father might have been part of the trap. And most probably, photographs would have been taken by the KGB in the hotel. The old, old honey trap that was rendered inconspicuous by the fact that the girl was not only an American but also a trusted member of Bobby Kennedy's staff. A position that would give an agent supreme importance. Which left Rust with two questions: Was Ell in the setup with her? And if not, why had he given her the agreed code?

"Go on, take your time," said Repson. "It's your turn to think up an alibi. Just make sure that it's a good one."

"Why did you give her the code, Ell?"

"I told you. I didn't."

"Okay, suppose you didn't. Could she have listened in on my London call to you?"

Repson glanced toward the telephone. "Yes, I suppose she could have, but why would she want to?"

"We'll come to that."

"Sure. As soon as you've cleared yourself of blackmail." Repson nodded toward a file on an octagonal wine table. "You don't deserve it, but you're entitled to see the evidence."

Rust flipped over the cover. There was a photograph, enlarged from a probably blurred, amateurish negative. She was kneeling in front of him. Rust remembered the words. "I don't know what it is. I'm craving for your sperms. I want them inside me. Everywhere." Rust looked at her. She avoided his eyes and stared out the window. Why had she given Ell the reversed blackmail story on her return from Long Island?

"Do you deny that it's you in the picture?" Repson asked.

"No. But that's no blackmail."

"It wasn't until you sent it to her with your demands."

"And you have my demand note, I suppose."

"No."

"No?"

"I burned it at the time," she whispered.

"Pity. It would have been ever so useful."

"We don't need it," said Repson. "It's all there."

Rust put the photograph back into the folder, only to be confronted with a copied set of his bank statements for the past six years.

"The FBI got those for me yesterday. Look at the ones marked with a red tick." Repson gestured with the gun. "Can you tell me who the source of those payments was?"

"Yes, you."

"Really?"

"Yes, and you know it."

"I know nothing of the kind. I mean, I knew nothing of it until yesterday. Why should I have paid you, anyway?"

"For the information I sent you from time to time."

"If you were one of my anonymous informers, you'd have claimed money for it."

"But I didn't. Because I didn't do it for money."

"No. You just accepted these anonymous payments."

"Yes. Partly because I knew that they could only come from you, and partly because the cash kept me a professional instead of a fucking amateur. It gave me a sense of belonging. It kept me in the game."

"A likely story. But the truth of the matter is that I've never sent you a dime. Nor did I authorize any Company payments to you. On the other hand, all these sums can be traced as payments from Anna's private account. There—see it for yourself."

"Okay, so you covered up the payments by putting them through her account."

"I didn't."

"Besides, you must admit, Ell, that if I was a blackmailer,

I was dabbling in small potatoes if these paltry sums were my reward."

"That's just the point. When you called Anna on Sunday, you increased your demands. You wanted a lot more. You thought she could lay her hands on a small fortune. But you miscalculated."

"Her word against mine."

"Precisely. But would you deny that you still have the negatives of those photographs?"

"Yes. I've never had any such photographs or their negatives."

"Well, let me tell you something. Two agents are on their way back from Miami. They'll be here soon. They've searched the Upstairs, and they've found the negatives. I wasn't there, Anna wasn't there, only the feds were there together with the Company station chief. Do you feel all right, Helm? You do look a bit pale."

Rust remembered the other raid on the Upstairs. The one Charles had been talking about. It was no search for evidence from Moscow. It had to be a proof-planting operation. Somebody had reported to Anna—or Ell, for all that!—that Rust might cause problems if he ever got out of the Soviet Union, so precautions had to be taken. Which would explain the date of the raid. Hal's presence was unexpected and the raiders shot him.

"You'll look even paler, Ell, when I tell you why she's invented this pack of lies."

"You're a filthy bastard, Helm," she hissed furiously, "and I'll see you rot in jail even if they drag me through the courts with you, and even if your beloved brother also gets a taste of the dirt." She spun around to spit in her husband's face: "I thought you'd be man enough to stand up for me, but then I must have forgotten that you're a cripple. God only knows why I loved you, why I went on and on, trying to cover up for that foolish mistake I made in Leningrad, paying Helm to keep you out of a scandal that might have ruined your career. At least now I know, it wasn't worth it."

"You've been under tremendous pressure for days, honey. Take a Valium, lie down, and let me deal with this the proper way."

"Don't you patronize me."

Rust leaned a little forward. His muscles strained as he prepared to lunge at his brother at the first sign of his deciding to use that gun under her provocation. "She's right, Ell, she doesn't need any patronage. So you'd better keep us both covered with that gun. Because she's KGB. She had me tortured. And she may still have a trick or two up her sleeve." Rust noticed that for the first time, his brother looked startled by what he had said. "She took me to that isolated house on Long Island to make sure that my screams would not be overheard by anyone when they used a centipede on me. That thing didn't travel from the East Indies for nothing. They knew, and Anna must have known, too, what agony it would cause. But nothing mattered, not as long as they retrieved all the info I'd brought out of Russia. And they wanted all the names of people who'd helped me over there."

"Rubbish," said Repson. His voice lacked total conviction.

"Don't you find it a hell of a coincidence that Anna has a sudden urge to confess our old affair, and the blackmail and the payments, just when I'm about to disappear without a trace after telling you that I'm carrying some vital information?"

She smiled. "And who do you think will believe this lungful of shit?"

Repson's eyes kept jumping from him to her and back.

"Nobody will believe me, sweetheart, not until Jake Schramm and Sir Charles and Company security get here—any moment now." Rust stopped. Suddenly he could foresee the whole scene. And he was sorry for his brother. He wanted to see him embarrassed. Now that he did, the sight made him feel uneasy. Anna turned her back on them. Rust ignored her. "You know something? It'll take a long time to clear yourself, Ell. And I could suggest to you to get out of the Company as soon as they let you. Save yourself the troubles of fighting. Don't shorten your life by years. Avoid the ulcer and the rest. It would be wise counsel, I know, but I won't suggest it. Because if I did, I'd make the same mistake as you made when you suggested just that wise course to me six years ago. Remember? It came soon after I'd found my father. You said I must get out of the Company. You warned that they'd hound me out. Or even worse, they'd drag me in completely. Until then, I only looked like good agent potential with a cover of journalism. But then, out of the blue, I could have become an important puppet. You warned that I'd soon lose my independence no matter how dear it was to me. Not because I'd find it so great to belong to the CIA, but because espionage was the most contagious of all games, and once I was infected, I'd be ready to do just about anything for the privilege of remaining a player. You even warned that if I didn't get out fast, they'd pressure me to turn that poor, shivering old man into an agent. And I listened to you. Because it made sense. Because it would have been unfair to infect that helpless old man and endanger his last few years. So what happens now? It turns out that he may be a player in his own right!" He laughed. And it hurt him. "So I won't suggest that you should get out and brood for the rest of your life. Put up a fight. Clear your name if you can. And remain a player whatever the consequences."

Repson looked disturbed. Then slowly the worry creases in his face dissolved in a smile. "You know something? I've never heard you say so much in one go."

Rust could not help smiling with him. Despite all the pain, doubts, animosity and accusations, an almost forgotten comradeship was rekindled for a few seconds. They were brothers against the world, two little boys taking on parents, school, neighborhood gangs, all comers. "You know something, Ell? I think you . . ."

"I know what you think."

"And I know what you think that you know what I think."

"And I know what you know and I think you stink."

They both laughed without a single sound. It was hardly more than a belly convulsion killed in its infancy by parental frowns of disapproval across the breakfast table.

"I wish you luck, Ell. You'll need it, too, if you're a traitor. But even if you're not, it'll take a lot of scrubbing to be rid of the stink Anna's touch has left on you."

"How very touching," said Anna. "Particularly when coming from a blackmailer."

Two men entered through the door at the far end of the room. One of them carried a tape recorder. "That'll do, sir," he said to Repson.

"Is it all on tape?"

"Yes, sir. And we can authenticate it in addition to your and Mrs. Repson's statements. You won't need the mike anymore."

Repson rested the gun on his lap and reached under his tie. He removed the hidden clip microphone and handed it to the agent. "He'll need a lawyer, I guess."

"It's up to him, sir. He'll be cautioned properly."

"I want to see your badges," said Rust.

Both agents identified themselves. They were FBI. Or so it seemed. But Rust remembered O'Connor, the bearer of his father's message, who claimed to be CIA. And then Mann and George. Who also pretended to be Company men. It would be pointless to argue with these two. Schramm must have thrown a tight net around the house by now. They would soon verify if these were bona fide agents. He hoped they were. It would help to prove Ell's innocence. A buzzer sounded. It elated him. With Anna caught, with Mann and George dead, with Charles and Jake proved trustworthy, there was every reason to hope that Yelena was safe, no matter what the pain had squeezed out of him.

Repson flicked the switch of the intercom. "Yes?"

"Mr. Adams to see you, sir."

"Adams?" Repson looked perplexed. Adams was the deputy director of CIA Security. "Of course. Ask him to come up, will you?"

The silence was almost total. Rust noticed that Anna moved noiselessly a little farther away from the group. She had always been a light mover. Repson switched off the intercom: it sounded like a minor explosion.

Adams came in, accompanied by Schramm, Charles and three other men. "Can we have some more light in here, please?" he asked softly. He viewed Anna and each of the men in turn. His eyes settled on Rust. "Thank you, Helm. I guess we may owe you quite a bit. I mean, if you have done what you seem to have done."

"Please don't jump to easy conclusions, sir," said Repson. "You ought to consider the documents in this folder first, then listen to the tape recording—"

Adams stopped him with a wave of his hand and turned to Schramm: "You got the tape?"

"Yes, sir." Schramm took a cassette out of his pocket. "We found it in an upstairs room on Long Island. The place was wired crudely but effectively. These are a woman's recorded screams, begging for help, the things she could be expected to shout when in trouble. If it was played through a speaker and heard through several doors, it would sound muffled, but very realistic." He looked at Rust, who nodded. Adams turned to Anna: "The voice will be subject to the usual ident process, of course. Do you wish to make a statement on this, Mrs. Repson?"

"I don't know who's screaming on your tape or where it comes from, but I can tell you now that I haven't been to New York for months."

"Suit yourself. We also have your fingerprints from that house."

"Why shouldn't you? If somebody tries to frame me, nothing is easier than to deposit a few things anywhere with my prints on them."

Adams was about to say something, but Repson interrupted him. "Were you or were you not in that house, Anna?" he asked her.

"What house?"

"You must tell me, Anna. Did you go to New York to meet Helm at Idlewild? How did you find out the code? And why? Why did you go there?"

"I've told you. I wasn't there. Helm's a liar."

Schramm stepped forward. "It's no good, Mrs. Repson. These two of my men were there, waiting for Helm at Idlewild. They saw you two together, right?"

The two agents confirmed it. "That was her, all right. We lost them at the tollgate at ..." He was fishing some notes out of his pocket. "At, er ... I can give you the exact time, sir, if you just bear with me for a moment."

Everybody in the room was watching the agent and waiting for him to complete his statement. Rust tried to detect any sign of emotion on Anna's face but could not. Nobody but Rust paid much attention to the squeak of a wheel—not until it was blanked out by a loud report. Blood spurted from Anna's neck and sprayed Rust, who had flung himself at his brother's arm. Repson was still firing, but the second and third bullets punctured only the Afghan run in front of the wheelchair. With her eyes unable to focus, Anna's dissipating gaze fell somewhere between the brothers. "Whatever it may seem ... I've loved you ... I ..." Blood flooded her mouth and drowned her voice. There was no way to tell whom she had addressed.

· Thursday, October 4 ·

De Gaulle threatens to resign if referendum rejects his proposal for direct election of President. U.S. Secretary of State
Rusk presses friendly countries to introduce at least limited
boycott of fast-growing Cuba-bound shipping; some support, but outright opposition by Canada and Brazil. Jim
Clark [Lotus] wins U.S. Grand Prix.

BACK FROM HIS HONEYMOON, CIA DIRECTOR MCCONE
was confronted with the astonishing discovery that western Cuba had not been overflown for almost a month. A special
session of the Committee on Overhead Reconnaissance was
convened right away. The urgent need of information ought to
have been obvious to all COMOR members, but advocates of
the "play safe" principle emphasized the risks in the resumption
of regular U-2 flights with full coverage. Alternative proposals
were examined. Sending unmanned balloons or remote-control
drone planes would involve no gambling with human lives, but
such techniques would be no substitute for the intelligence-

gathering superiority of the U-2s. The meeting was unable to break down the opposition to the spy flights because, particularly in the suspected areas, the Cubans were already known to possess an almost fully operational network of surface-to-air missiles. It was decided that more expert opinions should be invited; the question of overflights would then be given further consideration at the next meeting, almost a week later.

The decision bugged McCone. He could have invoked Presidential backing for the immediate resumption of overflights, but he was not convinced that he had a good enough case against the experts. Besides, to seek urgent, direct contact with the President—away briefly on the Congressional campaign trail—would place undue emphasis on the previous month's delay, and damage the Company which was far from being JFK's favorite anyway. Better wait until a natural opportunity arose, such as bumping into Bobby Kennedy at the French embassy dinner.

Before leaving for the embassy that evening, the Director inquired about the microdots that had reached Langley by some round-about way with the help of an outsider by the name of Rust. They were being developed and evaluated, he was assured, and could be in his hands with a full report within an hour or two.

Over drinks before dinner he managed to snatch a private word with the Attorney General about the special session of COMOR. Kennedy fired a volley of uncomfortable questions at him. "Is it possible that somebody on COMOR has sabotaged the program?"

"I wouldn't think so. No single individual has that sort of power on the Committee."

"Would anybody be able to exert that kind of indirect influence to achieve the long gap in overflights?"

"Well, anybody putting up a convincing enough argument would have some influence."

"Do you admit then that somebody might have done it deliberately with malicious intent?"

"Admit is a strong word, Mister Attorney General."

"Is it or is it not conceivable?"

"It's not inconceivable." The Director did not try to conceal his annoyance. "Are you bent on changing our traditional roles?"

"In what way?"

"Suddenly it's you who sees spooks and saboteurs everywhere. It used to be *you* who associated *us* with that kind of paranoia."

The conversation was interrupted by the Ambassador's wife who blasted them with an avalanche of party-talk. McCone was rescued from her a few minutes later when he was asked to answer an urgent call from Langley.

Jake Schramm had a distinct sensation that soon he would go crazy. He had never felt so completely gagged and bound by red tape. He had seen the blown-up pictures from the microdots in Rust's dictionary, but since he had handed them over through the proper channels to the Directorate of Operations, there was nobody who would tell him about their fate and evaluation or even the projected follow-up action, if any. Yet Rust kept pressing him all day for just such information. Although Schramm had great respect for regulations governing essential secrecy, he felt that Rust, in view of his trouble over the delivery of the microdots, was entitled to know if they were considered to be worth anything.

In his own mind, Schramm had no doubt about the value of the pictures. One was a map showing the Cuban locations of projected medium- and intermediate-range missile sites. Three pictures came from Odessa. In two of these, the loading of crates and missile trailers aboard Russian freighters could be seen. The third depicted the "restricted" outer port area where the freighters of the first two pictures were berthed. One photograph was a close-up of a huge, peculiar crate on the open deck of the *Poltava*. Identification should be no problem for trained CIA crate-ologists. The rest of the eight pictures were from Cuba. They showed the unloading of crates and missiles in two, possibly three, Cuban ports. Yes, Schramm understood the problem: the photographs might well have been produced by the KGB disinformation department to serve some as yet unfathomable espionage maneuver. And yes, it was possible that Rust had been used as an unsuspecting pawn in some mysterious game, although that could be contradicted by the desperate KGB bid to capture and interrogate the messenger. But surely such doubts should not be a reason for treating Rust as a suspect. Yet this exactly seemed to be the case. He was in the hands of counterintelligence. On medical advice, he had been moved to a small sanatorium, used almost exclusively by the Company, hidden among trees on a private estate, and conveniently situated only three miles from Langley. His room in an isolated bungalow was under constant surveillance. Schramm was allowed free access, but he had a feeling that the aim was to listen in on his conversations with Rust. He tried to arrange permission for a visit by Sir Charles, but failed. Now he had to drive back into town to break the news.

"I'm sorry, Charles, no go." He expected the older man to hit the roof. He was wrong.

"I understand, dear boy. It's in the nature of counterintelligence to live up to its name and run just such a course. One wonders if 'subintelligence' would be a more appropriate name. Give him my regards, will you?"

"If they still let me see him."

"How is he?"

"Enjoying a routine post-mission high, I guess, but it won't last long. The shrinks want to put him under a few days' sedation to avoid the risk of a nervous breakdown. But debriefing is considered to be more urgent and important."

It was almost 10:00 in the evening when Schramm arrived back at the sanatorium, but Rust's room was still crowded and lively. Apart from the two men who had conducted his debriefing all day, Repson was there. He looked pale and drawn, and Schramm knew why: in addition to the shock of the revelations about Anna, he himself might be subject to lengthy and harrowing investigations from which he might never recover fully even if cleared. He was probably allowed to visit his brother only because their conversation and nonverbal exchanges would be monitored closely as well as taped and filmed.

"How's Anna?" Rust asked.

"Do we have to?" Repson's face was twitching.

"Please."

"She'll live."

"Good. I want to be there when they strap her in the chair. Are you coming?"

"I'd have preferred it if you hadn't interfered."

"I'm sorry, Ell, but you went crazy at the time."

"I know. That's why my first shot failed to kill her."

"Fortunately, I'd say. Because you know as well as I do that it's important to have a chance to interrogate her."

"I know. Anyone but her husband would think of that right away. But I am her husband, I'm sorry to say."

"Did the bullet go right through her throat?"

"Almost. She may lose her voice."

"I'll always remember her screams."

"So will I. I heard the tape." Repson's voice was hardly audible.

"Pity they didn't tape me, too." Rust turned to Schramm: "Are you sure there wasn't a tape of the interrogation?"

"Pretty sure. Why?"

"It would be good to know how much I told them. I can't even remember their questions. Do you think they might have forwarded information to Moscow right away?" None of the men volunteered an answer. "I didn't give Yelena away. I couldn't. I don't even know her real name. Or anything about her. She was careful. She knew I'd give away everything if caught. That's why I wasn't supposed to know anything that wasn't essential." Fears, doubts and halfhearted self-assurances were gushing out of him. Schramm watched him sadly. For a second or two, Rust appeared to be on the verge of tears but then pulled himself together. The two counterintelligence men listened impassively. The one calling himself Peter asked Rust:

"Would you like to go through it again?"

"I've told you everything I could remember."

"It's worth a try," said the man calling himself Paul.

Their double act was annoying. They maintained a disinterested, strictly nonemotional attitude so zealously that it began to resemble the disguised hostility of a policeman trying to appear objective toward a child molester. Rust stared right through them. His eyes looked inward, reflecting some old horror. His knuckles whitened as his grip on the arms of his chair grew tighter. Schramm decided he would not like to bet whether Rust or the chair would crack up first. Peter and Paul noticed none of this. Noting but not noticing was part of their interrogation technique. Rust began to sense that their duty might not be mere debriefing. But he dismissed the thought. It was ridiculous.

"Did you get me a copy of the pictures?" he asked Schramm.

"No. Er, not yet."

"They're still being processed," said Paul, and Peter nodded in agreement.

"Just don't be long with them. There's no time."

"We realize that," said Peter, and this time it was Paul who did the nodding.

"No, you don't. You don't seem to realize that every minute may count. If the information is correct, those ships are coming in as fast as they can burn their diesel, the erectors are all trying to win their Stakhanov medal for overfulfilling their norms, and missiles may be raising their nuclear warheads all over Cuba before you could say 'being processed' three times. Yelena was clear about that." He paused, but nobody reacted. The silence seemed to disturb him. Schramm noticed that he was getting dangerously agitated as he continued his monologue. "She knew the timing. She knew that Khrushchev was in a hurry. That's why she risked everything. Even her life." The memory of her face brought him a smile. "And believe me, she might romanticize the thought of martyrdom, but she'd hate to be an actual rather than potential martyr."

"Then why would she risk her life?" Peter asked.

"I've told you. She hates Khrushchev."

"Millions and millions of Russians do, but they do nothing about it," said Repson.

"Perhaps she hates him more."

"Why?"

"I don't know. Perhaps because he once ruled the Ukraine and she's convinced that he was personally responsible for her husband's death in Kiev. Yes, come to think of it, her accent might have been Ukrainian. Which could explain it. But then maybe she's driven even more by her love of peace. It sounded pompous and pretentious when she talked about it. But she meant it. She cared about peace. And she cared about her country. And she cared a lot about Khrushchev's grip on her country. That's why she was anxious to help us. To force Khrushchev's missiles out of Cuba before they become operational. Because if we're late, it will be disastrous."

"You mean war?" asked Schramm.

"No. Compromise."

Repson shook his head. "Out of the question. The President was most emphatic about that."

"Yelena thinks the President is bluffing. She thinks that Khrushchev is convinced that the odds are in his favor. He's going to win something on this gamble unless Kennedy puts his foot down now!"

"Your Yelena wasted time by turning to you," said Peter.

"Weeks. She wasted weeks," added Paul.

"She was desperate. She had already tried to send us the information through various channels, including a suspected CIA agent."

"How would she know about anybody like that?" asked Repson.

"I don't know."

"She must be KGB or GRU."

"Maybe. I've already discussed this with Peter and Paul. Several times. And we haven't got anywhere with it." Rust's hand began to shake. He had to loosen his grip on the arm of the chair.

"We don't mind talking about it again," said Paul.

"Let's," said Peter.

"You think she wants to work for us?" asked Repson.

"No. Definitely not."

"But she's ready to help us."

"She doesn't give a shit!" Rust laughed. "Not a shit." He seemed unable to stop laughing. "That's what she said—and I·believe her."

"I wouldn't," said Schramm.

"Neither would I," chimed in Repson. "She must care a lot if she's willing to become a traitor."

That stopped Rust's laughter. "She'd kill you for that word. She doesn't see herself as a traitor. She sees it as her patriotic duty to help oust Khrushchev, who's wrong for her country. When I called her a traitor, it made her cry." He looked from one man to another. He thought he saw nothing but animosity in their eyes. "It did, I'm telling you." He felt cold. He did not seem to realize that the shakes had spread from his hand to all over his body. "Is there no heat in this damned room? Jake, you look shiverish. You must keep warm." Their silence made it even worse for Rust. He tried to retreat, pushing his chair back. He almost fell off it. "She's no traitor. We shouldn't treat her like one. She's honest. Don't you believe me?"

Peter had already pressed a panic button. A doctor and a nurse came running. They gave Rust an injection. "You'd better let him sleep now," the doctor advised.

"See you later," said Peter, and Paul nodded.

"I'll be around if you need me," said Repson.

Rust's eyes were desperately scanning the room: was there a centipede anywhere in sight? Schramm wanted to say something but could not. He was about to leave the room when Rust called him back. "Jake!"

"Yes?"

"What chance do we have to get them out?"

"Who?"

"Yelena and my father."

"I don't know."

"I might have a way. I mean they know the way." Rust's voice sounded tired. "She knows the way. And with a little help from us, from me I mean, when the time comes . . ." His speech slurred slightly. The jab had begun to take effect.

"Do you think he'd want to come over?" Schramm was thinking about the misleading information Rust had gotten from his father.

"I don't know. Talk to Chles. He's a gdm."

"A what?"

"A gdm."

Schramm guessed he might mean "good man." It was pointless to press him. Or to tell him that the Company had not authorized Charles to come and visit him. "I'll talk to him."

• Sunday, October 7 •

Guatemalan President reveals deal: He permitted use of his
country as training ground for Cuban invasion—now it's
America's turn to honor its half of the bargain and support
him in dispute over British Honduras. New York attorney
negotiates with Castro in Havana to swap captured Bay of
Pigs invaders for drugs and baby food. U.S. Assistant Naval
Attache is "caught red-handed" examining "military targets"
and carrying spy equipment (camera and maps) in Leningrad; he is roughed up and made *persona non grata*.

MAJOR BOYCHENKO WAS WELL SATISFIED WITH HIS PRES-
tigious new office. Thanks to his progress with the
investigation, his transfer to the Spetsburo had been finalized,
and the difference it made to his status could be felt everywhere: in the information he suddenly had access to, in the
way people greeted or saluted him, in the privileged purchases
he could now make in the KGB store, in the quality of his
chair and the size of his desk, in his own family's new respect

for him, but above all, in the things he could *do* with no
questions asked. While waiting for the file he was at last to
see, he decided to attend to three minor matters that had been
tucked away in his subconscious for weeks. A thought made
him smile. He had always prided himself on his memory.
From now on, nobody, but nobody, would be entitled to
count on his forgetfulness.

First he signed a "recommendation of transfer." A young
lieutenant, who had been in charge of the arrest and shooting
of old Rostonov, causing a bloody spectacle in the glass cage
of an elevator, was to be transferred to camp duty in Siberia.
It could be almost as bad as being an inmate of those camps.
Too bad, thought Boychenko, and reassured himself that it was
a mere coincidence that the same lieutenant had been in charge
of his own interrogation.

The second minor matter concerned Zemskov, the retired
Records clerk. Boychenko signed a note, already typed, saying
that Zemskov's handling of certain documents six years ago
had not been in strict accordance with regulations, and therefore
"his continued residence in Moscow is undesirable." Boychenko did not particularly care where they would send him:
the man would be expelled from the capital and deprived of
the luxurious accommodation he clearly did not deserve.

Finally, he made a telephone call. He thanked his daughter's
boss in Foreign Trade for the comradely help and encourage-
ment she had been given. It would ensure quick promotion for
her.

There was a knock at the door. He grunted approvingly and
his orderly brought in a file. Boychenko scrutinized Kolya and
found that the man's spic-and-span appearance was an accolade
to his own new status. He dismissed him with an impatient
wave of two fingers, then concentrated on the dossier: RUST,
Helm, 1956. It was essential to know the facts before starting
a potentially lengthy interrogation that might lead to revenge
on the man who had almost ruined his career.

The missile photographs and the report on their source were
studied by members of COMOR, and although there were certain doubts about their validity and the circumstances of their
delivery, there seemed to be a sufficiently strong argument in
favor of moving the next committee meeting up to October 9.

* * *

The consensus of medical opinion was satisfied with Rust's health. He had come out of heavy sedation in the morning, and appeared to be sufficiently cheerful and hungry throughout the tests. His mood changed considerably when two strangers from the CIA were brought in to see him.

"Just a few questions to clear up, hope you don't mind," they said. "For simplicity, call us Peter and Paul, if you wish."

"What happened to the other Peter and Paul?"

"Transferred to other duties, I suppose," said the senior of the two, who laid a thick file on the table and opened it.

Rust noticed the markings on the top sheets inside. One was a "201," his overt biographical data kept by CIA archives. The other was marked T for "trace." It would set out all known facts, allegations, suspicions, confidential reports and assessments concerning his past.

"Am I under some sort of suspicion?"

"Not at all. Just routine. We have to verify a few points and clarify the role you've played in this affair. You understand, I suppose."

"What's happening to the info I've brought out?"

"Let's get these papers out of the way first, shall we?"

From the details of the first few questions Rust could tell that this was not going to be a quickie. These two were bent on covering the entire ground all over again.

• Tuesday, October 9 •

Cuban President Dorticós at the UN claims the country can defend itself with "weapons we'd have preferred not to acquire and which we do not wish to employ." U.S. Ambassador Stevenson: "The maintenance of communism in the Americas is not negotiable." U.S.-assisted Alpha 66, an exile organization, raids Cuban port.

ELLIOTT REPSON WAITED IN THE PRESIDENTIAL AIDE'S ROOM for the session of COMOR to end. At last the aide returned with the news that the decision had been made: the U-2 flights were to be resumed all over the island. "Trouble is that the weather isn't all that favorable just now," he said. "But it's high time we got some real surveillance instead of those peripheral flights, agree?"

"Sure."

"I hear it was your brother who brought back those microdots."

"Half brother."

"You think that Keating's seen those pictures?"

"No idea."

Senator Kenneth Keating, who had just stirred up Congress with a statement that according to his "one hundred percent reliable" private sources six intermediate-range missile sites were under construction in Cuba, refused to disclose those sources to anyone. The presidential aide did not quite believe that Repson had "no idea." He was not alone in the suspicion that somebody at the CIA had leaked the pictures to the Senator. Damn spooks, damn cripple, he thought. He had never forgiven Repson for Anna's refusal of his advances. "How's Anna?"

"Fine, thanks."

"See you both at the party tonight."

"She can't go. I'm sorry. She has some trouble with a, uh, bunion. It hurts." Repson could not bring himself to attributing anything more serious to her state of health. He was not supposed to divulge the truth as yet. For it was a policy decision by CIA Security not to reveal to anyone that Mrs. Repson had been unmasked as a Russian agent. For the same reason, Repson was to continue all his normal duties and activities despite the shock he had suffered.

"And you say that this doll, this Yelena, referred to the KGB as the 'neighbors,' right?"

"Right."

"And she used the word *taynik* for mail drops, right?"

"Right. We've been through this umpteen times."

"And the guy who called himself Florian—you think that was his real name?"

"I don't know."

"What's your guess?"

"I can't guess. Put a yes and a no in a hat."

"And you say he used a Tokarev 7.15."

"Yes."

"You'd recognize it if you saw one."

"Right."

"Can you describe it?"

"For Chrissake, I know the damn gun. I've looked down

its barrel from both ends." Rust was pleased with himself that he was able to control his temper. But he was less and less sure how long he would be willing to. This kind of detailed interrogation ought to be concentrated on Anna if anyone.

• Wednesday, October 10 •

Russian assassin on trial in Karlsruhe, West Germany, demonstrates to court the working of poison gas pistol, his weapon from the KGB. British shipowners, Brazil and Sweden disapprove of U.S. restrictions on non-military trade with Cuba. Alpha 66 threatens to fire on merchant ships trading with Cuba. *Izvestiya* criticizes great "glamour wear scarcity": Moscow (population 5 million) receives only 650 pairs of nylons a day.

RUST WAS ABOUT TO REACH THE END OF HIS TETHER. ONE set of Peter and Pauls had been replaced by another, but the questions and the ground to be covered remained the same. They were checking only his memory, they claimed. No, it should not take long now. No, he was not a suspect, of course not. Why should he be? Could he think of any reason why he should be? Or at least the reason that made him think that he might be? No, there was no news for him from Sir Charles or

Repson or Hal or Schramm, nothing about Anna or the fate of the microdots.

Then Repson arrived. The hallmark of sleepless nights was stamped all over his face. He had stunning news for Rust: "Anna's been turned."

"You mean she's ready to work for us?"

"Yes."

"She may be a plant."

"Maybe. But she's singing. Well, it's a mixture of writing things down and whispering. They don't want to rush her. Or push her too hard. She's too important."

"Wish I was, too."

"You must understand. She may become an active double for us."

"You mean she might get away with it and escape the chair?"

"Right. I can imagine they'll prosecute me instead for damaging her!"

"She's a traitor."

"But right now, she's on our side. She's already given us the name of a KGB agent at the UN. He has diplomatic status, but he'll be declared persona non grata."

"Makes you puke."

"It's the game, Helm. One must be pragmatic about these things."

"Not me, mate. In my book, she's just a common criminal."

"That's just the point. They don't want you to show her— well, not too blatantly, at least—how you feel."

"I don't want to see her. Not without a nine-inch centipede in my hand."

"You'll have to. Security wants you to question her about your own involvement with her."

"No."

"I'll also have to be present."

"Even more disgusting."

"We'll have to be impersonal about it."

Her room was in a clump of bungalows, not far from Rust's. It was bright, full of flowers, with a good view of the forest. Heavily bandaged, her figure gently outlined on the crisp white top sheet, breathing cautiously as if timed by the steady drops of the intravenous tube, Rust found her so beautiful that it hurt. Hurt because it would have made a simpler, more manageable world if bad character were always twinned with inevitable ugliness. She smiled when the duty officer opened the door to let the brothers in, Rust pushing Repson's wheelchair. Neither of them could help wondering to whom her supposedly dying confession of love had belonged. But the question was not asked and she did not volunteer an answer.

Conversation with her was an arduous process, and they were reminded repeatedly that she was not to be exhausted or pressured.

"Are you Russian?" Rust asked her.

"Half." And after a pause: "But born here." She struggled to speak. "I've lived here all my life."

"That's been dealt with, Mr. Rust," the duty officer cut in, "but I can give you the gist of it. She's what amounts to being a second-generation agent. Her grandparents escaped from Russia via Shanghai and Hong Kong, and settled over here. Her mother quarreled with them, became a Communist and married a Communist. They were recruited by the KGB during the war. They themselves trained Anna for the job, but she was not activated until 1955, when both her parents were already dead. Please don't bother her with questions about the earlier period, not just now, if you don't mind."

"Not at all. Why should I? I'm as anxious as the next man to molly-coddle this delectable young lady, our newly found ally." Rust stared at her hard. "Pity we weren't on the same side just a few days earlier."

"I'm sorry. I didn't know what those two men would do to you."

"How did you know the code?"

"I listened in on the phone."

"Ell would have heard and recognized the click when you picked up the extension."

"She didn't use the extension," said Repson. "She had an extra earpiece connected to the line. It was hidden among her clothes, and whenever the line was in use, she could just listen. It had a cover fitted so that it wouldn't be heard chirping if, for instance, she was speaking on the line and I happened to look for something in the bedroom or even in her closet."

Rust listened to him but never took his eyes off her. "Were you sent to Leningrad only to pick me up?"

"No. I had to be briefed for the job. And to meet you, yes."

"Is that why I got permission to visit the closed part of the Hermitage? To bring me within your reach?"

"Yes."

"But why? You never even tried to recruit me."

"No, you were being set up for recruitment by some other KGB Directorate or perhaps the GRU, I don't know. But after I'd met Ell and he wanted to marry me, it was decided that you must be eliminated from CIA work."

"Why?"

"You were too close to Ell. You might have noticed things. You know, oddities about him. Something that might lead to his fall. We, I mean they, well, we, in fact, had to protect him. He'd be pushed hard to get promotions, and with our help—"

"Whose help?"

"Sapphire. It's a separate network."

"What network?"

"KGB. Not even the Washington Resident knows it. I certainly don't."

"We'll have to try and prod your memory."

Anna looked at the duty officer, who, in turn, warned Rust, "Please don't question her about her contacts, superiors and lines of communications. That's being dealt with by others."

Rust shrugged his shoulders. "How was I to be eliminated from Company work?"

"Somebody studied your past and behavior pattern. It was thought you'd resign."

"Because of our affair?"

She nodded, but avoided his eyes.

"And if not?"

"You'd be blackmailed into it."

"With the pictures?"

"Yes."

"Why did you suddenly reverse the blackmail idea?"

"Orders from the Center."

"Why?"

"I didn't know then that you were on the run from Moscow. But they foresaw that you might get to Ell and cause an embarrassment to me."

"So you arranged that the pictures should be planted at the Upstairs."

"Yes."

"Did you know what would happen to my friend Hal?"

"No. We thought the house was empty."

"When did you receive your orders?"

"Oh, about the eighteenth or nineteenth."

"September?"

"Yes. But it was only a precaution. Nobody thought you'd get out of the Soviet U—I mean, Russia. But they didn't know what other contacts you had in Moscow."

"What do you mean, 'other' contacts?"

"Apart from the embassy."

"Do you know that Holly was killed?"

"Who's Holly?"

"The man I contacted at the embassy."

"I'm sorry."

"Who was your man at the embassy?"

"I don't know."

The duty officer raised his hand. "Please stick to your own area of involvement."

Rust started to walk up and down the room. When he was passing the bed, he suddenly stopped and leaned over Anna. "Why did you claim that you craved my sperms?"

"I . . ." She stopped, closed her eyes, took a deep breath which seemed to hurt her, then tried to outstare him. "It was part of my instructions in Leningrad."

It shamed him that he was still so bugged by that sentence. Damn male vanity, he thought. Her instructors had certainly known how to plant a painful verbal time bomb that would be remembered. He turned to Repson with an apologetic half-smile. Repson nodded, saying. "It's not your fault," and busied himself with the handbrake of the wheelchair.

"What was your main assignment? Spying on Bobby Kennedy?" Rust tried to sound as impersonal as possible.

"Please," the duty officer reprimanded him.

"It's essential. Please answer," Rust insisted.

"Yes. I was to pick up as much intelligence as possible. But it was even more important to help Ell's promotions. It was hoped that one day he would be in a really top job and I'd be there, with him. In a position of trust."

"You mean his bed."

"Yes."

"How did you know that I was in Moscow?"

"I didn't. Not until about the eighteenth. That's why they asked me to find out where you were."

"Who asked you? The Center?"

"Yes."

"Why would they be interested in me or my whereabouts at the time?" Rust noticed that the duty officer pricked up his ears and looked toward a mirror. It must be a two-way, Rust guessed.

"Because of the message from the defector...I mean, the Russian sailor who tried to defect in Cuba."

"Tried?"

"He was caught."

"And questioned?"

"Probably."

"And he talked?"

"Probably."

"What the hell do you mean, probably? You know damn well that they all talk. I mean *we* all talk. Your people are kind of persuasive."

"Not *my* people. Not anymore."

"Why not?"

"I left them, didn't I?"

"Why? Why have you turned?" She was silent, and he grabbed her shoulders. *"Why?"* The officer did not interfere. "Why?" He shook her. Tears appeared in her eyes. *"Why?"*

"I lost my faith in them."

"So suddenly?"

"Not suddenly."

"I don't believe you."

"I was hoping that Communism would be different under Khrushchev."

"It wasn't. But that didn't make you change sides. You didn't come over voluntarily. You turned your coat only when you were caught."

"I was afraid."

"Of them?"

"Of them. And you. All of you. I didn't want to be tortured."

"We don't torture people."

"Don't you?"

Tears rolled down her cheeks and woke him to the fact that

he had been squeezing her shoulders mercilessly, just where the flesh curved into forming her neck. "I'm sorry." He drank some water to give himself time to cool down. "Okay. What do you know about that sailor, defector, call him what you like, and the message he brought out?"

"Only what the message was. Somebody had been ill but was better now. Something like that."

"What were you supposed to do with it?"

"To get it to you and report back your reaction."

"So you sent O'Connor to me, right?"

"Who's he?"

"He brought me the message. Posing as CIA."

"I wouldn't know. I didn't know who'd take the message. I only conveyed the Center's orders. I left them in a mail drop. It would be picked up by someone who'd then make his reports to me through another drop near Harvey's, the fish restaurant on 18th Street."

"Used to be one of our favorites," Repson mumbled.

Rust ignored him. "Well, I have news for you, sweetheart. You were not so clever after all." He was bent on hurting her, at least with words, and did not feel ashamed. "That poor, wretched man, whose balls were probably torn out when he was probably questioned probably by your friends, that sailor tricked you probably with his last breath. He changed the name in the message, and that was a warning signal to Yelena and my father and eventually to me, too!" It made him feel better. At least he had paid tribute to the memory of a fellow victim.

Anna appeared to be very tired. Her breathing was erratic. A doctor was summoned, and it was thought best to discontinue the interrogation.

"I don't believe her," said Rust to his brother when the door closed behind them. "She's trying to save her skin by offering to work for us."

"She didn't offer it. She was forced to."

"And if we set her up as a double on that basis, you think we could ever trust her?"

"No, I don't think so. Her actions will have to be watched all the way. But don't underestimate our own people. This decision was made at the highest level. The risks and the odds must have been assessed carefully." He took a deep breath as Rust pushed his chair through self-closing doors into the dusk that smudged the edges of trees and buildings. "I only wish I wasn't involved emotionally."

"But you are. And I must congratulate you, Ell."

"Why?"

"Because you didn't throttle her a few minutes ago. I know what a struggle it must be to restrain yourself."

"And it's going to be much worse."

"How can it be?"

"Through daily exposure."

"Daily? You mean . . . you're crazy!"

"It's not my choice, Helm, believe me. But she's potentially the most important double we've had for years. To play her will be a game of great skill and tremendous excitement. The main thing is to keep up the appearances. Nothing, but nothing, must seem to change in our lives."

"You mean she remains your devoted wife?"

"She must."

"And you're willing to continue living with her."

"No, I'm not. But I'm willing to continue living with the new game. I'm a player. I don't opt out easily."

"Thanks."

"I didn't mean that."

"Didn't you?" Rust was pushing the wheelchair faster and faster along the narrow garden path. "Goddam squeak. Why can't you get it fixed?"

"I keep forgetting it."

"It's awful." And it became even more irritatingly prominent when they entered the corridor of the building where Rust's room was.

"What's your next move, Helm?"

"Wish I knew."

"They really ought to reward you."

"For what?"

"Well, whatever else there may be, you've certainly exposed Anna. So I'm sure you'll land something big. After a while, I mean. Hasn't anybody approached you to discuss it?"

"Not yet."

"It'll come."

"How long will they keep me here?"

"I don't know. The longer the better."

"Why?"

"It's safer for you. You must have made some pretty obstinate enemies over there."

"I'm not important anymore."

"Don't bank on it, Helm. I guess our people must have turned the Upstairs into a fortress by now."

"What for? I'm not even sure that I'll ever go back there."

"You might have to."

"Nobody's telling me what I must do."

"The Company may."

"You're forgetting something, Ell. I've opted out. I'm a free agent."

"Sure. Nobody's disputing that. But I know that some people are thinking a lot about your future."

"Tell them to leave the thinking to me."

"That's just what I told them. Especially when I heard a bit of gossip."

"What?"

"That somebody had a bright idea of sending you to Cuba."

"Are they crazy?"

"Must be. Mind you, they said it would be quite a unique opportunity for you."

"What opportunity?"

"I don't know."

"Tell them to go and fuck themselves. All of them."

"I'll tell them. In fact, I think I have a much better idea."

"What?"

"To recruit you for my little outfit. It would be great to work together, wouldn't it?"

"Depends."

"Naturally. And, of course, the scheme would have to be devised very carefully. But with your Cuban contacts . . ."

"Forget it, Ell." They reached the room. Rust sat on his bed. No one was there, but someone was no farther away than the receiving ends of the bugs that must be hidden in every corner, every piece of furniture. Rust glanced around with open disgust. Repson nodded in agreement. "It's ridiculous," said Rust. "They trust her more than me."

"I don't know. But the important thing is that it should seem so to the Center. Don't forget, it'll be monitoring every move she makes. It'll scrutinize every word in every communication from her. It'll have to be convinced that although you might have killed their man on Long Island, you're not suspecting her, that although you might have delivered the message from Moscow, our people don't quite trust you because the blackmail trick has worked. It'll expect to see that you're in a bit of disgrace."

"Sounds great."

"It's our only way to sell them the double bluff. Even you and I won't be able to see one another for a while. I must seem to be furious with you."

"Naturally. I've fucked and blackmailed your beloved wife, haven't I?"

"That's how they devised the trap, and that's what they must see us falling into."

"Count me out, Ell."

"Sure. At least you won't have to share my predicament. Living with her, living with the temptation to kick her and beat her and . . . fuck her, yes, fuck her, no matter what. Because I still want her, and it's shitty and humiliating."

"I understand."

"How could you? You're a free agent. With all the glory of getting information out of Moscow and helping to prevent Khrushchev from arming Cuba with nukes."

"Yes, I could have done that in July. With that shopping list from Castro's desk."

"That's why Anna must have stolen it."

"I thought she was denying that."

"She was. But when we reminded her of the *porokhovyye konfety* on the list, she remembered and admitted it."

"Pity I didn't choose a different channel."

"You wanted to help me, Helm."

"Several people would still be alive if I hadn't."

Soon after Repson had left, Schramm arrived.

"Come on, Helm, our celebration dinner is long overdue."

"Have you brought sandwiches?"

"We're going out."

"Outside?" Rust asked with mock astonishment. "You mean I can be trusted?"

"Yeah. As long as you're protected."

"That's one way of putting it, I suppose."

"I've reserved a private room in an excellent Georgetown steakhouse."

It was a chauffeur-driven car, and they were following a civilian motorcyclist. Rust glanced back over his shoulder. An unmarked car seemed to be sitting right on their tail. Perhaps he was not trusted all that much. It infuriated him, but he chose to wait and see. He did not need to wait for long. Halfway through dinner, Schramm said he had a message for Rust.

"From whom?"

Schramm's index finger stabbed toward the ceiling.

"Really?"

"The very top. They want you to know how much your work is appreciated."

"Will they follow up the info?"

"Only bad weather is delaying it. U-2s will look at every microdot you brought us. They're very grateful. You've helped to settle an argument in high places."

"So what's the catch?"

"No catch."

They were finishing dinner when the door opened and Sir Charles walked in. "Good to see you, Helm."

"Good to see you, too. What a coincidence. You walking in here of all places."

"The place is famous for its Calvados. Can I have a glass with you?"

They drank, and Charles began to explain why in his opinion, Calvados was a better after-dinner drink than Cognac, but Rust lost his patience: "Okay, we've had the spiel, now let's have the facts of life."

"Right," said Schramm. "You've done well. You've earned the right to a hell of a lot of privileges. For the time being, I've been given the full-time job of looking after you and helping you do whatever you want. So what's your plan?"

"I haven't got one. I'm still living from one interrogation to the next."

"That's coming to an end. We can start preparing your future. We've got some ideas."

"Such as sending me to Cuba?"

"That's out. You're much too valuable to risk."

"You mean you've never thought about it?"

"Somebody had that half-baked idea, but it was dismissed right away. It would be crazy. How did you hear about it?"

"Ell mentioned some gossip."

"He shouldn't have."

"He's my brother."

"But not in charge of your case. He shouldn't have discussed plans with you."

"And you're talking bullshit, Jake."

Charles put his hand on Rust's arm. "Take it easy. You're talking to friends."

"Then talk like friends. That's what you owe me, if anything."

"That's why I've brought in Charles," said Schramm. "He and I have found a dream of a liaison job for you."

"At least until things clear up and you're ready for a major step up," Charles chimed in.

"No thanks."

"You can't rush these things, Helm."

"I know. I must be seen to be in disgrace, at least for a while, right?"

"Is that your idea?"

"No, but it's logical."

"Did Ell suggest it?"

"Yes."

"Once again, it was not for him to say that, but if he thought about it, he must have come to this conclusion because he's a pro."

"Whereas I'm still an amateur, is that what you mean?"

There was an almost imperceptible pause, then both men said, "Yes." And Charles added, "To tell you the truth."

"Good. I'm proud of it."

Schramm ordered more drinks, then asked Rust how he saw his future.

"Right now I have only one idea. I hear that Jus'-juice is out of the hospital. He suffered because of me. It's only fair that I should look after him until he recovers."

"Where? At the Upstairs?"

"Where else?" Rust thought he saw them exchange glances. "Any objections?"

"Well . . ."

"Well what? I owe him that much." He did not want to say that it would be essential for him to stay at the Upstairs for a while. Only there could a message from his father or Yelena reach him. If they needed somewhere to run to. If they wanted to.

"You're a great friend, Helm," said Charles, "we know that, but do you realize the risk?"

"You must have a lot of enemies," added Schramm. "The kind that never give up. Their own loyalties and discipline are built on revenge. They might come after you. Have you thought about that?"

"That should please you. If you watch my back properly, you may even catch them. Those whom Anna's refused to name and those she's never known. Like Sapphire."

"It's an idea."

"You should have kept quiet, Jake. Your voice was too delighted. But I don't mind. Because there's something else. I don't believe that Anna was the only ace in their pack. She could spy in Ell's bed and in her job, but she couldn't have pushed her husband up and up at the speed Ell was advancing. And the tidbits he had from me must have helped, but couldn't be enough. So there must have been others behind her. And if they go for me, we might find them."

"True."

"Then I'll play sitting duck for you on the condition that if anything comes of it and I live, I'll know the truth."

Charles laughed. "I think I can hear the last breath of your amateurism."

"Pity. I still don't want to see life as a game."

"Why? Do you see yourself as an idealist?"

"You both know me better than that. But being skeptical doesn't mean I can't trust friends. And despising politics doesn't mean I can't be inspired by a young President and his New Frontier men."

"Ah! You've managed to salvage the old loyalties."

"Without them I wouldn't be human."

"Without them you'd be a pro," said Charles. The laughter had disappeared from his eyes and voice without a trace, like May-morning frost. The way he said "pro" had a long-lingering echo. It kept reverberating in Rust's ears: if anything, he loathed cold professionalism and the game; if anything, he secretly longed to become a cold professional and a player in the game.

• Sunday, October 14 •

Kennedy predicts Castro's early fall from power. England receives assurance that U.S. will not sanction assaults by Cuban exiles on British or other Havana-bound vessels though it cannot be guaranteed that such incidents will not occur. British court to try Admiralty spy Vassall. Jackie Kennedy's new wardrobe is predicted to be a "tremendous surprise."

EKATERINA FURTSEVA HAD NO INTENTION OF SOOTHING her lover: the radiogram, delivered by special Kremlin messenger, had infuriated Khrushchev, and she thought it served him right. She had warned him about rumors that some of his generals and closest associates were trying to torpedo his game with *konfety* in Cuba. He should have ordered a full investigation right away. Now it might be too late.

With the telephone pressed to his right ear, Khrushchev stood at the window of her bedroom, staring down at Granovsky ulitsa, the endless row of waiting black Chaikas and Zils, the Bureau of Passes sign on No. 2, and the curved gray horn, now silent, on the corner. He listened to Biryuzov's apologetic voice, and wondered if the young missile general was one of those who might have wished to leak his plans to the Americans.

"We're almost ready, Nikita Sergeyevich, I can assure you. The delay's been due only to some limitations of port facilities and the traditional Cuban *mañana*. We have no way of cutting out at least limited use of local labor."

Of course not. Khrushchev knew that only too well. Castro's pride had to be observed: Cubans had to be seen helping with the construction of the missile sites. Khrushchev cut the general short: "You know there's been an overflight."

"Yes, Nikita Sergeyevich. It was a U-2 aircraft. There could be no mistake." The implication was clear: Khrushchev himself and the KGB at the highest level had assured Biryuzov that construction work could be carried out without wasting time on any special camouflage or protection from air reconnaissance because the Americans would not want to risk a serious incident and would therefore refrain from missions over western Cuba. So was their information wrong, or had there been a change in American policy?

The same questions vexed Khrushchev, too. But he went further. If there was a change in policy, what had brought it about? Had somebody succeeded in leaking information? How much information? Would Kennedy be willing to go to war over Cuba after all? If so, would he do it if missiles with nuclear warheads were already operational in Cuba? Or would he still be willing to comply with the Russians' minimum demand and guarantee noninterference as a reciprocal gesture for the removal of the missiles? It was all a matter of timing, so time had to be gained. "Are the current U-2s any different from the one we shot down?"

"There's no essential difference. As easy as the Gary Powers flight was."

"And what exactly is our Cuban surface-to-air readiness?"

"We could shoot them out of the sky at six hours' notice."

"So we could bring one down if there were more overflights."

"Yes, Nikita Sergeyevich, we'll be ready in six hours precisely."

"No, we won't! I didn't ask you to make policy decisions for me, did I? You just carry on and wait for orders."

Khrushchev flung the phone down and missed the cradle. Madame Furtseva picked up the receiver and placed it on the set. "Why is it that every tinpot general believes that he understands politics, and everything else for that matter?"

"Because few people can argue with them. We've given them the right to pull rank on reason."

"Some people might say the same one day about politicians, or even the party itself."

"What makes you think they don't? I'm sure they whisper. At least behind our backs."

"The way some bastards call me Catherine the Third."

"Do they really?" Khrushchev resisted the impulse to laugh, and wondered if her nickname was an understatement. After all, he himself had enough trouble controlling her now and then.

"It's dangerous to tolerate such signs of disrespect," she kept droning. "Nicknames may only be the beginning of more serious breaches of discipline." She did not need to spell out the threat: he knew about the halfbaked conspiracies to oust him, but unlike Stalin, he chose not to kill his suspected or potential rivals. This new socialist legality was his only hope that they would also let him live if and when they ever succeeded. And he knew that she as well as many others despised him for it—despite their hatred of Stalin's memory.

The small, sparsely furnished room was hot, full of cigar smoke, and overcrowded with Schramm and the six Cubans who listened intently to Rust. Two of them were Bay of Pigs survivors, ready to go in and risk their lives again. Operation Mongoose appeared to be a better-prepared, more serious venture, and Rust's advice on the use of the smuggling routes was well received.

"Would you come with us on the next hit-and-run raid?" one of the swarthy men asked.

"It's not up to me," Rust said.

"What if it was?"

"I doubt if they'd let me."

"What if they let you?"

Rust shrugged his shoulders.

"Would you take us as far as Cay Sal?"

Cay Sal. It brought back unpleasant memories of the string of coral dots, so many barren deathtraps, separated from Cuba by the narrow Nicholas Channel. "It's not up to me."

"Helm is here only to brief you," said Schramm, who had arranged this meeting in Miami because Rust was anxious to help in some way. But Schramm was not at all happy about his involvement. He claimed he would have preferred to keep Rust at the Upstairs under well-organized protection. This was only their third day back in Florida, and they had already had several fights. One because of Hal "Jus'-juice" Sheridan, whose recovery and keep-fit technique involved Rust in endless rum-guzzling and target-shooting sessions. Another two major arguments were triggered by Rust's insistence on walking around in Little Havana. Rust kept saying that if nobody knew he was back, no Russki hit man would show up, and it made sense, Schramm had to admit, but not without angry reservations. Then there was Rust's boat, the *Half Pint*, an irristible invitation to "proving trips" along the coast allegedly "to check out the engine" that appeared to be as reliable as a new bucket in any case.

After the briefing session and the subsequent inevitable bar-hopping, they were back now at the Upstairs. Rust and Hal settled down to some serious consumption of golden Bacardi. Hal was pouring more and more generously, and his remarkable recovery was emphasized by his steady hand: he did not spill a single drop even when a scream came through the open window and made Schramm hurl himself at the light switch. "Get down and stay down. Hal stays with you," he rasped and was gone.

"Bullshit," said Rust unemotionally and, glass in hand, followed Schramm through the door.

At the junction of several flashlight beams, a girl lay on the curved, creaking stairs, her shin, thighs, belly and breasts pressed uncomfortably into the treading edges. A light frock clung to her back, annihilating the possibility of anything remaining hidden between her skin and the floral pattern, but two guards held guns to her head, and a third man seemed to be bent on doing his utmost to discover if she was armed. When Rust appeared at the top of the stairs, it was this third man who

shrieked, "Fucking bitch!" because the girl had bitten his du-
tifully searching hand.

"You touch me again and I bite your head off!" She yelled
with a strong Spanish accent, then looked up and noticed Rust.
"Chico!"

At first he failed to recognize her. Then a sudden tightness
in his groin reminded him of that long day in Cuba when he
had tried to rest in her bed and live with the advice from
Morales: "Don't let your prick talk when your head knows
better what not to do." She lay there, dressed in the lucky
pillow she clutched to her belly—yes, it all came back now.

He stepped over the bodyguards and helped her to her feet.
The dress was ridiculously ill-fitting, much too tight at all the
wrong or maybe right places depending on the viewpoint, glued
to oily skin probably by a film of sweat. Another dummy lover,
thought Rust, savoring his memory of that envied pillow. She
stuck her mouth out, expecting to be kissed, but Rust ignored
it. Her visit could not be accidental. Morales must have sent
her. "You're late," he said and noted Schramm's astonishment.

"Am I?"

Rust knew that she was puzzled, but luckily her question
sounded merely provocative.

"You know you are. Come inside."

"I have a—"

"Kiss for me?" He could not think of anything better for a
quick interruption. She smiled. Her offer was still open, and
this time, if the pretense was to be continued, it had to be taken
up. He kissed her hurriedly.

"Won't you introduce me?" Schramm asked.

"Oh, yes. Sorry. This is Jake." Rust realized he did not
even know her name. He gestured toward her and said the first
name that came to his mind. "And this is Sylvia."

"Nice to meet you, Sylvia. I'm sure Helm will forgive you
for being late."

She looked blank and startled, not knowing what to say.
Conversation was obviously not her forte, but she sensed tension, chose to snuggle up to Rust, and she knew how to snuggle
up to a man. Rust took her hand to lead her into the house,
but Schramm stopped him: "Can I just keep you for a second,
Helm?"

"Sure. Go ahead, honey. One of these nice men"—he nodded toward the bodyguards—"will be pleased to offer you a drink."

"What's up?" Schramm asked when the two of them were left alone at the top of the stairs.

"A date. Any objections?"

"I didn't know."

"Do I have to tell you? I didn't realize you were supposed to guard my morals, too."

"You know what I'm talking about. When did you manage to fix up the date? We've been together all the time."

"Not when you went to the john and left me propping up the bar."

"Which bar?"

"El Paraíso."

"I don't remember."

"Nobody'd expect you to unless each time you piss is a memorable occasion in your life."

"Very funny."

"I wasn't laughing."

"And you say you managed to pick her up and fix the date before I could give it a final pull."

"I didn't say I picked her up. She's an old friend."

"A lucky coincidence."

With Schramm's suspicion aroused, Rust did not want to talk to her in the house. If what "Sylvia" had for him was a message from Morales, it might be better to receive it in the privacy of the boat. Schramm insisted that they must remain in sight, no more than fifty yards from the jetty.

"Are you becoming a voyeur in your old age?"

Schramm ignored his feeble joke. "Fifty yards. And no swimming."

Rust stopped the *Half Pint* some fifty yards out and waved to the men on shore. He switched to his creaky Spanish. "We'd better lie down before you say anything." She smiled, and he hurried to point out that it was only for the sake of appearances.

She reached for the hemline of the dress. "Would it help if I took it off?"

"Not unless you first tied a knot in my prick."

She peeled herself up to mid-thigh before he could stop her. "Why, *chico*? Don't you like me?"

"Morales is my friend." He paused. "If you're still with him, that is. Are you?"

"He's been very good to me."

"And to me." They lay side by side in the confined space, and the boat rocked to knock their bodies together. "Did he send you?"

"Yes. Now let me get this right. He said the *Bucca-neer* . . . no, not *Buccaneer* . . . *Buchaneer* . . . damn . . . he said it's a big town in Roman . . ."

"Roman? Rome?"

"No. It's a country."

"Rumania?"

"You're clever." She kissed his cheek. "How did you get that scar?"

"Stick to your message. Big town in Rumania. Bucharest."

"That's it, *chico*. It's a tanker. *Bucharest* is a tanker and it has a tank on board and it'll be in Cuba in about ten days."

"With a tank on board."

"Yes. Must be Russian. Only Russian tanks come to Cuba."

"Good thinking," said Rust. There was no need to tell her that it could only be the tank for baby crocodiles and it must contain his father or Yelena or both. "And I'm very grateful for the message. Now how will you get back to Cuba?"

"I'm not going."

"Oh yes you are. Morales expects you back, I'm sure, and you'll take my message to him."

"Tell him yourself. He's in Miami."

"What?"

"We left five days ago. For good. He was in trouble. As soon as we got here, he tried to find you, but there were too many guards around your house. Then he saw you in a bar." She kept chattering on but Rust was not listening. The news was a blow. He had always counted on it that if Yelena used the escape route, Morales would arrange her passage from Cuba to Florida. That plan now collapsed. It would be unfair even to try to persuade Morales to return home and risk facing whatever dangers he had escaped from. And Rust knew nobody else he could trust with the task.

"Tell Morales I want to meet him," he said.

"He's going to be away until the day after tomorrow."

"Okay, tell him to be in the john of El Paraíso at, say, four in the afternoon."

"In the john?"

"That's what I said. He must wait for me in there. And you sit at the bar. I'll see you there."

"Okay." Her mission completed, she relaxed, closed her eyes and let her mouth open slightly: she had once been told that men liked the shadowy shape of her tongue in the cage of lips and teeth. When nothing happened, she looked up. He was staring out to sea. "Are you tired, *chico*?" It was a genuine whisper of concern without any trace of resentment.

"No, I'm not. And I want you very much, you must know that. But he's my friend. An old man. You're probably his last love. We can't do it to him."

"Whatever you say. It's only that I was so pleased that you remembered me."

"You're a memorable girl, sweetheart." He did not want to call her sweetheart. But it would have been cruel to ask her now what her real name was.

· Tuesday, October 16 ·

Monday television interview with McGeorge Bundy, special assistant to the President, is quoted by the press: "I know there's no present evidence" or likelihood that Cuba and the Soviet Union "would, in combination, attempt to install a major offensive capability. . . ."

THE SHIPPING AGENT WITH ACCESS TO LLOYD'S MARITIME intelligence searched the available reports diligently but drew a blank on the *Bucharest*. He could have left it at that, except that he owed a favor or two to Rust, who would telephone him again later in the morning. Why Rust was interested, why he had asked for speed and secrecy, why Rust had called from a public phone instead of dropping in, the agent did not want to know. He looked through the Lloyd's list, found the Istanbul agent's number, and put through a telephone call. He spoke to a young man who, judging from the trill in the voice, must have been tickled pink by the transatlantic inquiry. His conclusion was correct. Young Ercihan, looking out across the

Bosphorus, was anxious to savor every second of his own importance. Only his knowledge of the cost involved persuaded him not to demand an explanation for the slightly irregular approach. "No, it's not surprising, kind sir, that the sailing of the aforementioned tanker is not making an appearance in the list, because it has passed through our esteemed view only two hours ago."

When Rust called the shipping agent once again, he was told that the *Bucharest* was on her way and would probably reach a Cuban port in about eight to ten days. I must be crazy, thought Rust, but he could think of no excuse for not going to Cuba. There was something suspicious about his father, but he had to be rescued if he was on the run. And Rust was uncertain what urged him to help Yelena. It might be love, lust or infatuation. Or a debt to be paid.

The fresh U-2 photographs were proof beyond doubt to the photo analysts of the CIA. The four-slash configuration on the ground was just like that in the pictures of intercontinental ballistic missile sites in the Soviet Union. In the light of these, the four-to-six-week-old photographs of Soviet ships attained additional significance. Both the *Omsk* and *Poltava* in the pictures were "long-hatch" freighters. Both rode unusually high in the water, indicating relatively light but space-demanding "bulk cargo" in the sealed holds. Both had trucks and other ominously shaped objects under canvas on their decks. The final interpretation was: missiles on board, missiles that were much larger than the defensive SAMs.

Internally, the CIA owed apologies and lavish praise to the analyst whose early warning had been ignored. Also internally, CIA Security assigned immediately an officer to investigate who if anyone had possibly been responsible for the disregard of the warning and who if anyone had deliberately delayed/limited/sabotaged the U-2 program by that potentially disastrous suspension of missions over western Cuba.

Yet the main problem was to submit the evidence to the President. Would he believe it? He was known to be suspicious of all CIA offerings ever since the Bay of Pigs venture. "Once burned, twice shy" was the way some senior Company operatives described his attitude, and nobody could blame him for it: the Pentagon, individual generals, Senators, special-interest lobbyists and, indeed, the CIA itself had at various times tried to fry their own bacon in the Cuban campfire.

Defense Secretary McNamara was not convinced that the evidence was sufficient to alert the President. "A missile is a missile. It makes no great difference whether you are killed by a missile fired from the Soviet Union or from Cuba," he said, demonstrating his disbelief in Penkovsky's reports that Moscow was still incapable of hitting America from Soviet soil. Yet at 8:00 on that Tuesday morning, special presidential assistant McGeorge Bundy was briefed by analysts in a cramped basement office of the White House. He felt that the President must be told and took the private elevator to Kennedy's bedroom. The pajama-clad President, sitting on the edge of his bed, dropped the morning papers and read the fresh report. He decided that further detailed evidence must be pursued without delay, that a pretense of continued ignorance must be kept up at all costs, and that a most secret committee to deal with the problem must be set up right away.

At 11:45, in a windowless room, a group of top men met in utmost secrecy. With the President and Bobby Kennedy playing leading parts in the discussions, this group was to gather several times a day from now on. It was to become known as EXCOM, the Executive Committee of the National Security Council, but temporarily, it would have to remain "nonexistent." Its task was to decide if World War III was about to begin. Members, even ministers, were to take their own notes and type their own reports. Concerning the confetti in Cuba, their options were summed up by the President: "The alternatives are to go in by air and wipe them out, or to take other steps to render the weapons inoperable." A showdown between the champions of peaceful and military solutions had begun.

Two bodyguards traveled with Rust as he drove along U.S. Highway 1. Leaving the main road, they met Schramm for lunch in a small restaurant near Sausage Tree, overlooking Biscayne Bay.

"Two bits of news for you," said Schramm. "One is that I've picked up some very hush-hush vibes that your information and efforts seem to have been fully vindicated. Congratulations."

"What's the other?"

"You seem to be very edgy this morning."

"Then give me the other bit of news."

"Ell's coming out here."

"Visiting?"

"Maybe a transfer. At least temporarily."

"Could mean one of two things," Rust pondered aloud. "They may want him to work with me or Mongoose. He's an expert on both."

"He'll have nothing to do with us—I mean, you and me—at the moment."

"So it's Mongoose. Is it going ahead?"

"Looks like it."

"Full invasion?"

"Don't know. My guess is as good as yours. But there's a lot going on."

At 4:15 in the afternoon, their car stopped at El Paraíso. The bar was almost deserted, and Schramm decided to stay in the car. Only a bodyguard followed Rust inside. The Cuban girl was already there, perching on a shaky stool, sipping some pink and fruity concoction through a straw. Rust ordered a drink, then excused himself and nodded toward the bodyguard: yes, stay put, I'm only going to the bathroom.

Morales was waiting for him, but Rust could tell he was not pleased: It was not the most agreeable place to wait for someone. Rust apologized both for the delay and for having no time to chat. "I'm delighted you're here and out of danger. You'll have to tell me what happened."

"It's simple, really—"

"Not now. Not here." Seeing his disappointment, Rust felt a dash of brazen flattery was called for. "But I must say, you still have one hell of a girl. Wow! Don't you ever grow old? At your age, how can you keep her so happy and satisfied?" The appeal to his *machismo* clearly did the trick.

"Don't waste time, *amigo*," Morales reprimanded him. "What's up?"

"I expect someone to arrive at the crocodile farm."

"The *Bucharest*?"

"You must have guessed."

"Male? Female?"

"Maybe both. And I must get them out."

"Ouch. I can't go back."

"I know. I'll go myself."

"No way."

"Not unless you help me. I want to join the next raiding party."

"What raiding party?"

"Come on, Morales, let's not waste time. Mongoose. That's what I'm talking about. They'd welcome me because I know the waters between Cay Sal and the coast. You arrange it."

"It's not enough for you to get into Cuba, *amigo*. How'll you get about? How'll you get to the crocodile farm? Your Spanish isn't good enough."

"I'll manage."

"And then all the way back. With your fugitives. You must have a guide."

"Are you volunteering after all?"

"The trouble is that my presence would be an added risk rather than help. But I'll see what I can do."

Rust gestured to silence him because there was some noise from outside. "I'll be in touch," he whispered and slipped out.

"Sorry I kept you waiting, sweetheart," he said to the girl at the bar, remembering only now with anger that he had forgotten to ask Morales what her name was.

Khrushchev was determined to maintain the pretense of "no offensive weapons in Cuba" no matter what the Americans' aerial photography might have discovered. His hopes that the U-2 had found out nothing were not unjustifiable. It had been two days since the overflight and there were no angry shouts coming across the ocean. He summoned U.S. Ambassador Kohler and gave him a bellyful of jolly assurances.

Time and more time was needed in the race to complete the missile sites. No amount of deception was to be too much to achieve that. A full range of Soviet diplomats from foreign minister downward were ordered to give signs of goodwill at all public and confidential levels. Kohler's report would only serve to corroborate the all-around cover-up.

· Thursday, October 18 ·

In Washington, Premier Ben Bella of Algeria appeals to Kennedy personally for urgent U.S. aid, then flies to Havana where he calls U.S. shipping restrictions "a blow to Cuban independence" and issues communique with Castro demanding the abandonment of American Guantanamo base. New Russian rocket "for space exploration" tested in the Pacific. Khrushchev drops heavy hints: he wants another summit with Kennedy; he is ready to go to UN in November.

FLORIDA WAS ROCKED BY RUMORS. SWANK HOTELS AND pensioned-singles-only hunting grounds were filled up with marines and Airborne troops in the vicinity of Miami and Key West. Baseball parks were turned into motor pools. All roads carried truck convoys. Heavy transport aircraft kept landing at all hours. Civilians self-imposed a hurricane alert: sandbag screens went up to protect school windows; there was a run on candles, water containers and canned food. The departures of submarine squadrons, destroyers and motley other vessels of war depopulated all the thoroughfares of honky-tonk establishments. Along Miami's Biscayne Boulevard, near the refugee offices, swarms of Cubans swapped rumors for canards day and night. The Spanish-speaking U.S. Army unit and the Cuban Revolutionary Council were suddenly swamped by volunteers.

Rust had established contact with Orlando, his Cuban smuggling partner, and a raiding party had agreed to take him to meet Orlando on Cay Sal on Monday, October 22, but now all the arrangements had to be reviewed in the light of the upsurge of military presence. The ceaseless naval activity indicated the possibility of some sort of invasion or blockade, and Rust was worried that he might not get through in time to meet the *Bucharest*. He had to consult Morales at once, but it was hard to avoid Schramm's watchful eyes. Yet he was determined not to let his old friend or anyone else know about his plans.

You must be paranoid, you've lost the ability to trust anyone, he scolded himself repeatedly, but the warnings remained ineffectual. And for the first time, he sympathized with Charles and Ell and Schramm, whose actions seemed to be guided by the recurring signs of incurable and pathological suspicion. A suspicion of everything and everybody at all times. I'd hate to live like that, Rust concluded and began to live just like that.

He used Morales and his girl shamelessly, and misled the leader of the raiding party about details of the arrangements with Orlando. The lies to Orlando himself were inevitable: the smuggler would never show up at the rendezvous if he knew that others but Rust were to be present.

"We must bring zero hour forward," he said to Morales in the lavatory of El Paraíso.

"Can't be done."

"Must go in on the twentieth."

"Impossible."

"Tell them I'll be waiting for them as arranged, at twenty-three hundred hours, but on the twentieth. Tell them it's no go otherwise. Tell them it may be their last chance to grab a bit of glory and show that the Cubans are men, not only America's puppets." It was below the belt, and he knew that Morales might just walk out on him. But that was a risk he had to take.

* * *

U-2 missions photographed the progress of Cuban missile installations six or seven times a day. The Wednesday pictures revealed at least sixteen and possibly thirty-two thousand-mile missiles which could apparently be fully operational within a week. According to military assessment, a few minutes after their being launched eighty million Americans would be dead.

The windowless room on the seventh floor of the State Department was in almost continuous use: the leather armchairs that lined the huge mahogany table were semipermanent homes for members of EXCOM. The hawks, suspected of playing down or actually withholding information about missiles until too late to prevent their installation, demanded an immediate military solution. They argued for options ranging from pinpoint bombing raids to take out the missiles to outright invasion. They claimed that diplomatic moves would only be ridiculed by Khrushchev, while a full naval blockade of a Cuba already bristling with missiles would only be bolting the door after the horse had been stolen. The President was disinclined to shoot first. He refused to do "a Pearl Harbor in reverse" because it was estimated that even if surgical precision was achieved, the pinpoint bombing would kill at least 25,000 Cuban civilians.

McNamara drew up a provisional list of requirements for a full-scale invasion. It contained a quarter of a million men, Marine and Airborne divisions, a hundred naval vessels and at least two thousand air sorties. The President sat tapping his front teeth with his forefinger; Bobby, the Attorney General, sat opposite, twisting his shirt into knots and tapping his teeth with his thumbnail—the familiar gestures were clear signs that the brothers were irritated by all the military options. Then the latest batch of photographs arrived. These left hardly any room for diplomatic maneuvers: the pictures showed that some missiles might become operational in eighteen hours—and several might have a two-thousand-mile range, capable of hitting any major centers as far as southern Canada and California. Inevitably, American war preparations were forced into top gear.

In the afternoon, Soviet Foreign Minister Gromyko was received by the President; in the evening, he was dined by the State Department. On both occasions, he kept lying through his teeth: no, there were no offensive weapons in Cuba. On both occasions, the Americans exercised tremendous self-control in not telling him they knew and could prove he was lying. Unless, of course, even he was kept somehow in the dark by Khrushchev, who would thus create yet another digger for his political grave.

• Sunday, October 21 •

First anniversary of Stalin's removal from Red Square mausoleum; Yevtushenko poem in *Pravda* appeals to government to "double, treble the guard at his gravestone so that Stalin cannot rise again." President Kennedy interrupts campaign tour and returns to Washington. U.S. ambassadors in Western Europe get mysterious instructions to go alone and armed to meet special presidential emissaries at obscure airports.

RUST'S *HALF PINT* AND THE RAIDING PARTY'S TWO POW-erful V-20 boats raced through the night and reached the string of coral shoals forming the Cay Sal bank by dawn. Rust found the rendezvous island without too much difficulty — yes, it was just as uninviting as he remembered it. They hid the boats on the scrub-covered side where they would be invisible from the Nicholas Channel, then settled down for a long wait: Orlando was not expected until the night of October 22.

In the morning a violent storm drenched them. At noon, a

small, ancient boat with torn square sails drifted by aimlessly. The youngest of the Cubans wanted to go out and investigate if there were people on board.

"There's no sign of life. No good to risk breaking our cover," said the leader of the raiding party, a tense, slight man who was said to have lost all his family in Castro's jails.

"They may be sunburned and lost and dying with no water and cracked skin and open sores and swollen and infected," the other tried to argue. "I know what it's like!"

"So do I," said the leader of the party. "I was the sole survivor on my boat when I left Havana. But we can't risk the mission for the sake of saving a couple of lives."

"Then what's it all about? What are we fighting for if we can't help our own people?"

It seemed obvious that every word had stung the frail leader of the group. And he was on the defensive now. "The boat may already be watched. One of the Komar class patrol boats may show up from behind an island any moment now." Nobody argued with him anymore, but the silence was hostile. He finally put it to the vote. Rust was pleased he had no vote on the matter. The young man turned away and began to cry. The others said nothing. Nobody voted against the leader, but everybody was ashamed of it. They resented the fact that he was right.

Rust walked away from them, climbed into the *Half Pint*, lay down and closed his eyes. He knew what it was like to be resentful of somebody else's correct judgment.

"Chico."

He looked up. "Sylvia" smiled at him. She moved her shoulder and tilted her head, asking for permission to join him. He did not react. She took it as an invitation. She lay down next to him, carefully avoiding any contact, although her hip was only an inch away from his hand. Damn you, thought Rust as he closed his eyes again. Damn you, damn me, damn the world. Memories flooded his brain. He could visualize Morales quite clearly. The old man had looked older than ever before at zero hour the previous night. Rust had pressed him all evening to reveal what arrangements he had made for a guide in Cuba. Then at almost the last minute, Morales had told him: "Your guide is already on board with the rest."

"Who is he?"

"It's a she, *amigo*. Take care of her for me." He led Rust to the boat and kissed his girl goodbye. Kissed her on the cheek, Rust noted.

"She's not going in," said Rust. "Or else I stay."

"I've tried every other possible solution, believe me," said Morales. "She's the only answer to all the problems. She knows her way about, she has all my contacts, and I can trust her."

"It's too big a risk."

"And don't I know it?" The old man's voice was harsh and hateful. "But it's that sort of a goddam world." He quickly crossed himself with an apologetic half-glance toward the sky, but could not resist adding a whispered "goddam it all," hoping that it would not be heard above.

Rust wanted to refuse her help, but at the same time, he wanted to kick himself for the urge to argue: it would have been an insult to Morales because it would have implied that the old man was acting callously without calculating the risk to his girl, without weighing possible alternatives, without the tacit recognition that Rust's mission might be, must be, very important. Rust also longed to make impossible promises and to thank him for a gesture he would never be able to repay, but could say nothing, and that made him even more resentful. "And damn you, too," Rust heard the old man shout over the roar of the powerful engines. It would have been another wrong moment to ask her name.

"Great! Fantastic! I hope you're proud of this glorious and monumental fuckup!"

Schramm listened to Elliott Repson's outburst without a word. He had no defense. He had allowed Rust to slip away, and he had no excuses. He looked away only to meet Sir Charles's reproachful eyes. "I'm sorry."

"That's not good enough. I hope it won't be good enough when you have to explain it to Langley."

"But it won't help if we keep shouting at each other," said Charles soothingly. He had just arrived at the Upstairs for a further debriefing session with Rust. "How much do we know?"

"Much too little," said Repson.

"He picked up some information and went to Cuba probably to act on it." Schramm addressed only Charles.

"How did you find out?"

"Heard it from a Cuban revolutionary contact."

"You mean informer?"

"If you like."

"What was Helm's information?"

"Don't know."

"How did he go in?"

"Private arrangement with a raiding party. I guess he traded some help from his smuggling contacts."

"Has he reached Cuba?"

"We don't know."

"Why didn't your informer contact you earlier?"

"He said he heard it only after they'd left."

Repson wheeled himself between the two. The squeak was an annoying conversation stopper. "Good show, boys, a marvelous double act. Have you considered a regular late-night slot on the tube?"

"Very funny."

"Not funny at all, Jake. It's my brother's life you're playing with."

"I'm sorry. You know I'm as upset as you are."

"Are you really? You mean you really don't know what he's up to? And you, Charles. You really haven't given him a little incidental assignment on the side? Well, I don't believe you. Because he's just where you wanted him to be, you bastards. Because you knew that he was good on his own, when he had to operate without any backing but free of control. And you wanted him to do something for you in Cuba from the start."

"That's not true, dear boy, just not true."

"Are you calling me a liar?"

"I was referring to your statement, not your character. So how's the delectable Anna, dear boy?"

Schramm and Repson exchanged glances: was Charles fishing for information? "A drink, anybody?" Schramm picked up a bottle of rum. "Some genuine Cuban."

"Here's to absent smugglers—and Anna," said Charles.

"She's well," said Repson. "She had a minor ailment affecting her vocal chords. A fleabite, no more. In fact, she may join me out here for a holiday."

"Just the place. Your Mongoose will protect her even from snakebites."

Yes, Charles was definitely fishing, Schramm concluded, and the thought irritated him. For the first time he was under strict orders not to level with Charles on anything concerned with the Cuban situation, military preparations, invasion plans.

• Monday, October 22 •

Penkovsky is arrested in Moscow. Vassall is jailed for 18 years. Soviet Union demands admission of China to UN. America condemns Chinese aggression against India. Successful U.S. high-altitude nuclear test over the Pacific. Two huge Russian nuclear tests over Central Asia and in the Arctic region. A Russian wins clay-pigeon-shooting world title in Cairo.

AMERICA WAS READY. MUSHROOM CLOUDS MIGHT BLOT out the sun whichever part of the globe it was meant to shine on in any minute of the days to come. Missile crews were on red alert, their ICBMs ready to be fired. Almost two hundred vessels of war were deployed in the Caribbean. The Strategic Air Command underground headquarters near Omaha issued orders to disperse its entire force to widely scattered civilian airfields to reduce vulnerability. Bomb-bay doors of B-52 aircraft were closed: the nuclear bombs had been loaded. A maximum force of these bombers was now to be in the air at all times—one would take off whenever another came in to land and refuel.

Friendly governments received top-level briefing from the President's emissaries. U-2 pictures and photo interpreters were made available to America's main allies.

Rust and the raiding party were too close to Cuba to notice any of the unusually heavy traffic beyond the Bahamas. They listened frequently to Spanish and English news broadcasts from American stations to pass the long hours of waiting, but nothing startling was announced. Inactivity helped to fray the nerves. The battered sailing boat was still visible occasionally on the horizon. Orlando was not expected much before midnight. Arguments seemed to flare up at the slightest provocation. The 6:00 news mentioned Gromyko's departure from Idlewild and quoted his stock farewell clichés of peace and mutual friendship. Because of it, the Cubans almost came to blows. Rust kept well out of it. Some of them argued that despite all the military activities in Florida and all the elaborate preparations for Mongoose, the current CIA-backed Cuban invasion plan, "Kennedy might still sell us down the river."

"That's a lot of crap."

"Who're you to call my opinion crap? Don't you remember the Bay of Pigs? Didn't he sell us out then? Why should it be different now?"

"Because Mongoose is his plan." Rust felt compelled to intervene. "Didn't Bobby Kennedy himself come to see the preparations a couple of months ago?"

That silenced them. But it was an uneasy silence. The leader of the group dispersed the men into defensive positions.

At 7:00, they gathered around the radio again, but instead of regular news, the President himself was heard. In a speech of spine-chilling simplicity, he revealed the evidence about the missiles in Cuba. He detailed the threat and catalogued the long list of Soviet deceptions. He declared his initial countermeasures. Naval quarantine was to be the first step. "All ships of any kind bound for Cuba from whatever nation or port will, if found to contain cargoes of offensive weapons, be turned back."

The Cubans cheered. Rust swallowed hard: war could be an arm's length away. And did the blockade mean that the *Bucharest* would be turned back? If yes, it would probably be the death sentence of anybody hidden in that crocodile tank. Yelena might starve to death. His father might come out, give himself up and scream for mercy. What was the point in entering Cuba and waiting for a tanker that might never come or might deliver only two decomposing bodies?

Kennedy went on. Surveillance. Threats of retaliation. Diplomatic moves. Appeal to the United Nations. Appeal to Khrushchev, urging him to move "the world back from the abyss of destruction," to honor his own word given so solemnly not to put offensive weapons in Cuba, and to withdraw the missiles already there. Until then, ships would be challenged. Any Russian ship trying to run the blockade would be sunk.

Then, as commentators began to fight their own battles, the Cubans on Cay Sal faced their most immediate problems. Would Orlando still show up? Was it still worth their while to carry out the raid?

Rust had never asked them what exactly their mission was, and he did not want to know now. "Whatever happens, and whatever your own decision is, I'm going in," he said quietly.

They cheered him. "And we take you, as agreed!"

Orlando arrived long after sunset. Rust waded into the water to meet and embrace him. "I thought you'd never come."

"Why?"

"You might have heard Kennedy's speech."

"I have. That's why I'm here. I thought you'd need warning to turn back."

"I can't. I must go into Cuba with you."

"No." Orlando viewed the Cubans standing in a half-circle. "You said you'd be alone. Who are these people?"

"Friends."

"You said you'd be alone. It's the second time you haven't played straight, *amigo*."

"It's very important that these people make it. That's why we're going together."

"You and them, okay. But not together with me."

The Cubans argued in flowery language. Most of their words were too big for Rust's taste. Words about Orlando's historical role. The fate of the world being in his hands. The service to Cuba and mankind he could perform. Orlando kept shaking his head but, Rust noticed, with less and less conviction. He was beginning to be impressed by his own importance. His waning resistance might be only to prolong his moment of glory. It was now only a matter of time. Clouds swam across the moon. It was almost midnight.

· Tuesday, October 23 ·

Nothing but ominous silence from the Kremlin; Khrushchev may be playing for more time. A long, sleepless night for millions of Americans; the mood: high noon at midnight— the gunfighters are still walking to reach shooting distance. Front pad small ad in the London Times: "Middle-aged lady. Fluent Russian and English. Work required. Write BOX P. 1492."

A T 12:40 IN THE MORNING, THE CUBANS WERE STILL arguing on Cay Sal. There was now a mild hint of threat. Orlando sensed it. They might force him to take them. Better to consent. That called for rum. There was plenty on Orlando's beached boat. They were going to get it when a strong light mowed a wide swathe through the night. Water and flying fish glittered, men and fish dived for cover. Then the engines could be heard approaching. The spotlight picked out ghostly features of coral outcrops. There was no time to hide Orlando's boat.

Any movement now would attract attention. The raiding party's best hope was that the boat might look just like part of the island from the distance.

The girl crawled with Rust under some prickly shrubs. Three of the Cubans shared their cramped spot of safety. The light scanned southward and left their island. The leader of the Cubans signaled to his men to spread out more and retreat to higher ground. The moon came out and lit up the patrol boat with its heavy machine gun and another boat in tow. It was the old sailing boat. "It must have been unmanned when they picked it up," the Cuban told Rust, "and now they're looking for survivors."

"Let's hope they won't risk a landing," said Orlando. His hope was short-lived. The light swung around and picked out his boat. The engines were stopped at once. Although the patrol vessel was still moving, the light remained glued to the raiders' island.

Rust and the others knew that if they picked the right moment, they could probably sink the patrol boat, but the captain might still have a chance to radio and alert Cuba. In which case they could do nothing but run for it.

The leader of the party turned to the girl: "If they land, you go and talk to them. Say you're a smuggler, here to meet your contact, who hasn't shown up. Offer to bribe them if they let you go."

"No," said Rust.

"Okay," said the girl.

"It's the only way," said Orlando. "She's a clever girl. I know it from Morales."

The patrol came right up to the beach. The searchlight examined the surrounding shadows, then a burst of machine-gun fire raked the shrubs nearest to Orlando's boat. When nothing happened, two men waded ashore. Three more pairs followed. One soldier stayed on board manning the machine gun. An officer examined Orlando's boat. Then four of them took up defensive positions while two two-man patrols prepared to search the island.

Sylvia crept away from Rust and his group. "Don't shoot!" she screamed as she stood up and took a few hesitant steps toward the beach. Her hands were high up in the air.

"Come down here. Slowly. All of you."

"I'm alone."

The foot patrols delayed their search, and everybody talked at the same time, all the time, when she reached the group. The initial menace disappeared from the tone of their hubbub. From time to time, Rust could make out a clear sentence or two about bribes. "And what else would you give me?" one of them asked her. It was a joke.

"I'd tell you if we were alone," she said, and it was another joke.

A couple of the men laughed. But another tried to embrace her. She pushed his hands away. The young officer stood with outstretched arms: he pressed a submachine gun to one breast and fondled the other. There was silence now, and the scene froze. Only that one hand kept moving. Then one of the men sidled up to her and drew with one finger her bodyline from neck to knee. Only two soldiers and the man on board kept watch now. The others dropped their weapons.

Rust moved. The leader of the raiders touched his shoulder. Think of the mission, he seemed to say.

"I know her well, *amigo*," whispered Orlando. "Believe me, she can take it."

"But I can't." Rust nodded toward the patrol boat. "I take out the machine gun and the light." And slithering backward, he was gone.

A couple of minutes later, he was swimming on his back to keep a couple of grenades dry in his hands. He was hoping that there were no sharks in the shallow waters. The girl was yelling. Men laughed. The coral reefs kept slashing Rust's clothes and flesh. He managed not to cry out, but pain forced him to jerk. The soldier on board paid no attention to the splash. He was too busy watching the scene developing on shore. Rust popped the grenades on board and ducked. He preferred to be cut up even more than stay exposed to the blast.

The explosions and flashes in quick succession paralyzed the men on shore. The machine gunner was killed. The two guards fired blindly. It gave their positions away. Both were shot. The remaining six men surrendered. By the time Rust appeared from behind the wrecked boat, they had been lined up and gunned down.

"There was no need," he said.

"How would you know?" retorted the leader of the raiding party contemptuously.

Rust asked the girl: "You okay?"

She shrugged her shoulders. "I could have handled them."

Rust turned away. He refused to feel guilty or like a fool.

The Kremlin remained silent. Khrushchev was stalling throughout the night. Stalling, but why? What was he preparing? War? Compromise? Capitulation? Kennedy could not be sure. Then came a blast of denials of having any aggressive weapons in Cuba. Khrushchev accused America of piracy, criminal threats and lies. In the Security Council, too, the Russians denied everything. Missiles? What missiles?

Some people doubted Kennedy's statements. Was he just electioneering? The Organization of American States and even the sometimes quarrelsome NATO allies came out with full support for the U.S. U-2s photographed Cuba and the sea routes. The pictures revealed frantic work and considerable progress on the missile sites. Others proved that twenty-five Soviet ships were continuing on their way to Cuba—their course had remained unchanged for twenty-four hours. The *Poltava*, now a known transporter of missiles, was among them. The Kremlin issued a threat: the *Poltava* and other ships were approaching the pickets; they would definitely defy the blockade no matter what.

As night fell, the Washington equation—night-time is party-time—still held. The Russian military attache was throwing a lavish reception. The First Lady was entertaining "as arranged." But there were a few subtle and not so subtle changes to be noted by those in the know.

At the Russian embassy, over buckets of caviar and vodka, guest of honor General Dubovik joked that the ships would sail through the blockade or be sunk: "I've fought in three wars, and I'm looking forward to fighting in the next." Nobody laughed. And the absence of Ambassador Dobrynin made people feel even less comfortable. "He's been delayed," they were told.

The Kennedys' pre-crisis invitation for a private dinner-dance still stood. But the dance part of it was now canceled. And Bobby Kennedy missed dinner, too. "He was delayed," guests were told. In fact, he was with Dobrynin who denied any knowledge of a Russian threat and blamed America for the crisis.

Bobby Kennedy then went to the White House. Although it was 11 P.M., the lights were on in almost every office. He found his brother, away from his guests and social chatter, in a private study talking alone to an old and trusted friend, British Ambassador Sir David Ormsby-Gore. The President's famous calm was only skin-deep. He talked incredibly fast, in short bursts of fiery sentences.

Bobby Kennedy reported Dobrynin's argument: "His line is that if the President has some evidence of offensive missiles in Cuba, why didn't he mention it to Gromyko when they met?"

"What did you say to that?"

"I told him that Gromyko must have known the truth, and you were so shocked by his blatant lies that you concluded that in these circumstances, no intelligent exchange of views would be viable."

A bottle of fine old Napoleon brandy was opened, and the three men talked about the two gravest, most immediate risks: ill-considered, hastily issued directives and some blind, stubborn, trigger-happy men in command of ships on both sides. Evidently, Khrushchev might need more time to think and convince his own hawks in the government if he was at all willing to back down. But to give him more time would be just the premature backing off the President could not afford. It was a vicious circle with the opponents paralyzed in a self-imposed pugilistic stance. Ormsby-Gore rose to the occasion. He pointed out that the quarantine line had been fixed at eight hundred miles from Cuba to keep the Navy outside the Cuban MIG fighters' range. His suggestion was to withdraw the ships quietly, and station them five hundred miles from the island— maintaining a strict, uncompromising blockade, but giving the freighters more time on course.

"You've earned your next cognac and perhaps the world's gratitude, David," said the President and called McNamara right away. The Defense Secretary was located at a dinner party where, with his host's permission, he used the privacy of a bedroom telephone to issue new orders to the blockade task force.

• Wednesday, October 24 •

Cuba complains to Security Council. Warsaw Pact forces are placed on full alert. Kennedy sends Dean Acheson on Paris visit to brief NATO on U.S. security measures against Cuba. Khrushchev answers Bertrand Russell's pacifist appeal with assurance that the Soviet Union "will never make any reckless decisions." Four ambitious newcomers, calling themselves the Beatles, make the pop charts at No. 48 with "Love Me Do."

WAITING, WAITING AND KNOWING NOTHING ABOUT THE outside world was the worst. Rust had only a .38 gun, a couple of hand grenades and a loaf of bread for company all day. Sylvia went into Havana trying to make contacts and find out about the *Bucharest*. After they had separated from Orlando and the raiders, she installed him in a dilapidated hut behind Morales's small, deserted house, because she hoped it was the least likely place where anybody would look for them. In the few days since Morales's escape the house had been reduced

349

to an uninhabitable ruin. It bore all the hallmarks of repeated searches by counterintelligence, systematic pilfering by the members of the political police, who would have first choice, and then by neighbors, friends, enemies and passersby. There were no doors left. Some windows were broken, others were missing lock, pane and frame. When Rust shook his head sadly at the sight, the girl urged him not to judge her people too hastily: "Their needs are great with nowhere to turn for help."

By midafternoon, Rust felt jittery. Every time a dog barked somewhere out of sight or a truck passed by, he kept peering out between two broken planks until his eyes began to hurt. The sun went down, and there was still no sign of the girl. If anything happened to her, he would have to try to reach the crocodile farm on his own. If she was caught, she would soon tell them where he was hiding. And from the hut it was impossible to see all the approaches. He left the hut and hid among bushes on the marsh behind. Wet, cold and worn out, he felt unsure about everything. What was the use of risking everything and saving his father or Yelena or both when there would be war anyway?

Washington, too, had a day of waiting and more waiting. The fleet know as Task Force 136 took up the assigned position encircling Cuba at a five-hundred-mile radius. The latest reports confirmed that all the Soviet ships were still on course.

At 10:00 in the morning, a radio message reached the President: the presence of an enemy submarine had been detected among the Soviet ships. Was *Essex*, the nearest aircraft carrier, required to contact it by sonar and use depth charges to force it to surface? Naval confrontation, the first positive step to war, was some twenty minutes away. At 10:15, orders had to go out: the quarantine line was not to be crossed without American permission. Permission would not be granted to any ship without certainty that no offensive missile was on board for Cuba. At 10:20, six ships and the submarine below were still approaching Task Force 136. Among the ships: the *Poltava*. Ten to fifteen minutes to go. At 10:25, the six ships stopped dead in the water. It was a good sign.

U Thant, Acting Secretary General of the United Nations, appealed to Kennedy and Khrushchev simultaneously. He asked for restraint on both sides and urgent negotiations. Khrushchev returned Kennedy's quarantine proclamation as unlawful and unacceptable, but sought private contacts to the U.S. administration, as if he could not trust his own official diplomatic channels. Was he just maneuvering or was he fighting his internal opposition? By now six Russian submarines were detected and harassed in the quarantine area.

Rust decided to wait for the girl's return until midnight. Beyond that, the risk of staying there would be too great. It was shortly before midnight that she arrived back. A man Rust failed to recognize was with her. He introduced himself as Miguel. He was the manager of the crocodile farm who had arranged the Odessa escape route. "Our latest information is that the *Bucharest* is still on course."

"When would she get here?" Rust asked.

"Tomorrow afternoon if all goes well. Maybe evening."

"And the tank is on board."

"As far as I know."

"Who's inside it?"

"Wouldn't know."

"How many people?"

"No idea."

The ship was expected at Matanzas. The crocodile tank would be put on shore and might be left there for days, even weeks. Alternatively, it might be taken by road to the farm right away. If it was left at Matanzas overnight, it would be best to free the refugees at once if possible. They agreed to wait for the ship's arrival at the port. But the question remained: would she ever arrive?

• Thursday, October 25 •

Stock market steadies. For the first time, with three days'
delay, *Pravda* publishes "groundless American lies" that
Moscow has installed offensive missiles in Cuba. Russians
are informed that America has declared war on little defenseless Cuba.

RUSSIAN SUBMARINES WERE FORCED TO SURFACE. THEN
at 7:50, the *Bucharest* approached the line of warships
and received instructions to identify herself by radio. Her captain declared that the ship carried nothing but petroleum. At
8:00, she was permitted to pass through the quarantine zone.
Five minutes later, an East German ship with fifteen hundred
passengers on board was allowed to go through. Navy reconnaissance reported that twelve Soviet ships had definitely turned
back. But Cuban overflights brought worrying news: work on
the missile sites progressed relentlessly, with extra labor, faster
than ever.

The confrontation shifted to the session of the U.N. Security
Council. Adlai Stevenson challenged Zorin, the Soviet repre-
sentative: "Do you deny that the USSR has placed and is placing

medium-and intermediate-range missiles and sites in Cuba?"
Zorin tried to stall. "Yes or no?" Stevenson pressed him. "Don't
wait for the translation. Yes or no?" Zorin protested that this
was not a court of law and he should not be questioned in
prosecutor style. But he sensed that something much more
devasting than debating power was to hit him. Stevenson produced the photographic evidence. Zorin chose to ridicule the
pictures and their validity. Those enlarged dots, blobs and
shadows could be just about anything. Scratches on the lens
or ice-cream vans on the ground. But it was obvious that his
words were only for the record. He fooled nobody—not the
delegates, not the TV cameras.

"We'll use my truck," said Miguel and watched Rust, who
was changing into loose-fitting calico pants and shirt. "I have
papers for three to enter the port, but she'll sit with me up
front. She may need to sweet-talk us through checkpoints." He
handed a wide-brimmed raffia hat to Rust. "You're not to say
anything whatever happens. Your Spanish isn't good enough."

"I'll be deaf and dumb." He laughed and gave a few inar-
ticulate sounds, but it was not funny. "Even better—I'll have
a stroke." He was rummaging through his own clothes, which
lay in a heap on the floor of the hut. He found what he wanted:
a packet of chewing gum. He let one corner of his mouth drop,
popped in a stick of gum, and with the aid of his tongue, let
his saliva drip freely. He made an effort to say something, but
his drooping face and lazily searching tongue seemed to prevent
the formation of any intelligible word.

"Will do," said Miguel. "Are you armed?"

Rust hesitated.

"Don't be. They might search us at the entrance of the port.
You wouldn't have a chance to shoot your way through."

They hid Rust's clothes and gun. Rust climbed onto the
back of the truck. He could not suppress the surging *déjà vu*—
the ambulance, Yelena and Florian, the roadblock at the Moscow exit.

Much of the time they had the road to themselves, but near
Matanzas, they ran into a huge traffic jam. All the vehicles
were abandoned: people walked almost a mile down the road
to find out what was going on.

"It would look odd if we weren't curious," said Miguel. "Let's go."

Some four miles from Matanzas, Cuban soldiers and uniformly check-shirted civilians held the crowd back to ensure free passage for cumbersome, elongated transporters moving slowly on a crossroad. Their heavy load was under canvas. Missile trailers, Rust would have sworn. He noticed the road sign to the right: Cuevas de Bellamar. The endless maze of caves, famous for the beauty of their stalactite and stalagmite formations in massive halls—a safe and natural hiding place some two hundred feet underground. Rust looked at Miguel. The Cuban nodded. "The same's happening in the caves of the Valle de Viñales," he murmured on their way back to the truck. They must be trying to protect them from the eyes of the U-2s, Rust concluded with a touch of pride. The problem was how to rush the news to Washington.

Because of the long delay, it was well after nightfall when they reached Matanzas. The harbor was full of lights and bustle. Miguel's papers and Rust's intensely disgusting salivation helped them through the two checkpoints. To their dismay, they saw the *Bucharest* at anchor way out near the mouth of the bay.

"Stay here," said Miguel. "I'm going to find out what's happening."

Rust used his absence to discuss their route of retreat with Sylvia. She would contact her friends in the resistance and arrange their return to Orlando, who would take them as far as Cay Sal.

"How many are we taking?" she asked.

"At least one. Maybe two—I hope."

"Is she good, *chico*?" She made it sound a light and innocuous question. But Rust detected a touch of jealousy.

"What makes you think that it's a girl?"

"You fidget like a man waiting for a lover."

Miguel returned. "They'll unload the tank and take it by road to the farm."

Twenty minutes later, a floating crane sidled up to the *Bucharest*. The tank was lifted off and carried slowly, dangling in midair, to a jetty where a truck with a long, open platform was waiting. "I know where it goes," said Miguel. "It's better not to follow it but go the long way around."

They drove out of the port, down the Vía Blanca, then turned right toward Jaguey Grande and the Bay of Pigs. The stench of the swamps was familiar to Rust as they reached the Laguna del Tesoro, where, according to legend, escaping Indians had once sunk all their fabulous treasures. Rust stared at the murky waters and wondered for a moment if he was surveying his grave. "This is as far as you go," he told the girl. He saw she was about to argue, but his fingers gently sealed her lips. "And that's final. I'll need you on the lake. Be here at eleven tomorrow evening and wait for the light signal we agreed on. If I don't show up by midnight, come back the same time the following two nights. If you don't see my signal, don't try to find me. You must then get back to Morales and tell him about the missiles in the caves." Again he had to hush her. "It's more important than anything you can do for me. Believe me."

She left them without ever glancing back. Herons and pink flamingos stirred and escaped from her path through the reeds. She had a good hour's walk to the hut where a friendly fisherman would hide and feed her.

Miguel rowed in silence. His oars sank into the water, pulled at an even pace and reemerged noiselessly as he maneuvered the boat among the motionless gray bumps on the surface of the lagoon. This time Rust needed no warning not to tempt those "bumps" with a hand over the edge of the boat. Even so, occasionally a huge scaly body came to life. It would snap at an oar or slide purposefully under the boat and give it a mighty jolt.

"Are you never afraid of them?" Rust asked.

"Are you never afraid in your work?" Miguel reversed the question.

"Always," said Rust.

"Same here," said Miguel. "Except that your kind of work would give me heart attacks three times a day."

"Then why are you helping me?"

Miguel shrugged his shoulders. "I'm helping Morales."

"Why?"

"Fidel's cheated us. He promised a different revolution. Somebody must let him see that we know."

"Why you?"

"Why not me?"

The farm was in darkness; nothing moved. The jetty where they landed was deserted. Miguel held Rust's hand and led him along the shaky, creaking catwalks that crisscrossed the ground barely a foot above the seemingly lifeless long gray mounds. Whenever the moon shone through the gaps in the swirling clouds, flat, staring stoplight eyes mirrored a reddish glow. Miguel stopped outside a wooden shed on stilts like a Borneo longhouse. "Wait here," he said and climbed the two stairs to the door. He returned a few minutes later and beckoned to Rust. They entered a narrow corridor that led to door after door, stores, offices, first-aid station. Clanking of metal could be heard. Miguel raised his finger to ensure Rust's silence, then cautiously pushed some reed shutters aside to open a window. The metallic noise, combined with the whine of some motor, grew louder. In the distance, where the catwalks converged at a wide platform adjoining high ground, the crocodile tank was being unloaded from the truck with the aid of a mobile crane. The men, four or five of them, worked and moved about sleepily. It was a good ten minutes before they finished with the tank and boarded the truck. The driver raced the engine thunderously. It seemed to take ages until the night swallowed the noisy intruder and some excited crocodiles melted back into the landscape.

"We'll give it a few minutes," Miguel whispered.

They needed massive blocks of wood to reach the top of the tank. The huge lid, moving on hinges, opened fairly easily, but it was heavy, and Rust could well imagine the noise it would make if they let it drop. He had to hold it on his own while Miguel shored it up. He strained under the weight, and his palms began to sweat, Sylvia's words rang in his ears. Is she good, *chico*? You fidget like a man waiting for a lover.

Inside the tank, they faced a second lid. It was to separate the larger baby crocs from their younger brothers. Miguel tapped the metal three times. The hollow sound was answered immediately by three taps from inside. The second lid was lighter. Miguel held it open, and Rust tried to peer down into the almost total darkness. "Come on, hurry," he whispered in Russian. "It's Helm, come on." A hand reached up, and he caught it. Yelena. He helped her out. The moon broke through, and the sudden flash made her blink a few times. She then just stood dazed. Rust embraced her. No reaction. "Father?" She did not answer. He called into the lower compartment. "Father?" He glanced back at her. "Are you alone?" She stared at the sky in search of the light that had gone.

"No, she's not alone, Mr. Rust." The voice came from the compartment. It was accompanied by a strong flashlight beam. It was Rust's turn to be blinded. He screwed up his eyes to withstand the glare. Something glittered, and a large Tokarev entered the beam. Its barrel advanced until it touched Rust's nose.

"What's keeping you?" Miguel asked impatiently. But before Rust could answer, the whole scene was lit up. They were at the junction of powerful searchlights. From below, the man holding the gun emerged. "Don't do anything stupid, Mr. Rust. You might have overlooked our little reception committee, but it's all around you, I can assure you. Help me out."

Rust was tempted to push Miguel so that the lid would drop on the man's head, but as he looked up, he saw several submachine guns pointing at them from above. He helped the man out. He looked vaguely familiar.

"I'm Major Boychenko of State Security. You may not remember me, but we've met, well, sort of met a few times, and I'm delighted really to meet you, Mr. Rust, at long last." Rust looked at Yelena. She still seemed dazed. Maybe drugged. In her vacant eyes, no sign of fear or recognition appeared. "Moscow, at the airport, at the hotel, no? Oh well, perhaps my face isn't all that memorable. No matter."

"What have you done to her?"

"All in good time, Mr. Rust."

"What have you done to her, bastard?"

"Now don't be like that. You must have known what might happen to her when you gave her away."

"I didn't."

"Then how did I find her? Eh? How? You told us, that's how. Her Ukrainian accent. Her hatred for Comrade Khrushchev, whom she might hold personally responsible for her husband's death in Kiev—remember? We'll talk about it. But first we need a little rest. It's almost midnight, and it's been a very uncomfortable journey from the hold of the *Bucharest*. You should consider yourself lucky that you or this young lady didn't need to take the whole trip from Odessa." Boychenko looked up at the armed men above. "Help us out of here."

The handgrip of a submachine gun smashed into Miguel's

face. Two men held his feet and dragged him along the catwalk. His hands were flailing over the edge of the narrow path and caused excitement below. Yelena stared at Rust. For a second, there was a faint sign of recognition, but it was gone before Rust could say anything.

· Friday, October 26 ·

At 7:00 A.M., the U.S. destroyer *Joseph P. Kennedy* runs up flag signal "Oscar November." U.S.-built, Panama-owned, Lebanese-registered, USSR-chartered freighter *Marucla* understands message: heave to and stop. The ship is a diplomatic choice for first boarding. Unarmed boarding party finds no weapons. *Marucla* allowed to continue to Cuba. Vatican's dilemma: should Latin remain sole liturgical language?

IN A TINY OFFICE OF THE LONGHOUSE, RUST SPENT THE NIGHT in a state of shock and remorse. Occasionally, for a few seconds, he fell asleep, only to wake up to the cries and screams from somewhere a few doors away where Miguel must be being questioned. Under the floorboards, some crocodiles thumped the stilts with their tails. But in a peculiar way, Rust felt at peace with the world. He was in limbo, with decisions and action behind him, pain and death somewhere on the ill-defined horizon, even beyond care. A touch of insane euphoria made

him smile: it was clever of him to leave Sylvia behind; she
would take the news about the missiles in the caves to Morales,
who would pass it on...pass it on to whom? Panic set in.
Morales might choose the wrong man. As he himself had, at
least with some of the things he had said. But was it his fault?
How could he suspect them?

Throughout the long, hungry hours of dawn, Rust tried to
recall scenes in the sanatorium, particularly the day he talked
about Yelena and her possible motives, her personal hatred of
Khrushchev, her Ukrainian origin. Who was present? Repson,
definitely. Also those two sets of interrogators. And Schramm,
yes, he, too. He could not remember anyone else. But there
had to be others. Listening. In another room. Technicians.
Company security. Some invited audience. Charles, perhaps.
Yes, Charles appeared to be well informed during that first
dinner outside the security compound. One of all these must
have sent a message to Moscow. By then the KGB investigators
must have known a great deal about Rust's escape and the
people who had helped him. They would have an ever-short-
ening list of suspects. Then those few, seemingly safe and
innocuous words were reported from Washington. In the right
hands, they would reduce the list to one or two. To Yelena.
They would pick her up and take her to the Lubyanka. Accelerated, intense interrogation. She could not hold out for long.
She would give away his father. And Florian. But they would
demand more from her. They would want Rust. She would
give them everything when she broke completely. Everything,
including the Odessa escape route. That would appear to be a
promising way to get to him. They would force her to send
the message, set the trap, wait for his arrival and shoot him,
then round up all who had helped him. But why would they
send a KGB man from Moscow? They would surely have
executioners on the spot. And why send Yelena? Further interrogation? Confrontation? They could not hope to learn much
more from them. If only he could alert Washington that someone in that sanatorium had been working for the Moscow Center
all along. To whom could he send that message? Who could
be trusted?

At 7:45, at about the time the *Marucla* was boarded, Boychenko entered the room. Yelena followed him with a Canaan
of a breakfast tray but stopped at the door waiting for orders.

Boychenko snapped his fingers: "Put it down and go." Rust reached out to touch her arm, but the move alarmed her. She backed away hastily. Rust wondered if the damage they had done to her was irreparable.

"Help yourself," said Boychenko. "You start with that papaya? It's not for me, I must say, although the locals say it's very good. I'm too conservative to experiment. But perhaps you like it, do you?"

"I'd enjoy it more if I could choose my company."

"That was uncalled for, Mr. Rust. But, no matter. And before you try to go too far with such an unfriendly attitude, I must warn you that armed guards are watching us." He suddenly switched to Russian: "And they understand English. Do you mind if we speak Russian?"

"I don't give a shit. I share no secrets with you."

"Not yet, Mr. Rust, not yet. But I'm about to tell you something."

"Why?"

"Because you've created quite an impression in Moscow. And other places. We may be on opposite sides, but I'm full of respect for you. You're a good man to have as a friend. No, no, don't argue, I mean it. And we've made inquiries about you. You're an able operator and very, very loyal. It's the sort of loyalty we've always valued much more highly than the Company ever could. It's the loyalty of the man who thinks things out for himself. Why is it that Washington doesn't value it much more?" Rust finished his papaya and pretended to concentrate only on his breakfast. Boychenko carried on regardless. "And I admire your loyalty to friends. The way you took the risk to help Yelena. That's the name our Colonel Muratova used in Moscow, right? So let's stick to it. Yours was a definitely chivalrous gesture, and I respect you for that, too. In fact, I'd like to help you. Both of you. For I'm sure you'd do everything in your power to restore her health. The damage is curable, I'm told. And the great American medical science and psychiatry could do wonders for her."

"You want to trade her for something?"

"A crude expression, Mr. Rust. What I have in mind is not like that at all, I can assure you. But let's first talk about you. You have great respect for your President, haven't you?"

"What about it?"

"He's an inspiring figure. So is his brother. The whole family. Someone tells me that they account for much of the new American patriotism these days. Certainly in your case, I'm told."

"By whom?"

"And I can understand. President Kennedy is a great man. Full of youthful determination. Ready to fight us if we don't remove those missiles, right?"

"Stop bullshitting, Boychenko," said Rust, reverting to English.

The Russian laughed. "Stop bullshitting. Good expression. I'll learn that. Thank you." He ceased laughing as suddenly as he had begun, and continued in Russian: "What a pity that your President is cheating you now as he's cheated all along. So I'd better stop 'bullshitting.' I'm going to tell you something that very, very few people know about. At the moment, only Comrade Khrushchev and a dozen other people. Later today, your President will hear about it. But you'll know right now."

"I'm honored."

"Comrade Khrushchev is sending a most confidential letter to the President directly. It'll propose to remove the missiles from Cuba under American supervision. It'll promise not to send others to replace them. He'll do that if the quarantine is lifted right away."

"I'm sure it will be. That's all the President has demanded."

"But there's something else. We can't let our Cuban friends down. Kennedy must promise never to attack Castro and must guarantee Cuban independence."

"Guarantee, no matter what? No way."

"And I say he'll do it. And I have proof. That's just what I wanted to tell you. You and all those Cuban exiles in Florida have been used and cheated all along. You all thought that the Kennedys were committed to the 'liberation' of Cuba. But they were just bullshitting."

"Nonsense."

"People who worked for Mongoose. The raiding parties. All who died. They died for nothing. You suffered for nothing."

"That's what you say."

"Let's see what you say." With a flourish, Boychenko produced a sheet of paper and gave it to Rust. It was the photocopy of a memo to the President on Bobby Kennedy's notepaper.

Its date was April 19, 1961. The day when cheated and desperate Cuban exiles were firing their last bullets on the beaches near the crocodile farm, and the ignominious Bay of Pigs invasion was drawing to a disastrous end. The day that was still more than a year away from any Russian missiles going into Cuba. "If we don't want Russia to set up missile bases in Cuba," Robert Kennedy wrote, "we had better decide now what we are willing to do to stop it." The memo considered possible courses of action. Invasion with American troops, already rejected but perhaps to be reconsidered, was one of them. A strict blockade was another. International prohibition of all arms shipments was a third. And in order to enlist full international support, Robert Kennedy invented and recommended a trump card: "Guarantee the territorial integrity of Cuba so that the Cuban government could not say they would be at the mercy of the United States."

Rust was dumbfounded. "Bullshit," he mumbled at last. His eyes fell on the handwritten lines at the bottom of the page. "R.K. willing to trade guarantea for promise of no missiles in Cuba." The fat letters and cursive handwriting were Anna's, unmistakably. So was the spelling error. It proved the genuine origin of the memo. "How long has Khrushchev had this?" Rust asked throatily.

"There should be a date of registry at the top." Boychenko glanced at it. "There. April 23. Good going, I'd say. And without this bit of information, Khrushchev would never have ventured to send missiles over here. But he knew what would happen. And now he knows that his offer to swap missiles for guarantees will be accepted."

"Why are you telling me all this?"

"Oh, just a gesture of trust. I thought it's unfair that a man like you and many others should be forced to risk everything while being cheated all along. Think about it. In Moscow, a few people at the top are reading this memo perhaps at this very moment. And you may be the first American outside the White House to see it. That's how highly we think of you."

In London, a Cuban embassy spokesman declared: "It is a ludicrous idea, indeed, to think that Cuba has long-range nuclear weapons and that the Soviet Union could be interested in establishing such bases when it has been acknowledged that the USSR has a sufficient number of such weapons on its own territory to be adequate for its own purposes."

In Washington, the hawks were pressing for action all day. The facts were on their side. Reports were pouring in that the missile sites were now being completed one after the other.

Khrushchev's private emissary approached an ABC diplomatic correspondent to try to middleman a deal with the President.

The State Department prepared a crash program to set up a civilian government in Cuba immediately after a successful attack and occupation. Kennedy supervised everything, even the contents of the leaflets to be dropped over Cuba, the assembling of the invasion fleet, and the list of Cuban doctors in the Miami area in case they were needed. The casualties of an invasion were expected to be "very heavy." The President warned his immediate circle: "We must accept the possibility that when military hostilities begin, those [Cuban] missiles will be fired."

At 6:00 in the afternoon, the American embassy in Moscow started to relay a personal letter from Khrushchev. It proposed the withdrawal of missiles under supervision in return for non-invasion guarantees. It was a long, rambling disclosure pleading, hesitating, showing signs of alarm and indecision, offering to be "quite frank" with Kennedy. The style was informal, a frightened man wanting to have a real heart-to-heart. State Department specialists analyzed it in a seventh-floor office. The verdict was that Khrushchev must have been "tight or scared" when dictating it to a lone secretary off the cuff, without help or consultation, fuming, pacing up and down in his huge Kremlin office overlooking the Spassky Gate.

Evaluation of the letter was to be continued through the night. It was decided not to publish the text itself.

Rust was left alone with his thoughts all day. Again and again he tried to convince himself that Boychenko's flattering confidentiality was just a crafty device, and the memo was a fake. But could Anna's handwriting be faked? In the sanatorium, she would be watched at all times, she would not have a chance to write it herself. Step by step, Rust worked himself into a blind fury. He had been cheated. Those Cubans had been cheated. The money, effort and dreams invested in Mongoose had been wasted. The raiders had bled, the dead had died in vain. Castro's rule would be guaranteed, Khrushchev would seem to lose a battle but win the war and buy time to build better missiles that could hit Washington right from the shadow of the Kremlin wall. From about 8:00 in the evening, Rust's painful thoughts were punctuated by horrible screams coming from somewhere far away.

Rust did not consider his own suffering a waste. It was an acceptable price for delivering a last-minute warning about the missiles and thwarting the completion of Khrushchev's scheme. It also unmasked Anna and, perhaps, others. But Julia-Rosa, who had given her life for that shipping list, died in vain. It would hurt her to see that memo. Miguel's words echoed in Rust's skull. "Fidel's cheated us. Somebody must let him see that we know." Somebody must let Kennedy see it, too. Why me? Rust asked himself. Why not me? Because my motive would be hurt vanity. Or was there more to it? And what could I do? Stop the news about the caves from reaching Washington? That would be high treason. Could treason be justified by the discovery that one's idols and leaders were cheats? Was Miguel's act of defiance against Castro justified?

Rust fought off these thoughts as the distant screams died away. He was sure that even if the letter and the memo were real, Kennedy would never issue that guarantee.

At 10:00, the door opened and an armed guard allowed Yelena through. She was bringing Rust some food. Her gait was like a sleep-walker's, and the dishes kept rattling on the tray. But her eyes were alive this time. She flicked a glance of warning toward the door behind her. Rust understood. "Shut that door, bastard!" The guard shrugged his shoulders and left them. She quickly dropped the tray on the table and embraced Rust. "I love you, Helm, I love you, I love you."

He kissed her. "I thought you're . . . are you all right?"

"Yes and no. But there's no time to talk. I'm fighting for survival. For both of us."

"Where's my father?"

"It's not my fault, I swear to you."

"Where is he?"

"He . . . he wasn't your father."

It would have been difficult to condense more than two such blows in a short sentence like that. Stunned and relieved at the same time, questions flooded Rust's throat and drowned his voice. Memory fragments of vague suspicions about the old man floated like jetsam. Discrepancies in his behavior. His limited recollections of Helm's mother and Geneva. His apparently compulsive reminiscing about the Jeddo. Yes, somebody certainly had fed him with information, some of which must have been mistakenly too fresh to be real memories. And the worst for Rust was that he now had to face the fact: he had always suppressed his doubts in order to build himself a past, even at the cost of trusting the untrustworthy, only to give himself someone to belong to and care for. The old man was a cheat. Somebody's carefully planned and drawn mirage to be pasted on Rust's horizon. Who had devised him? Yelena? It did not matter. For cheat or no cheat, the loss of the father figure hurt Rust. And the past tense in "he wasn't your father" signaled the irrevocable, the destruction of a mere puppet perhaps, but a relatively innocent death nevertheless. "Wasn't?" he asked Yelena with the last of his hope.

"He's dead," she whispered hurriedly. "I'm sorry. But I swear he wasn't your father. I'll explain everything when there's time. I just had to warn you. I'm not sure what Boychenko wants from you. But don't argue. Pretend to play whatever his game is. Then perhaps they'll let you go."

"And you?"

"I don't know."

"Why did you bring him here?" She did not answer. As she stared at him, clinging to him, he thought she would cry, silently, as when accused of being a traitor. But there were no tears. She might have no more left. "Have they tortured you?" She looked away. "You didn't come on the *Bucharest*, did you?"

"We flew to Cuba. Then went on board and into the tank at Matanzas only to trap you. I'm sorry. I couldn't help it."

"I know."

"I'll tell you more about the old man if you want me to. Do you?"

"I don't know. But I'd like to mourn him."

There were footsteps outside. And voices.

"I love you," she breathed and broke away from him. Her eyes lost their sparkle, her body went limp. It seemed she had to make a greater effort to maintain sanity than to pretend cracking up. Her vacant gaze that greeted Boychenko was very convincing. When she was ordered to leave, she backed out of the room.

I must say something, thought Rust, anything to allay Boychenko's suspicions. "You . . . you really think she could ever be cured?" he asked as she was stumbling through the door, bumping into the guard outside.

"Some of our top men have assured me that a complete recovery is possible. Wish I could be so reassuring about another friend of yours."

"What other friend?"

"It's not my responsibility at all, I swear to you. She's in the hands of the Cubans."

"She?"

"It's quite unimaginably barbaric what they've done to her. She's dying. She's begged to see you and say goodbye. I'll take you to her if you promise not to go crazy."

Surrounded by half a dozen armed men, Sylvia's naked, savagely mutilated body lay on the floor of a bare room at the far end of the longhouse. Her eyes were closed. She was too weak to scream any more, but whined incessantly. Whole chunks of her body had been torn away, and she was bleeding profusely. No such horrid injuries could have been inflicted by humans. Rust knelt beside her. She cried out, "No, please, no!" and raised her arm to protect herself before opening her eyes. He did not think she would recognize him, but suddenly the whining began to make sense: "I didn't give you away, *chico*, I didn't. They knew about you. Please don't let me suffer anymore . . . please . . ."

With tears and fury in his eyes, Rust glanced around to see if anybody could interfere with his throttling her.

"I've been away all day. I've nothing to do with this," Boychenko protested. "Here." He pulled a revolver out of his pocket. After removing the magazine, he inserted a single bullet. The clicks of safety catches on automatic weapons could be heard all around the room. "Here," repeated Boychenko, "take it. Just don't do anything crazy. You want to live. You want to live."

The temptation was tremendous to kill one of the men. But which one? And what would it achieve? How would it help the girl?

Rust accepted the revolver, knelt down again, and kissed her. He then leaned back. Her eyes were on him as he moved the barrel slowly, outside her field of vision, to her temple. "You'll be all right, don't worry. You'll get well and be happy," he said and pulled the trigger. For her sake, too, he had to survive. With no time to mourn for her. Not now. He forced himself to say thank you to Boychenko.

Rust's hands and clothes were full of blood. Boychenko ordered a bottle of rum, a washbowl and a change of clothes to be brought to Rust's room.

"I'll be quite frank with you," he said while Rust was washing.

"Why?"

"I want to give you a chance to choose your own course of action. You must be fed up with people trying to manipulate you."

"I am. And I understand."

"What?"

"That you feel left out. You think it's your turn to manipulate me." Rust noticed that Boychenko kept looking at his watch.

"I don't blame you for being suspicious of everyone. They all cheated you. Even your friends and colleagues. Even Colonel Muratova—I mean, Yelena."

Rust filled a paper cup with rum and drank several large gulps. "Go on."

"Yes, Yelena, too. She invented your . . ." He paused. "You'd better drink some more."

Rust nodded. He knew what was coming. To protect Yelena, he had to prepare himself to show sufficient shock.

"The old man in Moscow was not your father. And he's dead now."

Rust drank. "But then . . . who was he?"

"He was Yelena's invention. It got her immediate promotion. She worked for our military neighbors—I mean, the GRU. Through an informer in the U.S. embassy they heard about you when you came to Moscow in '56. Then they heard that you wanted to find your father's grave. Confirmation of this came from our source in the British embassy. Apparently your British friend Sir Charles informed both London and the CIA about your plans and recommended that you should be transferred back home at once. But you weren't. And you know why? Because of your other friend, Schramm. He suggested using you as a guinea pig to monitor both your and our people. Schramm thought we might try to set up something to trap and recruit you. He wanted to observe our technique and, at the same time, test your loyalty."

Rust felt sicker and sicker. "I see," was all he could say as he poured himself another cupful. Hit back, hit back, hit them all.

"When you found your 'father' instead of the grave, your bosses weren't sure what to do. After all, if the man was your real father, you'd be a sitting target. Schramm would have to call you back and get rid of you. That's where Yelena's ingenious scheme had its basic fault. And not only that. Although she had found a perfectly plausible and dead-scared ex-German inmate of Stalin's concentration camps to play the part, and although she trained him not to discuss anything but 'safe' subjects with you, you would have discovered huge gaps in his 'memory' if you had enough time with him. That's why she planned to move him out of Moscow so that you could see him only once in a while, for a few minutes at a time, secretly at railway stations and places like that. It wasn't a bad idea, I admit, because it would have helped to get you out of Moscow and set you up."

"Yet she's never tried to recruit me."

"She never had a chance. Because we stopped her."

"We?"

Boychenko hesitated, then nodded. "The KGB."

"Why?"

"Because we're pros while the GRU's just a pain in the ass."

"But why did you stop Yelena's scheme?"

"My superiors must have seen a reason."

"You could have taken over the whole idea."

"I suppose so."

"Why didn't you?"

"How should I know? You can't expect me to know about every operation, can you?" Boychenko did not sound convincing on this point. It implied to Rust that he was not authorized to say anything about Anna. So they might not know that Anna's cover had been blown. Boychenko poured some rum for both of them, then gestured toward the tray. "You haven't touched your food."

"No." Rust chose to drink up. It helped to soothe his seething anger as well as keep down all his questions about the death of his "father," about Anna, about the beasts who had fed Sylvia to the crocodiles. In the momentary silence he heard those restless bodies moving around under the floorboards: their appetite had only been whetted. Then from somewhere farther out came a high-pitched sound. Like a squeak. "Okay," said Rust. "Let's stop playing games. What do you want from me?"

"I only want us to be friends. I mean, once you see how everybody's tried to use and cheat you, you might decide to reassess your choice of friends."

"Where does Yelena come into this?"

"She doesn't. She doesn't matter. We don't need her. You can have her if you like. As a sign of goodwill. We're very loyal to our friends, you know. And if you ever feel the urge to hit back at some people, well, you can tell me, I might even be able to help you."

"What if I want to hit back at Yelena?"

"It's up to you. But she's not important."

"It was she who set me up in '56 and again who got me into this."

"She had her orders. From traitors."

"Do you know who they were?"

"They've been shot."

"Who were they?"

"They had the nerve to insinuate that they had the blessing of some of our leaders at the very top of the party and in government. But they, too, were amateurs. Or else they wouldn't have used someone like Colonel Muratova, who knows nothing about real tradecraft." The way he said "tradecraft" revealed the professional's pride in his work.

"She certainly knew how to get me to Moscow."

"That was easy. All she had to do was to resurrect your file. All right, she helped you, but if it wasn't for your tenacity, her whole scheme would have collapsed and ended in Moscow, or at least in Leningrad. That's how we came to admire you. And despise her. And her henchman, who killed himself to avoid capture."

Florian. "I wouldn't have thought that he had the courage."

"You're right. He killed himself out of cowardice."

And out of love. He died to protect Yelena, thought Rust, but saw no reason to tell Boychenko, who looked at his watch yet again.

Boychenko raised his cup. "Shall we drink to friendship?" And when Rust said nothing, he changed the question: "How about a drink to the mutual respect felt by professionals?"

"We'll drink to that." That noise could be heard again. It was nearer now. And yes, it was definitely a squeak. Like a wheel that needed oiling. "Keep warm, major," said Rust and held out his cup for a refill.

"Please call me Andrey Anisimovich. Or Andrey, if you wish."

"Here's to you, Andrey."

"And to you, Helm."

"Let me tell you something, Andrey. You're right to believe that I'm astonished by that Kennedy memo. And that I'm shaken by what you say about Schramm's attitude. And Charles. They should have warned me. I can see that. And yes, I do feel like hitting back. But you must understand, I'm no traitor."

"Of course not. I wouldn't respect you if you were. But one's loyalty to one's country can be influenced by certain ideals. Principles. Even individual leaders. And sometimes it's more important to fight for principles than remain blindly, unthinkingly loyal. It's a matter of honesty. A matter of being true to yourself above all—wasn't that what Hamlet said?"

"Polonius, actually."

"Right. We'll drink to that."

The squeak was quite close now. It stopped outside the door. Rust was about to say something, but the words froze into a lump in his throat. He wished that door would never open. But it did. Two armed guards entered. Their fingers were on the triggers of submachine guns. Behind them the squeak started again. Then the wheelchair appeared. Rust's muscles tightened. Blood rushed to his head and blurred his vision. Ell's face was all he could see clearly. He felt dizzy. The implications of Ell's presence seemed endless. It would certainly explain how Boychenko had come to hear about Yelena's Ukrainian accent. Keep warm. Keep warm. Rust hid his shiverish shock behind a stony stare.

Repson seemed to understand. "Don't say anything, Helm. Just hear me out. Please."

"Do I have a choice?" Rust listened to his own cold, cutting voice as if it were a stranger's.

"I'm here to help you, Helm."

"I'm obliged."

"All I'm asking is that you should listen."

"What if I don't want to? Will your friends make me listen? Or will you fly in specialists with a centipede? You don't know what a show you missed at Long Island."

"It had nothing to do with me. It was Anna's doing. All of it."

"What's the difference?"

"A lot."

"Don't you work for the same firm?"

Instead of answering, Repson turned to Boychenko. "Leave us alone." Seeing that the Russian was reluctant to go, he added: "I'll be all right." He hooked his right thumb into his shirt, resting it between two buttons. Rust guessed that the pose gave him easy access to his gun.

When the men left, Rust had no doubt that they would be just outside the door, should Repson need them. He began to eat with great gusto. He could not think of a better way of showing his contempt. "So you're a traitor, little brother," he said munching noisily.

"Depends on your definition of treason."

"Oh yes, your Russki friend's already treated me to a brief morality lecture as applied by you to the other side."

"We won't go into that, Helm, not now."

"No, it's easier to remain a doer, I suppose, and ignore the meaning of your acts. Let's say we haven't got time."

"Let's. Because it happens to be true."

"Okay. So how do you propose to help me?"

"I can try to get you away from here."

"All right, try. Just tell me the catch, first."

"No catch."

"No? Just a sign of reciprocated friendship, right?"

"Sort of."

"Then let me tell you, Ell, your friend Boychenko has already sort of half offered to trade Yelena for my friendly attitude. You know who she is?"

"Yes. I hope she can be cured."

"You think he'd do it?"

"He might."

"And how friendly would I have to be?"

"It's up to you. I mean, it depends on how bitter you are. How you feel about your American idols and so-called friends. They cheated you and your Cubans. They used you all. You know that. And they're furious with you, I can tell you."

"Why?"

"Schramm discovered that you'd come to Cuba."

"I didn't expect it to remain a secret forever."

"They've never trusted you since your return from Russia."

"I know."

"They'll be even more suspicious if you get out of here. It means you could be finished. Even if they let you live. And accidents do happen."

"That's a chance I'll have to take."

"Sure. If you're all alone, that is. But why take chances? Why risk your life?"

"Are you proposing some insurance?"

"That's why I'm here. To help you."

"You mean you're so concerned about me that you've risked everything, blown your beautiful cover in Washington, and run away only to help me?"

"It's not quite like that." Repson looked at the tray. "Do you mind if I have some of that food? I haven't eaten all day and it's almost midnight."

"Help yourself." Rust poured some rum for both of them. He was anxious not to reveal his desperation. In the last few minutes he had begun to realize that his despair was not due only to fear and the hopelessness of his situation. His thirst for revenge on everybody was another key factor. Which made it even worse. "How friendly would I have to be to get the deal?"

"Three things. First you'd have to return home a hero. The man who got his mad girl out of Russia. Of course, if she was cured, she'd be cross-examined a lot, but eventually she could be with you, if that's what you both wanted. Your second job would be to deliver the bombshell that I've defected."

"Have you?"

"I had no choice. I came under suspicion because of you. They were about to arrest me but I was tipped off."

"By whom?"

"I don't know. But it must be someone very, very high up."

"How high up is very, very high?"

"I don't know. And wouldn't tell you even if I did."

"Okay. So what's in it for you if I report seeing you here?"

"It'll cause a hell of an upheaval at Langley. Their operations will be paralyzed. Everybody'll suspect everybody else. Everybody except you. And then it would be up to you. If you wanted to stay friendly with us, we could help you. We have a great deal of influence. My spectacular career would be nothing compared to the height you could rise to. But that would be strictly up to you. And your rewards in power and in the joy of being in the know would be fantastic. Great men on both sides would be your puppets. War and peace might depend on you at times."

"Cut out the big words, Ell. What's the third thing I'd have to do?"

"That's simple. Just to support your credentials, you'd deliver a piece of intelligence you'd claim to have picked up over here."

"What's that?"

"That some of the missiles over here are being hidden in caves."

Rust rinsed his mouth with rum. He hoped it helped him to conceal his astonishment as well as the fact that this piece of intelligence was already known to him. But why the hell would the Russkis want him to take that news, as if for once the spooks of this world were united against their own masters on opposite sides?

• Saturday, October 27 •

Castro threatens U-2 overflights. OAS backs Kennedy. Anti-U.S. riots in Argentina, Bolivia, Venezuela and European capitals. Kennedy answers Bertrand Russell's letter and protests against his one-sided criticism: "Your attention might well be directed to the burglars, rather than to those who have caught the burglars." Huge crowds are lured to London's great moth exhibition.

THE MORNING BROUGHT WASHINGTON PALE SUNSHINE AND no relief. Radio Moscow began to broadcast Khrushchev's letter to Kennedy. Not the one that was sent secretly on Friday. This second letter was in the traditional Kremlin style with all the hallmarks of Presidium group thinking. And Khrushchev was upping the price of missile withdrawal. In addition to the guarantee of Cuban independence, he now demanded the withdrawal of American missiles from Turkey. Had the Presidium found out about Khrushchev's "private" approach? Had they outvoted him? Was he still in charge at all?

This open letter went on to offer reassurance that all the Cuban missiles were controlled by Russians and therefore America had nothing to fear, there was no risk of any unthinking or accidental shooting. The broadcast was still continuing when Kennedy received a news flash from the Air Force: a few minutes earlier, at about 10:15, a U-2 had been brought down over Cuba; the pilot, Major Rudolf Anderson, Jr., was one of the two who had obtained the first pictures of the missile sites; he was now presumed to be captured or dead. So the SAMs were definitely operational. And if the broadcast was telling the truth, the shooting had been no accident, no bungling by hotheaded Latins, but a deliberate act by cool Soviet missilemen firing on the orders of whoever was in charge in the Kremlin at this particular moment.

The morning heat brought Rust no respite from the strain of the night and the sickly fumes rising from the lagoon. Emotionally drained, spoiling for revenge for himself, Yelena and Sylvia, tortured by suspicions and anxiety, by dawn he had stopped calling his brother a traitor. He listened with sadness to the cripple's endless explanations and self-justification.

Repson had the dignity to talk about his misfortunes and handicap without too much self-pity. He coldly recounted how life had cheated him out of so many things, including prospects of success and happiness. Rust disagreed, but Repson brushed aside his argument: "It's not debatable. That's how I felt, so that's what mattered." He went on to say that some people— though not he himself—held Rust responsible for everything, starting with the toboggan accident.

"At least they can't say that I've driven you into the arms of the Russkis," said Rust. They shared a strained laugh. "How long have you worked for them?"

"Oh, seven years now, just about. It all began when I was still in Monitoring. I sort of misappropriated a piece of information that had come into the office. It was to be no more than a touch of self-glorification, I swear to you. No more than what everybody else was doing in order to get ahead. Except in my case, Moscow Center found out about it. How? I don't know. But that in itself impressed me a lot. It meant they must have had people in top positions within the Company. They approached me. It was a clever mixture of soft blackmail, hard cash and lots of carrot. And it wasn't the threat or the money that tempted me. It was the fantastic opportunity. To be in the know. The joy of back-seat driving—having the power of influence without the burden of responsibility for decision-making. For a while, I even toyed with the idea of playing their game only to unmask them and be a hero, eventually. But they were too good to me. Good and loyal. They trained me, guided me, turned me into a real professional, and got me promotions through their men at the top. And they never, never treated me as shabbily as your friends treated you. They went to endless trouble to protect me. I never knew that they eliminated you from the Company only to safeguard me."

"Didn't you? I'm tempted to swear that it was you who planned it."

"It wasn't. I might have been instrumental in supplying information about your character and psychological makeup on which they based their scheme."

"It was clever. Anna made me resign of my own free will and disgust without ever suspecting the pressure or her involvement, other than sexually, of course. And a few well-chosen words from you about Father gave me the final push. But I find it hard to believe that you knew nothing about her role."

"It's true. She had been working for the Soviet Union long before we met. Then her main task became to love me, help me and safeguard me at any cost. She prepared that reverse-blackmail trick to discredit you if you ever became a threat to me. She stole some information that had come from you to make my position easier. It would have been much more difficult for me to withhold that Castro shopping list from Langley if it ever got to me. And she risked everything to prevent you from reaching me when you were on the run from Moscow."

"Risked everything? What? What did she risk apart from my life? They almost killed me on Long Island."

"And I almost killed her with the shot you diverted. Because I still had no idea that all along she was only protecting me. That's what you can expect from these people, total loyalty."

"Yet now you're ready to ruin her. Once you're in Moscow, she'll be exposed. She'll be no good to Langley. They might lock her up or dispose of her. Accidents do happen."

"That's true. And she knows it. It's part of her deal. She didn't take her assignment blindly."

"No, but if you stayed on, she'd still be working for Moscow."

"True. But she's the price we have to pay for me. I had to get out. I was more important. And I'll continue to be more important when I start working in Moscow."

"That's what you call loyalty."

"No. That's what I call a matter of priorities. You must be pragmatic about these things. I only wish you could see it my way. We'd be working together. Real players, not onlookers. Remember what you told me when you came to see me in Washington after Long Island? You said I must clear my name and remain a player whatever the consequences. Now we could do that together."

The moment came back easily. It brought back the comradeship of their childhood, brothers versus the world, two little boys taking on parents, school, neighborhood gangs, all comers. "You know something, Ell? I think you . . ."

"I know what you think."

"And I know that you think that you know what I think."

"And I think you stink."

The silly old schoolboy routine brought instantaneous but short-lived laughter. The silence that followed was grave. The game was for real now.

Boychenko returned and gave Repson a slip of paper.

"Was it on the radio?"

Boychenko nodded.

"Then show it to my brother. It's no secret."

Rust read it: Havana had announced that a U-2 had been brought down by a SAM. It was meant to be a lesson to the imperialists. But it could mean war.

In Washington, EXCOM was in nonstop session. It had to decide how the two Khrushchev letters should be answered. Bobby Kennedy suggested disregarding the broadcast, reacting only to the first, "private" approach, and accepting the offer. Missiles out for the guarantee of noninvasion. But the answer would also be an ultimatum: if the work on the missile sites failed to stop and the evacuation of offensive weapons did not begin at once, the consequences would be Moscow's responsibility.

"Now it can go either way," said the President and issued orders to call up twenty-four troop-carrier squadrons of the Air Force Reserve.

"But can't you see, you're not asked to cause any damage to America," Repson insisted. "In fact, the information about the caves should look quite useful to them."

"Then why do you want me to give it to Langley?"

"It's not for us to question the reasons. We're pros. We just gather and supply information and let others make the decisions."

"But if that info really is or may seem good to the Company, whose side are we on?"

"Does it really matter? Look, the Russians may have all sorts of reasons. Perhaps somebody wants to embarrass Khrushchev. Or give something to Kennedy, who'd hear about those caves sooner or later in any case. Or help Khrushchev against Castro, who may resist the idea of pulling all the missiles out of Cuba. Or make Kennedy demand the removal of missiles from the caves so that Khrushchev could then agree to that, too, for a price, and still leave some other missiles in mothballs over here."

Rust felt tempted to say yes to everything his brother wanted. What bothered him was that he could not make up his own mind about his motivation. Was he trying to escape and save Yelena as well as take a piece of intelligence to Washington, or was he trying to hit back at Langley and become a big-time player in one go?

· Sunday, October 28 ·

At 9:00 A.M., Moscow Radio announces Khrushchev's capitulation. The missiles will be crated and removed from Cuba. American guarantees will be accepted.

AFTER A NIGHT OF COLLAPSE IN TOTAL EXHAUSTION, RUST and his brother listened to the news on the radio.

"Kennedy's won a great victory for the history books," said Repson.

"And lost Cuba as well as his freedom of action."

"He lost nothing. He was always ready to give guarantees on non-invasion under pressure. The memo was no fake."

After a silent breakfast together, Rust accepted his brother's propositions. Boychenko was called in to make the necessary

380

arrangements. He embraced Rust and kissed him on both cheeks. "Wish we had more time to talk," he said, "but let's hope there'll be other opportunities for us in the future."

Rust did not want to involve and endanger Orlando. He claimed he had no clear plans how to leave the island. Boychenko promised to find a way.

November
1962

Bertrand Russell claims: mankind owes a "profound debt" to Khrushchev for his "sanity and magnanimity." China pledges support to Cuba. Mongoose is canceled. Shot down U-2 pilot's body to be returned home. Kennedy reveals: dismantling of missiles has begun. Castro objects to supervision of dismantling. Front page advertisement in The London Times: "Good country home is required for silver poodle bitch [phone number]."

THE ENGINE OF THE INCONSPICUOUSLY DECREPIT BARGE Boychenko had acquired broke down barely beyond the Cay Sal Bank. Because the blockade had been lifted but the tension over the Caribbean had not been dispelled, there was no traffic in the area. Rust and Yelena ran out of water by the end of the first day. Rowing and reaching even the nearest coral reefs proved to be impossible. They lay in each other's arms, talked little, and waited. There was no choice.

After three days of drifting they were spotted and picked up by an American patrol. The captain was reluctant but was eventually persuaded to radio Miami and get Schramm traced. The date was November 2, when Kennedy went on the air to announce that the Cuban missiles were being dismantled.

Schramm arranged for them to be flown to Washington by the Air Force. During the flight, Yelena slept and ate and slept and ate all the time. Rust sat with Schramm. An air of lingering mutual suspicion made it difficult for them to start talking. Rust was troubled by his own motives: when he made his report about the caves, would he do it as a patriot or a traitor? In a way, it didn't matter. The outcome, his information, would be just the same. He told Schramm about the caves. He first said that he himself had seen a transport on the way to Matanzas with Miguel. He then added what Miguel had told him about the other caves. He finally revealed that Ell was in Cuba as a defector and wanted him to convey exactly the same message. Schramm said nothing and tried to look inscrutable, but Rust knew him well enough to know that he was shocked. The gist of his report was encoded and radioed to Washington.

On arrival at Langley, Rust had to say goodbye to Yelena. Schramm was stiff and formal toward her, but made an effort to be friendly: "You'll be all right, colonel. If you're frank with us, you have nothing to worry about. Your debriefing may take a few months or even a year, but I hope that Helm will be able to visit you from time to time."

"Just tell them everything they want to know," said Rust. "This is no time for holding back. And soon we'll be together." He hoped he sounded convincing.

For six hours, a three-man committee and Schramm listened to Rust, who decided to tell them everything, including the approaches made by Boychenko and the scheme outlined by his brother. At first they listened to him in icy silence. Then minute signs of a change in mood occurred. He wondered if he was becoming a hero. Was Ell's scheme beginning to work? Eventually, he was offered a cool vote of thanks and congratulations. His report would now go higher up and would need to be evaluated. He was invited to take a well-earned rest in a room on the second floor, where he was plied with drinks and food. Nobody made a secret of the fact that he was watched and guarded at all times.

Twenty-four hours later, Schramm came to see him. For

the first time since Miami in August, Rust saw him wear his old jovial earth-moving-machinery salesman's smile.

"Helm, you've done a fantastic job."

Never guessed it would be so easy to become a traitor, thought Rust.

"It's a great victory."

"Is it?"

"Of course it is. And you know it." Schramm was definitely beaming.

"Does it mean that Khrushchev's agreed to remove the confetti from the caves, too?"

"You're to forget about those caves."

"They can't be ignored."

"Just forget them. We'll try everything to smoke them out if at all possible, but we've no direct way to check every one of thousands of caves in Cuba. Besides, Khrushchev has got to be allowed to retain a vestige of dignity. Otherwise he couldn't possibly retreat and would go raving mad. The venture has earned him only a few more years in power."

"And Cuba. Or isn't our guarantee serious?"

"Dead serious. Mongoose has already been canceled. The Cubans and all its other personnel are being disbanded."

"And I'm free to go—is that what you're saying?"

"If that's what you want. On the other hand, I've now been put into the full picture and I'm authorized to tell you that we want you—need you, in fact, more than ever. We'll work together with Charles and you'll have the key part to play in the big game that's about to begin."

"What game and what part? I've already confessed to you that I was on the brink of becoming a traitor. And I'm still not sure about my motives."

"That's fine. Just fine." Schramm was clearly enjoying himself.

"What about Yelena?"

"Ostensibly, she's under psychiatric treatment. But we must consider the possibility that she may be a plant. They know what she did for you, yet they let her come over. They must have a reason."

"I know."

"Which is just fine. You'll return to the Upstairs for a well-earned holiday, and she'll be allowed to join you there if that's what you want. Then we'll wait."

"For her to give herself away? Don't underestimate her, Jake."

"I don't. And I'm sure that even if she's a plant, she probably won't make a single move for years. But I bet there'll be a gentle or not-so-gentle approach made to you. They'll want you to repay their gesture of friendliness. And you will, I promise you, you will. And together we'll smoke out those friends of theirs, the Sapphire network, somewhere very, very high up in the Company. Because I'm authorized to tell you what I heard only twenty minutes ago and what must be our best-guarded secret of the past decade: that our man's succeeded."

"With what?"

"He's got himself installed in Moscow Center." The smile disappeared from Schramm's face. "Do you want a drink, Helm?"

"You mean . . . ?"

"Yes. It's Ell."

"You mentioned a drink."

"I'll join you," said Schramm. "We'll drink to his success."

"You've just been told?" Rust's voice was unusually weak. The thought of Ell in Moscow brought back the flavors of danger he had tasted not that long ago.

"Yes. But apparently he's been working as a double for us for almost seven years now. He knew nothing about Anna's role. And initially, your unauthorized Moscow venture was an inconvenience and risk to him. But then it grew into the opportunity he had been waiting for. The big spiel of trying to recruit you at the crocodile farm was for the benefit of anyone listening in. Now we can do nothing but wait to see how he goes about it and how they intend to use you."

Rust spent a day of initial briefing in a daze. He never had a chance to think about wanting or not wanting to play. It was taken for granted that nobody would want to miss an opportunity like this. And nobody would be allowed to, once being in the know.

The following day, tidbits about his success and heroic deeds were leaked out within the Company. They would surely reach the right ears. Officially, a brief announcement was made about his return from a "lengthy leave of absence" and his promotion. He was then flown to Florida for his holiday.

It was at the Upstairs that a postal messenger delivered a small express package for him. Complying with his instructions, he did not touch it until Schramm arranged a thorough examination for explosives. Then the two of them opened it together. The first thing to emerge was a typed note:

"I've just discovered that some fool took photographs of you. I wouldn't want them to fall into the wrong hands. So here they are; I suggest you burn them at once. Regards, Andrey."

There were sixteen photographs. All taken in the room where Sylvia was dying. One showed her raising her arm to defend herself from Rust, her apparent torturer. His profile could be seen clearly. Rust was not in all the pictures. Some of them focused on her injuries. Others detailed his bloodied clothes. He was flanked by armed men at all times. The final pictures formed a sequence—her execution step by step, ending with a close-up as Rust handed the revolver to someone whose face was blackened out by a shadow. It needed no caption. Debts were expected to be paid.

It took Rust two days to track down Morales and arrange to meet him at El Paraíso, where Julia-Rosa had died. Schramm objected to the meeting. There was an element of grave risk in telling the old Cuban about the death of his girl. He might blame Rust. He and his friends might seek revenge. Rust refused to argue. Talking to Morales was a debt he wanted to pay.

Morales was sitting up at the bar when Rust entered. The old man watched him as he approached, grew older and older with every step, and knew the truth by the time Rust sat down next to him, ordering two golden *añejos*.

They drank in silence. Rust could still not decide how and how much to tell him.

"Were you there when she died?"

"Yes." And after a pause, "I'm sorry."

"Not your fault, *amigo*." And after an equally long pause, "Is it?"

"No."

"Did she suffer?"

Rust swallowed. "No."

"Did she cry?"

"No. She was brave. She fought them all the way." He decided to let Morales develop his own memories of the scene.

"Was she still beautiful?"

"Yes."

"Very beautiful. You tell me."

"She was very beautiful."

"She was a good girl." Morales ordered another round of drinks. "Fantastic in bed." He drank. "Fantastic . . . wasn't she?"

"Wouldn't know." He owed Morales the total reassurance that his girl had died faithful to him. "She was yours."

"She was fantastic. Probably the last of many in my life. I'm an old man. Without a home. Who'd want me? But it's a good way; it's a good girl to end it with, right?"

"Absolutely."

"She was so sexy. So giving. And so demanding."

Wish I knew, thought Rust, when it began to dawn on him that the old man might be seeking quite another kind of reassurance.

"She was . . . she was . . . Tell me, *amigo*, did you sleep with her?" Rust was about to deny it when Morales raised his hand to silence him. "No! Don't tell me. Just that—was she good?"

"The best."

October
1964

China explodes atomic device. Soviet 3-man spaceship is launched. OAS condemns Cuba for terrorist attacks and subversion attempts against Venezuela. Gold medals galore for America at the Tokyo Olympics.

ELEVEN MONTHS AFTER THE KENNEDY ASSASSINATION, Khrushchev left for a holiday at Sochi. All members of his Politburo, including his latest great protégé, Brezhnev, assembled at the railway station to see him off. The same group met in great secrecy on October 14. The same day, Mikoyan was visiting Khrushchev, probably to reassure the leader that nothing important was happening in Moscow. Khrushchev talked on radiotelephone to cosmonauts aboard the *Voskhod* in space. He was jocular but seriously puzzled when he shouted: "And Comrade Mikoyan has just arrived. He doesn't let me talk to you. He's pulling the phone out of my hand!" When Khrushchev returned to Moscow, not a soul was at the railway station to meet him. He must have known then that he was out and Brezhnev was in.